Illustrator: Stephen Clifton
Studio: Staple Hill Art Studio, Bristol, UK.

Jordan Luck

Will Armstrong

iUniverse, Inc.
New York   Bloomington

Jordan Luck

Copyright © 2008 by Will Armstrong

All rights reserved. No part of this book may be used or reproduced by any means, graphic, electronic, or mechanical, including photocopying, recording, taping or by any information storage retrieval system without the written permission of the publisher except in the case of brief quotations embodied in critical articles and reviews.

This is a work of fiction. All of the characters, names, incidents, organizations, and dialogue in this novel are either the products of the author's imagination or are used fictitiously.

iUniverse books may be ordered through booksellers or by contacting:

iUniverse
1663 Liberty Drive
Bloomington, IN 47403
www.iuniverse.com
1-800-Authors (1-800-288-4677)

Because of the dynamic nature of the Internet, any Web addresses or links contained in this book may have changed since publication and may no longer be valid. The views expressed in this work are solely those of the author and do not necessarily reflect the views of the publisher, and the publisher hereby disclaims any responsibility for them.

ISBN: 978-1-4401-0139-7 (pbk)

ISBN: 978-1-4401-0140-3 (ebk)

Printed in the United States of America

My thanks to Jean and Janet Muir for their advice and encouragement. Thanks also to Ann Ewing and Maureen Brister for taking on the onerous but necessary task of proof reading, to Brenda Hoyle and Margaret Rhind for their support and assistance and to my friend, colleague and fellow author, Bill Clinkenbeard, for providing expertise and background know-how when it was required. Finally, my sincere thanks to Linda and Nigel who worked tirelessly to bring Jordan Luck into the world!

To Vi, with all my love. Thanks for all those wonderful years.

Contents

Chapter 1 1
Chapter 2 6
Chapter 3 14
Chapter 4 20
Chapter 5 25
Chapter 6 32
Chapter 7 39
Chapter 8 45
Chapter 9 51
Chapter 10 56
Chapter 11 62
Chapter 12 67
Chapter 13 74
Chapter 14 78
Chapter 15 81
Chapter 16 90

Chapter 17 96

Chapter 18 102

Chapter 19 109

Chapter 20 114

Chapter 21 122

Chapter 22 128

Chapter 23 135

Chapter 24 142

Chapter 25 151

Chapter 26 157

Chapter 27 165

Chapter 28 173

Chapter 29 180

Chapter 30 189

Chapter 31 198

Chapter 1

The five riders jogged quietly down the dusty street and swung left into Courthouse Square. They exchanged an occasional low-voiced remark, eyes everywhere.

Seated outside H.T. Haven's hardware store, old Jeff McGrath paused in his whittling and eyed them speculatively, the partially carved leaping cougar forgotten for the moment. Cowhands; between jobs mebbe, the grizzled old-timer mused. Then again, they could be from one o' the northbound trail herds camped outside the town. Remembering other trails, other towns, he grinned reminiscently. Comin' in for their share o' Fort Worth licker and wimmen most likely.

The white-haired ex-lawman lifted a hand in greeting as they cantered past. S' funny though. Most waddies generally wave. Some even say 'howdy'. Not this bunch. From beneath his forward tilted stetson, McGrath studied the riders covertly as they dismounted outside the Longhorn Saloon. That tall sandy-haired gent wi' the fancy vest seems to be the boss man. Mean lookin' cuss. Wouldn't want him as a ramrod. An' that big black-bearded fella. Bet he's a rough one in a brawl. Shrugging, he shifted his chaw of Henry Clay, spat into the dusty street and went back to his whittling.

✯   ✯   ✯   ✯

'You remember now.' Diamond Jack Anderson kept his voice low as he secured his horse to the saloon hitching rail. 'I go in first, then Dutch and Clint. Red, you and Whitey wait here. When we barrel out through that door I want you comin' fast wi' the horses.'

'Why can't they wait outside the bank?' Clint Anderson, his younger brother whined, wolfish features twitching nervously. 'Seems to me they'd be better there when we come out, 'stead o' havin' to come hellin' across the square.'

'Cause five horses an' two fellas'd look right suspicious outside a bank. Across here they ain't nuthin' but waddies stoppin' off at the saloon. All set now?'

The others nodded tensely.

Jack Anderson angled across the rutted square to the Cattleman's Bank. Stepping up onto the sidewalk he paused to brush the trail dust from his clothes. Something of a dandy, Anderson affected the dark suit, white shirt and string tie of the traditional gambler. This was no idle whim. All across the South-West, Diamond Jack Anderson was known as a card player who could match wits and skill with the best. That, allied to his speed with a brace of .45s made him a formidable opponent.

His only departure from tradition was the ornate vest that he habitually wore. Embroidered with an intricate lozenge-shaped design, it had earned him the name, 'Diamond Jack'. Finished, he set his hat firmly on his head and pushed through the bank doorway.

Behind him, Clint and the giant van Doren moved away from the horses and headed across the square.

Inside the building, Jack Anderson took a deep breath and scanned the room. Only himself, two customers and the three shirt-sleeved staff, two of them positioned at the long polished counter. Should be easy. Confidently he approached one of the barred windows. Walt Ames, the unoccupied teller, rose from his desk and came forward expectantly.

'Howdy. Name's Smith. Alamo Smith. Been runnin' cattle down on the Trinity River range. Plannin' to move up here right soon. Like to see the manager 'bout openin' an account.'

Ames nodded politely. 'Why sure, Mister Smith. I'll go get Mister Johnson right now.'

Jedediah Johnson; plump, well-barbered and unctuous, hurried from his office.

'Mister Smith, Pleased to meet you. Opening an account are you? Won't be no trouble; no trouble at all.'

Anderson nodded, watching from the corner of his eye as Clint and van Doren came quickly through the door. Carefully, they positioned themselves behind the two customers.

'That'll be fine.' His right hand flicked up and the long-barrelled Colt rose above the counter. 'Just do like I say and nobody's gonna get hurt. Now, tell this fella here,' he indicated the wide-eyed pale-faced Ames and slid a rolled up gunny sack through the hatch, 'to put the money in this.'

Colour drained from the manager's cheeks. 'But … '

The muzzle of the big revolver centred on him. 'No buts, mister. Just tell'm.'

'Do as he says.' Johnson's voice was high and shaky.

Further down the counter Clint was similarly engaged, while the two customers and the third teller lay prone on the floor, guarded by the menacing guns of van Doren.

✯   ✯   ✯   ✯

From the hardware store porch, McGrath shot another sidelong glance at the two remaining gang members, lounging against the hitching rail. Somethin' mighty funny there. He rose stiffly and eased quietly back into the shadowy cluttered store.

'Howdy, Jeff.' Hector Haven, burly, balding owner of the biggest hardware store in Fort Worth and one-time lawman, looked up from the ledger he was studying and eyed his ex-deputy curiously. 'You get tired o' settin' out there in the sun messin' up my porch?'

'Hush up, Hec.' McGrath gestured impatiently towards the big shop window. 'Take somethin' outa that there winder an' tell me what you make o' them two fellas at the Longhorn hitchin' rail. An' there's another three in the bank already.'

A big man, Haven could still move quickly in spite of his bulk. Extracting an ornate brass table lamp from the big display window he shot a cautious glance across the square. The old excitement welled up in him. 'Bank raid you reckon? Never had one before.'

Jeff snorted derisively. 'That don't mean nuthin'. There's a first time for everything.'

The big store owner nodded. 'That's true.' He broke off as a tall, angular, grey-haired woman entered the store. 'Mornin', Miz Jones.' Haven beckoned to his wife, a stout smiling lady, who had just appeared from the storeroom behind the counter. 'Emily, take Miz Jones through to the stockroom and show her that new range o' china we just got in. Like her opinion on it.'

'Jem!' He set the lamp on the counter and beckoned to the tow-headed youngster lethargically sweeping the floor at the rear of the store. 'Go out the back way real quiet and hightail it down to the sheriff's office. Tell'm we might have some trouble at the bank. Go on now.' He pushed the startled boy towards the rear door. 'And don't talk to nobody on the way.'

'Now;' he unlocked the big steel gun safe and lifted out two brand new Henry repeating carbines, 'let's be ready in case somethin' breaks.' Tossing one to McGrath, he placed a box of ammunition on the counter and commenced to load rapidly.

His lifelong friend did the same.

'Don't go shootin' less'n you have to,' Haven cautioned. 'Them's new guns. Gotta mark 'em down if they're used. 'Sides, them fellas might be alright.'

'Huh!' McGrath chambered a round and positioned himself just inside the open door. 'You believe that, you'll believe anything. Allus said this store life was makin' you soft. Get set.'

★   ★   ★   ★

'Right!' Clint Anderson, his face twitching nervously, gestured with the Colt. 'Let's have that bag!'

New to the job, John Stevens hesitated fractionally, pride in his recent appointment making him reluctant to comply. For a moment the two young men stared into each other's eyes, then Clint's brittle temper snapped and he squeezed the trigger. The explosion echoed and re-echoed in the confines of the room.

'Hell and damnation!' Diamond Jack cursed furiously as the young teller, still clutching the bulging gunny sack, collapsed behind the counter, mortally wounded. 'Gimme that money ... now!' He snatched the bulky bag from a white-faced Walt Ames, voice lifting in a shout. 'Let's go!'

The boom of Clint's .45 ignited a flurry of action.

'There!' McGrath brought up the Henry as Red and Whitey, vaulting into their saddles, raced the gang's horses across the square.

At the same moment Clint and van Doren burst from the bank, guns at the ready. Behind them came Diamond Jack, struggling with a bulging sack.

Haven centred on Malone's broad chest and squeezed the trigger. The red-bearded outlaw toppled from his saddle, dead before he hit the ground.

McGrath cursed as his first bullet clipped the hat from Whitey Roberts' blond head. Adjusting his aim he shot again. Roberts clutched at the saddlehorn, hard hit.

Clint and van Doren were in their saddles by now, but Diamond Jack, hampered by the money sack, was struggling to get mounted. 'Here!' He tossed the sack to Clint, just as Malone's riderless horse careered between them. The sack struck the panic-stricken animal on the head and was trampled underfoot.

'Come on!' Clint's mount was already settling into a pounding run. Close behind him came the wounded Roberts, trying desperately to stay in his saddle. Across the square, Haven and McGrath were pumping bullets at the fleeing outlaws.

Teeth bared in a fighting snarl, Diamond Jack and a cursing van Doren unleashed a storm of lead as they swept past the hardware store. Hank and Jeff ducked instinctively as the big display window disintegrated into shards of flying glass.

As the four riders, strung out in single file, raced down Main Street, Whitey Roberts gasped and toppled tiredly from his saddle. Looking back, a grim-faced van Doren saw the young outlaw being dragged some sixty yards, before his foot slipped from the stirrup and he sprawled unconscious in the dust.

☆   ☆   ☆   ☆

The hammering hoof-beats faded into the distance and silence fell in Courthouse Square. Shakily, McGrath and Haven rose to their feet. 'Damn me,' the feisty old-timer extracted a sliver of glass from his sleeve. 'All them years as a lawman an' nary a scratch. Then I near get killed wi' a store winder! Allus said them things wasn't safe nohow.' His eyes widened as he turned to Haven. 'What in hell happened to you?'

'Got caught wi' a piece o' glass.' The burly storekeeper dabbed gingerly at a long shallow cut on his forehead. 'That damned window cost me nigh on two-fifty dollars, what with cratin' an' freight charges. This is what you get for bein' a public-spirited citizen.' He turned as Jem and a tough looking young deputy sheriff dashed in through the rear door. 'Howdy, Cal. What happened to all that tinstar law Hank Baxter keeps braggin' about?'

Cal Fischer flushed. 'Sheriff Baxter and deputy Devlin are outa town. I come as soon as I could,' he said defensively.

The bank door eased open and Walt Ames peered out cautiously. People spilled from the Longhorn Saloon, talking excitedly. In the distance querulous shouts could be heard.

Haven grinned suddenly, the carbine cradled in the crook of his arm. 'Guess you did at that, son. Now, you bein' a duly appointed peace officer,' he winked at McGrath; 'I reckon you ought to take a look at the scene o' the crime, 'specially that fella I downed. Might be you got a dodger on him.'

Gritting his teeth, the young deputy headed across the square towards the bank, the two grinning old-timers bringing up the rear. They'd seen it all before.

Chapter 2

With an ease born of a lifetime's practice, Ma Jordan flipped the rolled-out pastry dexterously onto the big pie dish and kneaded it into position. Ma liked baking. Jim, her long-suffering husband, reckoned it was the only time that Mary-Lou's face softened and the bleak look disappeared from her cold blue eyes. Sensibly, he kept such thoughts to himself. As he had forcibly pointed out more than once to the family, when they were on the verge of rebellion against Ma's hard-nosed discipline, they were damned lucky. Anyone who, at the age of nine, had found their entire family massacred by a marauding band of Winnebago braves, was entitled to be somewhat ornery at times.

He could have added, but didn't, that the abduction of their youngest son, John, at the age of eight, by Comanches, had destroyed much of the healing work done by their marriage. His subsequent rescue and return to them ten years later, to all intents and purposes a Comanche brave, had served only to intensify Mary-Lou's hatred of Indians. However, as far as Jim Jordan was concerned that episode was now a closed book.

This morning though, with the spring sunshine slanting in through the kitchen window and the big stove drawing nicely, Ma was as relaxed as she was ever likely to be. Her keen gaze swept the yard. Even when everything was going well Ma never dropped her guard.

Satisfied, she cast a critical eye over the dough-lined dish. Edges need trimmin'. With the deft movement of long familiarity, Mary-Lou's right hand explored the table drawer in search of a knife. As her fingers closed round the bone handle the back of her hand touched the cold metal of the Paterson Colt, tucked away in its special compartment.

Ma's face hardened suddenly and the bleakness reappeared in her eyes. Through the open door she could hear Sara-Jane, her younger daughter, singing as she tidied up the big comfortable living-room at the front of the house.

The knife blade flickered quickly round the pie dish. Finished, Ma paused for a moment, frowning. 'Sara-Jane!' she called sharply.

'Yeah, Ma?'

'Hush that ... .' A jay rose suddenly from the wooded ridge behind the ranch buildings. Its raucous alarm call echoed across the valley. Ma's gaze locked onto the crest of the ridge.

Footsteps echoed on the wooden floor of the passage and Sara-Jane Jordan bounced into the kitchen. A tall, dark-haired sixteen year old, with a wicked sense of humour and a figure much too mature for her years, she was the girl that Ma had always wanted to be.

Wanted, but couldn't, because of those terrifying hysterical nightmares, which had persisted until well into her teens. Nightmares that had left her withdrawn and always on guard.

'Want me?' There was an underlying toughness in Sara-Jane's voice. She sensed her mother's resentment without knowing why.

'Yeah. Might be we got company back o' the ridge.'

Sara-Jane groaned inwardly. Not again! Doesn't she ever give up. Bet it's another scare about nothing.

'Go up in the loft an' check through the end window. Your eyes are better than mine. Where's Ellie-May?'

'Went down to the barn,' Sara-Jane said sourly. 'Pa asked her to check the team harness for the new wagon.'

'She got her gunbelt?'

'Sure. You ever see her without it?' Sara-Jane sneered as she made for the loft ladder. 'Reckon she sleeps with it on.'

Ma's face hardened at the jibe. 'Check the hideout shotgun when you're up there. Leave the window open, it'll help air the loft.'

That'll teach me, Sara-Jane raged inwardly as she climbed the ladder. I should have kept my mouth shut. I hate guns. Some day I'll get away from all this.

The loft was dark and dusty. Easing the casement window open, Sara-Jane took a long look at the ridge. Nothing moved in the spring sunshine. Another false alarm.

Down below, Mary-Lou was coming to the same conclusion. Still, she mused, with Pa, John and Jake away deliverin' them steers to Fort Worth, and Bull off on one of his bounty hunts, it's as well to be careful.

'Don't see nothin', Ma.'

'Checked the shotgun?'

'Just checkin' now.' Gingerly, Sara-Jane slid the double-barrelled shotgun from from its clips above the casement window. Why me, she thought bitterly. Guns and horses scare me, but I was born into a family that don't think of nothin' else.

Easing off the canvas cover, another of Ma's ideas, she broke the gun and checked that it was clean. Shells? Yes, there was the pouch hanging from the hook alongside. Carefully, Sara-Jane replaced the cover and secured the gun in position. Descending the ladder she found her mother clutching the Paterson Colt.

'All checked?' Ma spun the cylinder expertly.

'Yeah. Can't see nothin' on the ridge. Gun's clean and there's plenty of shells.'

'Mm.' Ma laid the revolver on the table. 'Could be just a varmint up there, but somethin' sure scared that jay.'

She came to a sudden decision. 'Go down to the barn an' tell Ellie-May to take care. An' if she sees or hears anything to come arunnin'.'

'Right.' Sara-Jane swung out of the door and headed for the barn. Ma pursed her lips disapprovingly as she watched.

She swings her hips just like a grown woman, she thought sourly, an' she ain't barely sixteen yet. That gal's goin' to be trouble 'fore she's much older. Scowling, she turned away to check the oven.

✶ ✶ ✶ ✶

'Ellie May!' Sara-Jane peered through the barn door into the cool shadowy interior.

'Yo.' Her elder sister laid down the bridle she was cleaning. Blonde, blue-eyed, slightly taller than Sara-Jane, and with a figure most women would have died for, Ellie-May's only interests were horses and guns.

Look at her, Sara-Jane fumed to herself. Two years older than me an' all she's thinkin' about right now is that old bridle. An' she wears pants just like a man. She's the only woman I know that does.

Aloud she said, 'Ma reckons we might have company back o' the ridge.'

'Sounds interestin'.' Ellie-May lifted her gunbelt from the wall hook and buckled it on. Bending over, she tied the bottoms of the holsters to each long Levi-clad leg, then straightened and looked enquiringly at her sister.

'Thinkin' o' ridin' wi' the Anderson gang?' Sara-Jane couldn't resist a dig. There was a cold arrogance about Ellie-May that galled her.

'Maybe.' Her sister's right hand moved suddenly and Sara-Jane found herself looking down the barrel of a Colt. She let her breath out in a long whistle.

'Whooee! I knew you'd been practising but I didn't think you were that fast.'

'Well, now you know.' Ellie-May flicked her hand and the gun was back in its holster. 'And you don't tell no one; understand?'

'Sure.' Sara-Jane turned to go. 'Oh, Ma says come arunnin' if you see or hear anything.'

'Yo.' Ellie-May glanced through the open door into the dusty yard, where the Rhode Island Red chickens, Ma's favourites, scratched listlessly. She lifted her gaze to the corral beyond, and the half dozen horses drowsing in the warm spring sunshine. Nothing. Shrugging her shoulders, the tall girl turned back into the barn.

✯   ✯   ✯   ✯

Jack Anderson eased back from the crest of the ridge and rose to his feet. Walking downhill he glanced up angrily at the squawking jay circling overhead.

In the shade of a clump of cottonwoods three saddled horses stood with drooping heads. Traces of sweat and dried lather on their shoulders and flanks showed that they had been ridden hard. The two dusty, unshaven figures, sprawled on the grass beside them, looked equally tired.

'Your brother don't look none too pleased,' Dutch van Doren, a black-bearded bear of a man, glanced quizzically at his companion.

'Naw.' Clint Anderson, a weedy youngster, scowled moodily. 'Jack ain't happy 'less he's got a deck o' cards in his hand. An' he's as tetchy as all hell 'cause this job went wrong.'

'Yeah?' Van Doren frowned darkly. 'Seems to me if you hadn't blasted that teller when he reached for the money, we'd have gotten clean away. As it is we got nuthin', an' Whitey n' Red are lyin' back there; dead most likely. Betcha half the folks in Fort Worth are trailin' us right now.' He spat disgustedly.

'Weren't my fault,' Clint whined, his weak, dirt-streaked face twitching nervously. 'I thought he was reachin' for a gun.'

'Oh sure,' the giant outlaw sneered. 'You'd just told him to hand over the money, an' 'cause he's kinda slow you blast 'im.'

'You gonna sit there gabbin' all day?' Diamond Jack was in an ugly mood. There was a coldness in his pale blue eyes as he glowered down at his younger brother and van Doren. 'Time we made a move.'

'Jack,' Clint wheedled as they scrambled to their feet, 'I been thinkin' ...'

'Since when,' his brother sneered. 'You ain't got the brains to think. If you had we wouldn't be in the mess we're in now. So shut up an' listen. There's some good mounts in that corral down there. Don't see nobody around 'cept an old lady and a young gal in the house, and a young fella in the barn.'

'A gal eh?' Clint's eyes glittered and an evil grin appeared on his unshaven features. 'Mebbe we could have some fun ... '

'Damn you to hell!' Diamond Jack's right hand dropped to the gun on his hip. 'You're worse than a boar hog,' he grated. 'I've lost count o' the fellas I've tangled with 'cause you'd been pawin' their wimmen-folk. Last time it was that homesteader's gal over by Jacksboro. I ain't likely to forget that in a hurry. You killed her; then you shot her ma when the old lady come at you wi' a pitchfork. Then I had to shoot her old man, 'fore he spread you across half the county wi' a load o' buckshot. Let's just hope nobody finds out where they're buried. Maybe the Injuns'll get blamed. So listen real good. You put a foot wrong when we go down there an' I'll kill you m'self. We go in, get some grub, change the horses an' blow. We got enough trouble as it is.'

Breathing deeply, he broke off a twig and sketched quickly in a patch of sandy soil. 'Now, here's the house, the barn an' the corral. 'Bout a mile back along the ridge there's a dry wash that leads into the valley. We'll ease down through the wash, then me an' Dutch'll drop off here, just back o' the house.'

'Why can't we just barrel straight down off the ridge?' Clint demanded impatiently.

"Cause I don't want no scared female blastin' away at us. 'Sides, sound carries a long way out here an' that posse could be a whole lot closer than we think.'

'Naw.' Clint shook his head disparagingly. 'That stoopid bunch ... '

Jack Anderson's open palm cracked against his brother's jaw. 'Shut up an' listen! Dutch'll take care o' the old lady an' the gal. I'll handle the young fella in the barn. You take the horses to the corral an' rope us three fresh mounts. Got that?'

'Yeah.' Clint's eyes watered, and his face stung from the impact. Some day you'll pay for that, brother or no brother.

'We'll ease along behind the ridge until we come to that dry wash. Then we'll head down it to the ranch. Now, mount up.'

A mile back along the ridge they angled down into the wash, their horses shuffling tiredly through the sandy bottom. Diamond Jack pointed ahead. 'This is it. You all set?' The others nodded.

☆   ☆   ☆   ☆

Sara-Jane sniffed appreciatively. 'That peach pie sure smells good.'

'Keep your hands off.' Ma closed the oven door. 'Get up in that loft and check the ridge again.'

Waste o' time, Sara-Jane mouthed silently as she climbed the ladder.

The squawk of an alarmed Rhode Island Red alerted Ma. Grabbing the Paterson Colt, she eased back from the table to a point where she could see the rear door, half way down the passage.

Big as he was, Dutch van Doren came in fast, the Plainsman Colt ready in his right hand.

'Ma!' Sara-Jane screamed, framed in the loft trapdoor. Van Doren flicked a glance up, and, for a split second, his attention was diverted.

The two shots blended as one. Ma ducked instinctively as a bullet smacked into the wall above her head. Dutch staggered under the impact of the .38 slug and tried to bring his gun up. Coldly, Ma shot again. Slowly, tiredly, he fell against the passage wall and slid down.

Halfway across the yard Jack Anderson heard the shots and hesitated a vital second too long. Ellie-May came through the barn door on the run, the gun in her right hand centring on the tall outlaw.

Desperately, Anderson tried to swing back, but he was too late. The first bullet took him high in the shoulder and his answering shot went wide. A second slug caught him low in the chest and the .45 fell from his grasp. Eyes widening in disbelief, Diamond Jack toppled forward to lie sprawling, full length, in the dust of the yard. Stooping quickly, Ellie-May grabbed his guns and ran for the house.

'Ma!' The shotgun cradled in her hands, a wide-eyed, white-faced Sara-Jane peered down from the loft. 'Ma ... you alright?'

'I guess so.' Slowly, Ma Jordan collected her thoughts. 'See anything?'

'Yeah!' Sara-Jane's voice rose an octave. 'There's another fella at the corral.'

'Give 'im a blast.' Ma had a grip of herself by now.

'Sure, Ma.' Shaking with excitement and fear, Sara-Jane loaded two rounds and, pushing the twin barrels of the shotgun through the open window, pulled both triggers. Only luck, and the fact that she was shooting blindly and high, saved Clint. A storm of lead plucked the hat from his head. With a yell of fear he dived behind the empty wagon.

'Ma, it's me, Ellie-May. I'm comin' in.'

'Come ahead.' Ma's voice was brisk and businesslike again. Ellie-May dived through the doorway and fell over Dutch's body. Her eyes widened.

'Dead?'

'I guess so. Sounded like you was havin' some trouble.' A bullet smacked against the rear wall of the ranch house.

"Nother fella at the corral,' Ma said succinctly. Her voice lifted in a shout. 'Sara-Jane! What's happenin'?'

'He's back o' the wagon!' The voice was high-pitched and shaky. 'Don't think I hit'm.'

'Shucks!' Ma scowled disgustedly. She called again. 'Aim low an' see if you can bounce the slugs off that rocky ground there.'

Sara-Jane reloaded and, aiming the shotgun at the ground between the wagon wheels, jerked both triggers. The boom of the explosion seemed to shake the loft as the stock smacked against her already bruised shoulder. A leaden hail ricocheted under the wagon.

There was a yell from Clint. 'Don't shoot! I give up.'

'Toss out your guns.' Ma was all business now. 'Then come out slow yourself, an' keep your hands high.'

Two long-barrelled Colts came skidding out. There was a pause. 'I can't get up. My legs is shot up bad.'

'Crawl then!' Mary-Lou was merciless. 'An' keep away from them guns.'

Groaning loudly, Clint hauled himself painfully out from under the wagon. 'Help me, I'm hurt bad.'

'Mister,' Ma's voice dripped acid. 'You're lucky to be alive. Ellie-May, I'll cover'm while you get his guns. If he moves, drill'm.'

'Sure, Ma.' Ellie-May eased through the door and faded out of the line of fire.

'Sara-Jane!'

'Yeah, Ma?'

'Check that ridge one more time. Then get down here an' bring that shotgun.'

'Sure, Ma.'

Clint groaned as Ellie-May approached. Warily, eyes on the wounded outlaw, she bent and picked up the two guns.

'Nuthin' movin, Ma.' That was Sara-Jane.

'Alright. Get yourself down here. I'm goin' out to have a look at this varmint.'

'His legs are bleedin' awful bad.' Ellie-May said worriedly.

'Tcha!' Mary-Lou was dismissive. 'Betcha they're only flesh wounds.'

'We got to do somethin', Ma! Can't just leave'm lyin', bleedin' like he is.'

'Should'a thought o' that when he come bustin' in here stealin' horses! That's a hangin' offence. Still, I guess you're right. Sara-Jane, you help Ellie-May drag'm into the kitchen. Then I'll see if I can get the buckshot outa his legs.'

'What about the other fella?' Ellie-May queried. 'Tall, well dressed gent, lyin' out in the yard. Ma, I think he's hit bad.'

'Land sakes!' Ma exploded. 'You think! Why didn't you make sure? Right now he could be drawin' a bead on us.'

Ellie-May shook her head. 'Don't reckon he's got a gun. I picked up his Colts when I come runnin'.'

'Alright.' Ma was somewhat mollified. 'We'll tend to him first. You two, get that old handcart Pa uses when he butchers a steer. It's in the barn. Heave'm onto it, an' tie his hands an' feet. He's a varmint, just like this'n. Remember, if we hadn't been ready we'd be the ones lyin' out there. Oh, an' leave me the shotgun. I'll watch this fella here.'

'He looks bad,' Sara-Jane gasped as they heaved the unconscious Diamond Jack onto the handcart.

'Sure does,' her sister agreed soberly as she lashed the outlaw's hands to the cart, 'but it was him or me. Let's get him into the house an' see if Ma can do anything for him. Tie his feet, Sara-Jane. I don't want no trouble with Ma. All set?'

Her sister nodded. Together, they wheeled the old handcart and its unconscious burden towards the house.

Chapter 3

Sheriff Hank Baxter shifted uncomfortably in his saddle and groaned inwardly. Gettin' too old for this foolishness. Time I was lettin' them young fellas take the strain, he thought tiredly. The bulky lawman squinted downhill at the ranch nestling in the valley below. 'Any of you know the Circle J folks?' He twisted in his saddle as he spoke. 'It's kinda off m'beat.'

'Called there a coupla times.' Mike Devlin, his tall lead deputy, eased a deep-chested Morgan gelding up alongside the sheriff's big dun. 'Name's Jordan. Seemed like nice folks. A mite standoffish though.'

'How come?' Baxter's gaze swept the ranch buildings comprehensively.

'Waal,' Devlin drawled. 'Jordan's alright, but there's somethin' mighty strange 'bout Miz Jordan. 'Member the first time I come through this way. I hailed the house like you always do at them outlying spreads.'

Baxter nodded. 'Yeah, I know what you mean. Saves stoppin' a load o' buckshot from some nervous female.'

Devlin grinned wryly. 'There ain't nuthin' nervous 'bout Miz Jordan. Like I said, I hailed the house, an' a woman's voice said to come in, but slow, an' with m'hands up. Well, I did just that. Went in the door an' along a passage to the kitchen. When I stepped inside I found m'self lookin' down the barrels of a sawnoff shotgun! An' she had a Colt, one o' them old Paterson models, lyin' on the table beside her! Reckon that's the most gun handy female I ever saw. 'Nother thing. If you ever get close to her look at her eyes. My guess is she'd gun you down and not think twice about it.'

There was a snort of laughter from Cal Fischer. 'Damned if she ain't got you scared,' the young deputy sneered. 'Never thought I'd see the day when Mike Devlin was scared o' a woman.'

Devlin flushed angrily, then, biting off a retort, he reached into his vest pocket for his tobacco sack and proceeded to roll himself a smoke.

'Shut up, Cal.' Sheriff Baxter's tone was mild enough, but there was an air of finality about it and Fischer lapsed into a sulky silence.

'What's she like to look at?'

Mike Devlin thought for a moment. 'Shortish, grey-haired, 'bout fifty I reckon. Tough lookin' lady.'

'Any family?'

'Yeah,' Mike struck a match and touching it to his cigarette, inhaled deeply. 'That's another thing. Two sons an' two daughters, an' before you say anything,' he added warningly, 'both daughters are real good-lookin' gals. Only don't come up on the elder one without lettin' her know you're there. Last time I was through this way I was trailin' Jake Eastman, the guy that held up the Ehrenburg stage 'bout a year ago. You remember? The sheriff at Brownsville got him in the end.'

Baxter nodded absently.

'Waal, I got in 'bout suppertime. Old man Jordan said to take m'horse down to the barn an' give him a feed o' grain 'fore I turned him into the corral. Reckoned he was a good-lookin' horse an' worth takin' care of. Said his elder daughter was down there an' would show me where everything was.' He patted the Morgan's glossy neck absently as he spoke. 'Anyway, I reckon I must have startled her. I just stepped in through the barn door and ... man oh man!'

'What happened?' Cal Fischer leaned forward in his saddle.

'You ain't gonna believe this, but there was this tall blonde gal dressed in cowman's rig. Shirt, boots, pants; the lot. And wearin' a gunbelt with twin, tied down, cutaway holsters. Next thing I knew I was lookin' down the barrel of a .44! I swear it was one o' the fastest draws I've ever seen. 'Course, she said she was sorry after; said I'd startled her. Maybe I did, but she sure scared the hell outa me.'

The dark-haired Fischer scowled. 'Don't seem decent to me somehow. A gal wearin' pants an' guns.'

Mike grinned. 'Cal, you got some gall talkin' like that! From all accounts you're a regular tomcat with the ladies, an' here you are gettin' all fired up 'cause a gal dresses like a man. Me, I reckon she can wear what she likes.'

'Tell you somethin' else. Don't waste your time with her. All she's interested in is guns and horses. 'Course, you could try for her sister, Sara-Jane. She's a mite young, but she'll be trouble when she's older.'

'What about the sons?' Baxter slapped at a horsefly on his mount's neck.

'One's a big mean lookin' gent, wi' a scar on his forehead. Heavy built, an' it's all muscle. Packs twin .45's an' looks like he could use them. Reckon he'd be right useful in a fight.'

'Say,' old Jim Davies pushed his mount forward. Nigh on sixty; white-haired, with a beard to match, he was still one of the first up when a posse was called for. 'That wouldn't be Bull Jordan the bounty hunter, would it? Big an' mean lookin'; scar on his forehead. He got a moustache?'

'Yeah, come to think of it, he has. Hell!' Devlin swore disgustedly. 'How come I never connected him? 'Course,' he added hastily, 'I ain't never seen Bull Jordan before.'

'Waal,' Baxter scratched pensively at his stubbled jaw, 'seems like you have now. Last time I saw him was up in Jacksboro, when he brought the Armstrong gang in. Man, that was something. Two o' them were dead and roped across their mounts. The two that were alive were shot up pretty bad and tied in their saddles. Reckon he picked up nigh on two thousand dollars reward money that time. Tell you one thing. You get Bull Jordan on your trail, you might as well give up. He just keeps comin'. How about the other son?'

'John?' Devlin frowned as he drew on his cigarette. 'He don't say much, an' that's a fact. When he does, it's that clipped way Injuns speak when they've picked up our lingo. Packs a .45 and a Bowie knife. My guess is he's right handy with both, 'specially the Bowie. An' he's got a throwin' knife slung round his neck, wi' the scabbard down 'tween his shoulder blades. Saw it when he leaned forward one time. Fair-haired, 'bout six feet tall, lean built, an' it's all bone and muscle.'

'Nother thing; there's a young fella; name o' Jake Larsen, works there. Fair hair, height 'bout five ten. A mite heavier build than John, though they could pass for brothers. He talks the same way as John when other folks are there, but I heard the two o' them on their own, gabbin' away in Comanche lingo. Don't reckon Miz Jordan cares much for him. Sure, he's just like one o' the family. Lives in the house, and eats with them an' all. Him and old man Jordan seem to hit it off, but I seen Miz Jordan watchin' him one time, when she thought nobody was around. Man, it was like lookin' into the gates o' Hell!'

'Reckon the Andersons would try this place?' Fischer queried.

Baxter dismounted stiffly and tightened his cinch. Satisfied, he paused for a moment before remounting.

'Waal, we been pushin' them some. Mebbe … ' he broke off and took another hard look down the slope before swinging into the saddle.

'What d'you make o' them three saddled mounts at the corral? Looks like they've been ridden hard.'

'Yeah.' Devlin squinted against the sun. 'Could be the Andersons' horses. But where's Diamond Jack and his boys?'

'Reckon we'd better get down there fast if I'm right.' Sheriff Baxter kneed the dun off the ridge. 'Spread out. If the Andersons are forted up in there we don't want to make it easy for them. An' no shootin' till I say so. Don't want any o' them Jordan wimmen gettin' hurt.' Every nerve tensed, the posse eased their way down the slope.

☆   ☆   ☆   ☆

Mary-Lou Jordan straightened her aching back and scowled at the groaning Clint Anderson. 'Hush your fuss,' she snapped tartly. 'I'm doing all I can for your brother. Leastways,' she amended, 'you say he's your brother. Don't look much alike to me. Sara-Jane, pass me that skinnin' knife. Might just be able to reach the slug in his shoulder.' She bent again to her task. 'Can't do nuthin' 'bout the one in his chest though. Hafta git'm to a doctor for that.'

Sara-Jane shivered as she watched her mother probe Jack Anderson's shoulder wound with the long thin blade. The outlaw's mutterings rose to a scream as the pain made itself felt.

'Hold still.' Diamond Jack gave a long shuddering groan as the knife grated against the bone. Fighting the rising bile in her throat, Sara-Jane watched the blood well from the wound.

'There,' Ma said triumphantly as the misshapen slug appeared. 'I knew it was lodged against the bone. Wipe the blood away, Sara-Jane. Then get a pad an' a bandage onto that shoulder.' She looked sharply at her younger daughter. 'You alright, gal?'

'I think ... I think I'm gonna be sick!'

'Not in here you ain't! Outside if you feel that way.'

'I'll be alright.' Ellie-May was keeping watch from the doorway, and Sara-Jane had no intention of being sick in front of her. She clenched her teeth and tightened the bandages round Diamond Jack's shoulder and chest.

'See anything, Ellie-May?' Ma called as she washed the blood from her hands.

'Nuthin'…, Ma, I been thinkin'. I reckon these fellas are the Anderson gang.'

'Do tell! Might be you're right. Waal, looks like they won't be troublin' nobody for a spell. Right, get in here and give us a hand to move this jasper onto them benches. Then we can tend to his brother.'

Fear flared in Clint Anderson's eyes as he strained at his bonds. 'You ain't touchin' me,' he snarled.

'Mister,' Ma's voice dripped venom. 'For all I care you could bleed to death. But you been messin' up my floor long enough. 'Sides,' she added, 'm'daughters wouldn't forgive me if I let you die. Now, hush up till we get your brother settled.'

'He don't look good,' Ellie-May said apprehensively as they eased the unconscious Diamond Jack onto the benches, which had been placed side by side.

'That's for sure,' Ma agreed tartly. 'Still, them owlhoots are tough. Could be he'll pull through. Now,' she palmed the Paterson Colt expertly, 'Let's have his brother on the table. You give us any trouble, mister, an' you're dead meat!'

Hatred and fear showed on Clint Anderson's face as he was eased onto the table, but fear was the stronger emotion.

'Right.' Ma gestured with the gun. 'Tie his hands and feet to the table legs.'

'But, Ma ... '

'Do as I say. He's liable to start kickin' when I'm diggin' them buckshot out, an' I ain't takin' no chances.'

'You can't do this,' a whitefaced Clint croaked as his arms and legs were secured to each corner of the table.

'Mister,' Mary-Lou slid the Colt into the table drawer, 'right now I can do anything I like. Now,' to Sara-Jane, 'pull off his boots and cut away them pants. Ellie-May, you get back on watch.'

'All set?'

Sara-Jane nodded numbly.

'Right. Douse some whiskey on that blade an' let's get started. Ellie-May, you see anything?'

'Nuthin', Ma.'

Clint Anderson screamed, a drawn out, high-pitched scream, as Ma probed with the long knife.

'You don't hush up I'll gag you,' Mary-Lou said shortly as she levered out a lead pellet. 'Clean up that blood an' let's try for another slug, Sara-Jane.'

Her daughter nodded wearily and bent to her task. How does she do it? she wondered dully. Look at her, has she any feelings at all?

'Riders comin', Ma.' Ellie-May called softly from the doorway.

Mary-Lou clicked her tongue in exasperation, as she probed for another pellet. 'Sure is gettin' right popular round here all of a sudden. You reckon you know any of them?'

'There's a heavy lookin' gent in front ... ' there was a pause, then Ellie-May called again. 'He's ridin' a big dun. Could be Sheriff Baxter, from Fort Worth. Saw him one time, in Greenhills.'

'Do tell,' Ma said sourly as she dug another buckshot from the groaning Clint's leg. 'Ain't that just like the law. Never around when you need 'em! Keep that shotgun handy!' she added sharply. 'We ain't come this far to make a mistake now.'

★   ★   ★   ★

'Say.' Cal Fischer eased his mount alongside Mike Devlin's Morgan; 'ain't that a gal at the door?'

'That's right,' Devlin drawled. 'An' if you look right close you'll see she's packin' a shotgun, so mind your manners.'

Thirty feet from the ranch house doorway, Sheriff Baxter reined the dun to a halt.

Ellie-May, shotgun cradled in her right arm, and left hand hooked in her gunbelt alongside the holstered .44, waited tensely.

'Howdy, miss. I'm Sheriff Baxter, from Fort Worth, an' this here's my posse. We're trailin' the Anderson gang. Seen any riders come through here lately?'

'Howdy, sheriff.' Ellie-May's cold gaze swept the posse. 'That's their mounts up at the corral. You'll find what's left o' the Andersons inside.'

'You mean ... ' Baxter's eyes bulged and he struggled to regain his composure.

'Yeah, one's dead an' the other two are shot up pretty bad. Anyway,' she added defensively, 'they shouldn't have come bustin' in here like they did.'

'You believe me now?' Mike Devlin whispered to Cal Fischer, who was staring at Ellie-May in open-mouthed amazement. He nodded wordlessly.

Hank Baxter eased his considerable bulk down from the dun and handed the reins to Jim Davies. 'Cal, you an' the boys water the horses an' hitch them at the barn there. Then come across to the house. Mike, you can side me till we get this business sorted out.'

'Ma,' Ellie-May moved to one side and called through the open door. 'Sheriff Baxter an' his deputy comin' in.'

'I hear you,' Ma sounded tetchy. 'Tell 'em to come ahead.'

'Help me, she's killin' me!' It was the cry of a weak, frightened man. Baxter looked questioningly at Devlin as they stepped over van Doren's body and entered the kitchen.

Chapter 4

The smell of disturbed dust hung faintly in the rain-washed air of the valley. Hardy Jordan drew the Winchester from its saddle boot as the giant roan gelding sidled uneasily beneath him. 'Easy, boy.' The horse snorted and stood still, while his rider's keen eyes raked the brush-covered slopes. Nothing moved. Satisfied, Hardy, better known to everyone as Bull, looked again at the tracks ahead of him.

Bull Jordan was big in every sense of the word. Six feet four and weighing two hundred and ten pounds, all of it bone and muscle, he was a bad man to cross. As his brother Lance had once jokingly remarked, 'he's as ornery as a Longhorn bull on the prod!' The name had stuck and there were few who disagreed with it. Brown-haired, with deep-set brown eyes, he favoured his father's side of the family, but his drive and determination came from Ma.

Now, he scowled as he studied the hoofprints in the dust. Four unshod ponies had angled down out of the timber onto the trail ahead of him, not all that long ago. The fact that the ponies were unshod and strung out in single file, pointed almost certainly to Indians, probably Comanches. What were they doing here? Four wasn't enough for a war party, so this was most likely a bunch of young bucks looking for some excitement.

Not for the first time, Bull cursed the whim that had made him decide to visit Fort Concho on his way back from the Border, on the off chance of seeing his elder brother, Lance. Here he was, with a bunch of hostiles up ahead and no way of telling when they might decide to double back and surprise him. He could detour, but that was just as dangerous. It would mean heading into broken country, where Red's speed and stamina, plus his own superior firepower, would be cancelled out. No, best to tag along behind. He'd give them some time to get further ahead.

Sliding the Winchester back into its boot, he checked his two Walker Colts in their cutaway holsters. Normally Bull carried them with the hammer riding on an empty chamber to avoid an accident, but now he loaded each gun fully. If it came to a showdown a couple of extra rounds might make all the difference.

Satisfied, he eased Red into a clump of brush and dismounted. Ears flattened, the giant gelding nipped playfully at his sleeve. Red was a one man horse; the only exception was John Jordan, whom he tolerated and no more. The rest of the family knew all about Red's unstable temper and gave the big horse a wide berth. Strangers who didn't learned quickly! Now, as he stroked the glossy neck, Bull let his mind drift back over that fruitless trip down into Mexico. Eight hundred dollars, he mused. I could have done a whole lot to the ranch with that money. As Ma Jordan had tartly remarked to her husband more than once, their second son sometimes acted as though he already owned the Circle J!

Jim Jordan's wry comeback to that had been that you could hardly blame him. Lance, their eldest son, had gone off to the war and then, when that was over, had signed on for a four year stint with the cavalry. Also, during these years John had been a prisoner of the Comanches. Throughout this period, apart from two years scouting for the Confederate Army, Bull had worked like two men to help his father keep the ranch going.

That was when his other talent as a bounty hunter had come to the fore. It had begun by accident. Early on in his army service he had shown a natural talent for tracking, and it had been allowed to develop.

Following the surrender of the South, Bull had found an immediate and profitable use for his new skill. A somewhat unwilling member of a posse trailing some rustled cattle, he had watched with exasperation and no little contempt, as their self-appointed tracker struggled to follow the outlaws' trail. Eventually, Bull had pushed his way to the front and taken over. The subsequent pursuit and recovery of the cattle, plus the capture of both rustlers, badly wounded, had established his reputation.

It had also established something else. Scanning the 'Wanted' dodgers in the local sheriff's office, Bull had realised that this was where money could be made. Big money. Money that he desperately needed if he was to be a successful rancher, something he wanted to be above all else.

Now, his name was known and feared throughout Texas. Outlaws who had ignored the efforts of the local sheriffs and town marshals to curb their activities, headed out of town and frequently out of the state, when they knew that Bull Jordan was trailing them. Those that stayed to shoot it out came back tied across their saddles. 'Dead or alive' invariably meant dead where Bull was concerned.

And all the time the reward money was channelled into the Circle J. Better breeding stock, better equipment and better buildings. The ranch might be small in area, but, as far as Bull was concerned, it was going to be the best in Texas. Little wonder that Circle J steers and saddle horses commanded top prices everywhere. This trip though had been a failure. He could still hear the sneer in the rurale captain's voice, when he'd shown him Mack McIvor's bullet-riddled body.

'I fear that there ees no reward for you thees time, Senor Jordan. He tried to rob the bank in San Carlos. Eet was hees bad luck that I and my rurales were in town at the time.'

What the hell! Bull shrugged and decided that he had waited long enough. Swinging into the saddle, he eased Red through the brush. Rested, the big horse fought for his head. Quietly, gently, talking softly all the time, Bull steadied him down. Carefully he guided his mount from one brush clump to another, so that they were in the open as little as possible.

The trail wound upwards to a ridge and Bull paralleled it. Something elusive reached his nostrils. It came again ... wood-smoke!

Just for a second Bull Jordan hesitated, then, with the sickening certainty that he'd waited too long, he kneed Red into a gallop. Breasting the ridge the big horse swept down the reverse slope. Low in the saddle, a .45 in his right hand, his rider urged him on.

Below them the small sod-roofed shack and the lean-to barn burned steadily. Close by was an empty pole corral, a dead pony lying just outside the gate. Bull brought Red round the end of the cabin in a tight turn and lit running, twenty feet from the door.

Diving through the open doorway he rolled over and came up, the big Colt at the ready. As his eyes adjusted to the gloom he saw the two bloody forms stretched on the floor.

Bull swept the room with a practised eye. Death was no stranger to him. Jaw set, he stooped over the bodies. A man and a woman, probably in their twenties; both had been scalped. They had been hacked to death and it was obvious that the woman had also been raped. Something in the corner of the room caught his eye. He straightened up and moved closer. A photo in a cheap frame lay there, the glass shattered. Bull bent and picked it up. It showed a smiling young couple and two serious looking, flaxen-haired little girls.

Fear, an emotion alien to him, laid a clammy hand on Bull Jordan, and he hunted feverishly through the tiny cabin. Nothing ... Betcha they've taken them, he mouthed silently, looking at the two hacked bodies. Blazing timbers fell from the roof, just missing him. Moving quickly, Bull swept the sheets from the bed in the recess and laid them on the dead couple. Then he piled the pitifully few pieces of furniture on top. Best I can do he thought, touching a lighted brand to the pile. No time to bury them. Anyway I reckon they'd want me to look out for their kids first.

Red snorted through flaring nostrils as Bull approached. The big horse sensed that something was wrong. 'Easy, boy.' Bull mounted hurriedly and took a last bleak look at the blazing cabin. Part of the roof fell in and a cloud of sparks billowed up. Yeah, he thought sombrely, they'd have wanted it this way. Without a backward glance Bull Jordan headed out onto the Comanches' trail.

Three unshod ponies and two heavier, shod horses. That took care of the dead pony at the corral and the nester's saddle stock. The two shod tracks kept close together. Reckon one's carryin' the youngsters.

All day he rode steadily, paralleling their trail and crisscrossing it at intervals. Nobody, unless he was a greenhorn, followed an Indian's trail directly. That was asking to be bushwhacked.

And still the trail ran south toward the Rio Grande. Mexico I guess, Bull ruminated. Mebbe meetin' up with some Comancheros to trade the kids. He spoke softly to Red and, as if sensing the urgency, the giant gelding lengthened his stride.

★   ★   ★   ★

Lone Wolf reined in his pony and looked back. Their empty trail stretched behind them. Satisfied, he waved the others on and took his place at the rear. Seated behind her sister on the old buckskin mare, five year old Mary Johnson raised a tear-stained face and eyed him apprehensively. Stunned, her mind did not fully comprehend the disaster that had befallen them. Now, with her arms wrapped tightly round her elder sister, she tried to shut everything else out. At eight, Sarah Johnson was old for her years. Cut off from other children, her parents had treated her almost as an equal. She knew what had happened to them and the tragedy had left her numb, just like Ma Jordan all those years before. All her thoughts were now centred on one thing only, survival. Survival for both her and Mary. With that in mind, she locked her hands even more firmly into old Kate's mane, and fixed her gaze on the lead rope held by the brave on her father's black saddle horse, Prince.

Big Eagle was a giant easygoing extrovert, who enjoyed life to the full. Let others do the thinking and planning, Big Eagle, not overly bright, was happy to carry out their orders. Contentedly, he looked over his shoulder at the two small girls astride the buckskin mare. Two small serious faces, surrounded by blonde curls, stared back at him. The Comancheros would pay well for two such girls. In turn they would sometimes sell them over the border in Mexico. Occasionally, they had even been known to trade them back to the Army, who paid handsomely and no questions asked.

Ahead of Big Eagle the two remaining braves rode side by side, one supporting the other. Long Knife had taken one of Dave Johnson's slugs in his chest. Now, only willpower and Tall Horse's strong right arm was keeping him on his pony.

Lone Wolf eased his pony alongside and pointed to the small creek ahead. 'We will camp here tonight. Tomorrow we should meet with the Comancheros.'

He urged his mount to the front and swung towards a clump of cottonwoods. The others followed.

*   *   *   *

Bull Jordan nudged Red out of the timber and dismounted. Leaving the gelding ground-hitched, he climbed the small hill directly ahead and peered cautiously over the top. Some two miles due south a camp fire twinkled faintly in the dusk. Slowly, he eased himself back below the crest and made his way down to Red. Standing beside the roan gelding he mulled the problem over. He could make a run for the camp, and trust to luck and his firepower to see him through. Waste o' time, Bull thought wryly. They'd kill the girls before he got there.

Then again, he could hang on until dawn and try to drift in quietly. Still be the same. The kids'll be just as dead. He took a deep breath; there was only one way. Wait until the camp was asleep, then go in on foot. The odds weren't good, but he daren't risk waiting another day. There was always the chance that the band would meet up with Comancheros and sell the girls. For all he knew they could be travelling to a rendezvous right now. That would mean even more trouble. The decision made, Bull set about his preparations. First, he walked Red another mile and ground-hitched him. The Winchester he left in the saddle boot. This would be a close range job. Next, he undid his bedroll and took out a pair of moccasins. Removing his boots he hung them on the saddle horn, then slipped on the moccasins. They felt amazingly light and he grinned to himself. Pity I ain't keen on dancin'!

His fingers explored the bedroll and eased the long knife from its hidden compartment. Thoughtfully he weighed it in his hand. Yes, he would need it. Carefully, he buckled the sheath to his gunbelt and manoeuvred it into position. A thought occurred to him and, removing his hat, he hung it beside the boots. Finally he replaced the bedroll in its usual position behind the saddle. For a long moment Bull stood beside the gelding stroking its neck, then he turned and started walking towards the creek. As he walked, his eyes and ears alert for the slightest sound, he ran through his plan again. Ease down to the creek bank, then come in from that direction towards the fire. From there it would be a case of kill or be killed. The darkness was complete now, and he heard the chuckle of the creek before he saw it. Away to his left the campfire flared briefly. Mebbe half a mile, Bull surmised to himself. He slowed again and dropped into a crouch. Bent low, he moved cautiously forward.

Chapter 5

Sarah Johnson lay staring into the night, her mind still frozen with the enormity of the disaster that had befallen her family. Beside her, Mary stirred restlessly and moaned in her sleep. Although they were both bound hand and foot, they had not been ill-treated in any way. When it came to small children, Indians could sometimes be surprisingly kind.

The campfire blazed up suddenly and Long Knife muttered feverishly as the pain of his wound made itself felt. Lone Wolf came awake quickly, like an animal, and scanned the sleeping camp searchingly. Nothing. Their ponies drooped tiredly against the shadowy background of the night. Satisfied, he sank back and drew his blanket closer.

A hundred yards out, Bull Jordan flattened himself into the grass and tested the breeze. It blew towards him. Slowly he started to crawl forward, the long knife clenched between his teeth. For such a big man he moved with amazing stealth. The distance narrowed to seventy yards, … then fifty.

Long Knife cried out sharply; Lone Wolf started and rose quickly. For a long moment he stared round the sleeping camp. Satisfied, he moved across to where Long Knife lay, and stooped over the prone figure. Sadness touched his features momentarily. They had grown up together, and now Long Knife was nearing his end. Deep in thought, the tall Indian made his way back to his position on the other side of the fire. A last look round the camp and he settled himself back in his blanket. The flames sank to a dull glow.

Thirty yards out, Bull Jordan peered through the long grass. Now he knew where he had to strike first. It appeared that at least one of the Indians was wounded; well, that improved the odds slightly.

Foot by foot he closed on Lone Wolf. Twenty feet, fifteen ... he rose and covered the distance to the sleeping figure like a giant cat. The knife blade glinted in the dull glow of the fire as it rose and fell. Bull threw himself on Lone Wolf. The Comanche jerked convulsively and was still.

Directly across the campfire, Sarah Johnson's scream split the night. Coming on top of everything else, the sudden killing had swept away the mental barrier that the slaying of her parents had left.

Bull Jordan spun and came up with a Walker Colt in each hand. Between the fire and the horses, Tall Horse and Big Eagle were also leaping to their feet. Gun thunder rocked the night. Hit squarely by two .45 slugs, Tall Horse died before he knew what had happened. Beside him, Big Eagle threw his tomahawk in a purely reflex action. Bull cursed as he felt the blade slice across the top of his left shoulder. The gun in his right hand boomed twice in quick succession and the impact drove Big Eagle to his knees. Slowly, the giant Comanche fell forward and sprawled full length in the grass. The Walker Colt boomed again. Big Eagle shuddered under the impact and was still.

A flicker of movement caught Bull's eye. He wheeled and shot instinctively. Long Knife toppled sideways and sprawled by the dying embers of the fire. The echoes died away into a brooding silence.

Breathing heavily, guns at the ready, Bull swept the campsite with a keen gaze. Nothing moved. Satisfied, he punched out the empties and reloaded. Becoming aware of blood trickling down his arm, he flexed it and grunted with relief. Flesh wound.

Quickly he crossed to the two small figures and knelt beside them. Two pairs of big eyes stared back at him. 'Easy, kids. You're safe now.' His knife sheared through their bonds and they clung to him instinctively. Gently, he disengaged them, then ... 'Tell me your names.'

'I'm Sarah, an' she's Mary. Don't cry, Mary. We're safe now.'

'Them shod horses your Pa's?'

'Yes.' A sob caught in Sarah's throat. 'The buckskin is old Kate, an' the black is Pa's saddle horse, Prince.'

'Right.' Working swiftly, Bull hoisted the two girls onto the old mare, then turned to survey the carnage. Four dead Comanches sprawled in the flickering firelight, mute testimony to his killing ability. This would be a good place to leave.

Grasping the mare's lead rein, he mounted Prince and headed away north. Dawn was beginning to lighten the eastern sky.

Half a mile out, he halted Prince and whistled. Faintly down wind came Red's answering call. Satisfied, Bull Jordan urged the black horse forward, the mare plodding stolidly at his side.

Ears laid back, Red watched them approach. He had an evil temper and he hated seeing Bull on another horse.

'Alright.' Bull swung down and walked towards him. Red snorted and snapped at his sleeve. The two girls watched with big eyes as Bull batted the gelding on the nose. The big horse whinnied softly and rubbed his head against his master's arm. The scent of blood came to him and he drew back snorting.

'Mister,' Sarah said hesitantly, 'Is he safe?'

'Red?' Bull removed the moccasins and pulled on his boots. 'Sure. He's just playful, like a kitten.'

He delved into his saddlebags and pulled out a clean bandanna. Removing the one round his neck Bull knotted the two together. Next, the big man slipped off his shirt and, taking his canteen from the saddle horn, washed his shoulder wound clean.

Satisfied that the wound had stopped bleeding, Bull laid the makeshift bandage over it, across his chest and under the other arm. Carrying his shirt he walked towards the girls. Turning his back towards them, he spoke over his shoulder. 'Tie the ends across m'back. Make it good an' tight.'

Sarah shivered involuntarily as she knotted the bandanna ends together.

'That's fine.' Bull eased into his shirt and buttoned it. He turned to face Sarah. 'What was your folks' name?'

'Johnson. Pa's first name was Dave, an' Ma's name was Amy.'

'Alright, Sarah Johnson. Can you ride that black horse?'

'Prince?' Sarah nodded.

'Right! You ride Prince an' lead Kate. Red don't like other horses too close to him. Time we was movin'.'

'Where are we going?'

'Fort Concho. My brother might be there. You got any kin in these parts?'

Sarah shook her head. 'Pa an' Ma ... ' her voice trembled, 'they came from back east.'

'Right. Fort Concho it is.' Gently, Bull lifted Sarah off the old mare and deposited her on Prince's back. He handed her Kate's leading rein.

Swinging into the saddle he eased Red into his stride and headed north. The girls followed.

✯   ✯   ✯   ✯

The saloon was deserted. Sergeant Lance Jordan loafed against the end of the bar and cast a disgusted look over the empty room. Leaning across the polished bar counter, he signalled to Sam Winter, bartender cum proprietor of the Lone Star saloon.

'Gimme a beer, Sam, an' where in hell is everybody?'

Big Sam drew a brimming glass and shoved it across the bar.

'Waal,' he picked up the proffered coins, 'there's been an Injun raid down in the Brazos country. Coupla ranches burnt an' folks killed. Sheriff Hinton deputised every available man an' lit out after them.'

'Damned fools,' Lance grunted morosely into his beer. 'Them Injuns'll be in Mexico by now. Either that, or they'll sucker the posse into an ambush, an' with Sheriff Hinton leadin' it that wouldn't surprise me none.'

'Yeah,' Sam polished a glass reflectively. 'Fat Man Hinton ain't no Injun fighter. Anyway,' he added pointedly, 'your bunch sure as hell weren't here.'

'Waal,' the big blond sergeant shrugged moodily, 'Captain McMillan took the company up north to sort out that trouble around Washita. Reckon I'd have been there m'self, but me an' young Pete Jensen were escortin' a coupla prisoners to Fort Davis. You ask me, the tribes are on the prod. Lots o' Injun sign down that way. I think ... '

'Riders comin',' Pete Jensen, a stocky dark-haired youngster, shoved through the batwing doors and made his way to the bar.

'Strangers?' Lance downed the last of his beer.

'Yeah, big fella an' two kids. Looks like they come a fair piece.'

'Say, mebbe some o' them ranch folks got away!' the tall sergeant pushed his way through the doors and squinted up the dusty street. Glass in hand, Pete joined him.

'Big guy, ain't he?'

'Sure is.' Something stirred in Lance Jordan's memory. His blue eyes narrowed thoughtfully. That big roan ... 'Red! Big Red. Hey, that's m'brother, Hardy!'

'You don't mean ... say, ain't he Bull Jordan, the bounty hunter everybody's allus talkin' about?'

'Yeah, only don't call him that, leastways not to his face! Some things he's awful tetchy about.'

Bull reined Red to a stop beside the hitching rail and got down stiffly. Pete Jensen stared at him with awe. So this is the great Bull Jordan. Man, he's somethin' else. Thought the sarge was big, but this fella must be all of two inches taller an' mebbe twenty, thirty pounds heavier. Mean lookin' as all hell too!

'Howdy, Lance. It's been quite awhile.'

'Yeah, too long. Looks like you been doin' some travellin'?'

'A fair piece.' Bull shrugged his shoulders involuntarily and winced at the pain.

'That blood on your shirt?'

'Yeah; Comanche tomahawk. Soon as I get them kids a place to stay, I'll get somebody to take a look at it.'

'What about their folks?' Lance queried.

'Dead, Comanche raidin' party cleaned out their place down on Devil's Creek.'

The cavalry sergeant gestured to the two wide-eyed little girls sitting on their mounts. 'How come?'

'Comanche took 'em prisoner. I got 'em back.' He closed his eyes for a moment. 'Don't think I'd want to do it again.'

Pete Jensen frowned. 'How many?'

'Four.' Bull turned back to his brother. 'Say, could you find a place for the gals to sleep?'

Big Sam intervened. 'Me an' Miz Winter would be proud to have them.'

'Thanks.' Bull lifted the girls down from their mounts. Mary Johnson clung to him.

'Mister Jordan!' Sarah stared up at the big man. 'You won't leave us, will you?'

'Naw.' Bull's voice was gruff with embarrassment. 'Once I get the horses down to the livery stable, I'll come back an' see you 'fore you get to bed.'

Behind him, Lance grinned. It was something to see Bull embarrassed. 'Lemme give you a hand.' Picking up Prince and Kate's reins, he followed his brother and Red up the street.

Annie Winter put an arm round each of the girls and swept them indoors.

☆   ☆   ☆   ☆

'That's quite a story.' Lance stared across the table at his brother.

'Yeah, waal ... ' Bull shrugged and winced.

'You get that shoulder seen to?'

'Sure, Miz Winter did a right good job. Just wonderin' what'll happen to them kids?'

'Dunno; mebbe the Winters'll take them.'

Bull scowled. 'Don't fancy that. Saloon ain't no place for kids.'

'Mm.' Lance took a pull at his beer. 'Why don't you take them back to the ranch? How are the folks makin' out anyhow?'

'They're alright, but I ain't sure it'd be a good notion. You know Ma?' Bull looked questioningly at his elder brother. 'She's still just as feisty as ever.'

'Sure, Ma'll raise hell, but it might be just what she needs.'

'Waal, mebbe you're right. I'll sleep on it. Tell you one thing, I'm goin' to miss that eight hundred dollars. Would've made a big difference to the ranch.'

The batwing doors banged as Pete Jensen re-entered the saloon.

Lance grinned. 'Can't win 'em all. There's still the Anderson gang. Last I heard they were up north somewhere.'

'Not any more they ain't!' The young trooper dropped into a vacant chair. 'They tried to hold up the bank in Fort Worth four days ago. Stage just brought in the news. 'Pears like they didn't get nothin' an' two o' them were gunned down. Killed a bank teller though. Anyway, the three that were left lit out south with a posse after them.'

'South you say?' Bull frowned heavily. 'Don't like the sound o' that. Pa an' the boys were runnin' some steers to Fort Worth this week. That'd leave Ma an' the gals on their own. If the Andersons came down the Trinity River trail they could have hit the Circle J by now. Damn, I don't like it at all!'

'Take it easy.' Lance drained his glass and stood up. 'No use gettin' in a lather. I'll go see Lootenant Jackson. With the rest o' the company away he's in charge. If I tell him what's happened he'll let me go with you. Him an' me go back a ways.'

'You sure it'll be alright?' Bull looked dubious.

'Yeah; we been meanin' to scout that area anyway. I'll just bring it forward a mite. Now, get some sleep an' be ready to ride come mornin'. Oh, one more thing, take them gals back to Ma. Night now.' The big sergeant shoved his way through the doors and disappeared up the street.

'Easy-goin' cuss ain't he?' There was a note of exasperation in Bull's voice as he stared after his brother.

'The sergeant you mean?' Anger flared momentarily in Pete Jensen's eyes. 'Mister, you may be the bounty hunter that has everybody runnin' scared. Mebbe you kill Injuns with your bare hands, but you sure as hell have a lot to learn 'bout that brother o' yours. He might look easy-goin', but he's the best damn sergeant in the company!'

'When he says him an' the lootenant go back a ways, that's only half the story. 'Bout a year ago Lootenant Jackson was leadin' a patrol down in the Big Bend country. I was in the patrol, an' your brother was sergeant. Well, we run into a bunch o' Comanches an' the looie stopped a bullet. That's when the sarge took over. He organised us an' fought the Comanches till they give up an' pulled out. Then he dug the bullet outa Jackson, bandaged him up, an' brought him back to the fort. The looie was laid up for quite a spell, but he pulled through. Now he thinks your brother is the greatest. Wanted to get him a medal, but the sarge just laughed an' told Jackson to forget it.'

Pete stood up. 'Mebbe I shouldn't have shot my mouth off, but I think a lot o' the sarge. G'night.'

The batwing doors banged behind him and he was gone.

Bull Jordan scrubbed his chin thoughtfully, a shamefaced grin spreading slowly across his face. 'I'll be damned! First time in years anybody's talked to me like that. Still, what the hell, mebbe I been needin' it.'

Big Sam cleared his throat nervously. 'Young Pete didn't mean no harm. It's just that he sets considerable store by your brother.'

'Me too, mister.' Bull flexed his bandaged shoulder and winced again. 'Now, I reckon I'll go get some sleep. Thanks for takin' care o' the kids. G'night.'

'G'night.' Sam watched the big figure mount the stairs. He shivered involuntarily. Pete, you dang fool, you'll never know how lucky you were. That is one dangerous hombre.

Chapter 6

▼

'There.' Ma tossed a lead slug triumphantly into the bowl at her elbow and grimaced as she straightened up.

'Only another couple I reckon, Sara-Jane. Oh…howdy, Sheriff. We ain't met before, but,' she pointed the long skinning knife at Mike Devlin, 'I remember your deputy from last time he was through this way.'

The two lawmen removed their hats carefully. Struggling to assemble his thoughts, Sheriff Baxter stared at the stocky figure with the blood spattered apron and the long knife.

'Howdy, ma'am. Mind tellin' me what's been happenin' round here?'

'Waal now, these fellas,' she indicated the moaning Clint and the unconscious Diamond Jack, 'an' the big gent you saw in the passage, come bustin' in here loaded for bear. Ellie-May, my elder daughter, reckons they're the Anderson gang, but I figure you'll know all about that.'

'Yeah; well it's them alright, we beeen trailin' 'em a considerable piece; but how come … ?'

'How come a bunch o' wimmen whipped a tough outfit like the Andersons?' There was a frosty gleam in Ma's eyes. 'I'll tell you. 'Cause we was ready for 'em. I shot the big black bearded gent lyin' in the passage. The tall fella with the fancy vest? Ellie-May gunned him down in the yard. And,' she concluded, bending once again over the moaning Clint, 'if Sara-Jane could fire a shotgun without jerkin' the triggers, we wouldn't be diggin' the buckshot outa this fella here! Alright, Sara-Jane. Swab off that last wound, an' get a pad an' a bandage on it.'

'Ma'am.' Sheriff Baxter indicated the unconscious figure laid out on the benches. 'This here's Diamond Jack Anderson. How bad is he?'

'Waal,' Ma pursed her lips judiciously, 'he ain't good an' that's a fact. I took a .44 slug outa his shoulder, but he's got another one in his chest. Reckon if you can get him to Oxbow without him dyin' on you, then that young doctor there might be able to do somethin' for him. Even then, I don't reckon his chances are all that great.'

'How about Clint here?' Mike Devlin pointed to the prone figure on the table.

'Him?' Ma snorted. 'He'll be all right. 'Course, he might not walk too good for a spell, but that's his problem.'

'Waal, ma'am,' Baxter scratched his head. ' 'Pears like you done our job for us. 'Course,' he added, 'there's a tidy bit o' reward money comin' your way. About fifteen hundred dollars I reckon.'

'Fifteen hundred dollars!' Sara-Jane gasped, 'but ... '

'There now, Sara-Jane,' her mother said sarcastically, 'looks like being prepared is worthwhile after all.' Sara-Jane flushed scarlet and bit her lip.

'Ma'am;' Sheriff Baxter broke the uncomfortable silence. 'Seems to me that if Diamond Jack is gonna stand trial, we'll have to get him to that doctor in Oxbow right quick.'

'Waal,' Ma paused in the act of washing her hands. 'I can loan you a team an' a wagon. Send 'em back when you're finished.'

'Thanks, ma'am. I'm beholden to you. An' would you mind if we buried van Doren here? It's a long haul to Fort Worth an' I doubt if he'll keep.'

Ma's eyes narrowed until they were chips of ice. 'Sheriff, you ain't buryin' no owlhoot trash on this ranch an' that's final! Once you're off Circle J land you can do what you like.'

Baxter shrugged and bit off the remark that was on his lips.

'Ma,' Ellie-May called from the outer doorway, 'Deputy Fischer here would like to talk to the sheriff.'

Baxter nodded assent to the query in Ma's eyes.

'Sure, bring'm in.' She untied her apron and folded it. 'Sheriff, if you an' your deputy move Clint here onto them benches beside his brother, I'll start fixin' coffee an' some chuck for your posse. Oh ... and tie his hands. I'd as soon trust a rattlesnake!'

Ellie-May, followed by Cal Fischer, came through the kitchen doorway in time to see Baxter and Devlin easing the cursing Clint Anderson onto the benches. Fischer's eyes bulged as he stared at the two sprawled figures and the blood spattered table.

'Ma,' Ellie-May indicated the startled deputy, 'this here's Deputy Fischer.'

'Howdy, son.' Ma finished washing her hands and dried them carefully. "Pears like deputies are gettin' younger all the time. Ellie-May, that new wagon; you got the harness ready like Pa asked you?'

'Sure, Ma. I was workin' on the last piece when them Andersons … '

'Right!' Ma cut Ellie-May short and switched her sharp gaze to Cal Fischer. 'You wanted to see the sheriff?'

'Yes, ma'am.' The young deputy removed his hat and swallowed nervously. Mike Devlin stifled a grin. 'Sheriff, the boys was wonderin' … '

'Tell them to quit wonderin',' Baxter said tersely. He felt that the situation was slipping away from him. 'The Anderson gang is all washed up. 'Pears like we ought to resign an' let these ladies here take over. Anyways, tell the boys to take that dead fella lyin' in the passage, outside. Miz Jordan is loanin' us a wagon an' a team to haul him an' the Andersons back to Fort Worth.'

'That's right,' Ma dumped her bloodstained apron in a bucket of water and straightened up. 'Ellie-May, you catch up the team in the corral an' take them down to the barn. This young fella can help you. Get the harness on 'em an' hitch 'em to the new wagon. Pitch some hay into the wagon bed. Should make the ride easier.'

'Yeah, Ma.' Ellie-May and Cal disappeared through the door, both looking relieved to be out of the range of Ma's eagle eye.

'Sara-Jane!' Her younger daughter, who had collapsed into a chair, started nervously. 'Get some old blankets outa the storeroom while I scrub this table. I reckon these two,' she indicated the Andersons, 'will need some cover in that wagon. Then you can help me get some coffee an' chuck ready for the sheriff an' his boys.'

Mike Devlin cleared his throat.

Ma looked at him inquiringly.

'Ma'am, if it's alright with you I could help your daughter get them blankets.'

'Ma'am,' Sheriff Baxter had seen the merest flicker of Mike's left eyelid. 'It might let us get away sooner, an' I wouldn't want Diamond Jack dyin' on our hands if I can help it. I'll keep an eye on the prisoners meantime.'

'Waal … ,' Ma deliberated for a long moment, 'seein' that it's you, deputy, an' seein' that you been here before … alright. But,' she added warningly, 'no foolin' around. That goes for you too, Sara-Jane.'

'Ma!' A scarlet-faced Sara-Jane hurried Mike Devlin out of the kitchen.

☆   ☆   ☆   ☆

'Thanks for everything, ma'am.' Tipping his hat to Ma Jordan and the girls, Hank Baxter swung up onto the big dun. 'Deputy Devlin'll bring your team an' wagon back as soon as we're finished with 'em. Adios now.'

He settled himself comfortably in the saddle and nodded to Cal Fischer. From his seat on the wagon the young deputy threw him a sullen look as he eased the team into a long-striding walk.

A stream of curses erupted from the bed of the wagon, as the wheels bumped over a projecting rock. Fischer's black cowpony, hitched to the tailgate, shied nervously.

'Shut your row,' Baxter scowled as he brought the dun up alongside. 'We're gonna do this all nice an' legal. I aim to see you an' your brother stand trial.'

'Waste o' time an' money,' Cal said sulkily. 'They're guilty as hell. Pity them Jordan wimmen hadn't finished the job.'

Prone on his back, Clint Anderson glared up at the lawmen. Beside him, Diamond Jack groaned fitfully.

Baxter shook his head sorrowfully as he rolled a cigarette. 'Son, you ain't never gonna make a good lawman 'less you stop thinkin' like that. Our job is to bring 'em in, alive if possible. What happens after that is up to Judge Smith. Right now we're gonna get these varmints to Oxbow an' see what that young doctor can do for 'em.

"Course,' he jerked his head at the shrouded body of van Doren, stretched out in the back of the wagon, 'there ain't nuthin' we can do for him. Miz Jordan seen to that. Still, at least we got the body. There's a five hundred dollar reward for him. With that, plus a thousand dollars for the Andersons, them Jordan wimmen did a right good bit o' business.'

'Yeah.' Cal Fischer shivered involuntarily. 'Tell you one thing, I believe Mike now. Them wimmen are as dangerous as a nest o' rattlers! This owlhoot bunch here was supposed to be a tough outfit, an' they never stood a chance. How come?'

Baxter grinned mirthlessly. 'That's another thing you got to learn. How to get information. Now, Mike, he talked to the younger Jordan gal. Sara-Jane you said her name was, didn't you?'

'Yeah,' Mike Devlin's face reddened as he nudged the Morgan up beside the big dun. 'There's quite a story there. Most of it bears out what I told you before. Miz Jordan's folks homesteaded up in Illinois, round about 1820. She was born the same year. There were two boys as well, but they were a lot older. One way an' another, I reckon it must have been a lonely life for her.'

Baxter nodded absently, his mind drifting back to his own childhood. 'Then what happened?'

'Waal ... ,' Mike paused, while Cal eased the wagon round a rocky outcrop, 'for a spell everything was fine. The Injuns were right peaceful, an' the local chief, Black Hawk, I think Sara-Jane said his name was, hit it off real good with Miz Jordan's pa.'

'Say!' Old Jim Davies twisted in his saddle, 'I remember Black Hawk. 'Course,' he added hastily, 'I was only a kid at the time, but m'folks used to talk about him. They come from up that way.'

'What about Black Hawk?' Cal interjected.

Davies hosed a stream of tobacco juice into the trail dust and kneed his mount closer to the wagon. 'Seems like Black Hawk was the war chief o' the Fox tribe. Round about then, lots o' settlers started crowdin' into the Fox River country. Black Hawk, he organised the local tribes, the Fox, the Winnebago an' the Sauks, an' fought them all the way.'

'An' yet,' Baxter mused, 'he left Miz Jordan's folks alone?'

'Didn't do them much good!' Mike Devlin commented sourly. 'When Miz Jordan was about eight years old, a band o' Winnebagos came to the homestead. Probably young bucks on the rampage. Miz Jordan was out in the woods at the time. Seems her folks were used to her roamin' round like that.

'Anyways, she came back to find all the family dead. Sara-Jane was kinda short on details, other than that they had been scalped. My guess is that there was a lot more to it than that, only Miz Jordan ain't told her gals.

'You figger what that did to an eight year old. She wandered in the woods for two days before a search party found her.'

'What happened then?' Baxter queried.

'Some cousins in Idaho took her in an' gave her a home. That's where she grew up. Years later she met Jordan and married him. They come here an' started the Circle J. Started a family as well. Everything was fine for a spell. Then, some twelve, thirteen years ago, a Comanche raidin' party from Ten Bears' outfit grabbed young John Jordan; he was only eight or nine at the time, an' took off with him.'

'Say!' Old Jim Davies chewed reflectively for a moment, 'I remember that. Fact is I rode wi' the posse that trailed 'em.'

'Did you come up wi' them?' the sheriff rolled a cigarette as he spoke. Absently, he scratched a match on his pants leg.

'Nah ... , we chased them Injuns right down to the Border, but they crossed the Rio an' we never saw hide nor hair of 'em again. Thought sure they'd sell him to the Comancheros.'

'Waal, they didn't.' The Morgan nipped playfully at the dun's shoulder. Devlin leaned forward and slapped its neck before continuing. 'Seems like Ten Bears took a fancy to the boy, an' brought him up as his son. That might have been the end of it, 'cept this old buffalo hunter, Sven Larsen, wintered with the tribe some three years ago, an' he got to hear about young Jordan. Dunno why he wanted to take a hand. Mebbe he figgered there would be money in it for him if he could get John back to his folks. By this time young Jordan was eighteen years old, a Comanche in everything but blood. Still, he must have had some memories o' his family, either that or old Sven was mighty convincin'. Whatever the reason, young John agreed to make a break for it.

'Now, Larsen had a half-breed Comanche son, Jake, or Runnin' Wolf, if you want to give him his Injun name. That's helluva unusual 'cause the Comanches don't hold wi' mixed marriages. Him an' John had become real close. Mebbe old Sven figgered this was the only way to get his boy back among white folks as well; who knows. Anyways, in the spring o' sixty-six the three o' them made a run for it. Ten Bears' bunch were camped below the Pecos at the time.'

'What happened?' Hank Baxter interjected.

'Waal, they got away alright, then things went wrong. Accordin' to Sara-Jane, a scoutin' party o' Ten Bears' braves caught up with them at the Pecos. Must have been some fight, 'cause when it was over the scoutin' party were all dead, but so was old Sven. The boys buried him an' lit out north for the Circle J. Seems Larsen gave them directions before he died.

'An' that was it?'

'No, not exactly. Ten Bears' boys trailed 'em to the ranch, an' there was a hell of a fight. The Jordans stood them off, an' then they got lucky.'

'How come?'

"Pears the Jordans have another son, Lance, the eldest o' the three. He's a sergeant in the cavalry an' stationed at Fort Concho. Waal, he was comin' through this way with a patrol an' heard the shootin'. They come up behind the Comanches an' mauled them pretty bad. Don't think all that many got away.'

Sheriff Baxter squinted into the distance. 'Didn't Ten Bears ever try again?'

'Seems not. Injuns can be queer. You beat them in a fight, like as not they'll walk away an' forget about it. Not like white folks. We'd carry a grudge an' want to get even. Mebbe pride came into it as well. If Ten Bears thought young Jordan didn't want to live with the band, he might not want him back.'

'Mm,' Baxter thought for a moment. 'How come that Jordan gal told you all this?'

'You mean Sara-Jane?' There was a long pause. 'Dunno. Mebbe she was just dyin' to talk to somebody an' I happened to be there. Shouldn't think she's got much in common with her sister, or her mother either come to that.'

☆   ☆   ☆   ☆

Ma Jordan and the girls watched the posse's dust cloud dwindle into the distance. 'Alright, seems like we've had enough excitement for one day. The pair of you start cleanin' up the kitchen. Looks like somebody butchered a steer in there. Me, I'll fix us somethin' to eat.'

She headed for the kitchen. 'Oh ... an' keep them guns handy. They say lightnin' don't strike twice in the same place, but you can't never tell!'

'Ma.' Bringing up the rear, Ellie-May spoke worriedly. 'What about the gent I shot? The tall fella with the fancy vest. Reckon he'll make it?'

'Mebbe,' Ma selected a pot from an adjacent shelf and part filled it with water. Setting it on the stove, she paused and looked sharply at her elder daughter. 'Be just too bad if he don't. He come in here lookin' for trouble an' he got it. Don't blame yourself, it was you or him. Anyways, there wasn't nuthin' more I could do for him here. If they get him to Oxbow in time, might be that young doctor there can fix him up. They say he's real good.'

Sara-Jane looked up from her floor scrubbing. 'Will we have to go to the trial?'

'I guess so,' Ma chopped some vegetables with neat economical movements. 'Sheriff Baxter said he was sorry, but he reckoned Judge Smith would want it that way. 'Sides,' she added, tipping the contents of her chopping board into the pot, 'we got to pick up that reward money. Fifteen hundred dollars'll come in right handy round here.'

Chapter 7

John Jordan eased the last of the bawling, thickset steers into the holding yard. Reining his walleyed pinto to a halt, he waited while Jake Larsen secured the big gate. The two young riders grinned at each other and turned to where Jim Jordan was listening, grave faced, to an animated Matt Machin.

' ... throwin' lead like it was goin' out o' fashion,' the stout cattle buyer was saying excitedly. He paused for effect. "Course, them old-timers was rangers 'fore the war an' they don't spook easy.'

The tall lean rancher nodded absently, mind assessing the implications of the raid.

'Pity they hadn't got the Andersons, or that big fella that rides wi' them; van Doren.' Machin chewed reflectively on a short black cigar, something he was rarely seen without. 'I reckon they'll be pizen mean, seein' as how they didn't get nothin' an' lost Malone an' Rodgers into the bargain.'

Jim Jordan thought for a moment. 'Which way did they head?'

'Uh, didn't I say? An incomin' teamster saw them take the Trinity River trail.'

'Trinity River, you say?' The rancher's interest sharpened and he turned to the two grave-faced young men. 'Don't like the sound o' that, not one bit. Headin' down that way could bring them right close to the Circle J. Wi' us up here an' Bull chasin' Mack McIvor, Ma an' the gals are on their own. Was plannin' to stay in town overnight an' rest the mounts, but we'll cut it short now.' He shook hands with Machin. 'Thanks, Matt. Nice doin' business with you.'

'Me too.' The buyer expelled a long streamer of smoke, eyes narrowed thoughtfully. 'Sure hope your wimmen-folk are alright.'

'Yeah.' Worry surfaced for a fleeting second in the cattleman's deep-set brown eyes. Untying the big Cleveland gelding from the corral fence, he eased himself up into the saddle.

'John!'

'Yeah, Pa.'

'Look in at the depot an' see if there's any mail for us. Jake!'

'Yo.'

'Head down to the livery stable an' say howdy to Abe Davidson for me. Tell'm we need enough grain to take them horses as far as Greenhills. Grazin' ain't all that good right now an' we'll be pushin' 'em hard.' He dug into his pocket and came up with a couple of silver dollars, which he tossed to the young half-breed. 'That should cover it.

'I'll head for the bank. When I've finished there I'll pick up some grub at Bateman and Jefferson's. Just enough to keep us goin'. We won't be eatin' fancy on this trip. Then, I'll meet you both at that new eatin' place on Santa Fe street. Might as well eat 'fore we light out.' He kneed the big Cleveland into motion. 'Let's go.'

Machin watched the three riders canter up the street. There goes a worried man. Can't say I blame him. Them Andersons is killers. Glad it ain't my worry.

* * * *

'Jordan?' The lanky counter clerk riffled through the pile of mail. 'Lemme see, nah ... just a minute. Mrs M.L. Jordan, Circle J Ranch, Fort Worth, Texas. She any kin o' yours?'

'My mother.' The words came out slowly, almost painfully.

'Right, mister.' The clerk slid the long official looking envelope across he counter and closed the hatch.

John stepped out into the spring sunshine and, untying the pinto, swung lithely into the saddle.

Standing outside the Lone Star Restaurant, Jim Jordan eyed the wiry pinto pony trotting towards him, his youngest son swaying easily in the saddle. John's a good boy, he mused, but he's still got a lot o' Injun left in him. Oh, he's a Jordan alright, even with them blue eyes and blond hair. That comes from Ma's side o' the family. Sure wish Mary-Lou could loosen up when she's talkin' to him.

Another rider appeared in the distance. Jake ain't been hangin' around, the rancher mused, but then, he never does. Just gets on with his job. Looks more like a Swede than an Injun, 'cept maybe for them dark eyes. Pity Ma hates Injuns like she does. Still, there it is. Guess I can't expect miracles. Some day, God willin', she'll change. After what Jake and old Sven did for this family, she'd better.

'Any mail?'

'Yeah.' John passed his father the long brown envelope.

'Mm.' Jim Jordan looked at it thoughtfully. 'For Ma, eh. Sure looks official, don't it? Anyways,' he tucked the letter into a vest pocket, 'it'll keep.'

'Jake.'

Young Larsen drew his rangy black pony to a halt.

Jim Jordan eyed the sack secured behind the youngster's saddle. 'You got the grain, I see.'

'Yo.'

'How's Abe makin' out?'

Jake grinned tightly. 'Alright, I guess. Says he ain't forgot how you bested him at poker, last time you were in town.'

The rancher permitted himself a fleeting smile. 'Yeah, that was quite a night.' Worry returned to his lined features. 'Light down an' let's go eat. We got a heap o' hard ridin' ahead o' us.' He paused while they dismounted and secured their ponies. 'I got a bad feelin' 'bout this one. Them Andersons are meaner'n lobo wolves.'

John and Jake exchanged glances as they made their way into the restaurant. It was rare to see Jim Jordan as worried as this.

✦   ✦   ✦   ✦

Hank Baxter squinted at the rising sun and motioned to Mike Devlin. The Morgan came up beside the dun and pranced sideways skittishly. His rider steadied him down and swore softly.

'Damn fool bronc never learns. Every mornin' he's got to work the kinks outa his system. I swear, one day I'll get rid o' him and buy a real horse.'

Sheriff Baxter grinned to himself. He knew that Devlin would never get rid of the Morgan. Not only had he raised it from a foal, but he had also spent long hours training the pony to obey all sorts of commands. It would come at a whistle, stop and lie down at a word, and many more.

'Any time you want to get rid o' him, lemme know. I'll give you top price.'

Devlin laughed. 'Star ain't like that plowhorse you're ridin'. He's built for speed, not weight carryin'.'

'Nuthin' wrong with Buck.' Baxter patted the big dun. 'Him an' me get along right well. Anyways, reckon we'll make Chambers Creek by midday. One more night on the trail, then home the next day.'

Mike Devlin nodded absently, then jerked his head in the direction of the wagon. 'What about ... ?'

'The Andersons? They'll stand trial as soon as we can get a circuit judge here. Good thing the doc at Oxbow was able to dig that slug out. Accordin' to him, the bullet just nicked a rib an' didn't do no permanent damage. 'Course, we'll likely hafta get them Circle J wimmen there for the trial. Reckon that's your job.'

'Me!' Devlin's eyebrows rose and he looked askance at Baxter.

'Sure,' Baxter rolled a cigarette and scratched a match on his pants. 'You just take the wagon back. The young gal likes you, her sister ain't shot you ... yet, an' Miz Jordan ain't had time to make up her mind 'bout you. 'Sides, she'll be glad to see the wagon again.'

Mike grinned. 'Yeah, reckon you're right. Say, what about the dead guy ... van Doren. Think there'll be any trouble?'

"Cause we buried him at Oxbow?' The sheriff drew heavily on his cigarette and blew a long streamer of smoke. 'Nah; when Miz Jordan wouldn't let us plant him on Circle J land there wasn't much else we could do. We been on the road five days now. He wouldn't have kept that long. 'Sides, we all signed a paper certifyin' that it was van Doren. Don't see what more we could've done. Nah,' he waved his cigarette dismissively, 'there won't be no trouble.'

'Riders comin',' Devlin pointed ahead.

'Yeah,' Baxter squinted at the oncoming horsemen. 'Three fellas movin' at a right smart pace. Know 'em?'

Mike Devlin grinned. 'Sure do. It's old man Jordan, that youngest son o' his, an' that young fella I was tellin' you about, Jake Larsen.'

'Howdy, Mister Jordan.' Baxter reined the dun to a halt. The posse piled up behind him.

'Howdy, sheriff,' Jim Jordan lifted a hand and looked inquiringly at Hank Baxter. 'Mind tellin' me what you're doin' with m'new wagon?'

'It's a long story,' the sheriff shifted in the saddle and winced, 'but worth hearin'.'

Ten minutes later the Jordans and Jake Larsen drew off to one side and watched the posse head north.

Jim Jordan removed his hat and scratched his head reflectively. 'If that don't beat all hell,' he muttered. 'To think that Ma an' the gals cleaned out the Anderson gang and earned themselves fifteen hundred dollars reward money.' He chuckled, then laughed outright. 'Betcha Bull will be fit to tie when he hears!'

Surprise, and pride, showed themselves briefly on John Jordan's face. It appeared that this mother of his was quite a woman. He looked again at his father. 'It don't worry you ... Pa ... ,' he stumbled over the word, 'that they were in danger?'

'It worries me like hell,' Jim Jordan looked consideringly at his youngest son, 'but there ain't nuthin' I can do about it. Your Ma has been goin' her own way ever since we got married, an' she'll never change. Now, let's get on home, there's work to be done.'

☆   ☆   ☆   ☆

'Riders comin', Ma.' Ellie-May peered into the kitchen. 'One's Bull for sure and one could be Lance, but I dunno what to make o' the other two. Seems crazy, but they look like kids to me!'

'Shucks,' Ma took a last look at the stew simmering on the stove. 'You sure all that excitement we had last week ain't gone to your head?'

Bull and Lance reined their tired mounts to a halt and swung down quickly. Ma came through the doorway to be enveloped in a bear hug by her eldest son.

'Lance!' Ma blushed as she struggled to free herself. 'Quit this foolishness right now, you hear me.'

Bull grinned at their mother's embarrassment. Lance was the only one of the family who could fluster her. The big man turned to find his two small companions regarding the scene gravely. 'Howdy, Ma. Meet Sarah an' Mary Johnson. Can you get them something to eat, an' I'll tell you how they come to be here.'

Ma opened her mouth, then shut it again as she watched Bull gently lift the two little girls down.

'You won't leave us, Mister Jordan?'

'Naw,' Bull mumbled, flushing crimson, 'this is where I live.'

There was an unaccustomed lump in Ma's throat as she swept the Johnson girls into the kitchen and seated them at the table. Her youngest daughter surveyed them with wide-eyed astonishment. 'Sara-Jane, this here's Sarah an' Mary Johnson. You get them some apple pie an' milk, while I go talk to Bull.'

☆   ☆   ☆   ☆

The stable was cool and dark. Bull stripped the saddle and bridle from Red and rubbed him down, talking as he did so. Ma stood in the doorway listening intently. Beyond them Lance worked on the other horses.

'So there you have it,' Bull concluded. 'Their folks dead, killed by Injuns. They ain't got no kin, leastways none they know about. Ma, I couldn't leave them ... I just couldn't.'

For a long moment Ma stood thinking. Then, swallowing slightly, she came to a decision. 'You did right. They can have a home here as long as they like. It's the least we can do. Now, I got to get back to the house an' get a room ready for them.'

"Nother three riders comin'.' Ellie-May met her mother halfway across the yard. 'Looks like Pa an' the boys.'

'My, my.' Ma rolled her eyes. 'Better get the big table laid. Seems like we'll be a full house tonight.'

'Howdy, Ma.' Jim Jordan climbed down tiredly from the big Cleveland. 'Fellas,' he handed the reins to John, 'put the broncs in the stable for the night. We been pushin' 'em hard. Now,' there was a twinkle in his eye as he turned to his wife, 'Sheriff Baxter tells me you been right busy round here. You aimin' to take over from Bull as a bounty hunter?'

'Shucks,' Ma shrugged dismissively, 'it just happened an' we was ready.'

'Mm,' Pa nodded meaningly. 'Waal, you proved me wrong an' no mistake. I'll never gripe 'bout your hideout guns again. Oh, I almost forgot. Got a letter for you. Official lookin' too.'

'Say,' Ma looked closely at the envelope, 'it's got a Tucson postmark. The only folks I know out that way are the Wilsons. You remember them, they own the Flyin' W ranch. Sure is a big spread.'

She slit the envelope and drew out a sheet of paper. 'It's from some lawyer in Tucson. Mm, mhm ... land sakes, I don't believe it!'

Jim Jordan turned sharply. His wife was standing with her mouth open and a look of blank astonishment on her face.

'They're dead, Jim. Aunt Jess and Uncle Dave. Died within a week of each other. An' they've left me the ranch!'

Chapter 8

▼

'Land sakes, Jim.' Ma Jordan sank into the big old rocking chair, the letter still clutched in her hand. 'Why would they want to leave it to me?'

"Pears like they had no kin.' The rancher knew that Ma was shaken, she wouldn't have called him Jim otherwise. If she called him anything at all it was usually 'Pa'. 'Didn't you stay with them after your folks was killed?'

A shadow crossed Ma's face. 'Yeah, that was before they moved to Arizona. Uncle Dave built hisself a big spread somewhere between Dorando an' the Border.'

'Seems like they remembered you. What else does the letter say?'

'Waal, these here lawyers want me go out an' see them. An' they'd like me to take a look at the ranch at the same time.'

'Mm,' Jim Jordan paused in the act of rolling a cigarette and cocked an interrogative eye at Ma. 'Lots o' Injun trouble out there. Cochise has been givin' everybody a hard time. You sure you want to go?'

Ma reflected for a moment, then nodded. 'Yeah, I'm sure. It's the only chance we'll ever have to leave a worthwhile spread to the family.' She saw the hurt look on her husband's face.

'Oh, I ain't sayin' we don't make a good livin' from the Circle J, but Dunc Paterson an' his Triple X outfit have us boxed in. We ain't never gonna get a chance to expand. An' you know as well as me that it's only Bull an' Lance's reputations that keep Dunc from pushin' us harder.'

Her husband sighed and drew a box of matches from his vest pocket. 'Yeah, that's true.' He fumbled for a moment, then, extracting a match, struck it on the side of the box. Applying the flame to the end of the cigarette, he inhaled deeply and blew a long streamer of smoke. Satisfied, he threw the match into the stove and looked at Ma.

'Alright, so you want to meet the lawyers an' look the spread over. Get Bull to go with you. The rest of us can manage here. Bull knows ranchin' better than any of us. He can drive the buckboard up to Fort Worth, an' you can pick up the stage from there. Last I heard, that Southern Overland outfit had taken over the Butterfield route, an' were just beginnin' to hit their stride.'

'Let's see,' he ruminated for a moment. 'Reckon four weeks should get you to Tucson. Then mebbe a week to see the lawyer an' look at the ranch. Say eight, nine weeks, all told. Anyways, let's eat, then we can talk to the family 'bout it.'

★   ★   ★   ★

'Well, folks.' Jim Jordan glanced round the table. Supper was over and the Johnson girls had been put to bed in one of the spare rooms, though that had only been accomplished on the understanding that Bull would say goodnight to them later. 'That's the way it lays. Ma's inherited this big spread in Arizona, an' the lawyers want her to go out there an' look it over.'

He looked at Ma sitting impassively on his right hand, followed by Ellie-May and Sara-Jane. Down the left side, Bull, John and Jake stared back at him.

Sprawled comfortably in his chair at the bottom of the table, Lance Jordan grinned at his father. 'Don't see this is any concern of mine. If it's alright with you folks,' he half rose as he spoke, 'I'll just go take a look at the horses.'

'You'll stay where you are!' Ma's voice had steel in it all the way through. 'You're family, an' this is family business.'

Jake Larsen rose hastily.

'Sit down, Jake!'

It wasn't often that Jim Jordan raised his voice, but when he did, everybody, including Ma, listened. 'We're all family round this table, an' don't nobody forget it.'

In the silence that followed, Jake sank back into his chair, his face red with embarrassment. Lance grinned at him and winked.

'Right! Now we got that settled, I propose that Bull goes with Ma. He knows ranchin' an' stock better than any of us.'

Bull shifted uncomfortably in his chair and reddened perceptibly.

'I agree.' John Jordan's face was impassive as Bull shot him a grateful glance.

'Anybody disagree?' The others shook their heads.

Bull cleared his throat. His father looked at him inquiringly. 'Just how big is this ranch?'

Jim Jordan nodded to his wife. Ma glanced at the letter in front of her. 'Accordin' to the lawyers it's some nine hundred sections.'

Round the table mouths opened in surprise. Bull took a deep breath. 'That's some spread!'

'Yeah,' Jim Jordan took a piece of paper from his vest pocket. 'If I ain't forgotten all m'schoolin', it's somethin' like half a million acres! Some bigger than the four thousand we got here at the Circle J!'

There was a collective intake of breath round the table. Bull swore explosively and was rewarded by a glare from his mother.

'Sorry, Ma, but that's a lot o' land.'

His father nodded. 'It sure is. That's why I want you to go with your mother an' take a look at it. Buildings, land, stock, the crew ... everything. Then come back an' tell us what you think. Pick up the stage at Fort Worth.'

'There could be trouble with the Apaches.' John Jordan said quietly. 'Cochise is on the warpath out there.'

'Yeah,' Jim Jordan nodded sombrely, 'an' there could be rustler trouble too. We'd be close to the Border. That means carryin' a fair-sized crew. How'd you feel about this, Ma?'

Ma sat for a long moment, the cold faraway look in her eyes. 'The Wilsons left me their ranch, an' no murderin' Apache is gonna run me off it!'

There was an awkward silence round the table. John opened his mouth to speak, then closed it as his father shook his head warningly.

Bull cleared his throat. 'You mind if I take Buck and Star for the run to Fort Worth?'

'The Clevelands? Nah, you'll make better time with them. They're a matched team. Leave them at Sandy Jackson's livery stable. Same with the buckboard. Sandy'll see to everything. Him and me go way back.'

✯   ✯   ✯   ✯

It had rained during the night and laid the dust. The sun still hadn't dried everything out and raindrops glittered in rows on the underside of the fence rails. Down in the yard the Rhode Island chickens scratched contentedly, and the only discordant note was the sound of Big Red kicking moodily at the horse pasture gate, having just been turned in there by Bull.

After breakfast, Bull hitched the Cleveland team to the buckboard and brought it round to the porch. Going into the house he picked up his blanket roll and rifle. Depositing them in the rig he turned round and found his father at his back with Ma's travelling bag, and a long, narrow, canvas holdall.

Jim Jordan grinned at his son. 'That's Ma's travellin' bag.' He tossed it into the buckboard. 'An' this here,' he held up the canvas holdall, 'is her knittin', at least that's what she says. 'Pears to me there's a sawn-off shotgun an' a box o' shells in there as well. 'Course, that ain't none o' my business.'

'You're right,' Ma said tartly, appearing through the door behind him. 'Just 'cause I like to have an ace up m'sleeve, ain't nobody's business but mine.'

Her husband laughed and placed the holdall carefully in the buckboard. 'Can't argue with that after what you did to the Andersons. Just take care, that's all.'

There was a clatter of hooves as Lance led his saddled mount out of the stable. Vaulting into the saddle, he jogged the buckskin across the yard to the front of the house.

Grinning, he eyed his mother climbing into the buckboard. 'All set, Ma? Leave some o' them Apaches for the cavalry.'

Ma paused in the act of adjusting her seat cushion and fixed her eldest son with a flinty stare. 'Ain't you got nuthin' better to do than sit there gabbin'. Thought you was supposed to be scoutin'?'

'On my way, Ma. On my way.' The bantering tone disappeared from Lance's voice. 'You take care now. You too, Bull.'

'Why, Ma.' Sara-Jane had come to see them off. 'You look right smart. That hat an' coat suit you.'

'Shucks,' Tough as she was, Ma was still woman enough to enjoy her daughter's compliment. 'Ain't had no reason to wear them in a coon's age. Don't want them Tucson lawyers thinkin' we're poor relations. Now you see to the chores, Sara-Jane, an' keep an eye on them two youngsters. You need any help, I've told Ellie-May to pitch in an' lend a hand.'

'Sure, Ma.' Sara-Jane hugged herself mentally. Nigh on two months without her mother's abrasive voice needling her. And that deputy had said he'd bring the wagon back soon.

Ma settled herself comfortably on the front seat of the buckboard. 'An' if that deputy comes back with the wagon, don't you go moonin' round him!'

'No, Ma.'

'Mister Jordan.' Bull turned to find two small faces staring up at him. 'You will take care?' Mary Johnson said anxiously.

'Sure will.' The big man bent down somewhat self-consciously and hugged both girls. Then he climbed onto the driver's seat and picked up the lines.

'Reckon we'll make Greenhills tonight. Likely put up at Hannah MaCrae's place.'

Jim Jordan kissed his wife; something which, with the exception of the grinning Lance, embarrassed Ma and the rest of the family more than it did him and stepped back from the buckboard. 'See you in a coupla months time.'

Bull flicked his whip in salute. It was only an ornament, the Clevelands could outrun any team he he'd ever seen. Ma clutched at her hat, and the buckboard whirled out of the yard.

Lance grinned down at Sara-Jane and his father. 'Reckon I'd better start earnin' m'pay if I'm goin' to scout the trail to Trinity by tonight. I'll look in on my way back tomorrow. Adios, Sara-Jane. Watch out for that deputy! Pa, you take care now. Let's go, Buck.' He kneed his mount and the horse bucked half-heartedly a couple of times, before stretching out into a mile-eating lope.

Sara-Jane turned from waving goodbye, to find her father looking at her with a smile on his face. 'Last I saw of Ellie-May she was pitchin' hay down from the loft. Then she was goin' to clean the mowin' machine. Still, I'll tell her what Ma said! Then I'd best go see how Cougar and Jake are makin' out with them mounts we're breakin' for the Army.'

His youngest daughter laughed. 'Don't worry 'bout it, Pa. Me an' the girls will manage fine. Ellie-May will just get in the way.' Grabbing the Johnson girls by the hands, she was on the point of whisking them indoors, when she stopped and turned to her father. 'Pa, what was that name you called John just now, Cougar ... ?'

Jim Jordan paused for a moment. 'Well, it's like this. John grew up with the Comanches. Now, they named him Yellow Panther, bein' that they reckoned he was as tricky an' dangerous as that beast. We shortened it to Cougar, which is what white folks call them cats anyway. Only thing is, Ma don't like it an' I only use it when she ain't around. Same with Jake. Injuns call him Runnin' Wolf. but I don't use it round Ma.'

'Sarah,' Sara-Jane put her arm round the little girl's shoulders. 'Would you take Mary into the house an' start tidyin' up. Start in the kitchen.'

'Pa,' she turned to her father, her face suddenly serious. 'what happened to Ma's folks? Oh, I know they were killed by Injuns years ago, but I've always felt Ma wasn't telling us everything.'

'Reckon you're right.' Jim Jordan stared into the distance, a faraway look in his eyes. 'Mebbe it is time.'

The rancher's face hardened perceptibly as he looked at his younger daughter. 'You know what happened to them two Martin gals, over towards Trinity? The ones that were taken by the Comanches?'

'Yeah ... I think so,' Sara-Jane paused uncertainly. 'Ellie-May heard that the elder one had an Injun baby ... Pa?'

'They were raped!' Jim Jordan's voice was harsh. 'Raped by a dozen Comanche braves. That's what happened to them. An' that's what happened to your grandma! Ma found her lyin' in the yard, after that Winnebago raidin' party had finished with her. Your ma was only eight at the time, an' what she saw that day has been with her ever since. The search party that found her said she must have been wanderin' in the woods for at least a couple o' days. They said that she seemed to be frozen with the shock. Couldn't speak, didn't want to eat, didn't care whether she lived or died. It was weeks before she began to take an interest in things.

'Even then, she wouldn't talk to folks 'bout what she saw that day. I was the first an' she didn't tell me until we were married. Then, just when I thought she was gettin' back to normal, John was taken by the Comanches. Nigh on nine years he was gone.

'Well, you know the rest. Can you blame her for hatin' Injuns? Can you blame her for bein' cranky an' wantin' a gun by her hand all the time? I sure as hell don't and I ain't aimin' to start now!'

'Pa,' impulsively Sara-Jane touched her father's arm. 'I'm sorry. Guess I could've been more help, but I just didn't think.'

"Tain't your fault,' Jim Jordan's voice was gruff, and he rubbed a hand across his eyes. 'Mebbe I should've told you an' Ellie-May years ago, but I kept puttin' it off, hopin' things would change. Now I'm beginnin' to doubt it.'

Sara-Jane took a deep breath. 'Pa, let's take one day at a time. Maybe this trip to Arizona will help. An' when she comes back I'll try not to fight with her as much. Now, let's get to work.'

Chapter 9

'Looks like a wagon comin',' Bull squinted into the shimmering heat haze ahead of them.

'Mm.' Ma wasn't going to admit that all she could see was trail dust. Automatically she unbuckled the canvas holdall and drew out the shotgun. Delving into the bag again she located the box of shells. Breaking the gun expertly, Ma inserted two buckshot-loaded rounds. Snapping the weapon shut she laid it across her lap, twin muzzles pointing at the mesquite on her side of the trail.

"Tain't ladylike, Ma.' Bull protested feebly.

'You hush up an' tend to the team,' his mother said sharply. 'After my folks was killed I swore that nobody would ever catch me out again, an' I ain't about to start now!'

Bull looked again at the oncoming wagon, and grinned. 'You can take it easy, Ma. That there's our wagon an' our team. I'd know old Paint an' Dusty anywhere.'

'Howdy, ma'am.' Mike Devlin drew the team to a halt and tipped his hat to Ma.

'Howdy, deputy.' Extracting the shells, Ma returned the shotgun to the holdall. 'I hope you been takin' good care o' that rig?'

'Sure have, ma'am.' Mike grinned at Bull. So this is the famous Bull Jordan, bounty hunter. Shoulda known when I first saw him. He's a big, mean lookin cuss. Can't say I'd fancy havin' him trailin' me.

'Trail clear?' He came out of his reverie with a start to find Bull talking.

'Mm ... ? Oh sure, nuthin' movin' between here an' Greenhills. An' I got a message for you, ma'am, from Sheriff Baxter. He's been in touch with circuit judge Smith. Accordin' to the judge, you an' your gals don't need to be at the trial. Judge says written statements will be fine. Seems like it's an open and shut case. I was to ask you all to write out the statements an' give them to me, but seein' as how you're headed somewhere ... ' he paused interrogatively and looked inquiringly at Ma.

'We're headin' for Fort Worth. I'll make a statement when I get there.'

'That would be just fine, ma'am. Sure would be obliged. Sheriff Baxter will likely want to settle up about the reward money at the same time.'

'Thankee, deputy,' Ma surveyed him coldly. 'Reckon I can fit that in. An' if you're talkin' to m'daughters 'bout their statements, you just keep to that, you hear me!'

'Yes, ma'am.' Devlin flushed angrily. Damn her, she makes me feel like a snot-nosed kid. Out of the corner of his eye he could see Bull grinning. The Jordans always enjoyed an outsider being rawhided by Ma's tongue. 'Oh, almost forgot. Jack Anderson made it. That young doctor in Oxbow dug the slug out. He's real good, just like you said.'

'So that owlhoot made it did he?' Ma Jordan settled herself comfortably. 'Reckon he was born to be hung. Anyways, we ain't got all day to sit here gabbin'. Let's get this team movin' if we're gonna make Hannah MaCrae's place tonight. Nice meetin' you, deputy.'

Bull spoke to the Clevelands and snapped his whip. The big horses hit their stride, and the buckboard was gone in a swirl of dust.

Mike Devlin shook his head and eased the wagon back onto the trail. What an outfit, he thought, and what a woman!

* * * *

Hannah MaCrae and Mary-Lou Jordan went back a long way. They had come into that part of Texas at the same time and circumstances had conspired to throw them together.

When Donald MaCrae had been killed by a roving band of Kiowas, Ma had been the first neighbour on hand to offer practical help and support. She had even assisted Mrs MaCrae to lay out Donald's body and prepare it for burial, something that Hannah MaCrae had never forgotten.

On her side, Hannah was Ma's closest confidante, probably the only one, other than Jim Jordan himself. She was also Ma's fiercest defender.

A tall, handsome lady, with a sunny disposition and a shrewd business brain, Hannah MaCrae enjoyed life to the full. The MaCraes had no family and, after Donald's death, Hannah sold their small ranch to the Jordans and moved into the little frontier town of Greenhills. There she had bought a run-down hotel and renovated it from top to bottom. Now she had a thriving business, with a state-wide reputation for good food and comfortable accommodation.

Coffee cup in hand, she smiled affectionately at the stocky, grey-haired woman, sitting opposite. 'Land sakes, Mary-Lou, you're a sight for sore eyes. I ain't seen you in a coon's age. I take it you an' Bull will be stayin' the night?'

A wintry smile flitted across Ma's face as she nodded. 'Yeah. Bull's taken the team down to the livery stable. Don't know when he'll be back.'

Any other woman friend of Hannah's would have been enveloped in a hug by now, because the big woman was both affectionate and demonstrative. But Hannah was also extremely shrewd. She knew that Ma hated such demonstrations of affection and she also knew why. So her welcome for Ma was always carefully low key. Ma knew this and appreciated it. If anything, it cemented an already strong friendship even more.

Now, the frostiness in her eyes thawed perceptibly as she looked at her friend. 'It's been a long time, Hannah. Seems like we're always too busy to visit.'

'Yeah,' Hannah MaCrae paused and drained her cup. 'More coffee?'

Ma nodded.

Both cups refilled, Hannah replaced the coffee pot on the tray. 'Yeah,' she repeated thoughtfully, 'if you can call capturin' one o' the most dangerous gangs in east Texas bein' busy, then you surely have! Sheriff Baxter an' his posse come through here a while back. Hank Baxter said that in all his years as a lawman he'd never seen anything like it.'

'Shucks,' Ma shrugged uncomfortably, 'It weren't nuthin'. You know me, Hannah. Always did like to have a gun handy.'

'Sure.' There was a faraway look in the big woman's eyes. 'And I know that Donald might have been alive today if he'd listened to you. Still, there it is, you can't turn the clock back. So, what other news you got?'

'Well,' Ma pursed her lips judiciously. 'Bull was down on the Border trailin' Mack McIvor. Only thing was, the rurales got to Mack first. Reckon Bull must have been fit to tie. Anyways, he figgered he might as well look in at Fort Concho on the way back. Thought he might see Lance. You know he's stationed down there.

'On his way there, Bull ran into a bunch o' Comanches who had two little gals with 'em. The Injuns had already killed the gals' folks down on Devil's Creek. Bull took out after them an' got the kids back. Then he brung them to the Circle J.'

Hannah MaCrae raised her eyebrows. 'And the Injuns?' she probed gently.

'Dead,' Ma shrugged. 'But you know Bull. He don't talk much 'bout that kinda thing.'

'Yeah,' The big woman reflected for a moment. 'So now you got two more daughters?'

'Seems like it,' Ma sipped her coffee. 'To tell the truth, Hannah, I ain't right sure I want the hassle. I'm gettin' too old to start all over again with a family. Still, I suppose we'll manage somehow.'

For a long moment Hannah MaCrae stared into space, then ... 'I could take them,' she ventured.

Ma shook her head. 'Thanks for the offer, but it ain't that simple. Them gals have taken a shine to Bull, an' the funny thing is he's the same about them. Reckon we're stuck with 'em.'

'I know what you mean.' Hannah added sugar to her coffee and stirred it. 'Still, if they ever change their minds let me know. Any other news?'

'Remember them folks I once told you about, the Wilsons?' Ma paused for effect.

'You mean the folks you stayed with after your family were killed?' Hannah nodded. 'Yeah, I remember you tellin' me. What happened to them?'

'They moved out to Arizona an' built a big spread for themselves, somewhere between Dorando and the Border. Now they're dead, an' they've left the ranch to me!'

'Land sakes! You goin' to take it on?'

'Their lawyers want to see me, Hannah. An' Jim wants Bull to look the ranch over. There's nothin' more to it than that at the moment. But I can't say I ain't tempted.'

Hannah MaCrae nodded.

There was the sound of voices downstairs, then, a moment later, a tap on the door. It opened to reveal one of the black maids who staffed the hotel. Hannah always maintained that they made the best workers, by a mile.

'Miz MaCrae, Mister Jordan is heah now. Will Ah lay the table?'

'Do that, Lydia. An' tell Mister Jordan we'll be down directly.'

★   ★   ★   ★

Sheriff Baxter stretched and stepped out onto the sidewalk. Glowing like a fire in the eastern sky, the sun was just beginning to lift above the Fort Worth rooftops. It was going to be another hot day.

He half turned and called through the open door. 'Cal, you mind takin' first shift while I get some breakfast?'

'Sure,' Cal Fischer came through the door buckling on his gunbelt and yawning widely. One of these days, Baxter thought sourly, he'll step through that door buckling on that gunbelt, an' some young gunnie will put a hole in him.

He was about to point this out when movement up the street caught his eye.

'Say,' Cal Fischer followed his gaze, 'Ain't that Miz Jordan comin' along there?'

Hank Baxter looked at the small figure stepping purposefully along the sidewalk, and the big man walking beside her. 'Yeah, that's her alright, an' that's Bull Jordan with her.'

'So that's Bull Jordan. Big mean lookin' cuss ain't he?'

'Mebbe, but if we had a few more like him Texas would be a safer place.'

'Howdy, Miz Jordan.' Baxter tipped his hat to Ma. 'Sure am surprised to see you here, ma'am. Maybe you didn't meet m'deputy? I sent him back with your wagon.'

'Sure we met him,' Ma said tersely. 'East o' Greenhills. Told us you wanted a statement, an' seein' as we got business in Tucson, I figgered I'd just call in when we was passin' through.'

'I'm right obliged, ma'am.' The sheriff ushered his visitors into the office. 'If the pair of you'd just take a seat I'll get a pen an' some paper. Then we can tidy this thing up all nice an' legal.'

He paused and looked thoughtfully at Bull. 'Mister Jordan, I take it. Don't think we've met?'

'M'son, Hardy.' Ma glared at Baxter. "Case you're wonderin', he's goin' to Tucson with me. Your deputy tells me that varmint Jack Anderson didn't die on you?'

'That's right, ma'am. That young doctor at Oxbow did a right fine job. We got Jack an' his brother in the cells back there. You want to see them?'

Ma thought it over, then shook her head. 'Nah, I don't hold no grudge. They made their play an' they lost. Let's leave it at that. What did you do with the fella I shot? van Doren I think his name was.'

'Waal, ma'am, seein' as how you wouldn't let us bury him on Circle J land, we had him planted at Oxbow. Doc Marshall signed a certificate sayin' it was necessary; the warm weather an' all, an' that was it. 'Course, it don't make no difference to the reward. The dodgers said dead or alive.'

Ma glared at him. 'Sheriff, I weren't havin' no owlhoot buried on Circle J land. Still, I 'preciate you was only doin' what you thought was right. Now, if you'll gimme paper an' a pen, I'll get this statement down for you.'

'Right here, ma'am.' Sweeping a corner of his desk clear, Baxter placed a blank form and a steel pen in front of Ma. 'Write it like it happened. Just in your own words.'

'Wasn't thinkin' o' nuthin' else,' said Ma sourly as she bent to her task.

"Bout the reward money,' Baxter rubbed his chin reflectively. 'The bank put it up, so you'll have to go along there to get paid out. 'Course, I'll have to vouch for you.' He grinned suddenly. 'Sounds like you an' them gals o' yours might just put B ... , I mean Hardy, here, outa business!'

Chapter 10

Abe Winters scowled moodily at the dun wheeler, as the station hand eased the big horse into position and hitched him to the Concord coach. Years of driving a team in all weathers, plus snatched meals, and the intermittent danger factor of road agents and marauding Indians, had soured both the tough old driver's disposition and his stomach.

Folks said the only reason the company retained him was his dour determination that the stage must get through. There was however a lot more to it than that.

To begin with, he had ridden 'Mail Route 12587' as it was officially known, since before the war. It was even said that he had helped lay out the route for the old San Antonio and San Diego Mail, the first company to operate on this line. The S.A. & S.D. as it was more commonly known, was a tough, hand to mouth outfit. Anyone who had 'cut his teeth' with them could command a driver's job anywhere, and nobody handled a team better than Abe. So it proved. When the Butterfield Overland Mail Company took over the route, in the fall of '58, he was one of the drivers asked to stay on.

From 1858 until 1861 Abe Winters steered his coach along the toughest stage route in the West. Floods, droughts, storms, Indians and road agents, they all came alike to Abe. Old-timers said that even John Butterfield, the legendary J.B. who had founded the company, deferred to Abe when he expressed an opinion.

Then, in 1861, war between the States erupted. John Butterfield, already in serious financial difficulties, decided to cut his losses and close his operations on 'Mail Route 12587'.

From being a stage driver, one of the aristocrats of the trail, Abe found himself hauling freight from the Butterfield way stations as they were closed down. Even the teams, his pride and joy, were sold off to local ranchers.

For a spell he drove for the Prescott Stage Company, a small-time outfit that operated two short-lived routes. One between Prescott and Phoenix, and another between Ehrenburg and Prescott. But it wasn't the same somehow. The rigging was poor and broke frequently. The coaches were shabby, and the teams were scrubby and half-broken. All in all, Abe wasn't sorry when the line folded and he found himself out of a job.

But not for long. President Lincoln had early on recognised the need for western gold and silver to finance the war. He also needed western political support, and the best way to obtain that was to provide a strong military presence in the area. And so, in 1862, Abe found himself driving a wagon for General Carleton's column, on their march across the South-West. Loyalty didn't come into it. The Union Army paid him, and gave him a team to drive. That was all that Abe wanted.

When the war ended, and the Southern Overland U.S. Mail and Express reopened 'Mail Route 12587' as far as Tucson, he was there, the lines in his calloused hands and just the glimmer of a smile twitching the corners of his mouth. Folks said it was the only time they ever saw Abe Winters looking happy.

Now, he hosed a stream of tobacco juice into the dust of the station yard and spoke directly to the big dun wheeler. 'Jericho, you knothead, I swear if you give me any trouble this trip I'll turn you into dog meat!'

The dun's ears flattened and there was a mean look in his rolling eye. Abe watched him carefully. Jericho could kick like a mule if he got half a chance.

'You're gettin' old, Abe.' Tall, rawboned Slim McDonald; guard, conductor and long time friend, grinned as he pitched his warbag and shotgun onto the high front seat of the coach. 'A man starts talkin' to his horses, reckon it's time he was thinkin' o' retirin'.'

Abe glowered. 'You reckon that piece o' scrap iron'll fire if we ever need it?'

The guard paused in the act of rolling a cigarette. 'Let me worry about that. Old Betsy ain't never failed yet. Anyways, we ain't got much of a load this run. Only six passengers, an' some freight for Tucson. Small stuff.'

Abe bit off a fresh piece of Henry Clay, and replaced the twist in his vest pocket. Settling the quid comfortably in his cheek, he chewed reflectively for a moment. "Pears like Cochise an' his boys got everybody runnin' scared.'

The tall man shrugged. 'Can't say as I blame them. I'm always on edge till we're through Apache Pass.'

He paused and scanned the waybill. 'Reverend Thomas Jefferson; Miss Loretta Svenson.' Slim rolled his eyes, 'She's one good-lookin' lady!'

Abe grunted non-committally.

'Miz M.L. Jordan. Mr H. Jordan.'

'Married couple?'

'Nah. I'd say mother an' son. Mother's a tough old bird, an' the son's a big hard lookin' guy. Then we got a Mr Cameron Walker, an' another lady, a Miz Louisa Jones. She's gettin' off at Tucson, same as the Jordans an' the Svenson woman. Walker an' the preacher are goin' all the way to San Diego, if they can get transport at Tucson. Here they come now.'

Abe looked at the small group approaching. The giant figure of Bull drew his attention immediately.

'So that's Jordan. Hey, I know him. That's Bull Jordan the bounty hunter!'

'That's Bull Jordan! I've heard a lot 'bout him.' Slim stepped back and turned. 'Tell you somethin' … '

'Look out!' Too late, Abe grabbed for Slim's shoulder. The dun jinked sideways and lashed out like a striking snake. There was an audible crack as Slim staggered and fell forward. Abe dived in and hauled him clear of the plunging Jericho.

'Damn it, Slim, you alright?'

White-faced, the guard clutched at his leg, and attempted to sit up. 'I think m'leg's broke.' Sweat beaded his brow. Dimly, Abe was aware of a shadow looming over him.

'Can I help?' Bull Jordan knelt in the dust. His giant hands explored Slim's leg.

'Mm, clean break.' He spoke over his shoulder. 'Ma, you got any bandages?'

'Sure.' As Abe watched in amazement, Ma delved into the carpet bag and produced three rolled up bandages.

Bull caught his eye and grinned. 'Never be surprised at anythin' Ma brings out o' that bag!'

'Now, mister.' He looked down at Slim. 'This'll hurt a mite.' Grasping the leg, he jerked suddenly. McDonald gasped and went limp.

'It's the best way.' On her knees now, Ma bound Slim's legs together. 'Right.' She rose to her feet, 'get'm to a doctor. Looks like a clean break. Should heal quick.'

Abe watched as Slim was carried across the road to Doc Henderson's. 'Thanks, ma'am. You too, mister. Trouble is, I need a guard for this run, an' now I ain't got one.'

'Sure you have.' Bull tossed his roll onto the front seat. 'I'll ride shotgun for you!'

Abe grinned. 'Mister, I don't know what the company's gonna say, but what the hell, I been breakin' their rules all my life. Throw down Slim's warbag. The boys'll see he gets it.

'Now;' he walked to the rear of the coach. 'All the baggage aboard an' sheeted?'

There was a chorus of assent from the roustabouts. Turning, he looked into the stage. 'You folks all set?' Nods all round; Loretta Svenson flashing a dazzling smile.

'Alright.' Abe swung up onto the driver's seat, gathered the lines with a practised hand and kicked off the brake. 'Let's roll.'

✯   ✯   ✯   ✯

Ma knitted another row and stared pensively at the passing scenery. Thirteen days of bumpy, rutted trails, and thirteen nights of scruffy way stations, lay behind them. Nobody could call the journey comfortable, but Mary-Lou Jordan had ridden hundreds of miles in Conestoga wagons, and a leather sprung Concord stage was luxury as far as she was concerned.

The main problem had been boredom. Boredom at the endless vista of chaparral and mesquite, plus the constant irritation of the pervasive dust. Even the way stations had a monotonous sameness about them. Buildings which had been erected in a hurry, with scant consideration for the passengers, or crews comfort. Only occasionally, where the siting of the station had coincided with some rancher's attempt to supplement his meagre income, did things improve. Ma blessed these brief interludes, with their evidence of a woman's touch. El Paso tonight, she reflected. Can't say I'll be sorry. Wish it had been Tucson.

Seated opposite, Louisa Jones smiled tentatively. 'It was good of your son to take over as conductor.'

Ma shrugged. 'Hardy hates to be cooped up. 'Sides, he's like me, in a hurry to get to Tucson.'

'Oh, you've got relatives there?'

'Used to, they're dead now.' Ma clicked her needles with a finality that precluded further conversation.

'Maybe your son's trailing somebody?' There was the slightest hint of a sneer in Cameron Walker's voice, and the burly, florid featured man looked challengingly at Ma Jordan.

Ma's blue eyes became glacial. Somewhere along the route Walker had found out that Bull was a bounty hunter. 'Shows how much you know 'bout such things,' she said sourly. 'You don't trail them kinda fellas on a stage!'

Sitting at the opposite end of the seat from Ma, the Reverend Thomas Jefferson, tall, patrician, and silver-haired, shook his head in a gesture of distaste. 'Hunting down your fellow man for money seems sinful to me.'

'Reverend.' Ma's tone was biting. 'If the law can't round up the evil doers, then it seems to me we ain't got no choice but put a bounty on their heads. 'Course, if we had more churches out here, we might not need bounty hunters!'

Reverend Jefferson flushed angrily. 'I,' he began carefully, 'am on my way to San Diego to spread the word.'

'Wish you luck, Reverend.' Ma rolled up her knitting and placed it carefully in the carpet bag. 'From what I've heard o' San Diego they need you right bad. Still, you come across any livewire young preachers there, send them out here to us. We could sure use 'em!'

Up top, Bull squinted ahead through the haze. 'How far to El Paso?'

'Bout another ten miles.' Abe cracked his whip menacingly over the team. 'You'll see Fort Bliss first, soon as we top the rise.'

Bull sniffed the breeze appreciatively. 'Country sure smells great. What is it?'

The old driver shifted his quid to the other cheek and spat over the side. 'Vineyards; they grow some o' the finest grapes in the world down here. Make right good wine.'

☆   ☆   ☆   ☆

It was late evening when the stage pulled into El Paso. Bart Allen, the plump, extrovert, local station agent for the Southern Overland U.S. Mail and Express, bounced down the depot steps to meet them.

'Howdy, Abe. You made good time. No trouble on the way? This way, folks. Got you fixed up at Miz Pullen's hotel, right across the street. Best in town. This way ladies.'

'Listen to him.' Abe Winters locked the brake and wound the lines round the handle. 'The original talkin' machine. An' he never listens.'

He climbed down stiffly from the coach, grimacing as he did so. Bull followed with his roll and the shotgun. 'I swear if I was to come bustin' in here one day, yellin' that Cochise an' the whole dang Apache nation was on my tail, Bart would just say, 'Sure, sure, an' step this way for Ma Pullen's, folks!"

Bull laughed as they watched one of the ostlers climb into Abe's seat and trundle the stage round to the stable yard. 'Hope he don't get on the wrong side o' Ma. She can be right fierce at times.'

Abe shrugged. 'Won't make no difference to Bart. It'll just bounce off him! Let's check in at the hotel, wash up an' get somethin' to eat. One thing I have to say for Ma Pullen's, the chuck is the best in town. Then we might head down the street to the Twin Peaks saloon, an' sink a coupla beers. What d'you say?'

'Sounds good to me.' Bull broke the shotgun and extracted the shells. Together they picked up their blanket rolls and headed across the street. Behind them the stable yard buzzed with activity as the roustabouts prepared the stage for the following morning.

Chapter 11

Cameron Walker tossed back the glass of rye whiskey, and gasped at the bite of the raw spirit as it hit the back of his throat.

Phil Hendrix, the young, pencil slim bartender, eyed him sardonically. Them Easterners, he sneered to himself; think they know it all.

"Nother one?' He poised the bottle invitingly over Walker's glass. 'Or mebbe you find our booze a mite strong?'

'No ... ,' Cameron massaged his throat tenderly. 'Think maybe it went down the wrong way.' He felt the warm glow spreading through his gut, filling him with brash confidence. 'Yeah ... sure I'll have another.'

Phil grinned inwardly. They were all the same. Suggest they weren't tough enough, and they would buy another drink just to prove you wrong. He poured a generous measure into Walker's glass.

'Thanks.' The surveyor pushed some coins across the bar, and sipped reflectively at his drink.

'Is it always this quiet?' He surveyed the almost deserted room. Apart from the desultory card game taking place at the furthest away table, and a couple of obvious cowhands talking in low tones at the other end of the bar, the room was empty.

The young barman shrugged, 'It's early yet. Anyway, ain't many folks travellin'. The Injuns see to that.'

'Is it that bad? We didn't see nothing coming in on the stage.'

Phil paused in the act of polishing the bar top. 'It's a funny thing. The tribes don't normally bother the stage line. If there is any trouble, it's usually a bunch of young bucks lookin' for a little excitement.'

The swing doors banged as two men stepped into the saloon. They paused briefly and surveyed the room, before making their way across to the bar, next to Cameron Walker.

'Whiskey ... twice. Need somethin' to cut the dust.' The taller of the two spoke with a husky East Texas drawl.

'Howdy.' Phil nodded as he reached for the bottle of rye. Uh-huh, strangers in town. Carefully, he flicked a glance at the shotgun under the bar. Might need it yet.

'Here you are. That'll be four bits.'

'Thanks.' The tall man pushed two quarters across the counter. 'Quiet place you got here.' A badly healed knife slash, running from the corner of his mouth almost to his left eye showed starkly in the lamplight. His companion, stocky and fair-haired, leaned against the bar and surveyed the room.

Warning bells rang in Phil's mind. Only owlhoots watched their backs like that.

'Yeah. I was just sayin' to this gent,' he indicated Walker, 'that the Injuns had scared off most of our trade. I take it you ain't had no trouble?'

The tall man glanced at his companion. 'Nah, we come down from Corona. Didn't see nuthin'.'

He turned to Walker. 'You passin' through, yourself?'

Phil held his breath. It was an unwritten law on the frontier that you didn't inquire into a man's background, but he doubted if Cameron Walker knew that.

'Yeah.' The whiskey was beginning to take effect. 'Come in on the stage. Walker's the name, Cameron Walker. I'm a surveyor, on my way to San Diego.'

The tall man nodded acknowledgement. 'Steve Weston, an' this here's m'sidekick, Jim Stevens. Stage busy?'

Walker shook his head. 'Only five passengers going through, well six, if you count the big guy ridin' with the driver. He took over when the guard got his leg broken at Fort Worth.'

'Mm,' Weston stared thoughtfully at his drink. 'Seems a right public-spirited citizen this passenger, eh Jim?'

Stevens shrugged non-committally.

'His name's Jordan.' The surveyor swallowed a mouthful of whiskey and winced. 'Bull Jordan. They tell me he's a bounty hunter.'

'Well, well.' Weston set down his glass carefully. 'So Bull Jordan's in town is he? An' ridin' shotgun for the stage.'

Something in his tone made Phil Hendrix look at him sharply.

There was a tenseness about the tall man, and a wildness in his eyes.

He caught Phil's glance and laughed wryly. 'Just thinkin'. Must be a right comedown for a famous bounty hunter to be ridin' shotgun.'

'He's only going to Tucson. Guess they'll have to get another guard there.'

'Mm; any wimmen on the stage?'

'Three ladies. Jordan's ... ' Walker broke off as Bull and Abe came through the saloon doors.

Lowering his voice he spoke again. 'That's him now, the big guy with the stage driver.'

'So that's Jordan; big mean lookin' cuss, ain't he! Well, drink up, Jim. Reckon we'll be ridin'.

'The night's young yet,' Stevens objected.

Weston downed his drink. 'We're ridin'. Got things to do. Adios, Walker. Nice meetin' you.'

He headed for the door. Resignedly, Jim Stevens downed his drink and followed.

Bull leaned against the bar and nodded to Phil. 'Evenin'. Two beers for me an' my friend here. Oh, an' ask Mister Walker there what he's drinkin'.'

'Thanks; 'nother whiskey.' The surveyor's speech was slightly slurred.

'You alright?' The big man frowned as he pushed three quarters across the bar.

'Sure,' Walker waved a hand indulgently. ' Just beginnin' to warm up.'

Bull shrugged and turned back to Abe.

✫   ✫   ✫   ✫

On the outskirts of the town, Weston and Stevens pulled off the trail. Satisfied that nobody was following them, they eased their horses round to the rear of the tumbledown adobe building set back among the chaparral. As they dismounted a dark figure materialised from beneath the dogtrot.

'Heard you comin',' Ed Weston chuckled. 'Didn't think it was you at first. Thought you'd be late back for sure.'

'Best ask your brother 'bout that.' Stevens snapped as he tethered his horse in the breezeway. 'Seems like somethin's needlin' him.'

Young Weston stared after Stevens as he shoved his way into the living-room where a small fire burned. Then he turned to his brother questioningly.

'What's eatin' Jim? Ain't like him to be all riled up like that. Did you bring a bottle back for me an' Sam?'

'No, I didn't.'

'Hell!' Ed swore disgustedly

'Shut up an' listen. Bull Jordan's in town! I saw him in the saloon.'

'Bull Jordan!' There was a sudden flaring interest in Ed's voice. You mean ... ?'

'Yeah, the same Bull Jordan that put Pa in the pen.'

'Think he's trailin' us?'

'Nah,' Steve Weston shook his head. 'It's only four days since we pulled that bank job in Capitan. Reckon they ain't had time to get word here yet. 'Sides, he's takin' the stage to Tucson. Doin' them a favour by ridin' shotgun that far.'

'Why didn't you blast'm?'

'Use your brains. We gun him down in town an' we'd have the law all over us. Anyways, I want to see him suffer like Pa did, 'fore he died o' TB in Austin. I want him alive. We'll get ahead o' the stage, an' hold it up where the trail narrows in Picacho Pass. Right now let's go in an' talk to Jim an' Sam.'

★   ★   ★   ★

It was still only half-light and dawn was a long way off, when Bull threw his roll onto the high seat. He turned to watch Abe supervising the hitching of the fresh team. There was a flurry of clattering hooves and muffled curses, as the roustabouts struggled to line up the fractious horses.

Abe had warned everybody that he planned an early start. Now, lights gleamed in the hotel windows as Ma and the others finished their hurried breakfasts.

Bull grinned as he thought of Cameron Walker. Too much whiskey and a long stage run didn't mix. The surveyor had looked very green when he had come into the dining-room that morning.

Tucking the shotgun under his arm, he walked across the stable yard to where Abe was standing.

'Mornin'.'

Abe grunted as he checked the hooks on the trace lines. 'Well, you can get up early, I'll say that for you.'

Bull grinned. 'Been doin' it all m'life. You all set?'

'Soon as we get them passengers aboard. That surveyor fella looked kinda poorly this mornin'.'

The big man shrugged. 'Shoulda thought o' that last night. Never touch the stuff m'self. Well, not often.'

'So I noticed.'

The first members of the party, Louisa Jones and Ma, appeared from the hotel.

'Mornin', miss. Howdy, Ma.' Bull tipped his stetson to Miss Jones as he assisted them into the coach. 'You have a good night's rest?'

'Yes thank you, Mister Jordan.' Louisa Jones settled herself in her seat and smiled gratefully. Forty and unmarried, she was at the stage where polite attention from any man made her day.

Ma sniffed audibly. 'I've seen beds that were a sight more comfortable. Mind,' she added grudgingly, 'that Miz Pullen sets a good table. I'll give her that. Here's the Reverend comin' now, an' that Walker fella. My, he don't look none too chipper!'

Bull smothered a grin. Ma's voice carried a long way, and he could see the surveyor flushing angrily.

'Mornin', gents.' Abe straightened up from his examination of a singletree, 'All set?'

'Good morning.' The tall preacher frowned as he climbed in and took his seat. Cameron Walker followed sullenly. 'What an unearthly hour to start a journey.'

'Sorry about that, Reverend,' Abe paused by the open door. 'We got sixty odd miles to travel, over some mighty rough country, an' we only got a couple o' way stations along this part o' the line. Now, if Miss Svenson was here we could roll.'

He turned to the agent hovering in the background. 'Bart, would you mind goin' across to the hotel an' seein' what's keepin' her?'

'Sure, sure.' The stout figure bustled across the street and reappeared almost immediately with Loretta Svenson in tow. He helped her into the coach and was rewarded with a brilliant smile.

'Sorry to keep you all waiting, but I declare, I forgot the time.'

'Right!' Abe slammed the door shut and followed Bull up onto the high front seat. Gathering the lines in a practised hand he kicked off the brake, and the stage rolled out on the run to Cooke's Spring.

Unrolling her knitting, Mary-Lou Jordan settled herself for a long session.

Chapter 12

High in Picacho Pass Steve Weston reined in his mount and nodded with satisfaction. 'This ought to do it.' He pointed ahead to where the trail wound between steep cliffs.

'Jim, get a rope on that deadfall there.' He indicated the lightning blasted dead tree, leaning white and gaunt against its neighbour. 'Snake it down across the trail. That ought to hold them till we get the drop on Jordan. Rest o' them don't count. Three wimmen, a preacher, an' that surveyor fella, Walker. Nuthin' there to give us any trouble, once we got Jordan an' the driver.'

Stevens paused in the act of shaking out his rope. 'Don't hold wi' revenge m'self,' he said slowly. 'Gets so you ain't thinkin' straight, then you got trouble. Still, we're pardners an' I'll go along. You never know, there could be cash aboard. We might get lucky.'

Swinging the loop round his head, he cast neatly and dropped it cleanly over a broken branch on the tree. Dallying the end of the rope round the horn of his California rig, he backed his mount a few paces to take up the slack. Gently, talking softly to the horse, he increased the pressure. There was a crunch of breaking branches as the dead tree slid clear, gathered momentum, and crashed across the trail. 'That ought to hold them. They'll get down to move it, an' then we'll get the drop on 'em.'

'Yeah.' Steve Weston chewed reflectively on his lower lip. 'Ed,' he turned to his younger brother. 'Me, Jim an' Sam,' he indicated the fourth member of the gang, a lanky rawboned Tennessean, 'will stash the horses back in the trees an' lay low among the rocks here. Leave your horse with the others and ease down through the trees to the end o' this stand o' timber.' He indicated the tapering line of trees extending back down their side of the trail. 'Wait there till the stage passes.'

'When Jordan an' the others get down to look at the tree an' try to move it, you cross behind the stage an' come up on the far side. Tell them wimmen to sit tight. Get any money or valuables they have, an' if they're carryin' a strongbox bust it open, if you can. The rest of us'll get the drop on Jordan an' his sidekick. You got that?'

'Sure, should be easy.'

Steve Weston took a long look at his brother and shook his head. 'Nothin' like this is ever easy, jest remember that. Right, let's get set. They'll be makin' good time since they changed teams.'

* * * *

Climbing all the way, the trail twisted and turned through the pass. Swaying easily to the motion of the stage, Bull scowled at the rugged, arid landscape stretching into the distance.

Poor cow country. Sure hope it's better down Dorando way. Wonder how Ma's makin' out. Grinning, he visualised the small feisty woman in the coach below, knitting needles clicking industriously. He glanced at Abe. 'How far to the next way station?'

Abe shrugged. 'Cooke's Spring? Mebbe twenty miles. Then another twenty to the Mimbres River depot in Deming.' He pointed ahead with his whip. 'The trail narrows quite a bit up ahead. Once we swing round this bend you'll see it.'

* * * *

Steve Weston raised his head and listened intently. 'You hear anything?'

Jim Stevens glanced sideways. 'Nah ... wait, yeah I can hear something now.'

Fifty yards back down the trail Ed Weston took a deep breath and tried to still the mounting tension within him. Times like these he wished he could be as cool as his elder brother.

Expertly, Abe swung the leaders into the bend. The trail opened up in front of them.

'What the hell!' The deadfall loomed directly ahead. 'Whoa ... ' Abe hauled on the lines and the team came to a plunging halt, some fifty feet from the tree.

'Think it's a hold-up?' Bull's eyes probed either side of the trail.

Abe shook his head. 'Doubt it. Never had one on this stretch before, but there's times we get the odd tree just like this. That's why I carry an axe.'

Below them the Reverend Jefferson stuck his head out. 'Why have we stopped?'

'Tree across the trail,' Abe said tersely. 'Just waitin' to see if anythin' happens. Alright, 'pears like we'll need Mister Walker an' yourself to help shift it.'

In the coach Louisa Jones's eyes widened as Ma opened the long canvas bag. Extracting the evil looking sawn-off, she rummaged again for the box of shells. Expertly she broke the gun and loaded two rounds.

'Do you think … ?'

'Maybe … maybe not.' Ma clicked the weapon shut with chilling finality. She settled herself comfortably, the loaded gun pointed at the door. 'But I sure ain't takin' no chances!'

'Right!' That was Abe. 'Let's have both of you an' we'll cut through this tree and move it. Ladies, if you all sit still, this won't take long.'

Muttering under his breath, Cameron Walker climbed down, followed reluctantly by the Reverend Jefferson. The four men walked towards the deadfall.

Ma's eyes roved and she came to a sudden decision. 'Can either of you handle a gun?' She delved into her bag again as she spoke.

Loretta Svenson put her hand to her mouth in horror and shook her head.

Louisa Jones nodded quietly. 'I can. My father was a cavalry officer. He taught me. I used to be a better than average pistol shot.'

'Praise be.' Ma extracted a bundle from the holdall and unwrapped it. 'This here's a Paterson Colt. You got to cock the hammer 'fore the trigger'll appear.'

The schoolteacher laughed as she took the proffered weapon. 'I learned to shoot on this type of gun!'

'Better still.' Ma took command. 'Cover that door an' I'll take this one. Miss Svenson, I suggest you get down on the floor.'

※　　※　　※　　※

'Right!' Abe took an experimental swing with the axe. 'Don't reckon this'll take long.'

The crash of the rifle shot froze them in their tracks. 'Throw down your guns an' hoist your hands!'

Damn! Bull thought furiously; suckered like a green kid.

Running low, Ed came up diagonally behind the stage and eased alongside to Ma's door.

'Howdy, ladies.' He gestured carelessly with the .45. 'You all sit tight an' everything will be fine. Oh, an' let's have any money an' valuables you got.'

The twin muzzles of the shotgun rose above the door. 'Don't move, son.' Ed chilled at the ferocity in Ma's voice, 'or the first thing you'll get will be two load o' buckshot. An' drop that .45, now!' Sullenly Ed complied.

There was a shout from the rocks. 'You alright, Ed?'

Ma gestured with the shotgun. 'Tell'm I'll blow your head off if he tries anything.'

'Steve!' Ed's voice shook. 'She's got a shotgun an' she says she'll blow my head off. She means it!'

'Damn.' Jim Stevens swore disgustedly. 'How in hell did he let that happen?'

'Shut up!' Steve Weston lifted his voice in a furious shout. 'Tell her I'll kill every man out here.'

'He says ... '

'I heard him, son. Tell'm you won't be here to see it. Tell'm ... now!'

'She says she'll kill me anyway. Steve, she means it.'

Louisa Jones swung round, her eyes wide. 'That's your s ...'

'Hush up!' There was a crushing finality in Ma's voice. 'You jest sit tight an' leave me to make the moves. 'Pears we got a stand off here. You see anything on your side?'

'There's movement in the rocks up ahead.'

'Anybody shows, get set to drill'm. Rest the gun on the window.'

'Alright!' Ma's confidence had got to Louisa. She steadied the Paterson Colt carefully on the window ledge and waited tensely.

'Stand-off!' Bull whispered to Abe and the others. 'Get ready to duck. Hell's gonna break loose in a minute.'

Back in the coach Ma was tense. She was pushing and knew it. 'Tell this Steve fella he can back off an' go, but you stay with us.'

'Steve, she says you can back off an' go, but I got to stay!'

'Damn her!' A killing rage swept through Steve Weston, and he came up shooting.

As the roar of the Winchester and the sharper bark of the Paterson Colt blended, the group by the deadfall threw themselves flat. Steve Weston staggered and fell forward. Bullets tugging at his shirt, Bull swept up the shotgun and triggered it twice. A hail of buckshot ricocheted through the rocks. Silence fell, broken only by the groans of the wounded.

A grim edgy Mary-Lou faced Ed across the door. Behind her she could hear Loretta Svenson sobbing hysterically on the floor of the coach.

'Ma,' Bull's voice rose in a shout. 'You alright?'

'Sure; how about yourself?'

'A bullet burn across m'ribs, that's all.'

There was silence for a moment, then his voice lifted again. 'Alright, come out slow, with your hands up.'

Ears flattened and eyes rolling, the team sidled away from the smell of blood. A voice spoke soothingly and they stood still. Abe appeared, a Walker Colt cocked in his right hand. Carefully he bent and picked up Ed's gun.

'Unbuckle your gunbelt.' Hastily Ed obeyed.

'You ladies alright?' Abe spoke without taking his eyes off the young outlaw.

'Yeah.' Ma squinted at Loretta Svenson, sobbing fitfully on the coach floor, and Louisa Jones, drawn and white, hunched in her seat. 'Mebbe a mite peaky here an' there, but we're fine!'

'Right.' The driver gestured with his gun to Ed. 'Walk across to where the others are. Keep your hands high, an' don't forget I'm right behind you.'

'Waal, seems like the excitement's over.' Ma turned in her seat and stopped abruptly. Louisa Jones was lying on the floor in a dead faint!

'Tsk, tsk.' She rummaged in her bag and produced a small red bottle. Removing the cork, she stooped and held the bottle under the schoolteacher's nose. Strong ammonia-based fumes drifted through the coach.

Louisa gagged and her eyes opened. Recognition returned and she tried to sit up.

'Take it easy,' Ma propped her against the seat. 'Everything's fine.'

'But I shot a man!'

'Happens all the time,' said Ma dismissively. 'It was them or us.' She looked thoughtfully at Loretta Svenson lying whimpering on the floor. Bending suddenly, she slapped the girl's face hard. The whimpering stopped immediately.

Anger flared in Louisa's eyes. 'Why did you strike her?' she demanded.

'Best treatment for shock,' said Ma unperturbed. 'I'd have done the same with you if you hadn't fainted! Now, keep an eye on her while I go see what's happenin' up front.'

Stepping down from the coach, she paused for a moment and turned back. 'What were you gonna say when I shut you up back there?'

'I was about to say ... ,' Louisa faltered for a moment. 'I was about to say that was your son out there!'

'Thought that was it,' Ma's eyes were bleak. 'An' if you had? It might just have tipped that young fella to try something.'

The teacher shook her head wonderingly as she watched the small, determined figure, shotgun tucked under an arm, make her way across to the group at the dead tree.

'Howdy, Ma.' Bull spoke over his shoulder. He was kneeling beside Cameron Walker, trying to staunch the flow of blood from a leg wound. 'Cameron's got a bullet in his thigh. Looks like it nicked an artery. Think you can help?'

'What about the others?' Ma indicated the prone figures by the side of the trail.

'The Reverend,' Bull indicated the preacher, lying on his side moaning softly, 'took a bullet in his arm. Went clean through an' never touched the bone. This fella,' he indicated Jim Stevens. 'His shoulder's tore up pretty bad with buckshot. The bearded gent there,' he pointed to Sam's motionless body. 'He's dead. Took a load o' buckshot in the face.'

'What about this Steve fella? Him that was doin' all the shoutin'.' She pointed. 'That him there? Seems like he was the boss man.'

'Yeah, he's dead too.' Bull sounded tired. 'Somebody drilled him plumb centre.'

'That was the schoolmarm; her pa was a cavalryman. He taught her to shoot. I gave her my old Paterson Colt. Your pa always did say it was the best gun he ever had. She was coverin' that side.' Ma frowned, 'Hardy, she ain't never done nothin' like this before. She's gonna take it hard.'

Walker groaned and struggled to get up. Blood welled through the bandage.

'Lie still.' Ma leant the shotgun against a rock and dropped to her knees beside Bull. 'Let's see. Mm, it ain't good an' that's a fact. We got to get a tourniquet on this leg. Get the schoolmarm an' the Svenson woman across here, Hardy. Tell them to take off their underskirts in the coach. We're gonna need 'em for bandages.'

She pointed to where Abe, gun in hand, was watching Ed Weston swinging the axe at the deadfall. 'Then give him a hand. The quicker we're rollin' the better. I feel like a sittin' duck out here.'

Gradually, under Ma's direction, things began to take shape. Louisa Jones and Loretta Svenson, the one white-faced and silent, the other sniffling uncontrollably, tore up their underskirts and bandaged the wounded. Meanwhile, Bull and young Ed, working in turns, cut through the dead tree, Abe keeping a careful watch on their prisoner all the time. Finally it was done, and they rolled the cut section to one side of the trail.

'Right.' Abe climbed onto his seat and brought the big coach up to where the women were working on the wounded. Carefully, Ma supervising, they loaded Jim Stevens and Cameron Walker into the Concord.

Ma was in her element. 'Put Mister Walker on the middle seat, an' this fella,' she indicated Stevens, 'sit him on the back seat. Tie him up an' rope him to the window tug.'

'That's barbaric,' Louisa protested.

'It's common sense.' Ma said toughly. 'He tried to kill us didn't he? As far as I'm concerned he ain't gettin' another chance. Same for the young fella. Tie him up an' put him in the other corner o' the back seat, roped the same way.'

'Now,' indicating the moaning Jefferson. 'The Reverend can sit between them. Help'm up. There ain't nuthin' much wrong with him anyway. An' what about them?' She pointed to the two bodies. 'Don't seem right to leave 'em here.'

'Alright.' Abe scrubbed his chin with a calloused hand. 'I ain't all that keen, but we'll put 'em on top.' Between them, Abe and Bull loaded the bodies onto the roof of the stage. 'That young owlhoot don't say much,' Abe remarked as they covered the corpses with a sheet.

'Nah,' Bull frowned. 'Reckon he's still shook up. Facin' Ma an' that shotgun ain't no fun. Now, I'll get them fellas' horses. They're stashed back in the timber.'

Down below, Ma was shepherding the other women onto the stage. She gestured with the shotgun. 'The two of you ride up front with me. Then you can change Mister Walker's bandages, while I keep an eye on them fellas in the back.'

There was a clatter of hooves as Bull led the four saddled horses out of the timber and secured them to the rear of the stage. Passing by the coach door, he grinned at Ma before climbing up beside Abe.

'All set now?'

'Yeah. Sure would hate to leave good horses out here.' Kicking off the brake, Abe eased the team into their stride.

Below them, Louisa Jones gave an involuntary shiver.

Ma looked at her. 'You alright?'

The schoolteacher shook her head. 'I don't think I'll ever be alright again!'

'Sure you will,' said Ma toughly. 'Someday you'll tell your grandchildren 'bout this.'

Louisa shuddered.

Chapter 13

Charlie Kenyon narrowed his eyes and squinted into the glare of the sun. 'That's them alright,' he muttered absently, 'but they're raisin' a hell of a lot o' dust. First time I ever seen Abe Winters this late.'

'Mebbe the trail was blocked.' Old Seth Parker, one of the change crew, paused in the act of tightening a strap on the fresh team.

'Mm ... you got that team ready?' Charlie had managed the Cooke's Spring relay station successfully for the past year, and he wasn't about to start making mistakes now. Seth nodded.

Abe hauled on the lines and the stage pulled up in a swirl of dust. Setting the brake he climbed down stiffly followed by Bull. Charlie came up on the run.

'Howdy, Abe.' He stepped aside hastily as the crew eased the tired team out of the traces and led them away. 'Where you been? Thought mebbe you had run into some o' Cochise's boys.'

Abe shrugged tiredly. 'It's a long story. This here's Bull Jordan, he's ridin' shotgun this trip. Road agents tried to hold us up. We got three wounded fellas an' a prisoner inside. Oh, an' a coupla bodies on top!'

Charlie's eyes bulged. 'What the hell you been doin' up there?' he gasped. 'Fightin' a young war?'

'Kinda seemed like that for a while. Now, can you take them saddle horses? We gotta make Deming tonight. One o' the passengers has got a bad leg wound.'

'Sure.' Charlie waved to the crew and issued swift instructions. Bull and Abe watched the outlaws' mounts being led away.

'Thanks, we'll have to roll if we're gonna make up any time.'

Kenyon raised his hand as they climbed back into their seats. 'Tell me about it next time you come through.'

Abe nodded as he kicked off the brake. The long whip cracked menacingly and the fresh team hit their stride.

☆   ☆   ☆   ☆

Sheriff Jud Breen was in a bad mood. A long tiring ride to check on some missing horses, only to find that it was a simple case of straying stock had not improved his temper. Now, he had been on the point of climbing into bed, when a breathless messenger had arrived to say that he was wanted urgently at the stage depot.

He frowned heavily as he looked at the young stable hand. 'You say the stage just got in? Must be all of two hours late. That ain't usual. It ain't usual at all.'

The boy shifted nervously. 'It's true though. An' there's three wounded fellas on it, an' a prisoner, leastways, they got him tied up. Oh, an' one o' the crew says they got a couple o' bodies as well!'

'Hell!' The sheriff swore disgustedly as he buckled on his gunbelt. 'Tell them I'm on my way. What about Doc Jenkins? Accordin' to what you say they're gonna need'm.'

'I give'm a shout. Reckon he should be there by now.'

'Good thinkin', son.' Breen snatched up his hat. 'Alright, let's go.'

☆   ☆   ☆   ☆

'Got to hand it to you, ma'am.' Doc Jenkins completed his examination of Cameron Walker's wound and rose to his feet. A spare, vinegary fifty year old, the doctor recognised a kindred spirit in Ma.

'That's a right smart piece o' work you done there. Neat bandaging, an' you say you been releasin' the tourniquet every so often? That's good. Lotta folks forget that, then you get complications. Mister,' he turned back to the groaning surveyor, 'you got a lot to thank this lady for.'

'Shucks.' It wasn't often Ma was embarrassed, and it showed now.

Watching out of the corner of his eye, Bull stifled a grin.

'It weren't nothin'. You run a ranch there's always somebody breakin' somethin'.'

The white-haired doctor nodded as he rolled up his sleeves. 'Seems like you ain't finished yet. Got to get this bullet out right away. Oh, howdy, sheriff. This here's Miz Jordan. She was a passenger on the stage. Did a right good job on them wounded fellas. Ma'am, this here's Sheriff Jud Breen, He's the law in these parts.'

'Howdy, ma'am.' The sheriff was rattled and showed it. 'Accordin' to Abe Winters, you're right handy with a shotgun as well! Seems like you took a quite a chance from what he says.'

Ma frowned. 'Reckon the law ain't never satisfied. If you back down to road agents, they say you ain't a public-spirited citizen. An' if you shoot first then you're takin' a chance. Anyway, I didn't do no shootin' back there.'

'No offence, ma'am.' Startled by the steel in Ma's voice, Sheriff Breen searched hurriedly for a way out. He indicated Ed Weston, firmly tied to a chair in a corner of the depot waiting room. 'Just as well you didn't get nervous when the shootin' started, else that young fella might have got the drop on you.'

'Well now, sheriff,' Ma poured hot water into a basin and set it beside Doc Jenkins. 'The only thing he would have got would have been two load o' buckshot in his face! So if you're worryin' 'bout me gettin' nervous, forget it.'

Doc Jenkins coughed suddenly and went red in the face.

'You alright?' Ma looked at him shrewdly.

'Sure, just caught my breath. You'll have to excuse us, sheriff, we got to get this slug out.'

☆   ☆   ☆   ☆

'That Miz Jordan .' Breen nodded to where Ma and the doctor were bent over Cameron Walker. 'She's awful tetchy.'

'Sheriff,' Abe Winters spoke warningly, 'this here's Miz Jordan's son, Bull Jordan. He's been ridin' shotgun with me from Fort Worth.'

'No offence, mister. Bull Jordan, hey... say, you that Texas bounty hunter I keep hearin' about? Kinda outa your bailiwick here ain't you?'

Bull scowled. 'I got personal business in Tucson, Sheriff.'

Abe intervened hurriedly. 'You got any idea who them fellas were? Didn't think they was any road agents round here. Thought Cochise's boys had 'em all scared off.'

'That the two stiffs?' Breen indicated the blanket-covered bodies.

'Yeah. Reckon the quicker you get the undertaker here the better.'

'Mm,' Jud Breen bent and twitched back the blanket. 'Say, I know this fella. Got a 'wanted' notice for him in my office. This here's Steve Weston. Don't know the other fella though.'

'Just a minute.' Bull walked across to where Ed Weston sat staring sullenly into space.'You any kin to that tall dark gent that was shot back there?'

'He was my brother,' hatred flared in Weston's eyes. 'Damn you, Jordan. You put our old man in the pen an' he died there. Now m'brother's dead 'cause he wanted to get even.'

'So you're Hank Weston's boy!' Understanding flooded across Bull Jordan's face. 'Shoulda known, I can see the resemblance now. Mister, your old man was a Comanchero, an' one o' the worst killers I ever run across. So he was your pa, but I ain't gonna shed no tears over him. Seems like your brother was headed the same way. Adios, friend. Looks like you're gonna see Austin yourself!'

Chapter 14

The outlying buildings of Deming dropped away behind them, and the coach headed out onto the winding desert trail. Abe flicked the lines and let the fresh team run. Contentedly, he shifted his chaw of Henry Clay from one cheek to the other as the six horses settled into a mile-eating gallop. Out of the corner of his eye, he glanced at his companion.

'What in tarnation's eatin' you?' Bull clamped his hat firmly on his head. 'You're sure in one hell of a hurry this mornin'.'

Grinning self-consciously, the driver eased the team's pace slightly. 'Easy now ... easy.' The horses steadied to a long-striding lope that they could maintain indefinitely.

'I hate towns, can't get out o' them quick enough.'

'I'd noticed,' Bull said dryly, 'but I'd like to make it to Tucson in one piece!'

Abe laughed. 'Don't worry about it, I ain't never broke up a stage yet. Anyway, we should make good time to Stein's. Ain't no grade to speak of on this section, an' the way stations all got good teams.'

'You mean they can vary?'

'Oh sure,' Abe nodded seriously. 'This is rough country. Ain't so many years back that Cochise had everybody buffaloed down here. Reckon it wouldn't take much to start it all up again. So the stations keep only the best teams. 'Course it cuts both ways. The Apaches get to know you got top quality horseflesh, an' once in a while they try runnin' them off.'

'What's it like for the ranchers on the Arizona side?'

'Kinda rough,' Abe glanced at his companion. 'You thinkin' o' ranchin' out that way?'

Bull shrugged. 'Might be. How about the range down Dorando way, that's on your route ain't it?'

'Nah, we swing just north o' it. Some right good grazin' round there. 'Course, down towards the Border it's brush country, an' real tough.'

'Mm, that's what I figured. You ever hear o' a spread down that way called the Flyin' W? Big outfit, stretches right down to the Border.'

Abe frowned. 'Flyin' W? Seems like I heard that name somewhere ... hey, I remember now. Rolf Peterson, the line's agent in Tucson, he buys the replacements for his teams from the Flyin' W. Got a runnin' contract with them.'

'What's their horseflesh like?'

'Peterson reckons they're the best. That's how they keep the contract.'

There was a long silence. Bull squinted into the distance. Then ...'What about them new passengers?' he said abruptly. 'Know anything about 'em?'

Abe cracked his whip and the team settled into their collars on a long uphill grade.

'Accordin' to Murphy, the agent at Deming, that big, well-dressed gent with the gold watch chain is a banker. Name o' McDevitt. He's bound for Tucson, got business there.'

'Them two young fellas, Davis and Clayton, they've been hired by the company as station hands. Easterners, lookin' for excitement. Waal, they're sure goin' to the right place! They're headin' for the Gila Ranch way station.

'Then there's that slim dandified gent. If I remember rightly, his name's Wallace. Got gambler written all over him.'

'How about the big lady?' Bull queried.

'Miss Schwartz? Seems she's goin' out to cook in one o' them Tucson hotels. Judgin' by her accent her folks musta been German.'

Bull thought for a moment. 'That's seven. You got room inside for two, three more.'

'Yeah. 'Course if them wounded fellas and Miss Jones hadn't stayed over in Deming, every seat inside would have been taken. Sure hope that lady feels better soon.' Bull nodded.

☆   ☆   ☆   ☆

Ma knitted another row and looked across at Miss Svenson. 'You feelin' better this mornin'?' she queried.

'Yes thank you,' Loretta eyed Ma warily. 'That was a comfortable hotel in Deming.'

'Mm,' Ma's needles clicked industriously. 'Wonder how them wounded fellas we left are makin' out?'

'Mister Walker didn't look good.'

'That's true.' Ma stopped knitting and stared at Loretta pensively. 'I didn't like the look o' that leg wound, not one bit. Should'a been cauterised.'

Loretta Svenson shuddered. 'I don't know how you can even think of such a thing. And the Reverend Jefferson too. He looked real poorly when I saw him this morning.'

'Him!' Ma said disgustedly. 'The bullet went clean through his arm an' didn't even touch the bone. He was just feelin' sorry for himself.'

'How can you say that!'

'Shucks.' The needles clicked again. 'One miserable little bullet hole an' he's dyin'. No wonder the churches can't get a hold out here!'

From his seat diagonally opposite, Clay Wallace smiled sardonically. 'I understand that you two ladies were involved in that hold-up in Picacho Pass?'

Ma looked at him coldly. The embroidered waistcoat, the black jacket, the pencil slim moustache and the pale complexion. He's got gambler written all over him.

'Yes,' Loretta Svenson shuddered dramatically. 'It was terrible. If it hadn't been for Miz Jordan I don't know what would have happened.'

Further along the seat the burly banker, Lincoln McDevitt, stirred and half turned to face them. 'Do I take it, miss, that you ladies had some say in thwarting this hold-up?'

'Why yes. Miz Jordan held up one man, and Miss Jones, the lady who stayed behind at Deming, shot another.'

The large lady sitting next to Loretta spoke. 'And you,' the accent was heavily Germanic, 'What did you do?'

'Nothing,' Loretta fluttered her eyelashes. 'I was terrified!'

'I was not aware,' McDevitt had the booming voice of the politician, 'that ladies travelled armed.'

'Oh yes,' Miss Svenson gestured graphically. 'Miz Jordan has a shotgun and a pistol in her knitting bag.'

Ma scowled angrily.

'Your servant, ma'am.' Clay Wallace tipped his hat admiringly. 'Remind me never to get into a poker game with you.'

'That ain't likely.' Ma's tone was tart. 'I don't hold with gamblin'. An' what I carry in this bag is my business, an' I'll thank you all to remember it!'

Chapter 15

Sam Harkness swung his mount into the stand of cottonwoods and surveyed his back trail tensely. Nothing. 'Clyde, old hoss,' he patted the bay's neck, 'mebbe we outsmarted them this time.'

Harkness you damn fool, he thought bitterly, how come you're in this mess, you that always figures yourself as a smart lawman? What were you thinkin' about, lettin' them Apaches sneak up on you like that?

Stocky, dark-haired, with a hint of grey, and tough weather-beaten features, Sam Harkness looked what he was, a highly capable U.S. Marshall.

Sent from El Paso to Hatchita to get a statement from a prisoner, he'd been on his way back when a band of roving Chiricahuas had jumped him. All morning they had manoeuvred him north, and it was only a matter of time before they got him out in the open and ran him down. His mount was good, but they'd just spread out and run their horses in turn until the bay was exhausted.

Now he waited patiently for a sign. There! Way down at the far end of the valley. The faintest spiral of dust. He bent forward and spoke softly to his mount. 'Alright old hoss, let's go. Mebbe we can outrun 'em yet.'

The bay plunged out of the trees and hit the long, punishing, uphill grade. It stumbled and Sam swore. If we can just make the ridge, he thought, might be I could hold 'em off.

A glance behind him dashed that hope immediately. Already, the pursuit, seven strong, was fanning out. Gonna try an' circle me, he thought grimly. Right, Clyde, it's up to you now.

The labouring bay lunged over the crest. A gentle downhill slope stretched ahead and there ... 'Glory be, it's the stage!'

Sam laughed exultantly as he leaned low along the bay's neck. If we can team up wi' them we got a chance.

'Rider just come over the ridge.' Bull cradled the shotgun in his hands. 'Goin' like all hell was on his tail. Should cut our trail by that clump o' mesquite.'

'Hold-up maybe?' Abe shot a glance out of the corner of his eye.

'Nah.' Bull was positive. 'He's ridin' like he's got trouble behind 'im. Uh-oh, here it comes. Six, seven Injuns just cleared the ridge. Ain't got a rifle anywhere have you? Shotgun's alright for close work, but it don't carry no distance.'

The driver cracked his whip above the leaders and the pace increased. He thought for a moment. 'There's a Big Fifty Sharps somewhere under the seat, an' a box o' shells if you can find them. Took 'em off a buffalo hunter in a poker game a year ago, but it ain't been fired since.'

Sam Harkness hit the trail some thirty yards ahead, and steadied the bay to allow the stage to catch up.

'Am I glad to see you!' He grinned up at them as the Concord rocked alongside. 'Thought them Apaches would get my hair for sure.'

'It ain't over yet,' said Bull sourly. Delving under the seat, he came up with the big Sharps. Bending again, his fingers gripped the box of ammunition. He opened it and cursed savagely. 'Five rounds! You sure as hell weren't aimin' to start no war.'

'Never had no need.' Abe said defensively, watching the trail ahead.

Bull snapped open the breech of the big rifle and scowled. 'Hell, you could plant corn in here.' He looked back. The Apaches were about four hundred yards behind and closing fast.

'Right,' he chambered one of the big rounds and slammed the breech shut. Swinging round he crawled along the stage roof and rested the barrel of the Sharps on the luggage rail.

Sighting carefully on the leader he pressed the trigger. The big gun boomed and Bull winced with pain as the butt smacked against his shoulder. Peering through the smoke he grunted with satisfaction. The leader's pony was down and the other riders had pulled up.

Below, the crash of the shot had alerted the passengers. Smoothly, Ma whipped the long bag open and extracted the shotgun. Clay Wallace watched admiringly as she deftly loaded two buckshot rounds into the gun and closed it. A movement caught her eye, and she looked up as the gambler palmed a short-barrelled pistol from inside his jacket.

'What you got there?' Ma asked caustically.

'Smith and Wesson .32.' Wallace thumbed rounds into the cylinder. 'Never needed anything heavier until now.'

'First time for everything,' Ma delved into her bag again. 'Can anybody else handle a pistol?' She held up the Paterson Colt.

Hank Davis, the slim, red-haired youngster, spoke hesitantly. 'I useta shoot squirrels with my pa's old army Colt.'

'Right.' Ma passed the revolver over. ' It ain't much use less'n they get in close, but it's better than nothin'.' She tossed a small box across. 'An' make them rounds count. I ain't got that many.'

Abruptly her gaze switched to the white-faced Loretta Svenson sitting opposite. 'You gonna be sick?'

The blonde girl shook her head wanly.

'Thank the Lord for that. I can't abide wimmen that's allus throwin' up when things get tough.' She turned to the banker. 'You see anythin' that side, mister?'

Lincoln McDevitt shook his head. 'I'm afraid not. Whoever is behind us is sticking close to the trail.'

'Ain't got much choice,' Ma peered out cautiously. 'Look at all that mesquite an' chaparral out there.'

The Sharps boomed again from above, blending with the sharper crack of the Winchester as Sam Harkness opened up.

'Don't reckon he'll hit much,' said Ma disparagingly. 'Shootin' from a runnin' horse is a chancy business at best.'

Up top Bull swore disgustedly. 'Damn!' Clean miss, an' only three rounds left. He breathed heavily into the breech and chambered another round. Below, Sam Harkness was firing rapidly. Anyway, one thing's for sure, they ain't gettin' no closer. The big man rolled over and looked ahead.

Not good. The mesquite and chaparral fell away on either side and the trail continued through open grassland. Well, he thought grimly, if they fan out now we got trouble. He eased back into position and steadied the Sharps on the rail.

Below, Ma studied the terrain thoughtfully. 'Open country now. Get ready, them Injuns'll try to come up on either side.' She gestured to Hank Davis. 'Son, you get right up to that window. Then if one of them comes in close you're all set.'

Clay Wallace grinned. 'Have you any last minute advice for me, ma'am?'

Ma looked at him frostily. 'You just tend to your side, an' leave me an' the young fella to tend to ours. Rest o' you, I'd advise you to get down on the floor. Watch out, here they come.'

Fanning out on the open grassland, the Apaches urged their ponies on in a last desperate burst of speed. Ma sighted carefully on a racing pinto and triggered both barrels. The pony went down in a rolling somersault and lay still, its rider pinned beneath it.

In the opposite corner Clay Wallace waited tensely. A flying black pony was coming into view, the rider draped over its off side and hidden from the taut gambler. Up ahead Sam Harkness's Winchester crashed twice in quick succession. The black pony sagged to its knees and fell sideways. Its rider came up running.

The Smith and Wesson barked from the coach and the Apache pitched forward to lie sprawling on the grass. The remaining braves swung away on either side. Suddenly it was all over.

Bull wiped the sweat from his eyes and looked again. The surviving Indians had halted by their two dead companions and were picking up the bodies. As he watched, they swung up onto the remaining ponies and headed due south.

'Chiricahuas for sure,' Bull grunted as he scrambled up to the front of the coach. 'Long ride ahead, an' each pony carryin' double. Reckon they'll think twice 'fore they try that again.'

Alongside, Sam Harkness grinned and waved. Bull waved back and eased into his seat.

'They gone?' Abe was concentrating hard. The excitement had triggered the team, and he had a runaway on his hands if he wasn't careful.

'Yeah.' Bull stashed the Sharps under the seat and settled himself comfortably. 'Picked up their dead and headed south. They got some explainin' to do to Cochise.'

The driver grunted. "Nother three--four miles to the next way station. Say, I heard a shotgun blastin' back there. That your old lady again?'

Bull laughed. 'Guess so. Ain't nobody else aboard got one, an' Ma hates to miss a fight. Oh, an' if you're gonna keep that Sharps, give it a clean an' buy some extra rounds. It ain't a bad gun at that.'

'I hear you,' Abe applied the brake gently. 'Got to stop them knotheads somehow, else they'll just keep goin'.'

Below them Ma packed the shotgun and the box of shells neatly into her bag. She looked across at young Davis. 'Pass that Colt, son, an' them rounds.'

'Yes, ma'am.' Reluctantly the youngster handed them over. He spoke hesitantly. 'You ... you wouldn't consider sellin' it?'

Ma shook her head decisively. 'Sorry son, me an' that pistol go way back. I wouldn't feel happy without it. Anyways, young fella like you needs somethin' heavier, a .44 mebbe.'

Clay Wallace tucked his gun inside his jacket and leaned back in his seat. His mouth twitched. 'Ma'am,' he bowed slightly in Ma's direction, 'it's been a privilege to see you in action.'

'Shucks.' Just for a second an answering gleam of humour flickered in Ma's eyes. 'You ain't so bad yourself, mister. Mind,' she added disparagingly, 'you could do with something heavier than that stinger!'

Lincoln McDevitt cleared his throat importantly. 'I shall be commending your action to the authorities,' he began sonorously. 'Such public-spirited zeal deserves some recognition.'

Ma paused in the act of unrolling her knitting. 'Reckon you mean well, mister, but if you're gonna live out here a gun would be more help than all them fancy words you been stringin' together.'

☆   ☆   ☆   ☆

Abe pointed ahead with the whip. 'Way station comin' up. Ain't much, but what the hell ... it's better than nuthin'.' The foam-flecked team steadied on the uphill grade. 'Easy now, easy.' They slowed to a canter, then a trot. Sam Harkness reined in the bay and dropped back out of the way.

The Concord rolled to a stop in front of the squat adobe station. Luke Ackerman, the tall, rangy station boss, came through the doorway, rifle at the ready. He raised a hand to Abe as the station crew swung open the corral gate and led out the fresh team. 'You're early. You been makin' good time ... ' Luke broke off and crossed to the rear of the stage. He reappeared clutching two arrows. 'Seems like you had a little trouble,' he held up the arrows.

'Apaches,' Abe grunted. 'Jumped us about eight miles out. They was chasin' this gent here,' he indicated Sam dismounting from Clyde.

'Howdy.' Harkness led the bay up to them. He looked at Abe. 'Thanks for savin' my hide back there. The name's Harkness; Sam Harkness, U.S. Marshall, out of El Paso. I was on my way back from Hachita when them braves jumped me.'

The driver shrugged. 'Was kinda busy savin' my own hide.'

Harkness laughed. 'I noticed!' He nodded as Bull came up. 'Sam Harkness. Thanks again. You're kinda handy with that Sharps.'

Bull grinned. 'Hardy Jordan. You're a fair hand wi' that Winchester yourself.'

The fresh team was eased into position and the hands coupled up the traces.

'Sorry we ain't got no way o' feedin' you,' Ackerman said quietly, 'but it's all we can do to hang on here. Injuns run our horses off twice in the past month. Still, you'll make Stein's tonight an' they got a good place there. Miz Jamieson's a mean cook.'

'Yeah, I know.' Abe glanced at Sam Harkness. 'You're travellin' the wrong way now. Got any plans?'

Harkness shook his head. 'Reckon I'm lucky to be alive.' He looked at the station boss. 'If it's alright with you I'll rest up here for a day, then start back.'

'Sure,' Ackerman waved his hand, 'it ain't much but you're welcome. Turn your horse into the corral. We'll feed an' water him. The eastbound stage gets in tomorrow. You can tag on with it to El Paso.'

The marshall watched Abe and Bull climb back onto the stage. 'Adios, fellas an' don't go tanglin' with no more Apaches.'

Abe shook out the reins and released the brake. 'We ain't aimin' to make it a habit.' He snapped his whip and the team surged forward. Dust boiled up in their wake.

★   ★   ★   ★

Stein's lay behind them. They were into the narrow pass in the Peloncillo Mountains, the team working hard on the uphill grade. 'Arizona now.' Abe spat and shifted his quid. 'San Simon station next. Then we head for Apache Pass an' Fort Bowie. Put up at Bowie for the night.'

'I hear the Pass can be rough?'

'Yeah.' Abe eased the team into a bend. 'Never had no trouble there myself, but it ain't no place to hang about in. Apache country. It's four miles through that pass an' they got you cold if they're feelin' ornery. Worst stretch in Arizona, but there ain't no other way in.'

Bull swept the country with a practised eye. 'Poor grazin'.'

'Gets better past Bowie.' Abe flicked the off leader with his whip. "Specially down by Tucson. Lots o' good gramma grass along there.'

'What about the Border country?'

'Depends.' Abe shrugged. 'Some good, some bad. Better than Alkali Flats though.'

'Yeah.' Bull reflected on the bleak plain they had crossed in New Mexico. 'Ain't much good for anythin' 'cept rattlesnakes an' scorpions.'

The driver grinned. 'Yeah, and Apaches.' They laughed tightly together.

★   ★   ★   ★

'You are going far?' Abigail Schwartz stared inquisitively at the small stocky figure opposite.

'Tucson.' Ma's needles clicked industriously. 'Got business there.'

'Might I offer you my card.' Lincoln McDevitt delved importantly into a pocket. 'Maybe I could be of some assistance.'

'Why thankee.' Ma took the proffered square of cardboard and peered at it closely. 'Lincoln McDevitt Esq. General Manager, Cattleman's Bank, Tucson.'

Blue eyes narrowed shrewdly, she looked carefully at the banker. 'Well thankee again, I'll bear that in mind.'

'I too am going to Tucson!'

Right determined lady, Ma thought. Aloud she said, 'you got business there too?'

'Yes.' The large lady nodded importantly. 'I am going to be cook at a big hotel. The owner, he is German, like myself and he wishes to taste German cooking again.'

Ma glanced at her carefully. 'You ain't from these parts?'

'I am from Fredericksburg in Texas. My parents settled there. I see this job in newspaper and I write.'

'Yeah.' Ma switched needles and started another row. 'I hear Tucson's a tough town.'

Miss Schwartz shrugged. 'My parents are dead. I am alone now and must find work. Also, he offers to pay well.'

'Mm,' Ma reflected for a moment. 'Well, I wish you luck.'

'Thank you.' Abigail leaned forward impulsively. 'You are strange lady, but very kind.'

'San Simon.' Abe pointed ahead. 'The old company built the station right close to the river, then they had to build an earth dam to hold water. It don't rain all that often round here, an' sometimes the river gets real low. Change teams here, then we head for the Dos Cabezas Mountains an' Apache Pass.'

Bull nodded. 'Could do to stretch my legs.'

'Sure.' Abe steadied the team. 'From here to Fort Bowie is a fair haul. We'll let the folks get a cup o' coffee here. Ed Parker's always got a pot on the stove. They don't feed you though. Only got enough supplies for themselves.'

✯   ✯   ✯   ✯

Mary-Lou Jordan climbed down from the stage and stared round grimly. Lord, she thought, I ache all over. Wish I was back at the Circle J. Wonder what I've let myself in for.

Ed Parker, the stout, balding station agent, bustled forward. 'This way folks. Got a fresh pot o' coffee ready.' He drew Ma to one side. 'Ma'am, could you speak to the other ladies. We got a little place out back,' he coughed delicately, 'where you can freshen up. It ain't much, but … ' he shrugged expressively.

'Mister,' there was a glint of humour in Ma's eyes. 'That's right nice of you. Thank you kindly. I'll pass the word to the other ladies.'

Hank Davis and Mike Clayton sipped the scalding hot coffee and stared at the busy scene. Wonderingly they watched as the station crew unhooked the tired team and led them away. Minutes later they were back with the replacements and were easing them into line.

'It sure looks easy,' Hank whispered to the slim, dark-haired youngster. 'Think we can do it?'

'We ain't got much choice,' Mike replied. 'We told that fella in St. Louis that we could, so we're out of a job if we don't.'

'Alright, folks.' Abe peered in through the open door. 'Take your seats. We're ready to roll. Next stop Fort Bowie. We'll put up there for the night.'

★ ★ ★ ★

The morning was cool and dry with a hint of the heat to come. To the east the sun was just beginning to wash over the horizon. There was a smell of sagebrush in the air. Bull sniffed appreciatively.

Abe leaned towards him. 'Sleep well?'

'Yeah. Best way station I've seen so far.'

Abe nodded. 'Bowie's always had a good name. 'Course, havin' the soldier boys there helps.'

'Mm,' Bull reflected on the gloomy, four mile long pass they had come through the previous day. He remembered how the clatter of the team's hooves had echoed off the towering rock walls. 'Them soldier boys have a tough job up there.'

'Yeah. Lot o' good men died keepin' that pass open.' Abe cracked the whip menacingly. 'We can stretch out now. Ewell Springs next. Then Dragoon Springs, an' through Ceurca Pass to the San Pedro station. We got to ford the river there.'

Bull looked at him. 'That's a fair piece.'

'Yeah, but it's open country. I can let the teams run. There ain't but one uphill grade between here an' Tucson. That's just before La Cienaga, then it's an easy run to Tucson.'

★ ★ ★ ★

Dusk was falling when they rattled into Tucson. Lights glimmered in the houses as they turned towards the stage depot at Pennington. The two carriage lamps, set one either side, just below and behind the drivers seat, cast long wavering shadows ahead of the tired team. Abe had lit them some miles back.

'Don't do no good,' he confided to a grinning Bull, 'but it's company rules an' I can't break 'em all.'

The stage clattered through the depot gates and slowed to a halt. Abe set the brake and dismounted stiffly. He watched with approval as Bull assisted the ladies to alight. Rolf Peterson, the tall blond agent, appeared with one of his clerks and gathered the passengers together. He spoke swiftly, gesturing to the lights of a building further down the street, and indicating that the young clerk would escort them there.

'Rolf's a good man,' Abe bent to pick up his blanket roll. 'Mind,' he added, 'he owns the hotel, so that helps.'

Straightening up, the tough old stage driver peered at Bull in the gathering dusk. "Case we don't see each other again, thanks.' He extended a calloused hand. 'You can side me any time.' They shook hands and walked on companionably towards the hotel.

Chapter 16

The appetizing smell of frying steak drifted through the dining room and Bull Jordan sniffed appreciatively. He glanced up at the diminutive waitress hovering at his shoulder and grinned.

'Steak and two eggs, miss. You got any potatoes?' The girl nodded. 'Fried potatoes as well then.' Movement by the door caught his eye; he saw his mother come into the room and look round. Bull waved. 'Oh, and a big pot o' coffee.'

'Sure.' The girl smiled and disappeared.

'Mornin', Ma.' He rose and drew out her chair.

'Thanks.' Ma seated herself comfortably. One thing you got to say for the boys, she thought to herself, they got manners. Always did say, you bring kids up right they'll turn out right.

The waitress reappeared with Bull's breakfast. He glanced across at his mother. 'How about yourself, Ma?'

'Ham an' eggs, an' some potatoes.' She poured herself a cup of coffee and tasted it. 'Mm, that's better.'

Bull looked up from his plate. 'All set?'

'Yeah,' Ma sipped the steaming liquid. 'Soon as we're finished here we'll look for them lawyers.'

The waitress set the laden plate in front of her.

'Looks real good ... say, can you tell me where I can find these here lawyers?' She consulted the letter. 'James and Sherman.'

'Why sure. Right out through the front door and turn left. It's about two blocks down the street.'

'Thankee, miss,' Ma looked across at her son. 'That's right handy.'

'Mm,' Bull mopped his plate with a piece of bread. 'Means we don't hafta go traipsin' all over town. Gives us more time to have a look at the ranch.'

✯   ✯   ✯   ✯

Together they made their way along the street.

'Tucson ain't all that much,' Ma commented sourly. 'Too many saloons for my likin'.'

'Growin' though,' Bull pointed across the street to where building was in progress.

'Mm ... say, this looks like it.' Ma craned her neck and pointed to the gilt-lettered sign on the front of the building: G.W. James & R.T. Sherman, Attorneys at Law. 'Yeah, that's them.'

'Can I help you, ma'am?' The young clerk looked up from his desk.

'Why sure, son. I'm lookin' for a Mister James, or a Mister Sherman.'

'Mister Sherman is away on business, ma'am, but Mister James is here.' The young man paused, 'What name shall I say?'

'Tell'm that Miz Jordan an' her son Hardy are here.'

The clerk disappeared through an inner door. There was an indistinct murmur of voices, then he reappeared. 'Right this way, folks.' Ushering them down a narrow passage to a door flamboyantly inscribed 'George W. James, Attorney at Law. Established 1858', he knocked.

'Come in.' It was a dry legalistic voice, with a hint of musty documents and copperplate writing. The young clerk opened the door and waved them through.

A tall white-haired figure rose from behind a cluttered desk and extended his hand.

'Good morning, ma'am, sir. Please sit down.' He waved them towards two comfortable armchairs, and resumed his seat behind the desk. 'I regret that my colleague, Mister Sherman, is not here as well. Circumstances have dictated otherwise.' His bushy eyebrows drew down in a frown. He seemed to feel that the circumstances could have been avoided.

'However, Miz Jordan, this does not prevent us from proceeding with the business in hand.' He picked up a folder lying on the desk. 'Namely, the last will and testament of your late uncle, David Wilson.'

Ma nodded. 'Mind tellin' me what happened?'

George James leaned back in his chair and reflected for a moment. 'Your aunt died about two months ago. It was very sudden, according to your uncle. A stroke I believe. As for your uncle,' sadness showed fleetingly on the severe features, 'he never really got over her death. They were very close. Of course, they had no family. That might have helped to cushion the blow.' Ma nodded.

'Anyway, about a week later he was riding into Dorando when it happened.'

Ma and Bull looked at him questioningly.

'The accident. It appears that something scared his horse, and he was thrown.'

'Don't seem like Uncle Dave somehow.' Ma interjected. 'He was a right good horseman.'

'Yes,' the lawyer nodded. 'But you must understand, he was much older than when you knew him. Also, he had put on a great deal of weight in his latter years. Anyway, that's what his foreman, David Sands, reckoned. He found him. Your uncle never regained consciousness. He lingered on for a few days, but seemed to have lost the will to live and,' again he consulted the folder, 'he passed away on the twentieth of April.'

'Mm?' Bull's eyes narrowed. 'This foreman, Sands ... he a good man?'

George James rested his elbows on the desk, and interlaced his fingers as he considered Bull's question. 'Well, I won't say there hasn't been talk. But Mister Wilson seemed to think highly of him. Beyond that I wouldn't like to say.'

'Now,' his eyes dropped to the document in front of him, 'your uncle left all his estate to you, Miz Jordan. The ranch, the stock, everything. The ranch extends to some nine hundred sections, or five hundred and seventy-six thousand acres if you prefer it that way. Some of the land is very good, particularly round the home ranch. Further afield it varies considerably.'

'As for the stock,' he shrugged. 'Difficult to say. According to last year's returns, which are by no means complete, there are approximately five thousand head of cattle and some six hundred horses on the Flying W.'

Bull looked at him through narrowed eyes. 'Don't know enough 'bout the grazin' an' water, but five thousand head don't seem all that many for a ranch that size. Lot o' horses though.'

The lawyer nodded. 'That's true, Mister Jordan, but there is a great deal of trouble with rustlers down that way. As for the horses, Mister Wilson had a remount contract with the Army, and he also supplied replacements to the stage way stations.'

'What size o' crew did he carry?'

The lawyer pursed his lips. 'Five years ago the Flying W carried a crew of twelve, now they're down to five. I know, I know ... ,' he held up his hands, 'it's not enough. According to what I hear, men won't stay since Sands became foreman. But as I said, Mister Wilson seemed satisfied with him.'

Ma stirred in her chair. 'Anything else?' she queried.

'Oh yes. There's some $10,000 in the bank. That's yours as well. At one time your uncle was an extremely wealthy man, but things seem to have gone downhill considerably in the last few years.'

'Since Sands became foreman you mean?' Ma's eyes were bleak.

James shrugged.

'Well thankee, Mister James.' She turned to Bull. 'Reckon it's time we got out there and saw things for ourselves.'

Her son nodded. 'Where could we hire a buggy?' he queried.

The lawyer thought for a moment. 'Tim Sheridan's livery stable. It's reckoned the best in town. Just across from the stage depot.'

'Thanks, mister.'

'My pleasure. Now Miz Jordan, if I can have your signature on one or two documents, that will complete the formalities. Oh yes, and I'll give you a letter of introduction to the bank.'

✯   ✯   ✯   ✯

Sheridan's Livery & Feed Stable was a substantial adobe building, set back from the street. Bull grinned as they surveyed the notices on either side of the main door. It was obvious that Tim Sheridan had a sense of humour. *City transfer & hack line. Expressing and hauling. Boarding horses a speciality. Horses let by the day, week, or month.* He switched to the other notice. *Carriages To Benson, Marana, Casa Grande, Dorando and all points of interest. Fine saddle horses.* The words stood out boldly.

'Well now,' Bull opened the door and waved Ma through. 'Seems like we've come to the right place!'

A short bow-legged man, with a swarthy complexion, rose from his seat in the cubicle which passed for an office and came towards them.

'Sure now, what can I do for ye?' The Irish accent was very pronounced.

Ma surveyed the stocky figure carefully. 'M'name's Jordan, Miz Jordan. This here's my son, Hardy. We're lookin' for Mister Sheridan. Want to rent a buckboard for a week'. She glanced at Bull.

'Yeah,' he nodded, 'at least.'

'Well now, I'm Tim Sheridan an' I have the very thing right here.'

He led them to a corner of the building where several rigs were lined up. A handsome, neatly painted buckboard caught their eyes.

'That's some outfit,' Bull surveyed it from all angles. 'Don't see many sprung like that.'

An expression of pride flitted across the small man's face. 'Begorrah now, that's true. A gentleman in Dorando had it freighted in, but the poor fella died before he could make use of it. Ah, it was a cryin' shame.'

'Right,' Bull nodded. 'We'll take it for a week. Now, how about a team?'

'I've got the very thing for ye. Bought them along with the buckboard. Matched blacks they are, an' so gentle an' easy to handle, sure the lady herself could drive them.'

'Wouldn't be the first time,' said Ma tartly. 'Alright, how much do we owe you?'

'Well now,' Sheridan rubbed his hands consideringly. 'Shall we say thirty-five dollars, an' five dollars for every extra day? Ye won't find better terms round here.'

Bull reflected for a moment. 'Seems fair.' He looked at Ma, who nodded.

'If ye don't mind,' Tim looked carefully at Bull who was peeling seven five-dollar bills off a roll, 'I'd prefer coin. No offence ye understand, but I never did like paper money.'

Ma thought for a moment. 'Take us another half hour,' she commented sourly. 'Still, can't say as I blame you. Alright. Hardy, we'll step down to the bank an' get some silver.'

Sheridan came to a sudden decision. 'I can see ye're genuine folks, so I'll break me own rule. I'll take yer paper money!'

'You sure?' Ma looked at him keenly. 'Well now, that's right nice of you. I won't forget this, mister.'

'Thank ye, ma'am. I'll get the boys to hitch the team up. Now, if ye wouldn't mind tellin' me where ye're bound? Just in case anythin' happens.'

'Sure.' Bull looked at his mother. 'Know anything 'bout the Flyin' W spread, down Dorando way?'

'That down on the Santa Cruz?'

Bull nodded.

'Runs clear to the Border,' the livery stable owner eyed them closely. 'That's rough country. Oh, grazin's alright, but ye'll have Apaches, Comancheros an' rustlers to contend with.'

'So,' he looked again at Bull. 'I'd heard that the new owner was a lady?' Bull grinned and indicated his mother. 'Me sincere apologies, ma'am. I wish ye all the luck ye'll surely need. Mister Wilson was a fine man, but his judgment could have been better at times.'

'So everybody keeps tellin' us.' Ma said frostily as they watched the stable hands hitch the black team to the buckboard. 'Only thing is, nobody'll tell us why!'

Sheridan shrugged. 'It would be better if ye made up yer own mind, ma'am, but I would advise caution. There's something wrong at the Flying W.'

'Now,' he handed Ma into the buckboard and stepped back as Bull picked up the lines, 'I'll wish ye a safe journey. Take the stage route back outa town. 'Bout ten miles out take the south fork. Ye should hit Dorando 'bout evenin'. Ye'll see the mines first. After that it's due east all the way. Adios now.'

Bull eased the buckboard out of the lot and turned south. The black horses picked up speed and he let them run.

Tim Sheridan resumed his seat. A faint smile played about his mouth as he filled a short-stemmed clay pipe and lit it. Well now, Mister Sands, he blew a stream of smoke into the air, I don't think ye'll bluff them folks as easy as ye did Dave Wilson.

☆   ☆   ☆   ☆

The team had run their high spirits off during the first hour, and were now settled into a pace that was eating up the miles. Bull pointed with his whip. 'Right good cow country. Plenty o' gramma grass.'

'Yeah,' Ma glanced at him. 'Water too,' she gestured ahead to the scrub marking the banks of the Santa Cruz.

Her son nodded. "Bout Sands. You thinkin' what I'm thinkin'?'

Ma frowned. 'I don't like the sound o' him, Hardy, not one bit. Still, we got to give 'im a chance.'

Bull grunted. 'Guess so,' he glanced at his mother out of the corner of his eye. 'That mean you made your mind up 'bout the ranch?'

'Yeah, reckon I have. We'll keep it. Don't reckon I ever had any doubts. Ain't sayin' your pa's gonna like it, but I reckon I can talk him round.'

Bull grinned. 'Reckon you can at that!' He pointed ahead. 'Rider takin' the same trail as us. Sure ain't in no hurry.'

The solitary rider looked over his shoulder as the buckboard swept up on him.

'I declare,' Ma looked up at a grinning Clay Wallace, 'sure didn't expect to see you so soon.' Gesturing towards Bull, 'my son Hardy … ' she paused inquiringly.

'Wallace, ma'am, Clay Wallace.' He raised his hat and nodded to Bull. 'I take it you're bound for Dorando like myself.'

'Yeah,' Ma thawed perceptibly. 'Might be we'll see you there.'

'I'll look forward to it.' He glanced at the eager team. 'I'd say you'll be there long before me, this old livery plug has only one pace. Still, I'm in no hurry.'

Bull nodded. 'See you there then.' He shook out the lines and the team were into their stride in a swirl of dust.

Clay Wallace watched them race ahead and laughed quietly to himself. What a woman!

Chapter 17

Bull shoved through the saloon doors. A quiet drink would round off the evening nicely. Also, he wanted to check their directions to the Flying W. They'd had dinner, Ma was settled in comfortably at the hotel, and the rest of the evening was his own.

'Gimme a shot o' bourbon.' He rested both elbows on the bar, 'an' a beer.'

'Sure.' The tall, lantern-jawed bartender poured the drinks and shoved them across.

'Thanks.' Bull dropped a Mexican silver dollar on the bar top and picked up the whiskey. He tossed it back in a long easy swallow and relaxed as he felt the warm glow spread through his stomach. 'Man, that's good whiskey.' Reaching for the glass of beer, he drank deeply and turned to survey the room.

'Kinda quiet,' he spoke over his shoulder. 'Guess it'll liven up later?'

'Doubt it,' Gus Faraday placed some coins at Bull's elbow. 'Your change. Things have been awful slow for the past month. Down this way Cochise has got everybody buffaloed.'

'Keep it.' Bull sipped his beer. Something formed in his mind. 'Know any good hands lookin' for an outfit?'

'Thanks.' Gus swept up the money with a practised hand. 'Waal now ... if you're lookin' for top hands, them fellas at that corner table might just fit the bill.' He nodded in the direction of the two cowhands talking quietly together over their beers. 'Names are Joe Masterson, that's the red-haired guy, an' Manuel Ortega. Rode for the Three Star brand, a big outfit west o' Dorando. It was owned by a company from back east an' they went bust. Joe an' Manuel drifted in here 'bout two days ago.' He looked at Bull meaningly. 'Reckon they're near broke.'

'Mm,' Bull drained the last of his beer. 'That's cattle companies for you.' He eased away from the bar. 'Thanks, mister.'

'Any time.' Gus flicked a hand and moved down the bar. Wonder why he's lookin' for hands, he ruminated. Quiet spoken, but I wouldn't like to see him riled. Big hard lookin' guy.

Bull paused by the table. 'Mind if I join you? Got a proposition you might be interested in.'

The red-haired cowhand shrugged and looked at his companion. 'Why not?'

'Si senor,' white teeth flashed in the brown face as Ortega gestured expansively. 'Why not? We have plenty of time and very little money; please sit.'

Bull grinned in turn and settled himself comfortably. He liked what he saw. Both men looked to be in their middle or late thirties. Clothes worn, but neat and tidy. Everything about them pointed to men who knew the cow business.

He realised they were waiting. 'Jordan's the name; Hardy Jordan. I'm from east Texas. M'folks are takin' over the Flyin' W spread,' he didn't see any need to go into details, 'an' I'm lookin' for hands. Pays thirty dollars a month an' found. You interested?'

The redhead whistled and flicked a glance at his partner. 'Sure we're interested. For that kinda money I'd go up against Cochise.' He extended a calloused hand. 'Joe Masterson, from Missouri originally. Worked with a few outfits before I joined the Three Star. Been up the Chisholm coupla times with Shanghai Pearce's outfit. That's where I met Manuel here.'

'Si,' the stocky dark-haired Mexican gestured expressively, 'we are compadres. I come from Sonora. When I was young and foolish I work the brush country. You know it? The brasada.'

Bull nodded.

'It is a hard life, a brush vaquero ... so I move north. Then I join up with Senor Pearce, and that is where I meet Joe.'

'Mister,' Joe glanced awkwardly at Bull. 'I know where there's a couple more fellas if you're interested. Good men, both o' them, they rode for the Three Star with us. Only thing is ... they're black!'

Bull shrugged. 'Don't bother me none. They could be green for all I care. Just so long as they know the cow trade. Where are they now?'

'Down at the feed barn, just back o' McQueen's livery stable. Can't get a place to sleep nowhere else.'

'Mm, what's their names?'

'Jeff Short an' Chester Jones. They was sergeants wi' the Tenth Cavalry.'

'Were they now?' There was a faraway look in Bull's eyes. 'I did some scoutin' for that outfit once.' He stood up. 'You got your horses an' gear?'

They nodded.

'Right, I'll see you at McQueen's stable, first thing in the morning.' Bull grinned, 'then you can meet the owner. You'll enjoy that!' He delved into a pocket and placed four big Mexican dollars on the table. 'Have a drink, or a steak, on me. Night, fellas.'

The two men watched him disappear through the swing doors. 'Think he'll go see Jeff an' Chester?' Joe queried.

Ortega shrugged. 'Who knows ... but we have tried, we can do no more.'

'Mm,' Joe grunted doubtfully, 'you know much about the Flyin' W?'

'Only these stories we hear about this man, Sands.'

'The foreman? Yeah; thought o' mentionin' it to Jordan, but he looks like he could take care o' himself. Strange, I reckon I've heard that name before somewhere. Aw hell, c'mon, let's head for that new eatin' house across the street. I'm dyin' for a steak an' all the trimmin's!'

☆   ☆   ☆   ☆

Grinning to himself, Bull Jordan turned into the feed barn entrance. Ma would give him hell tomorrow, but he knew he was right. There was something wrong at the Flying W, and it would be a lot safer to arrive with their own crew.

He peered into the dim office. The elderly storeman dozing in the chair woke with a start.

'You got a coupla fellas here, names are Short an' Jones?'

'Dunno.' The storeman shrugged. 'They's a coupla black fellas back there,' he gestured towards the lantern lit interior. Dimly, Bull made out two shadowy figures. They appeared to be braiding a rope.

The old man yawned. 'Was thinkin' o' closin' up soon. 'Course I shouldn't leave them in here ... ' he looked slyly at Bull.

Sudden rage gripped the big man. He dropped a silver dollar on the table. 'Them fellas ride for me,' he lied fluently. 'This take care o' a bed for them?'

'Sure, mister.' The grizzled oldtimer grabbed the coin hurriedly. He'd seen the wildness in Bull's eyes. 'Didn't mean no offence, they's right peaceable fellas.'

'Alright,' Bull had a grip of himself again. 'Mind if I talk to them?'

'Go right ahead.' The old man tucked the dollar into his vest pocket.

Bull made his way into the barn towards the two shadowy figures.

'Howdy, gents,' Two dark faces looked up at him. 'Which one of you is Short an' which is Jones?'

The man holding the riata jerked his head. 'He's Short, an' Ah'm Jones. Mind tellin' us what all this is about, mister?'

'The name's Jordan, Hardy Jordan. Just been talkin' to a coupla friends o' yours. Joe Masterson and Manuel Ortega. They said you might be interested in a job?'

The two negroes exchanged glances, then they looked suspiciously at Bull. This time it was Short who spoke. 'Cowhands jobs are kinda scarce right now. Who'd we hafta kill?'

Bull grinned. 'It ain't nothin' like that. M'folks are the new owners o' the Flyin' W, an' I'm lookin' for riders. I hear you're good. 'Sides, you rode wi' the Tenth. I scouted for them one time. Mighty good outfit. Alright, pays thirty dollars a month, an' found. You in?'

'Try an' stop us!'

'There's just one snag.' Chester Jones continued. There was a troubled look on his face, as he and Short exchanged glances. 'Your foreman, Mistuh Sands, he don't have no truck with us black folks!'

Anger flared again in Bull Jordan's eyes. 'You let me worry about Mister Sands. I take it you got your horses an' gear?' They nodded together. 'Right.' He handed them two silver dollars each. 'As of now, you're Flyin' W riders. Get yourself some chuck an' be out front here, come mornin'. The new owner'll be there as well. G'night, see you in the mornin'.'

'Waal now,' Chester flicked a dollar into the air and caught it, 'seems like we's eatin' after all. Sure lookin' forward to seein' Mistuh Sands's face when we rides in.'

'Ah ain't so sure.' Jeff said worriedly. 'That Sands is a mean one an' he's right handy with a gun.'

'Yeah,' There was a faraway look in Chester's eyes, 'but there's somethin' 'bout this fella, Jordan. Ah've heard that name somewhere before. Anyway, he don't seem worried none.'

✯   ✯   ✯   ✯

'So you been hirin' a crew.' Ma scowled at her son over the rim of her coffee cup. 'Kinda previous ain't you? Just remember I'm the owner!'

Bull grinned as he attacked his breakfast. 'I ain't likely to forget it. But we already agreed that we're gonna keep the ranch, an' I'd rather have a crew that we can trust. We been hearin' too many rumours 'bout this guy, Sands.'

'Yeah,' Ma conceded grudgingly. 'Mebbe you're right. Don't like the sound o' this fella at all.' She switched suddenly. 'You reckon these fellas you hired are good boys?'

Bull nodded emphatically. 'Mm, they're cowhands alright, right down to their bootheels.'

'Waal,' Ma rose from the table, 'Better get ready. Seein' that they're my crew, reckon I should look my best!'

★   ★   ★   ★

Joe Masterson rolled a cigarette and looked at Jeff Short. 'So Jordan came to see you last night?' He struck a match on his levis and inhaled deeply.

Jeff nodded. 'Just walked in an' asked us if we wanted a job. Seems an alright guy.'

Masterson nudged Short suddenly. 'Here he comes now. Say, that's a woman with him. Said he was bringin' the new owner!'

'Howdy, gents,' Bull grinned as he surveyed the four open-mouthed cowhands. 'This is the new owner, Miz Jordan. Ma, meet our new crew. Joe Masterson, Jeff Short, Manuel Ortega an' Chester Jones.'

Ortega was the first to recover. Whipping off his hat, he bowed slightly. 'Buenos dias, Senora Jordan. Welcome; I look forward to riding for the Flying W!'

'Thankee, mister.' Ma moved forward a step. 'Right nice to know that there's at least one gentleman here! Pleased to meet you all. Just one thing I want to say. You do right by me, an' I'll do right by you. Now, we got a fair ways to travel to the Flyin' W, so let's not waste time. Hardy,' she turned to her son, 'you go an' see about the rig, rest o' you get your horses. We're movin' out!'

★   ★   ★   ★

Joe secured his bedroll behind his saddle. 'Kinda fierce lady, Miz Jordan,' he ventured.

Bull nodded as he watched the hostlers hitch up the team. 'Yeah, she's tough alright, but straight. Just one thing. Watch out for that bag she carries!' He laughed and walked across to assist his mother into the buckboard.

'Wonder what he meant by that?' Joe tightened his cinch and warded off his mount's half-hearted attempt to bite.

Ortega smiled. 'Maybe there is more than one surprise in store for Mister Sands!'

★   ★   ★   ★

'Four riders an' a buckboard comin''. Lanky Jem Anson stuck his head into the room that doubled as an office in the Flying W ranch-house. There was anxiety in his voice. He'd sided Sands for the last five years, but he knew they were on dangerous ground this time. 'Just crossin the creek now.'

'Mebbe it's Sanchez's boys, for that next bunch o' horses we been holdin' for him. 'Course,' the thickset foreman frowned suddenly, 'it could be the new owner. Nah. That young clerk at the lawyers said it was some old lady from east Texas. Jordan he said her name was. She wouldn't have no crew with her. Queer about the buckboard though. Reckon old man Sanchez musta come himself this time.'

'Pity the rest o' the boys ain't here. Allus feel uneasy when them Comancheros are around.'

'You know why they ain't here!' Anger flared in Sands deep-set eyes. 'I want to throw a herd together an' run it north to Abilene. We been playin' penny ante stuff so far. Now, with old man Wilson dead that game's about played out. So, we take two thousand head an' blow. One last big killin'. What you beefin' about anyway? You been doin' well out of it up till now.'

※   ※   ※   ※

'Ain't far now, Ma.' Bull pointed ahead. The ranch buildings shimmered in the sun. 'Big spread. Well laid out too.'

'Mm.' Absently his mother delved into the long bag and extracted the shotgun.

'Ma!' Bull gestured to the four riders behind them.

'Shucks.' Ma loaded two rounds and snapped the gun shut. 'They can't see nuthin' back there. You're worse than your pa. Allus worryin' 'bout what folk'll think! Now,' she rested the twin muzzles on the end of the bag, and, unpinning her shawl, flicked it deftly over the shotgun, 'I'm all set. An' remember, this is my hand, an' I'll play it my way!' Bull's mouth twitched and he nodded.

Chapter 18

Dave Sands and Jem Anson stood on the porch watching the buckboard sweep round the corrals and up the slope, the four riders bunched behind it. Bull drew the team to a halt in a swirl of dust.

'Howdy, ma'am.' The foreman came down the steps. 'You lookin' for somebody?'

'Sure, mister. The name's Jordan, Miz Jordan. This here's m'son Hardy, an' these fellas are m'crew. We're lookin' for a fella, name o' Sands. You him?'

'Yeah, ma'am, that's me, Dave Sands.' Anger flared across the man's swarthy features as he struggled to control himself. 'Miz Jordan, we already got a crew!'

Ma looked at him coldly. 'Who's this fella?' She nodded towards Anson, standing open-mouthed on the steps.

'Jem Anson, top hand. Rest o' the boys are out on the range. Jem's been coverin' as foreman since Mister Wilson died.'

"Pears to me he should be out on the range. He ain't doin' nuthin' standin' there. Still, he can show the boys where the bunkhouse is.'

Hatred flared in Sand's eyes. 'I don't bunk with no niggers,' he snarled.

There was an electric silence, then Ma spoke with cold finality. 'Mister, you're fired! Tell me what I owe you. Fella like you got no place here!'

The foreman took a pace back. 'You can't do this!' His hand dropped to his gun.

'Hold it!' Ma flicked the shawl back and Sands stared at the twin muzzles. Slowly, carefully, he lifted his hand away from the big revolver. Bull eased out of the buckboard, .45 in hand, and moved round beside Ma.

'Turn round real slow, both of you. Now, unbuckle your gunbelts an' let 'em drop.'

'Boys,' he spoke without turning his head. 'Take Mister Sands down to the bunkhouse an' see he picks up his bedroll.'

'M'roll's in the house.'

'Is it now? Seems like you were plannin' to take over. Anyways, go with him. Soon as he's got everything he can saddle his horse, then bring him back here. You got that? Meantime, me an' Mister Anson got some talkin' to do.'

Bull picked up the two gunbelts and carefully removed the rounds from each gun. He spoke to Anson. 'Turn around real careful like.'

Jem did so.

'Now, just walk down the steps an' say howdy to the new owner.'

Anson approached Ma slowly, his eyes watching the shotgun all the time.

'Howdy, ma'am.'

Ma gestured with the gun.

'Right,' Bull cut in, 'Where's the rest o' the crew?'

Anson was silent for a moment.

'Rustlin's a hangin' offence,' Bull reminded him, 'an' from what I hear stock's been disappearin' off the Flyin' W. A jury might go easy on you if we was to say that you helped us.'

The cowhand thought for a moment. 'They're over towards Saddle Peak,' he said reluctantly. 'Musterin' steers.'

'Now we're gettin' somewhere,' Bull prodded gently. 'An' I take it you an' Sands been runnin' off stock.'

'It was Dave's idea ... .' Anson stopped suddenly, realising that he had implicated them both.

'Waal now,' Bull reflected. 'Mister, you're in big trouble.' He aimed the .45 directly at the startled cowhand. 'I could kill you an' claim it was self-defence. Ain't nobody here to argue.'

'Ma'am ... .' White-faced, Jem appealed to Ma.

Mary-Lou climbed down stiffly from the buggy. 'I'm goin' to have a look at the house,' she announced. 'Anythin' happens out here, I ain't seen it.'

'Now,' Bull looked carefully at Anson. 'You just tell it like it was, an' mebbe I won't shoot you.'

'Waal,' Jem collected his thoughts, 'it seems that Dave had a hold on Wilson. Somethin' 'bout his past, I think. Anyways, Dave came down this way lookin' for him. I met up with him in El Paso, an' we just sort o' drifted west. That was five years ago. So, we came to Tucson, an' Dave found that Wilson had become a big rancher down near the Border. That started him off again, an' we come on down here to the Flyin' W. Dave asked to see Wilson an' they had a long talk. Then they both came out, an' Dave said we'd been hired.'

'Wasn't long before Dave started interferin' in the ranch work; then he wouldn't take orders from the foreman. It come to a showdown, an' the foreman told Wilson that it was him or Dave. Wilson wouldn't back him, so the foreman went. Next thing I knew Dave was foreman. Things just went to pieces after that. Some o' the hands left o' their own accord, an' others Dave fired. They's only three left, oh ... an' the cook. He's out on the range with the others. These four are fellas that have been wi' Wilson for years. Reckon that's why they hung on.'

'Mm.' In the distance Bull could see Sands saddling up at the corral. Joe and Manuel were watching him carefully. Satisfied he looked again at Anson. 'When did the rustlin' start?'

Anson shuffled uneasily. 'It wasn't somethin' you could pin down. 'Bout three years ago Dave started shovin' the stock down into the brush country along the Border. I reckon he had something goin' with a bunch o' rustlers down there. They was probably runnin' the steers across the Border an' sellin' 'em. Anyways, he didn't tell me much about it.

'Horses now, that's different. They don't like the brush country, so he kept 'em up here, near the ranch. He was in cahoots with an old Comanchero called Sanchez. Sanchez's boys useta pick up twenty head here; we generally left 'em down by the creek; an' run 'em down south. Sold 'em to anybody that was interested. Allus a demand for good horses down there.'

'Yeah.' Bull eyed the approaching riders, Joe and Manuel on either side of Sands. 'Where does Sands keep his money?'

'In his saddlebags. Never lets them out o' his sight.'

'Mister Sands is all set to pull out, Boss.' Joe swung down and grinned at Bull.

'Mister.' Bull looked at Sands. 'You mind steppin' down.' The foreman dismounted slowly, his face twisted with baffled rage.

'Open them saddlebags.'

'I'll see you in hell first!' Cursing, Sands charged at Bull. There was a dull thud and Dave Sands was lying on his back in the dust. Bull rubbed the knuckles of his right hand and turned to Joe.

'Unbuckle them saddlebags an' empty them on the porch.'

'Madre de Dios!' Manuel stared in amazement at the silver stream cascading onto the ground. 'They are full of Mexican pesos!'

'Yeah,' Bull nodded sombrely. 'Don't reckon they'll pay for what he's done, but they'll sure help. Now, count out thirty dollars an' put them back. Judas got that much, an' I don't reckon this fella rates any more! Then buckle them bags on again.'

Sands groaned and stirred.

'On your feet, mister.' Bull hauled him up. 'Now, you listen good. My old lady set considerable store by the Wilsons an' that's the only reason I'm lettin' you go. The boys here'll see you down to the creek. Here's your gun, I've taken the shells out.' He jammed the empty gun back in the holster and hung the gunbelt on the saddle horn. 'You ever show up on the Flyin' W again an' I'll kill you!' Joe and Manuel shivered at the coldness in his voice.

'One more thing. I was christened Hardy but most folks call me Bull.' Sands started. 'I see you heard that name before. You give me or my kin any trouble an' I'll hunt you down like a dog!' He stepped back. 'Mount up an' don't look back.'

☆ ☆ ☆ ☆

Masterson and Ortega watched Sands splash through the ford. 'Compadre,' the vaquero built a smoke as he spoke, 'I think the Flying W will be a good outfit now.' He lit up and inhaled deeply.

'Yeah,' Joe watched the tiny figure dwindle into the distance, then he reined his mount round. 'Let's not sit here gabbin'. I sure wouldn't want that big fella lookin' at me the way he looked at Sands!'

'Si.' Manuel brought his mount alongside. 'Or the senora. Did you see her face when she threw back that shawl?' He crossed himself. 'If Sands had drawn his gun he was dead and he knew it!'

'Yeah,' Masterson reflected for a moment. 'Bull Jordan! Now I know where I've heard that name before. That's Bull Jordan the bounty hunter! Man,' he shivered, 'that's one dangerous hombre.'

Ortega shrugged. 'It is better we are on his side then.'

'Uh-huh. Wonder what he's plannin' to do with Anson? Sure glad it ain't me!'

☆ ☆ ☆ ☆

Bull looked at Anson. 'You know I could stretch your neck right here, an' the law would say I was right?'

Fear showed in Anson's eyes. 'Yeah.'

'Waal, you ain't whinin', that's somethin'. Alright, here's the deal. You work here for nothin' but your chuck till I reckon you've paid back what you owe.'

'But ... '

'You ain't in a position to argue. It's either that or the rope.'

Jem nodded shakily. 'Fair enough.'

Ma emerged from the house. The silver caught her eye. 'Land sakes, Hardy. Where did all them Mex dollars come from?'

Bull grinned. 'Mister Sands reckoned he oughta make a donation to the Flyin' W 'fore he left. Now, Jem here,' he indicated the red-faced Anson, 'he's decided to stay on an' work for his keep.'

Ma looked at Jem suspiciously. 'That right?'

'Yes, ma'am.' He coughed and looked embarrassed, 'I feel I owe you that much.'

'Waal,' Ma scrutinised him closely, 'guess you know your own mind best.' She turned to Bull. 'They got a cook round here?'

'He's out on the range ma'am,' Jem said hesitantly, 'with the rest o' the crew.'

'Tsk,tsk,' Ma said disgustedly. 'That ain't no way to run an outfit. It ain't round-up time.'

She paused in the doorway as Joe and Manuel loped into the yard. 'There's coffee an' beef in the kitchen. Gimme an hour or so an' I'll see what I can rustle up.'

'Right,' Bull motioned to Jem. 'Unhitch the team, give them a rub down an' a small feed o' grain, if there's any, then turn 'em into that fenced pasture I can see behind the corral. Joe, you an' Manuel unsaddle your mounts an' do the same. Then meet me at the bunkhouse. Chester an' Jeff are there already, an' I want to talk to you all.' He strode into the house.

'You heard the man,' Joe gestured to Jem. 'Let's go.'

*   *   *   *

'Ma!'

'In here.'

Bull made his way down the long passageway and peered into the kitchen. Ma was on her knees in front of the stove muttering to herself. 'Land sakes, if Aunt Jess could see her kitchen now. Son, this here's one o' them hay burnin' stoves.' She indicated two long, empty, spring-loaded containers. 'You mind loadin' these for me. There's a hay store just across the yard. Tamp it in good an' firm. I aim to bake some biscuits.'

'Sure Ma,' Bull grinned. One thing about bein' around Ma, she kept your feet on the ground!

*   *   *   *

Manuel turned his mount into the pasture and waited while Joe closed the gate. Together they walked towards the bunkhouse.

'Here comes the boss,' Joe indicated Bull just leaving the ranchhouse. 'Wonder what he's goin' to say?'

Manuel shrugged. 'We will know soon enough.' He turned to Anson, 'maybe our friend can tell us.'

Jem Anson shook his head. 'I sure don't know anything an' I got enough troubles of m'own.'

Bull ducked in through the bunkhouse door. 'Hafta get this doorway raised I reckon.'

He looked round the bunkhouse. The five stared back at him. 'Right. As of now Joe's foreman.'

There was an audible gasp from Joe and grins from Manuel, Jeff and Chester.

Bull noted that Jem was carefully non-committal. 'Tomorrow Jem's gonna take us out to meet the rest o' the crew. Any stock they've gathered we'll push up to the home range. Then we start gettin' the stock outa that brush down there.' He paused.

Manuel raised his hand. Bull looked at him.

'Senor, that brush, it is rough country. We will need chaparrejos, you know ... leather chaps, and leather aprons for the horses.'

"Nother thing,' Chester picked up his stetson and pointed, 'no hat strings. It's the easiest way to hang yourself on a snag. This way you lose your hat, but you ain't goin' back for it anyway. Not in there.'

'Yeah,' Joe nodded, 'an' we'll need spare mounts. Nothin' roughs up a horse quicker than that brush, 'specially if he's got to keep bustin' through it.'

Bull grinned. This was a good team. 'Alright, you know brush country, I can see that. Come mornin', Jem can take me an' Jeff out to where the rest o' the crew are workin'. Then we'll start shovin' the stock north to the home range.

'Joe, start gettin' ready for the brush country. Oh, an' watch out for Comancheros, there might be a bunch come prowlin' round.' He ducked through the door and was gone.

Joe Masterson rubbed his chin thoughtfully. 'Never figgered to be a foreman,' he muttered. 'This fella Jordan sure don't hang about. Still, I suppose I might as well start earnin' m'pay. Let's go see what kinda gear they got on the Flyin' W.'

'It's pretty fair,' Jem said cautiously as they made their way to the barn. 'Dave Wilson saw to that when he set up the spread.'

☆ ☆ ☆ ☆

Bull stared in amazement at the transformed kitchen. Biscuits were cooling on a tray and there was a pot of coffee on the stove. Steak sizzled in a large frying pan and the big central table was laid.

'Got to hand it to you Ma, you sure can fix things.'

'It ain't nuthin',' Ma's tone was offhand but Bull could see that she was pleased. 'Just got to put your mind to it. Get me another drum o' that hay. This here stove eats it. Then bring me a bucket o' water from that pump in the yard.'

'Sure.' Bull smiled to himself as he picked up the empty drum. Ma was a hard taskmaster.

*   *   *   *

Joe Masterson rose somewhat self-consciously from the table. 'Thanks, ma'am, that was a real fine spread.' There was a chorus of assent from the others as they pushed back their chairs.

'Si,' Manuel flashed his teeth in a grin of appreciation. 'I have not tasted food like that since I was a boy. Muchas gracias.'

'Well thankee, boys.' Ma looked flustered but pleased. 'It's right nice of you all to say so. Mind,' she added warningly, 'I ain't makin' a habit o' this. Sooner you get that cook back off the range the better.'

Chapter 19

In the dawn half-light, Jeff squinted at the big man riding beside him. A bad man to cross, he reflected. Wonder why he picked me to ride with him and Anson? Thought sure he would leave me back there with Chester. One thing's certain. Colour don't bother him none, or his ma!

Bull rode easily, swaying to the movement of the big grey he'd selected from the remuda. He ain't Red he thought nostalgically, but he ain't bad. Sensing Jeff watching him he grinned to himself. He knew that the black man was wondering why he had been selected to make this trip. This is the way I mean it to be, he reflected. There ain't gonna be no them and us! Reckon we got the makin's o' a good outfit. Wonder how John an' Jake'll fit in? His eyes swept the country ahead. Well, one thing's for sure. What with Apaches, Comancheros and rustlers we'll need a big crew. Twelve riders at least I reckon. Wonder what these fellas we're goin' to see are like? Old-timers accordin' to Anson. Still, plenty old hands can do a good job. That was another reason for bringin' Jeff along. Anybody got a gripe 'bout workin' with black riders, now's the time to sort it out.

Beyond him, Anson's mind was in a turmoil. Jem you dang fool, this is what you get for bein' a drifter. Pa allus did say you'd end up on a rope but you wouldn't listen. You just drifted in wi' Dave Sands, an' now see where it's got you. He shivered suddenly in the cold dawn air. Sure hope Dave don't do nuthin' stoopid. If he comes back to the Flyin' W Jordan'll kill him. That is, he thought wryly, if the old lady don't do it first! Now there is one tough old bird.

Tex Morton finished washing up and emptied the water into the brush. Pushing another branch into the fire he picked up a bucket and made his way down to the creek. Stocky, bowlegged, with a shock of iron-grey hair and a beard to match, Tex looked what he was, a typical, tough, hard-bitten old cowhand. He was also an above average cook, something that was appreciated by the crew of the Flying W.

Now, he filled the bucket and made his way up the bank to the camp. Wish water was always as handy, he thought. Sure makes a nice change. He pushed the branch deeper into the fire. Don't even have to look for firewood. Behind him, half-a-dozen horses, tethered to a rope stretched between two trees, stamped lethargically and swished their tails at the flies. Boys'll be in for fresh horses soon. Wonder what'll happen to the old Flyin' W now that the boss is dead? Likely be sold I guess. Damn that Sands, he's ruined this spread.

Three riders topped a distant ridge briefly and the old man squinted into the sun. That could be them now. He hung a can of water on the pothook, which in turn was suspended from the fire iron. Reckon they could use a cup o' coffee. He bent to his task. Funny though, one o' them usually stays wi' the herd.

☆ ☆ ☆ ☆

Bull eyed the brush stretching away to the south. 'You get any 'cimmarrones' down here?'

'Wild ones?' Anson nodded. 'Yeah, quite a few. Mostly Longhorns, but they's still one or two o' the old black cattle left. Coupla big old bulls in there, real mean ones. They'll kill you if they get the chance. Don't let them close to your horse, an' don't ever let them catch you afoot or you're dead! Mister Wilson, he'd been huntin' them for years, ever since one o' them killed a prize stock bull, but they was allus a sight too smart. Now they're real leery, an' they stay deep in the brush.'

☆ ☆ ☆ ☆

The riders were closer now. Dang, that ain't the boys. Quickly Tex reached into the wagon and hauled out an old Spencer carbine. Gun at the ready, he watched as they splashed across the creek and loped up to the camp.

'Howdy.' Bull reined in and waited.

'Tex,' Jem spoke hurriedly, 'this is Mister Jordan. His folks are the new owners o' the Flyin' W.' He indicated Jeff, 'an' this here's Jeff Short, he's ridin' for the Flyin' W now.'

'Dang me,' The cook stared at Bull. 'What happened to that Sands fella?'

'He left,' Bull said tersely.

'Well hallelujah!' Tex's bearded face lit up. 'Ain't that somethin'. Best news I heard in a coon's age. The name's Morton, Tex Morton. Nice to meet you. Rode wi' Colonel Goodnight when I was younger, an' scouted for General Jimmy Carleton for a spell. Light down you fellas, light down an' I'll get you a cup o' coffee.'

Bull grinned as they dismounted. The old cook was like a breath of fresh air. 'Rest o' the boys around?'

'Be in soon,' Tex busied himself round the fire. 'They come in to change horses. That brush is awful rough on horses.' He peered past Bull. 'Here's two o' them comin' in now. One o' them allus stays to see that them critters don't start driftin' back to the brush.'

Bull nodded approvingly. That was good thinking from thirty a month cowhands. He eyed the two approaching riders. Might have been stamped out of the same mould. Stocky, powerfully built, somewhere in their late forties he reckoned. The same weather-beaten square jawed features and deep-set eyes.

They swung down together and looked round inquiringly. 'Fellas,' Bull could see that Tex was enjoying himself, 'this here's Mister Jordan. His folks are the new owners.' He indicated Jeff, 'an' this is Jeff Short, he's ridin' for us now.

'Boss,' he waved at the two startled cowhands. 'These here fellas are Mike and Sam Alderson. The good-lookin' one's Mike! They're twins,' he added, somewhat unnecessarily.

The Aldersons exchanged embarrassed glances. Bull laughed as he shook hands with them. 'You boys get much hoorawing 'cause you're twins?'

'All the time,' Sam grinned sheepishly. 'Tex is the worst.'

'Yeah,' Bull looked at the two riders. 'You willin' to stay on?'

The brothers looked at each other. 'Boss,' Mike said slowly, 'it ain't as easy as that. Me an' Sam have had 'bout enough o' your foreman, Mister Sands.'

'You can forget 'bout him right now,' Bull said abruptly. 'He's been fired.'

The brothers looked at each other again and grinned. 'Well now,' Sam slapped his pants' leg, 'that's the best news I've heard in years. Sure we'll stay.' He punched his brother's shoulder. 'Let's change horses an' get back out there. Can't wait to see Anders's face when I tell him Sands ain't here no more.'

He saw Bull's look of inquiry. 'Anders Lindstrom, he's the third rider out here.'

'Swede?' Bull queried.

Sam grinned. 'Nah, he's a Dane, an' he don't let nobody forget it! Big guy, not far short o' yourself.' He looked consideringly at Bull. 'That's one o' the reasons I'm glad Sands ain't here no more. I could see it comin' to a showdown wi' him an' Anders. Anders ain't no gunnie like Sands, but he's a top hand with stock.'

This outfit's goin' to be somethin', Bull thought to himself. Coupla black riders, a Dane, a Mex, Jake, who's half Comanche an' half Swede, an' John who's more Comanche than white. Waal, it's a tough country out here, an' mebbe we need a tough outfit.

He watched the Aldersons change mounts quickly and competently. Good men; know their work. Draining the last of his coffee he stood up.

The Aldersons climbed into their saddles and looked at him expectantly. 'Alright, fellas. We'll ride out to the herd with you. Thanks for the coffee, Tex.' He put his foot in the stirrup and swung up. 'Let's go.'

Fording the creek, Sam turned downstream. 'Only 'bout half a mile,' he eased his mount alongside the big grey. 'Tex says you can't get clean drinkin' water less'n you're well upstream from the herd, and o' course,' he pointed towards the timber, 'there's wood here for the fire. We're holdin' the herd in some pasture down by the creek. It's part o' a little valley. Good grazin' and plenty o' water. Makes 'em easy to herd.'

'How many you got so far?'

Sam reflected. 'Reckoned 'bout four hundred head last night. Mebbe 'nother twenty this mornin'.' He gestured towards the brush. 'Still a hell of a lot o' beef in there.'

Bull nodded as the herd came into view. 'All Longhorn stock?'

'Yeah, Mister Wilson swore by them. Said they was the only stock that could survive in the brush.'

'Mm.' Bull knew that few old cattlemen could see past the Longhorn. Equally, he was convinced that they would have to change their views in the end. In the distance he could see a tall rider easing a recalcitrant steer back into the herd.

'Right,' he came to a sudden decision. 'We'll start musterin' what we got here, then we'll move 'em north to the home range, near the ranch. Mike, ask Anders to see me 'fore he goes back to the camp. Him an' Tex can bring the chuck wagon an' the horses in.'

'You packin' up out here?'

'Yeah, lot o' things I want to get straightened out. Want to sweep all the land from the creek up to the north boundary. Then we can start thinkin' about the brush country.'

Mike nodded and loped away round the herd. Bull sat for a long moment feasting his eyes on the scene. This is it, he thought exultantly. What I've always wanted, something to build on. We'll make this the greatest ranch in the whole South-West. He watched the tall figure of Lindstrom as he guided his horse through the outlying steers towards him. Big man, reckon I'd have my hands full with him.

'Mike tell me you want to see me?' The voice was deep, with a strong Scandinavian accent.

'That's right.' Bull looked at the man carefully. Nigh as tall as me I reckon. An' he'll weigh about the same. Thirtyish, mebbe. Fair-haired, tough lookin' hombre. He extended his hand. 'The name's Jordan, Hardy Jordan. My folks are the new owners.'

They shook hands. First time I ever met somebody with hands as big as mine. Betcha he's a mean guy in a fight.

The giant Dane laughed. 'You are strong man. First time I ever feel grip like that. Well now, my name is Lindstrom, Anders Lindstrom. Some day I like to wrestle you.'

Bull grinned and flexed the fingers of his right hand. 'Some other time maybe. Right now I want to know if you'll stay on?'

'Why yes, I will stay. Mike says you have got rid of Sands. That is all I need. He is one bad man. Some day maybe I kill him.'

Bull glanced at the scabbarded Bowie knife on Lindstrom's left hip. Yeah, he thought, you just might if you get close enough.

The Dane leaned forward and stroked his horse's neck.

Something caught Bull's eye. I'll be damned! He noted the distinctive grip of an Arkansas throwing knife protruding from a scabbard at the back of Lindstrom's neck. That's an Arkansaw Toothpick. Mebbe he wouldn't need to get close after all. Looks like him an' John'll have somethin' in common.

Lindstrom waited expectantly.

'Anders, when you go back to camp, get somethin' to eat. Then you an' Tex bring the chuck wagon an' the spare horses in to the ranch.'

Lindstrom looked at him shrewdly. 'You have other plans?'

Bull nodded. 'Yeah, big plans. See you at the ranch.' He kneed the big grey and took off after the herd.

Lindstrom watched him go, then he reined his mount round and headed upstream. Leaning forward, the big man spoke softly to his horse as it lifted into a canter. 'By golly hoss, you know somethin'? I think maybe the old Flyin' W not finished after all!'

Chapter 20

Bull Jordan threw down the pencil and swore softly.

'I heard that,' Ma said sharply, placing a cup of coffee on the end of the desk. 'The good Lord don't look kindly on folks that take His name in vain!'

'Sorry, Ma.' Her son rubbed his eyes wearily. 'It's just that I seem to be gettin' nowhere. As that James feller said, the returns over the last few years ain't too clear. Reckon we'll have a better idea when Joe an' the boys finish musterin' the north end o' the range.'

'Mm.' Ma frowned. Faintly through the open window came the rhythmic clang of hammer on iron. 'Anders seems right busy?'

Bull sipped his coffee and nodded. 'This bein' a big spread it paid to have their own blacksmith. Seems your uncle built his own forge, an' when he took Anders on he taught him how to shoe horses.'

'That's right.' There was a faraway look in Ma's eyes. 'Uncle Dave's pa was a blacksmith, and he taught him the trade.'

'So that's how it was? Anders set considerable store by your uncle. Accordin' to old Tex, Anders's folks were drowned crossin' a river somewhere up north. There weren't no other family an' he just drifted south. Fetched up in Tucson. Your uncle found him workin' as a swamper in a saloon, an' offered him a job. That's why he hates Sands. He reckons Sands is to blame for your uncle's death.'

The enraged squeal of an angry horse drifted up from the corrals. 'That's Sam an' Mike. They're pickin' mounts for the boys an' givin' them a workout. I want each rider to have a string o' six horses to work with. Seems like everythin's been let go round here. We're usin' that herd that was grazin' down by the creek.'

'Seen anythin' o' them Comancheros Anson mentioned?'

'Nothin' so far. Could come anytime.'

'Mm. What about Anson? How's he makin' out?'

'Alright,' Bull shrugged. 'He does his work an' don't say much. Can't ask for more.'

'Just watch 'im,' Ma disappeared through the door.

Bull stretched. She always has to have the last word. He rose and reached for his stetson. Might as well take a break now. I'll go see how Sam an' Mike are makin' out. Pausing for a moment in the doorway, he retraced his steps and picked up his gunbelt. Reckon Ma's makin' me leery, he thought, as he buckled it on and tied down the twin holsters, but it don't pay to take chances. He stepped out into the warm sunshine.

☆   ☆   ☆   ☆

Sam Alderson looked up at his brother. 'You all set?' Mike nodded. Beneath him he felt the black horse quiver tensely.

Deftly, Sam whipped off the blindfold and ducked through the corral rails. For a split second the horse stood motionless, then Mike kneed him gently. The black took off round the corral, bucking half-heartedly.

'How're they workin' out?' Sam turned to find Bull at his side. The stocky cowhand gestured toward the circling gelding, now settling into a run.

'Right good. 'Course they're saddle broke stock anyways. It's just that, with there bein' so few riders, they ain't been rode in over a year. The boys chose a couple each when we brought them in, then told us to choose the rest o' the strings.' His brother cantered the snorting black up to them and dismounted.

'Howdy, Boss.'

'Hi, Mike. Sam says they're workin' out right well?'

'Yeah,' Mike patted the black horse. 'This is a good bronc, got weight an' muscle.' He looked at his brother. 'Reckon we'll put him in Anders's string.'

Bull laughed, 'Save me that big grey I was ridin' the other day. He ain't a bad horse. Leastways,' he added, 'he'll do till Red gets here. Red's one hell of a horse. Trouble is he don't take kindly to anybody else, an' he can be real mean.'

'Yeah?' Mike was unsaddling as he talked. 'Open that gate, Sam. I'll run this fella into the pasture an' rope another one in here.'

Bull eased away from where he had been leaning on the corral rail. 'Leave you to it. Guess I'll go see Anders now.' He strode away in the direction of the forge.

'He's an alright guy.' Sam swung open the gate into the horse pasture.

Mike nodded as he removed the bridle and watched the black canter away. He uncoiled his rope and headed for the corral. 'Let's see what else we got.'

☆   ☆   ☆   ☆

The big horse, tethered to the wall-mounted ring, turned his head and surveyed Bull placidly as the rancher stepped through the open door.

'Howdy, Anders.'

Bent over a rear hoof, which he held cradled between his knees, the giant Dane was hammering the last nail of a new shoe into position. Satisfied, he reached over and twisted off the protruding end. A few final taps before lowering the hoof to the ground, and he straightened his back with a satisfied grunt.

'Mornin', Boss. This job is not good for us tall men.'

'Yeah,' Bull chuckled. He jerked his head at the big animal. 'Lot o' draft horse there.'

' Mister Wilson, he liked to have one heavy team. Used them to haul feed an' lumber, things like that. They are half Conestoga I think.'

'Mm. You could be right. How about bar iron for shoes? You got plenty?'

'Yeah, when things were going well, Mister Wilson, he lay in a good stock.'

'You thought a lot o' Mister Wilson didn't you?' Bull queried.

'He was like a father to me. All this,' Lindstrom waved a giant hand towards the glowing forge, 'he taught me how to use. Without him I am nothing.'

Bull nodded. 'Yeah, that's how my old lady feels.'

'Riders comin', Boss.' Sam Alderson peered in. 'Five o' them, 'bout halfway down the ridge at the back o' the ranch.'

Bull stepped into the yard and eyed the long slope. 'I can see 'em. Could be the Comancheros that Anson mentioned.' He thought for a moment. 'Pass the word to Mike an' Tex that we got company.' He looked again. 'They're ridin' easy so they won't be here for a while yet.'

'How about Miz Jordan?'

'Alright, only shout good an' loud. I don't want you stoppin' a load o' buckshot!' Sam grinned and disappeared.

☆   ☆   ☆   ☆

Standing by the open window, Ma watched the approaching riders as they rounded the end of the ranch buildings. Mean lookin' bunch, got the look o' Comancheros alright. Shotgun ain't no good, it'll spread too much. Got to stick to the Colt. Clutching the revolver, she settled herself and waited. The riders clattered into the yard and halted.

'Howdy, gents.' Bull, followed by Anders, stepped into the open. 'Lookin' for somebody?'

'Dave Sands.' The leader, a heavily built individual with a black moustache and a long jagged scar down his right cheek, leaned forward and scowled. 'We got business with him.'

'Sands has gone,' Bull said shortly, 'an' he ain't comin' back.'

'He owes Sanchez a passel o' horses an' we aim to collect.'

'Them horses weren't Sands's to give.' Bull's voice was bleak. 'Ride on, an' I don't want to see you on Flyin' W range again.'

'Waal now,' A wild-eyed youngster next to the leader grinned derisively. 'I don't see no army here. We can just take the horses an' blow.'

Bull looked at him coldly. Wild kid, gunnie lookin' to make a name. He set himself, every sense alert. 'You ain't takin' nuthin', son. Fellas like you are a dime a dozen. Turn your horses an' ride!'

'Damn you!' The youngster went for his guns. Bull's hands blurred and the .45s roared almost as one. The young gunnie slumped sideways and toppled out of his saddle. Simultaneously, Anders flicked the slim knife from its neck scabbard and threw. The scar-faced leader dropped his gun and clutched at his chest. From the house, the Paterson Colt barked twice in quick succession. One of the three remaining riders swore and grabbed at his arm. Hurriedly, the others raised their hands.

'Dang me!' Tex Morton hobbled out of the cook shack brandishing the Spencer. 'Everything happened so dern quick. Didn't get a chance to take a crack at 'em.'

'Usually does,' Bull said tiredly. 'Watch them fellas.' He removed his hat and scowled at the neat hole in the crown. 'Nother inch lower an' there wouldn't have been no more dreams! Maybe I'm gettin' old.'

The Alderson twins dashed round the end of the cookshack, guns at the ready.

'Where you been?' Bull asked sourly.

Sam and Mike glanced uneasily at each other. 'Boss, I'm real sorry 'bout this,' Mike licked his lips nervously. 'Fact is, since we was workin' them broncs, an' bein' at the ranch an' all, we didn't figger we'd need our guns, so we left 'em in the bunkhouse. Sure am sorry.'

Bull frowned. 'Yeah, I nearly made the same mistake myself. Alright,' he indicated the three survivors. 'Get them fellas tied up. Looks like one o' them has a busted arm.'

He turned to find Anders at his elbow. 'This is a tough outfit now, by golly!' Bull watched as the big Dane walked across to the body of the dead leader. Stooping, he jerked the long, evil looking knife free, and, wiping it carefully, slid it into the neck scabbard. He paused for a moment and took a long look at the young gunnie sprawled in the dust. 'Boss, that sure was some shootin'! You hit him twice, dead centre.'

'Yeah,' Bull shrugged. 'He didn't do m'hat much good though. Tell you somethin', you're a fair to middlin' hand wi' that knife.' He turned as Ma appeared, the Paterson Colt clutched firmly in her right hand.

'Land sakes, Hardy. You got a hole in your hat! You fellas alright?'

'Yeah, Ma.' He indicated one of the Comancheros who was clutching an arm. 'Seems like you winged this fella. Reckon you'll have to dig the lead outa him now!'

'Shucks!' There was a note of regret in Ma's voice. 'Pity I couldn't have used the shotgun. Too risky though. Might've hit you fellas. Sure pays to be ready. Right, I'll get a knife an' some bandages.' She disappeared into the house.

Behind her the twins exchanged embarrassed glances and their faces reddened.

Damn! Bull thought for a moment. Now we got to go see the sheriff. 'Anders,' he turned to the Dane, 'you finished shoein' the heavy team?'

'Yeah. They are still in there though.'

'Hitch them to the wagon. We'll get them fellas fixed up an' then you can take them into town. I'll come with you. We sure as hell ain't goin' to be popular, turnin' up wi' a coupla dead bodies an' three prisoners.'

Lindstrom shrugged. 'Sheriff Dawson is a good man. An' he hates Comancheros. Says they're worse than Injuns. He won't give you no trouble.'

'Waal ... maybe,' Bull said dubiously. 'Anyways, get the wagon.' He indicated the two bound Comancheros and the bodies. 'Load them fellas an' the two stiffs. Soon as Ma fixes the other jasper we'll ride.'

★   ★   ★   ★

Standing on the steps of the jail Sheriff Dawson grinned as he surveyed the loaded wagon. "Pears to me you did a right good job on this bunch. Either of you know any of em?'

Bull and Anders shook their heads.

'That scar-faced fella there,' the burly sheriff indicated one of the bodies, 'reckon I've seen him before somewhere. Joe!' he raised his voice in a shout, 'Get out here, we got customers.'

He turned to Bull. 'So you're Jordan, hey? Your folks own the Flyin' W now. Been kinda hopin' to meet you. Shame 'bout Dave Wilson, he was an alright guy.'

'Yeah,' Bull dismounted and tied the grey to the rail. 'My old lady was reared by the Wilsons, after her folks was killed. She set a lot o' store by them.'

A tough-looking, elderly deputy appeared through the door. Scott Dawson waved his hand. 'Joe, this here's Mister Jordan o' the Flyin' W. These fellas here,' he indicated the prisoners and the corpses, 'tried to hold up the Flyin' W this mornin''

Joe leered wolfishly, "Pears like they didn't do too good a job.' He unhooked the wagon tailgate and motioned the three Comancheros to get down.

'Yeah,' The sheriff rubbed his chin, and looked closely at Bull. 'You musta got a real salty outfit out there now. Reckon when word o' this gets around folks are gonna think twice 'fore they tangle with the Flyin' W.'

Bull nodded. 'I sure hope so. Seems like they's a lot o' stock missin' out there.'

'Heard rumours.' Scott Dawson ushered Bull through the jail door. Anders hitched the team and followed. "Course I never had no official complaint, so there wasn't nuthin' I could do about it.'

'Right, fellas.' He rummaged in a desk drawer. 'If you can just write down what happened, an' I'll look at them dodgers I keep in my desk.'

Anders shuffled his feet and coughed uneasily.

Scott Dawson looked at him inquiringly.

'I do not write too good,' the big man said haltingly.

'Mm.' Dawson frowned. 'Can you sign your name?'

The Dane nodded.

'Tell you what then. Mister Jordan, here makes a statement, an' you sign it with 'im. That should about cover it.'

Silence fell, broken only by the scratching of Bull's pen, and the dull clang of the cell doors as Joe secured the prisoners.

'I knew it!' Bull raised his head sharply at the sheriff's exclamation. Dawson waved a poster. 'That big scar-faced gent. He's Charlie Casner, a real bad hombre. Accordin' to this dodger here, he's old Domingo Sanchez's segundo. An' that young fella,' he riffled through the pile of notices and paused, 'seems he's John Adair.' He read carefully from the notice, "More commonly known as the Navajo Kid". Account o' his mother bein' one o' that tribe. A real hardcase Border gunnie, just startin' to make a name for hisself.

There's a reward o' four hundred dollars for Casner, an' three hundred for the Kid. Nothin' on the others.' He glanced shrewdly at Bull. 'The Kid as fast as they say?'

'Yeah,' Bull nodded sombrely. 'Too fast for my likin'. He didn't do my hat no good.' He signed his statement and passed the pen to Anders.

'Better that than your head,' said Dawson unsympathetically as he watched the giant Dane signing with teeth-clenched determination.' That'll do, Anders. You ain't brandin' a yearlin'!' Picking up the statement, he read it carefully. 'Yeah, just fine. See Miz Jordan was sidin' you.' He looked at Bull. 'That your mother? Must be right handy with a gun?'

Bull nodded. 'She put Jack Anderson an' his brother in the Austin pen.'

Dawson's eyes opened wide. 'Say, I heard that story. How them wimmen wiped out the Anderson gang. Never did understand how a bunch o' hardcases like the Andersons got caught thataway.'

Bull looked at him coldly. 'Sheriff, there's a lot o' things me an' Ma don't see eye to eye on, but when the chips are down there's nobody I'd ruther have sidin' me!'

Scott Dawson grinned and held up his hands. 'No offence, mister. Just surprised, that's all. Now, if you'll oblige me by takin' them bodies down to Hen Wills, the undertaker, that'll be just fine. Anders knows where his place is. Look in 'fore you leave town an' I'll settle up this reward money with you.'

The deputy came in and nodded to Bull. 'Got a prisoner back there would like see you. Fella by the name o' Wallace. Gamblin' man.'

'That's right.' Dawson picked up a paper from his desk. 'Claims he was pistol-whipped on his way from the Silver Dollar saloon to the Grand Hotel, an' that all his money was taken. Reckon he's tellin' the truth, got a bad cut on his head. Trouble is, Miz Le Mayne, that's the owner o' the Grand, she says he owes her for five days' room and board. Then the livery stable says he owes them for boardin' his horse.' He looked closely at Bull. 'How come you know him?'

'It's a long story. He was on the same stage from El Paso. We had a brush with some Apaches on the way.' He shrugged. 'Wasn't no war, but he pulled his weight. Mind if I talk to him?'

'Sure. I owe you one anyway, seein' as how you cleaned out that bunch o' rattlesnakes.'

'Thanks.' Bull made his way down the passage.

'Mister Jordan, I believe.' Clay Wallace, a red-stained bandage round his head, raised a hand tiredly. 'How is your mother?'

Peering through the bars, Bull grinned. 'Howdy. She's in a sight better shape than yourself right now. What the hell you been doin'?'

'Not watching my back for a start. Somebody pistol-whipped me like a greenhorn. Took all my money. So you see, I am in a somewhat difficult situation.'

'Yeah,' Bull reflected for a moment, then he came to a decision. 'How much do you owe the hotel an' the livery stable?'

Wallace shrugged and winced. 'According to Sheriff Dawson, some fifty-five dollars all told. Don't tell me you're the Good Samaritan in disguise?'

Bull laughed. 'Nah, but Ma seemed to take a shine to you an' that's good enough for me. I'll go see the sheriff an' square this with him. Then I got work to do. Adios, friend.' Back in the office he paused beside the sheriff's desk. Dawson looked up. 'Sixty dollars take care o' everything for Wallace?'

'Yeah, why not?'

'Take it out o' the reward money?'

The sheriff nodded.

Chapter 21

Henry Wills, a pint-sized black-suited individual, with wispy grey hair combed carefully across a pink scalp, rubbed his hands. 'Right nice bit o' business you brought in, mister.' He indicated the two bodies. 'Work's been kinda slack lately, so I'm real glad to see you. The county'll pick up the tab, so I got no worries about gettin' paid.'

Bull grimaced. The man was like a ghoul.

☆ ☆ ☆ ☆

Sheriff Dawson unlocked the safe and counted out seven hundred dollars. 'Bank in Tubac put up the reward. Seems like Casner an' the Kid pulled a hold-up there a coupla years back. Shoulda remembered earlier. Sheriff down there sent me a letter 'bout it. They killed a teller, then rode down a woman makin' their getaway. She's been a cripple ever since.'

Bull shook his head. 'Them kind spread trouble everywhere.'

'Well, they won't do it no more.' He peeled off sixty dollars from the roll and offered the remainder to Bull. 'Just sign here.'

The big rancher shook his head again. 'Gimme two hundred an' forty. The rest goes to Anders. It's his by right.'

'Boss!' Lindstrom's face reddened and he shook his head violently. 'I do not ... '

'You'll take it!' Bull cut in sharply. 'A man fights for the Flyin' W, he gets paid his dues.'

Scott Dawson grinned as he passed the roll of bills to the embarrassed Dane. 'Sign here, Anders. You're sure gettin' some practice!'

'What about Wallace?' Bull shot a glance at the sheriff.

'Gettin' himself cleaned up. Should be finished soon.' He looked up. 'Here he comes now.'

Clay Wallace stepped through the connecting door. He had shaved and his hat was carefully arranged so that as little as possible of the bandage showed. 'The Good Samaritan again! What can I say other than thanks.'

The idea that had surfaced in Bull's mind grew sharper. He straightened up and looked directly at Wallace. 'You can come out to the Flyin' W with me. I got a proposition to put to you. First of all though, pay your debts in Dorando.' He looked at Dawson. 'That alright with you, sheriff?'

'Yeah. Joe!' The lean deputy peered into the office. 'You go with Mister Wallace here, and see that he settles his accounts with Miz Le Mayne, and McQueen's Livery Stable. Then come back here.' He handed the small roll of dollar bills to Wallace.

★ ★ ★ ★

'Wasn't all that sure you'd come.' Bull glanced sideways at Clay Wallace as he spoke. They were riding together, about fifty yards ahead of Anders and the wagon.

The gambler smiled. 'I wasn't all that sure myself. 'But ... beggars can't be choosers, and I must admit I'm curious.'

'You know anything about accounts?'

Wallace laughed. 'My father was an accountant. He wanted me to follow him into the business. I stuck it for three years, but I couldn't stand the monotony. One day I walked out and never went back. I headed west and just kept drifting. Then one night I got into a card game and found I had a natural talent for the cards. Maybe my accountancy training helped. Anyway, I just kept moving west and finally I ended up in Dorando.'

'Mm.' Bull was silent for a spell. 'Like you to take on a job for me,' he resumed slowly. 'The ranch tally books ain't been kept properly for the last two to three years. Think you could fix them?'

'Bring them up to date you mean?'

Bull nodded.

'Don't see why not. Take a little time, that's all.'

'Right. Ten dollars a week, plus room and board, how does that grab you?'

Clay Wallace laughed, showing a flash of white teeth. 'Sure, why not. I've nothing else in mind anyway. It's a deal.'

★ ★ ★ ★

It was late when they reached the ranch. The sun was just dipping behind Saddle Peak and the blue shadows were starting to lengthen. Splashing through the ford they breasted the slope and turned into the yard. Bull saw his mother watching from the porch. He grinned to himself as they dismounted. Ma, you got a surprise comin'!

Together they watered their tired mounts at the trough and led them into the stable. In the yard Sam and Mike had materialised from nowhere and were helping Anders to unhitch the team. Removing the saddle and bridle, Bull hung them on wall pegs. Buckling on the halter he began to groom the grey. In the adjoining stall Clay Wallace was also busy.

'See you ain't forgotten how to take care o' your horse.'

Wallace paused, brush in hand. 'Once a cavalryman, always a cavalryman! You don't forget it.' He turned again to his mount.

'Yeah.' Bull brushed steadily. In his own good time Wallace might tell him more. That was up to him.

★ ★ ★ ★

'Anders,' Bull straightened up from the grain bin, a laden scoop in his hands. 'Grain the team an' bed them down in here tonight. Boys,' he waved his hand at the busy gambler. 'This here's Clay Wallace. He'll be around for a spell. Clay, this is Sam an' Mike Alderson.' He emptied the scoop into the manger in front of the eager grey and passed it to Wallace. 'Sam, you mind beddin' our mounts down while I take Clay here up to the house.' Sam nodded and lifted a pitchfork.

★ ★ ★ ★

'Got a visitor for you, Ma.' Bull peered into the kitchen where Ma was stirring something in a steaming pot. 'You remember Clay Wallace from the stage?'

'Evening, Miz Jordan.' The gambler removed his hat and gave a slight bow. 'It's a pleasure to meet you again.'

'Land sakes!' It wasn't often that Mary-Lou Jordan showed her surprise, but this was one of the few occasions. 'What brings you out here?'

Clay flicked a glance at Bull and waited.

'It's a long story, Ma. Tell you all about it at supper. I've asked Clay to stay for a spell.'

'Supper'll be ready soon. He can have that room next to yours. Show'm where it is an' be back here right smart.'

'Your mother is a remarkable woman!' Clay Wallace pitched his roll onto the bed and grinned.

'Yeah,' Bull agreed. 'An' we'd better get back there right smart or you'll see just how remarkable she is!'

☆　　☆　　☆　　☆

'So there it is, Ma.' Bull drained his coffee cup and set it down. 'Clay can straighten out them accounts while I get out onto the range an' start gettin' this place goin' again.'

Ma pursed her lips and looked closely at Wallace. 'You figger you can sort out them books?'

'Yes, ma'am. I was a good accountant. Trouble was I hated being cooped up.'

'You're gonna be cooped up here.' Ma pointed out shrewdly.

Clay grinned at her. 'Yes, but not for life.'

'Alright,' Ma rose from her chair. 'Seems like you know what you're doin'. Right now I got to get cleared up. 'Nother day tomorrow.' She lifted a pot and poured water into a basin.

'Ma'am,' Clay Wallace had his coat off and was rolling up his sleeves. 'If you're going to wash these dishes I'll dry.'

'Well thankee, Clay!' Bull grinned to himself. It was rare for Ma to use someone's first name so quickly. 'You're right mannerly, more than I can say for some folks!'

☆　　☆　　☆　　☆

Joe Masterson leaned forward and patted his horse's neck as he and Bull watched the herd disperse. 'Waal, that's it, Boss. Better than we'd hoped. Reckon they's nigh on four and a half thousand head on this north range. 'Course, with three gathers we might have overlapped some, but I reckon we're close. Now we got to tackle the range south o' Saddle Creek.'

'Yeah,' Bull nodded. 'You done a good job, Joe, an' the boys too.'

'Shucks,' Joe removed his hat and ran a hand through his flaming red hair. 'They're a good bunch. I just point 'em in the right direction.'

Bull smiled inwardly. Joe was working hard to prove himself and the whole outfit was responding.

'We'll move camp today. Tex can restock the chuck wagon at the ranch, then you can head south. Me, I got to see 'bout gettin' Ma back to the Circle J. That's m'folks spread.'

Joe pondered for a moment. 'What you aimin' to do?' he queried cautiously.

'They'll sell up an' move out here. There's a big rancher who's been itchin' to buy the Circle J for years, so there won't be no problem there. Then, they got a lot o' good stock. Horses an' cattle. Expect Pa'll want to bring them an' that means a trail drive.'

There was a long silence. Together they watched Manuel and Chester cut out a limping steer. The vaquero and his pinto cow pony were stylists. Lariat in hand the Mexican raced up on his quarry and dropped the loop neatly over the steer's horns. Manuel flipped the rope to one side of the bawling animal and the pinto cut away sharply. Hind legs swept from under it, the steer went down and rolled. The pinto sat back and took the strain as Manuel dived out of the saddle, pigging strings in his hand.

Bull nodded approvingly as he watched Ortega secure the animal's legs, while Chester kept a careful watch in case one of the herd bulls decided to take a hand.

'Tie-fast, grass rope man,' he said as Manuel checked the steer's hooves.

Joe laughed. 'Yeah, he's a vaquero from the brasada alright. Shanghai Pearce reckoned he was one o' the best, an' Shanghai weren't often wrong.'

Manuel opened his big clasp knife and probed. The steer bawled angrily. They saw the Mexican rider hold something up and speak to Chester.

'Rock, or piece o' hard wood.' Joe surmised.

Bull nodded. 'Wedged in the cleft.'

Manuel called to the pinto and it moved up, ears pricked. He flipped the loop free and walked towards his mount coiling his rope. Chester flicked a heavy quirt tentatively and waited. Gently, Ortega eased the pinto into position beside the prostrate steer, then he whipped the strings loose and was up into the saddle and gone. The steer lumbered to its feet, tossed its head, and took off after the herd, bawling angrily. Quirt still dangling from his wrist, Chester loped after Manuel.

Bull whistled. 'We got the makin's o' an outfit here, Joe.'

Joe nodded. 'Even Anson's shapin' well. The boys are gettin' used to him now.'

'He ain't got much choice,' Bull grunted. 'It was either that or the rope. Still, I'm glad I was right.'

"Bout your folks,' Joe ventured tentatively. 'If they're headin' west they'll likely use the Goodnight-Loving trail, at least part o' the way. Man, that is one tough trail. Between Fort Concho an' the Pecos there ain't no permanent water, an' that's a ninety mile stretch. Comanches, Lipans, an' rustlers along there too, so it's a tough haul.'

'Yeah, I know,' said Bull gloomily. 'Still, we need that breedin' stock. One thing, it won't be a big herd. Pa'll sell the steers before he pulls out.'

Joe shrugged, 'No sense in meetin' trouble half-way. I'll start gettin' the outfit back to the ranch.' He touched his mount with his heels and loped off.

✯   ✯   ✯   ✯

'That was an excellent meal tonight, ma'am.' Clay Wallace rose from his chair. 'Now I'm sure you and Mister Jordan have a great deal to discuss. I've finished the accounts,' he indicated the pile of books on the side table, 'so I'll bid you goodnight.'

'Sit still, Clay.' Bull said hurriedly. 'Sure we have a lot to discuss but it concerns all three of us.' The gambler sank back into his chair, a surprised look on his face.

Ma put her knitting down and looked at him thoughtfully. 'I guess you know that I aim to keep the ranch,' she began. 'Uncle Dave left it to me an' I reckon my mind's been made up all along. Now I got to go back an' tell the family. Then we'll have to sell up an' bring any stock an' gear we want to keep, out here. This'll take time, an' we feel that it'd be best if Hardy stayed here an' I went back. I don't mind travellin' on my own, but trouble is I got to pick up our buckboard an' the team at Fort Worth.' She scowled. 'It ain't that I can't handle a team, but them Clevelands'll be jumpin' out o' their skins, an' I ain't as young as I used to be.'

'Yeah,' Bull interjected quietly, 'an' I'd be a lot happier if there was somebody with you. It's nigh on two hundred miles from Fort Worth to the ranch. Clay, I'd take it right kindly if you'd escort Ma to the Circle J.'

Clay Wallace sat silently for a long moment, then he smiled. 'Clevelands eh? Back home our carriage horses were Clevelands. Ma'am,' he rose and bowed formally to Ma. 'I'd consider it an honour to be your escort!'

Chapter 22

Sarah Johnson scattered a final handful of grain among the Rhode Island Reds, and stood for a moment watching the scurrying chickens. A movement across the yard caught her eye and she turned. Ellie-May came out of the stable carrying a pitchfork and headed for the barn. She waved briefly to Sarah who waved back. Through the open kitchen window she could hear the voice of Sara-Jane, who was trying to bake and cope with endless questions from Mary, Sarah's young sister, at the same time. Sarah smiled, she liked Sara-Jane. There was something about her that drew children like a magnet, and the Johnson girls were no exception. She's nice, Sarah thought, just like Ma. Her eyes filled with tears at the memory, and she rubbed them with the back of her hand.

High above the barn Ellie-May appeared briefly in the loft doorway. She scanned the surrounding range for a moment and then vanished again. Watching her, Sarah frowned. She was still somewhat unsure of the tall blonde girl who wore Levis and a gunbelt. When I grow up, she thought, I'm going to wear nice dresses, just like Sara-Jane. Not pants, and belts with guns, like Ellie-May. She sniffed. I wish Mister Bull was back. He promised he would, but he's been gone a long time. He makes me feel safe.

'Sarah,' Mary called from the doorway. 'Sara-Jane says would you like a glass of milk and some biscuits?'

'Yes please!' Her depression lifted, Sarah Johnson ran towards the house.

★ ★ ★ ★

Jim Jordan slouched comfortably in his saddle and surveyed the milling herd. Reckon I was right, he mused. That Durham blood makes them cattle easier to handle. Good calf crop this year too. Figger we been doin' alright. Wonder how Mary-Lou an' Bull are makin' out? Nigh on two months since they left. Guess Ma will want to make the move. She's got plans for the kids. Me, I'd leave them to live their own lives. Still, she's been a good wife, an' a good mother. Maybe, he reflected wryly, we ain't as close as other couples, but that ain't her fault. Just wish she could show a bit more feelin' at times.

He grinned. Betcha her an' Bull have it all worked out. Bull sees hisself as another John Chisum. Waal, ambition ain't no bad thing. Trouble is, where do the rest o' the family fit in?

Lance now, he ain't no problem, not like when he was a wild kid. Still, that's over an' done with. We made our peace an' I'm glad.

Across the backs of the bawling cattle he could see John and Jake easing the point of the herd between them, and counting the cattle as they drifted through.

The rancher rubbed his chin absently. There's the problem, them an' Sarah-Jane. Ellie-May? He grinned. Give her a horse an' a gun, an' she's happy.

Sara-Jane? Well, mebbe that talk I had with her'll help. Just wish Ma wouldn't bear down on her so heavy. She's a good kid at bottom. Might be I'll have to take a hand there.

He frowned as he watched the herd drifting between the two distant figures. Damned if I know what to make o' that pair? They're here an' yet they ain't. It's like they're in a world o' their own at times. An' when they drop back into Comanche talk they've got me beat.

Nudging the big Cleveland with his heels, he started to drift the stragglers towards the gap. Hell, I can only keep tryin', even if it means bearin' down on Ma at times. They were comparing tallies when he rode up. 'How did you make out?' He grinned at the two serious young men.

'Five eighty-four all told.' John looked at Jake.

His partner nodded. 'That's right. Six bulls, Two eighty-nine cows, an' two eighty-nine calves. Coupla late calvers but they're balanced by two sets of twins.'

Jim Jordan nodded. 'Saw them myself a week or so back. Waal, it's been a long day. Let's head back.'

They turned their horses and fell in beside him.

'Pa.'

Jim Jordan looked at his youngest son. 'Yeah.'

'Jake an' I have been been talking. This move to Arizona, do you think it is a good thing?'

His father shrugged. 'Can't rightly say. One thing's for sure, it'll be different. But your Ma's keen, so it's up to the rest of us to make the best of it.'

'Bull seems to think it is a good idea,' John said cautiously. He looked at his father out of the corner of his eye.

'Yeah,' Jim Jordan laughed. 'Bull wants to be a bigtime cattleman, like Dunc Patterson. Me, I can do without the hassle. Still, it's what's best for you young folks that matters. Big spread like that, you can all have a good life.'

They rode on quietly, each busy with his own thoughts.

★ ★ ★ ★

Sara-Jane peered into the oven. The savoury smell of roasting meat wafted through the kitchen. 'Mm, smells good.' She looked up to see her sister, gunbelt draped over her shoulder, step through the doorway. 'Well,' Sara-Jane straightened up, 'I think I'm gettin' the hang o' this stove at last. See anything o' Pa an' the boys?'

'Yeah.' Ellie-May filled a basin with water and rolled up her sleeves. 'Saw them just toppin' the ridge a while back. Should be comin' up from the creek 'bout now. 'Course,' she soaped her hands carefully, 'the gals are playin' down at the barn. By the time Pa talks to them an' they tell him 'bout everything that's been happenin' round here, an' the boys hafta do all the unsaddlin' an' the groomin', it could be 'nother half-hour 'fore we see them.'

Sara-Jane laughed. 'Well, it'll be 'nother half-hour an' more 'fore supper's ready.' She paused and looked sharply at her elder sister. 'What you got against them kids anyway?'

The blonde girl shrugged. 'Nothin', 'cept that they're kids! Oh,' she reached for a towel and dried her hands carefully, 'they're nice enough youngsters, got good manners an' all, but they ask so many fool questions.'

Sara-Jane's temper flared. 'An' I suppose,' she snapped furiously, 'you just woke one mornin' an' all that know-how 'bout horses an' guns was there. You never stopped askin' Pa an' Bull. Yeah, an' if John had been here you'd have asked him too! Anyway, I heard you talkin' to him the other night 'bout knife throwin'.'

'Well,' Ellie-May buttoned her sleeves, 'mebbe I was a mite hard,' she said lamely.

'A mite hard!' Sara-Jane said derisively. Her eyes flashed. 'Them gals saw their folks killed, an' worse likely,' she added darkly, 'though nobody's said nothin' 'bout that. Then they was captives for a spell. An' in the end they saw Bull kill the Injuns that did all this. You know what somethin' like this did to Ma. An' all you can say is mebbe you been a mite hard! Ain't you got no feelin's? Now get, an' leave me to fix supper.'

For a moment Ellie-May looked as though she was about to say something, then she shrugged and disappeared down the passage to her room.

Breathing deeply, Sara-Jane turned back to the stove.

Hannah MaCrae drained her coffee cup and set it down carefully. Leaning back in her chair she looked pensively at her friend. 'Land sakes, Mary-Lou! That's quite a story. An' you've made your mind up? You're goin' to move to Arizona?'

Ma shrugged tiredly and nodded. 'Yeah, it's some spread. Big house, lot o' land, an' the grazin's fair to middlin'. Don't see how we can do better.'

'Mm.' The widow looked thoughtful. 'What about this fella that come back with you? Clay ... Clay Wallace I think you said his name was? Seems a real gentleman.'

'That was Bull's idea,' Ma sipped her coffee and reflected. 'He wanted to stay behind an' get the ranch movin' again. 'Course,' she added defensively, 'I agree with him. It's just that ... ' she paused.

Hannah poured more coffee and replaced the pot. 'You'd best tell me, Mary-Lou. It ain't often I've seen you like this.'

'It's Sara-Jane,' Ma said worriedly. 'She ain't never met somebody like Clay Wallace. Suppose he turns her head? He's a smart lookin' fella, right mannerly an' all. You seen what he was like when he met you.'

A faint smile played round Hannah MaCrae's mouth, as she remembered Clay Wallace bowing over her hand when they met. 'Yeah, I know. Couldn't help wishin' then that I was thirty years younger!'

'Hannah!' Mary-Lou was scandalised. 'You see what I mean. If he's got you thinkin that way, what's Sara-Jane gonna be like?'

Hannah smiled. 'Why don't you talk to him 'bout it. He seems a right thinkin' fella. Just tell him you don't want Sara-Jane upset. Where is he right now anyway?'

'He's down at livery stable. I left him there. Never saw a fella so taken wi' anythin' as he is wi' that team.'

The widow shrugged. 'Seems to me it'd be best just to have a quiet word with him 'fore you get to the ranch. How old d'you reckon he is anyway?'

Ma pursed her lips and considered. "Bout the same age as Lance I should think, or Bull mebbe.'

'Makes him a fair bit older than Sara-Jane,' Hannah reflected.

'Sara-Jane's always been way ahead of herself when it comes to bein' a woman!' Ma said tartly.

'Mary-Lou,' Hannah MaCrae hesitated and then continued. 'It ain't no business of mine, but from what I've seen, an' what you've said to me, you seem to be a mite hard on Sara-Jane. You got any special reason for treatin' her like that?'

'She's a wild one,' Ma said defensively, 'an' she don't like ranch life.'

'So she likes a little fun, an' she wants to grow up. I don't blame her, I was just the same when I was young. Mary-Lou, you got to lighten up on that gal!'

There was a long silence. Remorse filled Hannah MaCrae. I've finally done it, she thought ruefully. I'm the only friend she's got and I've destroyed that friendship. She looked across at Mary-Lou Jordan and was surprised to see tears in the other woman's eyes.

Ma spoke hesitantly. 'Hannah, I wanted to be like Sara-Jane, to laugh an' have fun, but I couldn't, not ever. Every time I tried I kept seein' Ma's body lyin' there in the dust, all bloody an' with her clothes ripped off... an' I'd just freeze up.'

The big woman rose and walked across to sit beside her friend. Gently she put her arm round Ma's shoulders and held out a handkerchief. 'Your mother was raped wasn't she? You never told me but I guessed. That's what's been eatin' at you all those years. Didn't you ever tell anyone?'

Ma dabbed her eyes. 'I told Jim,' she said defensively.

'You told Jim! He knew what was wrong with you, but he couldn't do nothin' about it. How d'you think he felt? Land sakes, Mary-Lou! A lot o' men would have given up on you long ago!'

'I can't help it. I keep hearin' them screams an' then I see them painted devils ridin' off whoopin' and yellin'. When I ran into the yard there they were, Pa, the boys an' Ma, lyin' in the dust. They were all cut up an' bloody, butchered like steers. An' I keep seein' the flames an' hearin' the fire cracklin' as the house burned.' She stopped and sobbed uncontrollably.

Hannah waited patiently.

'They told me I'd wandered in the woods for a coupla days before they found me. Don't remember nuthin' about it.' Ma twisted the handkerchief in her hands. 'When they picked me up I couldn't speak an' I couldn't think either. I was just numb. Then Aunt Jess and Uncle Dave took me in. They were good folks, but they couldn't get through to me an' in the end they just give up.'

'And then you met Jim?' Hannah probed gently.

'Yeah.' There was a faraway, softer look in Ma's eyes. 'An' for a spell I thought things were gonna be alright. Then the Comanches took John an' it all came back worse than ever.'

'But you got John back!'

'Yeah,' Ma shivered, 'as near a Comanche as makes no difference. An' Jake's half Comanche anyway. I hate when they talk to each other in that Injun lingo.'

'You could try rememberin' that if it hadn't been for Jake's father you might not have got John back.' Hannah said sharply.

'I know. Jim keeps tellin' me that. He says Jake lost his pa gettin' John back to us an' that he's part o' the family, but I can't forget what them red devils did to my folks. Every time I look at Jake I hear them screams again.'

'Mary-Lou!' The big woman spoke forcefully. 'You got to put this foolishness behind you right now! There's good Injuns an' there's bad Injuns, just the same as white folks. Them Kiowas killed Hank, but I don't hate the whole tribe. From what I hear they got good reason to hate us too. 'Stead o' bein' full o' hate you ought to be thankful that Ten Bears brought John up right.'

'An' I suppose,' she added sharply, 'that's why you've always got a gun handy?'

Ma nodded. 'I swore that nobody would ever take me alive, an' I meant it.'

Hannah frowned thoughtfully. 'I ain't goin' to argue with you on that. You've been proved right too often. But,' she added warningly, 'lighten up on the family. Get rid o' all that hate.'

'I'll try,' Mary-Lou said hesitantly, 'but I can't promise nuthin'.'

'Well,' the widow smiled, 'it's a start anyway. 'Now, you tidy yourself up an' we'll go down to the dining room.'

✯   ✯   ✯   ✯

The greying barman, polishing half-heartedly at the bar top glanced at the slim well-dressed customer toying with his empty glass. Sure-fire gambler he thought, noting the embroidered vest and the slim, well kept hands. You can tell 'em a mile off.

'You fancy a hand o' poker?' He indicated a table across the room. 'Boys are always pleased to see another player. Small stakes too,' he added encouragingly, 'so there ain't no need to get out o' your depth.'

Clay Wallace smiled and shook his head. He could feel the old familiar tingle in his fingers. Drink wasn't a problem, but cards now, that was different.

'Mebbe you think that the game ain't big enough for you?' There was a barely-concealed sneer in the bartender's voice.

Always somebody pushing, Clay reflected wryly. How can I tell him that I'm scared to sit down at the table in case the gambling fever grips me again. I told the Jordans that I left accountancy because I couldn't stand the monotony, but that was a lie. Father threw me out when I wouldn't stop gambling. Now I've got a chance to straighten out and I don't want to blow it.

'It isn't that,' he looked at the clock on the wall. 'I've another appointment in an hour's time and I wouldn't want to spoil the game.'

'Shucks.' The grey-haired bartender was friendlier now. 'That ain't a problem.' He raised his voice. 'Gent here says he can sit in for an hour. That alright with you fellas?'

There was a muttered chorus of assent from the four card players. The barman flipped his hand. 'All yours, mister.'

'Thanks.' Clay Wallace downed the remainder of his drink and set the empty glass on the bar. Shrugging, he walked across to the table. Maybe now was the time to find out if his newfound resolve was equal to the test.

'The name's Wallace, gentlemen. Clay Wallace.' He looked down at the players. 'As our friend said, I have one hour. If that's agreeable to everybody then I'll sit in?'

There were nods all round. 'We play for small stakes anyway.' The speaker, a heavily-built cowhand with thick greying hair, indicated the empty chair. 'Can't win or lose much in an hour, so you ain't gonna hurt anybody. Sit in.'

Clay nodded and settled himself comfortably.

An hour passed quietly, punctuated only by the muttered calls of the players. Clay raked the pot towards him and glanced at the clock.

'Gentlemen,' he checked his winnings, 'I'll drop out now. Reckon I'm about four dollars up.' He rose to his feet.

'Thank you for an enjoyable game. You'll find a drink waiting for each of you at the bar. Now,' he tipped his hat, 'I'll bid you all goodnight.'

The four watched the slim figure weave between the tables on his way to the bar. 'Real nice fella,' the grey-haired cowhand chewed reflectively on a tooth-pick. 'Wonder where he's from?'

His opposite number grinned. 'Sure ain't from round here with manners like that. Reckon he's from back east.'

The burly cowhand frowned. 'Somethin' else queer 'bout him. He don't seem to care whether he wins or not. Coupla times I reckon he could have lifted the pot, but he just didn't seem interested. Aw, what the hell, you gonna deal them cards, Slim?'

Outside in the dusk, Clay Wallace smiled triumphantly to himself as he strode towards the hotel. It was a beginning, a small beginning maybe, but a beginning just the same. The gambling fever was still there, but tonight he had been able to control it. Now he had a chance to put the past behind him.

Chapter 23

'All set then?' Hannah MaCrae smiled at Ma. 'You won't forget what I said?'

'No.' Mary-Lou looked fondly at the big woman. 'An' thanks for the advice, Hannah. I needed to talk to somebody.'

'Any time.' Hannah put an arm round Ma's shoulders. She noticed that Mary-Lou didn't flinch. Well, it was a start. 'Think I hear Clay with the buckboard. Don't forget, talk to him 'bout Sara-Jane. He's a right nice fella. I sure enjoyed his company at supper last night.'

'Yeah.' They stepped out onto the porch just as Clay Wallace brought the Clevelands to a plunging halt.

'Whoa, fellas ... whoa now.' He flashed a grin at Hannah and Ma. 'Morning, ladies.' Setting the brake, he swung down and picked up Ma's bag. 'All set, ma'am. I guess I'll be hard pressed to hold the team in.' He set the bag in the buckboard and handed her up.

'Mm,' Ma settled herself comfortably on the sprung seat. 'Jim always did say that they could outrun anything in Texas.' She placed the long canvas bag beside her, handily within reach.

Hannah MaCrae smiled to herself, some things would take a long time to change.

Clay swung into the driver's seat and eased off the brake. Hannah waved and the Clevelands hit their long flowing stride, a pace they could keep up for miles.

Busy with her thoughts, Ma swayed to the movement of the buckboard. Maybe things would be better after all.

Jim Jordan leaned against the horse pasture gate and kept a wary eye on Big Red, who was grazing his way up the side of the high rail fence. 'I know what you're aimin' to do, you big ornery mule. If you can get close enough you'll swap ends an' try to catch me with a kick.'

'Talkin' to yourself, Pa?' Sara-Jane had come quietly up behind him. 'That's the first sign you're gettin' old,' she teased.

'I'm talkin' to that big slab-sided lump o' horseflesh there.' He indicated Red, who laid back his ears and tossed his head. 'Thank the good Lord that he lets John ride him, or he wouldn't have done nothin' while Bull's been away. I tell you, Bull an' him are two of a kind.'

Sara-Jane laughed. 'Bull ain't so bad.' She laid her hand impulsively on her father's arm. 'You're worryin' about Ma an' him, ain't you?'

There was a long pause then Jim Jordan turned and faced his daughter. 'I ain't worried exactly,' he began. 'Bull can take care o' himself. So can Ma if it comes to that. Only ... it's nigh on nine weeks since they left. 'Bout time they was showin' up.'

'That why you been comin' up here last thing most nights?'

'Well ... ,' her father grinned shamefacedly. 'It's a fair piece from Hannah MaCrae's place in Greenhills. When they do come,' he looked at the sun dipping behind the hills, 'it'll likely be late like this when they get here.'

'Don't look like they're gonna be here tonight.' Sara-Jane linked her arm in his. 'Come on in. I've got the gals in bed an' Ellie-May's made a pot o' coffee.'

'Glory be! Ellie-May makin' coffee. You sure it's safe to drink?'

'Pa!' Sara-Jane laughed. 'Ellie-May's right handy in the kitchen, when she tries.'

Her father grinned. 'Trouble is she don't try very often!'

Big Red neighed challengingly. Jim Jordan turned quickly. Head up, ears pricked, the big horse was staring towards the west.

'Somethin' on the ridge trail. Movin' fast too. Your eyes are better than mine, Sara-Jane. Can you see what it is?'

Sara-Jane shaded her eyes. 'It's a wagon ... or a buckboard.'

'Bet it's them. Yeah, ain't no team round here can stretch out like that. Go an' tell Ellie-May that we're gonna need her coffee. An' tell John an' Jake that they can give Bull a hand to unhitch the team.'

✯   ✯   ✯   ✯

'That's the ranch now.' Ma pointed ahead. "Course, it ain't nuthin' like the Flyin' W, but it ain't a bad little spread.'

Clay Wallace spoke gently to the big horses and they slowed perceptibly. Ma watched his hands as he eased the lines, still talking.

'You're good with a team ain't you?' she observed.

'Yes, ma'am.' Clay grinned as the team slowed to a canter. 'My father had Clevelands, but this is the best team I've ever handled.'

'Now,' Ma looked at him anxiously, 'you won't forget what I said?'

'About Sara-Jane?' He nodded. 'No, ma'am. I won't forget. Trust me.'

✯   ✯   ✯   ✯

Standing together in the yard, the little group watched the buckboard sweeping down the last stretch to the ranch.

'That ain't Bull!' John said suddenly.

Jake nodded. 'That's right, but whoever he is he sure can handle a team.'

'Wonder why Bull didn't come?' Jim Jordan said worriedly. 'Sure hope nuthin's happened to him.'

The buckboard whirled into the yard and drew up in front of the porch. Jim Jordan helped his wife down and hugged her.

'Pa!' Ma was pleased but flustered. 'This here's Clay Wallace, he come with me 'stead o' Bull. Clay, this is m'husband, Jim.'

'Howdy, Clay. I take it Bull's alright?'

'Why yes, he wanted to get things going at the ranch, so he asked me to escort Miz Jordan on her journey. Now, if you could show me where you want the buckboard, I'll unhitch the team.'

'I like that,' Jim Jordan nodded approvingly. 'A man who thinks o' his horses first. Still, tonight John an' Jake'll take care o' them for you. Now, this here's John, our youngest son, an' this is Jake Larsen, another member o' the family.' They shook hands. 'An',' the rancher waved towards the girls, 'these are our daughters, Ellie-May and Sara-Jane.'

Clay Wallace smiled and tipped his hat. 'Nice to meet you both.' He picked up his roll and followed Ma and Jim into the house.

'Good-lookin' fella, ain't he?' Sara-Jane whispered to Ellie-May. 'So mannerly an' all.'

Her sister shrugged. She watched John and Jake open the barn doors and run the buckboard inside. 'He can handle a team,' she said grudgingly.

'Shucks,' Sara-Jane scowled at her. 'Is that all you can think about? Horses. C'mon, let's go see what they're sayin' in there.'

Ellie-May frowned. 'Think I'll go help the boys.' She strode away across the yard.

'Tcha!' Sara-Jane shook her head in exasperation and hurried indoors.

Ma looked up as she entered. 'Sara-Jane, I was just tellin' Clay here that he could have Bull's room while he's stayin'.' She looked hard at Wallace. 'Would you show'm where it is.'

'Yes, Ma.' They disappeared down the passage together. Ma watched them go.

'Sure hope I done the right thing bringin' Clay here,' she said worriedly.

Her husband looked at her shrewdly. 'Seems a nice enough fella to me. What's troublin' you?'

'Sara-Jane.' Ma said succinctly. 'Clay's from back east. Right mannerly an' all. An' he's had a good education. Jim, she ain't never met nobody like him before.'

Jim Jordan grinned. 'First time for everything. Anyway, she's a sensible gal. Tell you somethin' else. She's done a real good job while you been away. Ran the house, fed us, an' looked after them Johnson kids right well. Reckon you ought to lighten up on her some.'

'Hannah MaCrae told me the same thing.' Ma sipped, and frowned. 'Her coffee ain't all that special though!'

Her husband laughed. 'That's Ellie-May! But don't say nothin'. So you been talkin' to Hannah. Waal, I allus did say that she'd more sense than most men.'

✦   ✦   ✦   ✦

Sara-Jane opened the bedroom door. 'This is Bull's room, though from what you been sayin' it don't seem as though he'll be usin' it again. Hope it's alright.'

'It's fine, thanks.' Clay dropped his roll on the chair beside the bed. 'Guess it won't be long before I turn in. It's been a long day.'

'Better come an' have somethin' to eat first. Ma won't let you go to bed without it.'

'Your mother is quite a lady, isn't she?'

'Ma?' Sara-Jane paused for a moment. 'Guess she is too. Funny thing is, I think I know her better now that she's been away for a spell.'

Clay Wallace nodded. 'Same with me and my father. I haven't seen him in years, yet I feel I understand him better than when I was at home.'

Sara-Jane lingered in the doorway. 'You want some water to freshen up?'

'Mm? Oh, yes please.'

'Right, I'll bring some along. Then I'll give you a call when supper's ready.'

✦   ✦   ✦   ✦

'An' that's how it is.' Ma leaned back in her chair and looked at the family. Supper was over and Clay Wallace had made his excuses and gone to his room.

Her husband rubbed his chin thoughtfully. 'Sure makes the Circle J seem small. Take some time to get used to the change. An' you reckon 'bout six thousand head?' He looked at Ma.

Mary-Lou shrugged. 'Accordin' to Clay, anyway. He's been through the tally books an' the accounts. 'Course, they's a lot o' beef down in that brush country which ain't been accounted for. That fella Anson says they was pushin' cattle down there, so that the rustlers an' Comancheros could run them over the Border.'

'I'm surprised Bull kept 'im on,' Jim Jordan mused.

'Waal, he did tell us what had been happenin', an' he's workin' for nothin'. I think Bull didn't want to cross the sheriff this early. Mebbe just as well seein' that trouble we had wi' them Comancheros.'

'Mm.' Jim looked at the others. 'Anybody else want to say somethin'?'

'Ma,' Sara-Jane eyed her mother carefully. 'What about Tucson and Dorando? What kinda towns are they?'

'Didn't see all that much o' them, but I'd say they're your usual run o' cowtowns. Dorando's flashier, but I reckon Tucson's got more business folks. You ask me, some day Tucson'll be a big town.'

'What about the Apaches?' John queried. 'Is there much trouble?'

There was a long silence before Ma spoke. 'We had that brush wi' them on the stage run, but things seemed quiet enough at the ranch. Joe Masterson reckons that Cochise is tryin' to control the young bucks, but some o' the wild ones go on the rampage every so often.'

Jim Jordan looked closely at his wife. This ain't the usual fiery way Mary-Lou talks when she's discussin' Injuns. There's been a change an' I reckon I got big Hannah to thank. Waal, best to keep quiet for the moment. He yawned. 'Reckon it's time to get to bed. Guess we got a lot more to talk about come mornin'.'

There was a chorus of goodnights as Ellie-May, John and Jake disappeared to their rooms.

Sara-Jane paused for a moment. 'Ma.'

'Yeah?' Ma looked up from her chair.

'It's nice to have you back.'

Ma's eyes glistened in the lamplight. 'It's nice to be back, Sara-Jane, an' thanks for everything. Mebbe I've been a mite hard on you in the past but I'll try to make up for it now.'

Her husband smiled to himself. Things had changed and for the better.

★ ★ ★ ★

Wiping his bloody hands on the grass, Chester straightened his back. Jem Anson withdrew the glowing branding iron from the fire and pressed it firmly on the calf's quivering flank. The smell of burning flesh and hair filled their nostrils. There was a plaintive bawl from the calf and its mother bellowed an anxious reply. Quirt in hand, Bull swung the grey round in a tight turn, cutting off the cow's attempt to reach her offspring. The quirt slashed along her flanks and the Longhorn took off towards the herd, tossing her head and bellowing angrily. Jeff and Anders released their hold and rose hastily. Bawling loudly, the calf staggered shakily to its feet and trotted after her. Joe Masterson marked the tally book, while Bull pulled the grey to a halt and grinned at him.

'Lookin' good.' He gestured toward the herd where the Aldersons were circling, while Ortega and his stylish pinto dragged in another protesting youngster.

'Yeah.' Joe watched Jem and Chester throw the calf and pin it down. The ex-sergeant flicked Manuel's rope loose and waved.

Coiling the lariat, Ortega neck reined the pinto round and took off toward the herd.

'Reckon we're doin' a lot better than I thought we would. Sure must be a lot o' beef in that brush.'

'Waal,' Bull reflected, 'Jem said they'd been pushin' stock down there for a long time.' He paused for a moment. 'See many scrub bulls?'

Joe frowned. 'Yeah, they's a good few. What you plannin' to do with 'em?'

'We got to get them out first. Say, we could try that old trick, sewin' up their eyelids wi' thread. 'Course, we got to think what we're gonna do with 'em afterwards. Don't like cuttin' them at that age. Too much risk o' infection.'

Joe nodded. 'They's that army post just bein' built, between the north range and Dorando. Camp Crittenden, I think they call it. You could sell them there, providin' the price is right. Army's allus lookin' for cheap beef an' you want to get rid o' them critters anyway.'

Bull punched his shoulder. 'That's right good thinkin'. Now I can see why I made you foreman. I'll ride over there first chance I get an' talk to the boss man. Oh, you seen anythin' o' them old 'cimarrones' you were tellin' me about?'

'Them two old bulls?' Joe shook his head. 'Nah, an' I hope I don't either. They're hid up in the brush an' I aim to have a rifle handy when I meet 'em. Met an old fella once who'd scouted for the army in the '47-'48 war. He told me that there was lots o' them around then. Said the troops hated 'em, 'cause when they started to come for you, you had to kill 'em every time. Anyway, I got work to do. Them fellas'll roust me if I mess up this tally.' He made another entry in the dogeared book and passed the glowing iron to Jem.

I was lucky, Bull thought. Got a damned good foreman there. Need to think 'bout another coupla riders to make things easier for him. 'Course, once the family's here we'll have John an' Jake. Pa, as well, though I reckon it's time he started easin' up. Hope Ma an' Clay got back alright. Now there's a right handy fella. Educated too. Mebbe he would stay.

He watched a cow break out of the herd and head towards the branders. Kneeing the grey into a gallop he swept in, quirt cracking, and cut her off. Some day he thought, as he watched her trot sullenly back to the herd, this is gonna be the best damn spread in the whole South-West!

Chapter 24

Perched on the corral rail, Jake Larsen watched John Jordan ease the saddle onto the tense bay gelding. Talking softly, John tightened the cinch. Then he held the young horse's head firmly and blew softly into its nostrils. The gelding shivered and stood still. Jake nodded to himself. Ten Bears was right. He said that Yellow Panther had the gift of the great horseman and that he could gentle the truly wild ones. I am good, but Yellow Panther will always be the best.

John leaned against the corral rails and looked up at him. 'We will give him some time to get used to it.' He spoke in Comanche, something he and Jake always did when they were alone.

The fair-haired young half-breed nodded. 'It is good.' He gestured towards the horses in the adjoining corral. 'Only another six and we will be finished. Then your father can sell them.'

'That is true, though he may wish to keep them if he decides to go to Arizona.'

'Do you think he will?'

John shrugged. 'Who knows? But I think, yes. My mother is strong. She will want to go, and so will Bull. As for my father; he will agree.'

★   ★   ★   ★

Jim Jordan pushed the piece of paper towards his wife. 'There's how I see it, Ma. If we get mebbe twelve thousand for the ranch, plus another thousand for that hundred steers an' this year's calf crop, that gives us a total o' thirteen thousand dollars. The breedin' stock an' the horse herd I'd want to take with us.'

'Yeah.' Ma looked pensive. 'There's just one snag.'

'Dunc Paterson you mean?'

Mary-Lou nodded.

Her husband frowned. 'Yeah, you're right. Once Dunc knows we got to sell he'll drop his price, an' there ain't nothin' we can do about it. You got any ideas, Clay?'

Across the table Clay Wallace looked at them both thoughtfully. 'You know I wasn't keen to be in on this discussion,' he began. 'But you wanted my opinion as an accountant. Isn't there anyone else who would be interested in buying the Circle J? Someone who would give Paterson a little competition. Who is he anyway?'

'Ain't as easy as that.' Jim Jordan rose and walked across to the map hanging on the wall. 'Dunc Paterson is the big wheel in this part o' Texas. His Triple X outfit's got us boxed in on three sides.' He pointed. 'On the fourth side there's the creek. Across the creek is the Rockin' H, Cliff Henderson's spread. Cliff's smaller than us, an' he's had a run o' bad luck these past few years. Right now he ain't doin' much more than hang on. Nah,' he shook his head, 'reckon we can forget Cliff.

'The only reason we were able to buy the MaCrae spread after Hank was killed, was 'cause Hannah MaCrae don't scare, leastways not easily. An' the fact that Bull an' Lance both got reputations. It don't pay to cross them, especially Bull. That's why Dunc ain't never leaned too heavy on us.'

'Supposing,' Clay said slowly, 'there was a possible buyer, from back East? Somebody with financial backing?'

The Jordans stared at him. 'Ain't a chance o' that,' said Ma decisively. 'Any kin we got back East is just homesteaders. An' we don't know no city bankers.'

'Supposing Paterson thought you had a buyer back East. What would he do then?'

'Waal,' Jim Jordan rubbed his chin. 'Dunc's a hothead. He'd up the ante right away.'

Clay Wallace grinned. 'That's what I thought. Alright, you have a buyer ... me!'

They gaped at him. 'You're joshin' us,' Jim said slowly. 'Oh, I don't mean no offence, but ... '

'But I haven't got that kind of money? You're quite right, I haven't, but Paterson doesn't know that! All you have to do then is pass the word round that you have a possible buyer from back East staying with you. That should be enough to push the price up.'

Ma frowned. 'That's lyin' an' I can't agree with it!'

Jim Jordan nodded regretfully. 'Got to go along with Ma there.'

'Alright.' Clay pondered for a moment. 'Where does Paterson hang out when he's not at his ranch?'

'Crockett, mostly. It's a small cowtown, near enough surrounded by the Triple X. They reckon it's their town. Dunc an' his boys ride in most Saturday nights. Dunc's never married. Guess he's been too busy buildin' hisself a cattle empire.'

'Don't reckon any woman would have him!' Ma said tartly.

Jim Jordan laughed. 'Come on, Ma. Dunc ain't so bad. He'll have one, mebbe two drinks at most, an' then he'll play poker, but only for small stakes. I go there myself occasionally. Just to be neighbourly,' he added hastily.

'Right,' Clay Wallace tapped the table. 'Here's what we do. On Saturday night we ride into Crockett. We have a quiet drink in the saloon. Then you can introduce me to Paterson. I'm Clay Wallace. From Atlanta, Georgia. My folks have a large accountancy and real estate firm there. Leave the rest to me. I assure you I won't lie to him.'

'There's just one flaw in your scheme.' Jim Jordan looked at him shrewdly. 'Dunc ain't no fool. Suppose he goes to Fort Worth an' sends a wire to Atlanta? He ain't gonna take it very kindly when he finds we been foolin' him.'

Clay laughed. 'That's the whole point. If he wires Atlanta he'll find that my father, Jefferson T. Wallace, is president of Wallace, Baker and Vincent. Accountants, Real Estate and Property Developers.'

There was a long silence. 'You mean...' Ma began.

'Yes, it's all true. Also, the fact that I walked out on my father is not common knowledge. My parents,' he said bitterly, 'would not admit that their only son and heir had left home, so they told everyone that I had set up in business out West.'

'I'll be damned.' Jim Jordan slapped his thigh.

Mary-Lou glared at him.

'Sorry, Ma, but it's just so neat.' He looked anxiously at Clay. 'Think it'll work?'

'Don't see why not. Oh ... there are two points I would like to make. First, what we have discussed is confined to the three of us.'

The Jordans nodded.

'Second, when the sale has been agreed on, I leave and head back to the Flying W. If I hang around here it will only make Paterson suspicious and I'm sure you would rather part amicably.'

Ma looked at him. 'It's real neat, but why'd you want to go back to the Flyin' W?'

Clay Wallace smiled. 'Ma'am, you may not believe this, but I owe you and your son a great deal. Between you, you changed the course of my life. Before we met I was just drifting. Now, I believe in myself. I might set up in business in Tucson, or I might go back East. First though, I'm going back to the Flying W. Your son took a chance on me and I mean to repay him. He plans to build that ranch into an empire and he'll need financial advice. I intend to see he gets it.' He stopped and looked embarrassed. 'I'm sorry, I didn't mean to make a speech.'

The Jordans looked at each other. 'Reckon you didn't son,' Jim grinned, 'but you did a fair job just the same. Mebbe we all learned somethin' today.'

★   ★   ★   ★

' ... an' they all lived happily ever after ... there!' Sara-Jane closed the book with a decisive snap. 'Now,' she smiled at the two small serious girls sitting beside her on the old couch, 'time you were in bed. Kiss Ma, an' I'll take you along.'

'Land sakes!' Ma surfaced from their embraces. 'You'll smother me. 'Night now.'

'Sara-Jane.' She looked up from her sewing as her daughter returned. 'You've done well by them gals. I'm proud o' you.'

'Why, Ma!' Sara-Jane blushed. 'That's right nice of you.'

'Ain't no more than you deserve,' Ma said gruffly. 'They're shapin' real good.'

'Are we takin' them with us?' Sara-Jane asked cautiously.

'Ain't got much choice. Don't think I'd like to face Bull if I turned up without 'em.'

Her daughter smiled. 'I'm glad. They ain't got nobody an' they're happy here.'

Mary-Lou nodded. 'Yeah, it's for the best.'

'Ma, why did Pa an' Clay head off to Crockett this evenin'?'

'Waal,' Ma paused uncertainly, 'you know that for a long time Dunc Paterson's been keen to buy the Circle J? Your Pa's hopin' to see him an' take him up on his offer.'

'Mm?' Sara-Jane thought for a moment. 'Then why did he take Clay with him?'

Her mother bent over her sewing. 'Mebbe he felt Clay could help, him bein' an accountant an' all. Anyway, we'll know soon enough. Now,' she listened thankfully, 'I can hear Ellie-May an' the boys comin' up from the stable. Think you could make a pot o' coffee?'

✱   ✱   ✱   ✱

'Quiet, isn't it?' Glass in hand, Clay Wallace leaned back in his chair and surveyed the almost deserted room. In one corner a slim dark-haired youngster strummed softly on an old battered piano, while at a couple of tables, poker games were just getting under way.

'Yeah,' Jim Jordan grinned as he nursed a glass of lemon squash. 'When Dunc first started comin' here he told Mike Bodell, that's the owner, that he didn't want to see no hell-raisin' an' no dancehall gals in the place. Now this here is Triple X territory, an' what Dunc says goes. But Mike was smart. He built a big saloon, down the street a ways. You want dancehall gals, big card games an' general hell-raisin', you go there.' He laughed. 'You'll find most o' Dunc's boys down there. Suits Dunc fine. He gets a nice quiet drink, an' a nice quiet game o' poker. An' it suits Mike. He ain't got no competition. Anybody thinks o' startin' another saloon, Mike just speaks to Dunc. Dunc leans on them an' they forget all about it.'

Clay smiled. 'That's quite a setup.'

'Mm,' Jim Jordan nodded. 'You see, Dunc reckons it was Triple X money that built Crockett, an' he figgers that entitles him to make the rules.'

Wallace grimaced. 'Even if those rules aren't legal?'

The rancher shrugged. He lowered his voice. 'Remember what I told you 'bout Jud Moore an' Fitzgerald. Dunc controls this neck o' the woods. The rest o' us are two bit outfits compared to the Triple X.'

Clay Wallace frowned thoughtfully. He still found it hard to believe the story that Jim Jordan had told him, on the trail to Crockett. It had begun when he'd inquired about Paterson's background. 'Where does he hail from?'

'Lotta folks would like to know that, Clay.' The rancher had looked at him worriedly. 'Reckon I ought to level with you, so that you know what you're gettin' into. Dunc is awful close-mouthed 'bout his past. Sometimes, when he's had a few drinks, he talks about the California goldfields, but ... I dunno.'

'You don't believe him?'

'It ain't that exactly. When John was took by the Comanches we kept in touch wi' the rangers. They often picked up white youngsters that had been wi' the tribes for years. Anyways, after the war them northern carpetbaggers wasn't havin' no ranger outfit policin' Texas. So they was disbanded. 'Course, we still useta run into some o' them once in a while. 'Bout three years ago Bull met up wi' this fella, Charlie Glidden, an' they had a drink together. Charlie had rangered some in the old days, mostly down around Brownsville. Bull happened to mention Dunc, an' old Charlie got right interested. 'Pears like he'd seen a dodger one time, 'bout a fella name o' Dave Peterson. Seems this Peterson was the guard on a cash shipment out in California, when it disappeared. The money was a mine payroll. Charlie reckoned the description could have fitted Dunc, though he admitted it wasn't all that good. 'Course, wi' the rangers disbanded an' all their records to hell an' gone, there wasn't a lot he could do 'bout it.'

'So what happened?'

'Nothin'. Charlie was plannin' to come up here an' take a look at Dunc. Next thing we heard he'd been killed in a gunfight in Brownsville. Likely somebody payin' off old scores.'

'And that was it?'

'Yeah. Dunc was well established round here by then. Wasn't much we could do on hearsay. He'd come in around '58 and bought the Triple X. Some Eastern outfit had let it go all to hell, and the story is he got it dirt cheap. Wasn't very long before he started crowdin' other ranchers. Tell you one thing. Folks that cross Dunc generally regret it. Whatever happens round here, the Triple X allus comes out on top. A few years back there was an English fella ranchin' west o' Crockett. Fitzgerald his name was. He'd a horse ranch, the Cross Crescent. Now, Dunc, he was expandin' at the time an' he wanted that spread so bad he could taste it! He made Fitzgerald a real good offer, but Fitzgerald wasn't interested. He had remount contracts with the Army an' he was doin' right well. So he turned Dunc down flat. Next thing you know Comancheros start runnin' off Cross Crescent stock. Waal, accordin' to Sheriff Lane they was Comancheros.'

'And the sheriff is Paterson's man?'

'Uh huh,' Absently, Jim Jordan had rolled a cigarette as they jogged on together. 'Seems he rode for Dunc in the old days. Anyway, things went from bad to worse, an' in the end Fitzgerald headed out to the Triple X to have a showdown wi' Paterson. So Miz Fitzgerald testified at the trial. As it happened Dunc was out on the range, but Jud Moore, his foreman, was there.

'Now, Moore is one mean hombre. Story goes that he hails from Arkansaw, that he killed a coupla fellas back there an' had to leave town in a hurry.' The rancher had shrugged and struck a match on his Levis. "Course there's always stories 'bout fellas like Jud, but he is a gunhand. Anyway, accordin' to Moore, him an' Fitzgerald had words. Fitzgerald went for his gun an' Moore had to kill him in self-defence. So he said. Sheriff Lane reckoned it was an open and shut case, an' Jud was acquitted.'

'No witnesses?'

'Mm? Oh yeah. Young wrangler who was gentlin' some horses at the home ranch. He testified that Moore's story was true.'

'Is he still around?'

'Nah. He left the Triple X right after the hearing. That was the last anybody round here saw of him. Miz Fitzgerald sold out to Dunc an' went back to England. After that, folks played it real careful when they was dealin' with Dunc.'

The batwing doors banged and he came out of his reverie with a start. Two men entered.

Jim Jordan spoke quietly from the corner of his mouth. 'The big heavy guy's Paterson, an' the tall slim one's Moore.'

Clay surveyed Paterson cautiously. Around six feet, weight maybe two-thirty, just beginning to run to fat, but still a lot of muscle there. High colour, bull-necked and barrel-chested. A bad man in a brawl, he mused. He turned his attention to Moore as the two men made their way to the bar. About six two, around a hundred and eighty pounds, scar on his right cheek. His eyes flicked to the twin .45s in tied-down holsters. Gunhand, he shivered slightly. There was the smell of danger about this one.

The two men picked up their drinks and headed directly towards them. Paterson paused by the table and looked down.

'Howdy, Jim. Ain't often we see you in here.' It was a strong arrogant voice, the voice of someone accustomed to giving orders and having them obeyed.

Jim Jordan shrugged. 'Howdy, Dunc. Come an' sit a spell. Figgered I ought to have a night out once in a while. This here's Clay Wallace, young fella from back east. He's stoppin' over for a few days. Clay, meet Dunc Paterson o' the Triple X, an' his foreman, Jud Moore.'

'Evening, gents.' Clay nodded to them both and sipped his drink.

Jud Moore looked at him closely. 'What sort o' business are you in, Mister Wallace?'

'I'm an accountant by profession, but I also dabble in property developing and real estate.'

Dunc Paterson frowned heavily, looking for all the world like an angry bull. 'What fetched you out here then?'

It was the height of bad manners in the old West to ask someone their business, and a measure of the rancher's arrogance that he would do such a thing.

'I met Mister Jordan's son Hardy and Miz Jordan, in Tucson. They suggested that I should return with Miz Jordan. There's been a lot of talk about the possibility of silver down this way, and I wanted to look at the territory for myself.'

'An' what d'you think?' Paterson's tone was challenging.

'Well.' Clay paused for a moment. 'As you probably know, there was a certain amount of exploration done in Texas before the war. The signs were promising, so it is possible. If there is silver in this area then land values round here would increase dramatically. Anyone who owned land and struck lucky would stand to make a fortune. That's where I come in.'

'Ain't no land for sale round here!'

'Waal now,' Jim Jordan said hesitantly, 'That ain't rightly true, Dunc. You see, Mary-Lou's been left a big ranch in Arizona an' we're sorta plannin' to move out there. 'Course, we'd hafta sell the Circle J.'

'How come you ain't mentioned this before?' Paterson's temper was beginning to build. 'You always said I'd get first chance if you decided to sell out.'

'It ain't like that at all, Dunc.' Jim Jordan managed to introduced an anxious note into his voice. 'Mary-Lou just got back, an' we ain't no more than agreed to move. Aside from Clay here, nobody else knows.'

'An' I suppose he's just made you an offer?' Dunc Paterson sneered.

'You got it all wrong.' Jim said reproachfully. 'I told Clay when we was talkin' about it that you had to get first chance.'

'Waal,' the rancher was somewhat mollified, 'reckon you always been square wi' me at that. Like to think about this for a few days. I'll drop by your place 'bout the end o' the week an' let you know then.'

Jim Jordan nodded. 'That'll be fine.'

'Right, see you then. Now, we got a poker game waitin'.' Paterson and his foreman rose.

'Mister Wallace.' Clay looked up into Moore's cold stare and felt the hair on the back of his neck prickle disturbingly. 'I'm kinda interested in this real estate business. Could be the comin' thing. You know anybody I could get some advice from?' The foreman smiled, the thin-lipped, mirthless, calculating smile of the waiting predator.

Clay shivered inwardly. 'Let me think.' He set his glass carefully on the scarred table and frowned as if deep in thought. 'Tell you what ... ' delving into his breast pocket he produced a small gilt-edged card. 'Seeing as you're interested I'll let you have this.' The young Easterner allowed a note of pride to creep into his voice. 'That's my father's firm, always looking for clients.'

'Uh-huh,' Moore took the proffered card and tapped it thoughtfully. 'Atlanta eh? Well, well. Thanks. You plannin' to stay long?' He raised his hand in acknowledgement as Paterson beckoned impatiently.

'Depends,' Clay frowned judiciously. 'Our main interest is minerals, and some of the signs are quite promising.'

'Mind how you go then.' For a moment the foreman's long slim hand rested on Clay's shoulder. 'This is the frontier out here. Wouldn't want nothin' happenin' to you 'fore you get back to Atlanta.'

'I'll bear that in mind. Nice meeting you.' He watched as Moore wove his way between the tables to the waiting rancher.

'That touch wi' the card was real sneaky.' Jim Jordan said admiringly as they watched Paterson and his foreman ease into their game. 'Lucky you had it with you.'

There was a touch of bitterness in Clay's laugh. 'Thanks. You don't know how lucky. It was the only one I had! Don't know why I kept it, except maybe as a reminder of the old days.'

'Reckon he believed you?' Jim Jordan queried quietly.

'Maybe. Anyway, we'll know come the end of the week. You were pretty good yourself.'

'Shucks,' the rancher grinned tightly, 'it just come natural. When you been around Dunc for a spell you get used to agreein' with him. It makes life easier. Let's drink up, then we can drift out quietly.' He looked at Clay closely. 'Less'n you want a hand o' poker?'

Wallace shook his head. 'If I was to take a hand Moore would recognise me for a professional gambler right away. You can't disguise it, and he's no fool. I started gambling at college and it developed into an obsession. In the end my father gave me an ultimatum. He said I had to choose between the business and gambling. I chose gambling and walked out. As it happens I was pretty good at it and I just drifted west. Maybe I'd have gone on drifting if I hadn't met your son. He changed my views on life, gave me something to aim for. Some day I'll go back to my father's business, but not just yet. I've got things to do here first.' He drained his glass and stood up. 'Alright, let's go.'

Jim Jordan grinned wryly to himself as he followed the young man through the door. Just goes to show, he reflected. Who'd have figured that Bull could get through to an educated gent like Clay.

Chapter 25

The five-man cavalry patrol jogged quietly along the ridge trail, dust rising from each hoofbeat. In the lead, Sergeant Lance Jordan wiped the sweat from his brow and gazed down at the Circle J. *Sure is nice to see the old place again. Wonder why I couldn't settle when I was here?* He grinned wryly as he remembered the furious arguments between himself and his father. Arguments which had culminated in a blazing row, and had led to him leaving home in a blind fury. *Well, that was all behind him now. Sure am glad me an' Pa made our peace. Reckon I'm gonna miss the family if they head out for Arizona.* He frowned. *Though if the Flyin' W is a halfway decent ranch then they'll be goin' anyway. Ma'll see to that. An' Bull ... he's got his sights set on bein' a big time rancher, an' ain't nothin' gonna stop him.*

He raised his arm and the patrol closed up behind him. 'That's m'folks place, the Circle J, down there. We'll grain an' rest the mounts, get something to eat, an' then head south for Trinity. My old lady can be kinda fierce but don't let that worry you.'

Pete Jensen grinned. 'Allus wanted to meet your ma. Any lady that can whip the Anderson gang rates high in my book.'

'Yeah ... well don't go makin' a big thing 'bout it, leastways, not round Ma. She's liable to tear your fool head off! Alright, let's go.'

★   ★   ★   ★

The pinto flinched as John Jordan eased himself into the saddle. The young rider urged the pony forward gently and it bucked half-heartedly, before setting off at a canter round the corral.

Seated on the corral fence, his father turned to the silent figure beside him. 'Damned if I know how you two do it, Jake. Most fellas can't break horses without raisin' hell an' dust everywhere. But the pair of you got them cayuses eatin' out o' your hands.' He gestured towards the circling horse and rider. 'This here's Comanche style ain't it?'

Jake Larsen nodded. 'Yes, this is how the Comanches train horses. Ten Bears say you must never break a horse's spirit. A horse trained the Comanche way is worth much. Ten Bears also say that John has the gift of understanding when it comes to horses.'

'Yeah? Son, you're pretty good yourself. I've watched you both an' I wouldn't like to bet my life on which o' you was best. One thing I do know. The two of you, workin' together, are the best I've ever seen with horses. Captain McMillan, at Fort Concho, is goin' to be right pleased wi' this bunch.'

Ellie-May cantered up on a walleyed blue roan. 'Riders comin', Pa.' She pointed. 'Five of them on the ridge trail.'

Jim Jordan squinted into the distance. 'Yeah, you're right. Any idea who they might be?'

His elder daughter shrugged. 'Reckon they're cavalry. They all look the same. Was anybody else, they'd all have different gear.'

Her father nodded. 'Mebbe you're right. Could be a patrol. Might even be Lance. Say, you seen Clay anywhere?'

'Yeah. Him an' me moved the horse herd down to the bottom land next to the creek. Right now he's unsaddlin'. Should be up here soon.'

'You told Ma we got company?'

Ellie-May nodded. 'Clay said he'd pass the word.'

★   ★   ★   ★

The patrol clattered into the yard and reined to a halt. Lance grinned down at his mother. 'Howdy, Ma. Reckon you get purtier every time I see you.' He swung down off his mount.

'Less o' your nonsense!' Ma was pleased just the same. 'Just means you ain't seen me very often lately!'

Her son laughed. 'Seems like Arizona done you good. Oh ... meet the boys. Pete Jensen, Mike McGee, Jeff Wilde an' Steve McCall.'

They tipped their hats gravely.

Lance turned to his mother. 'Ma, we're aimin' to water the mounts an' grain them. Cup o' coffee would taste right good too.'

His father came round the corner of the ranch house.

'Hi Pa, you're lookin' right chipper.'

'Howdy, son. You want to rest your horses? Put them in the stable an' take the saddles off. It's cool in there. Then bring the boys up to the house.'

'Alright,' Lance waved his hand. 'Let's go.'

✶   ✶   ✶   ✶

'Ma'am.' Pete Jensen looked diffidently at Ma. 'I'd like to thank you for the meal. That apple pie was somethin' special.' There was a chorus of assent from the others. 'Ain't tasted pie like that since I left home.'

'Right nice of you to say so.' Ma kept her face carefully deadpan, 'but I didn't bake it. Sara-Jane did.' Sara-Jane blushed in confusion. Minor details like that didn't usually bother Ma!

'Waal, ma'am.' Pete searched carefully for the right words. 'All I can say is she had a real fine teacher!'

✶   ✶   ✶   ✶

'So you come back from Arizona with Ma?' Lance and Clay leaned against the hitching rail in front of the house and stared into the distance.

'Yes.' Wallace shot a glance at the big sergeant. 'Your brother wanted to stay behind and get the ranch going again.'

Lance laughed and turned to look at his companion. 'Yeah, I can imagine that happenin'. Bull's been waitin' all his life for a chance like this an' he ain't about to pass it up now.'

'What about yourself? Not interested in the cattle business?'

His companion paused in the act of rolling a cigarette. 'Look at it from where Bull stands. Supposin' you had a brother that took off an' joined the army. Then, at the end o' the war signs up for a four year hitch in the cavalry. All this time you'd been bustin' a gut helpin' your old man to keep the place goin'. Would you take it kindly if he was to come back when things was lookin' good?'

Clay thought for a moment. 'I guess not. Would you come back?'

Lance blew a long streamer of smoke and shook his head. 'Nah. Guess I got the cavalry in my blood now. M'hitch finishes next year an' I'll have to start thinkin' 'bout what I aim to do next. I wouldn't mind a spell sheriffin', though that can be a chancy business, 'less you got backin'. Reckon I might be as well stayin' where I am. Say, there's a coupla riders comin' down the ridge trail.'

Clay Wallace took a long look to the north and smiled. 'It looks like Dunc Paterson and his foreman. I reckoned it would take about a week. Seems like I was right after all.'

"Bout what?'

'It's a long story, but I think Paterson's here to make an offer for the Circle J. Like to ask a favour from you.'

'Shoot.'

'Could you hang around for a spell? I don't trust Jud Moore.'

Lance looked at him keenly. 'Reckon you got a nose for trouble. Run across a U.S. marshall a while back. He come down from Arkansaw to look at a Comanchero we picked up. Turned out it wasn't the fella he was lookin' for. Anyways, I mentioned Moore to him an' it seems like this lawman knew Jud. Accordin' to him Jud was the local bad man. Killed a young fella an' claimed self-defence. Witnesses didn't agree. The local sheriff didn't like it much either an' arrested Jud on suspicion. Come the trial the witnesses had changed their stories. 'Nother thing, this fella reckoned there was a lot o' Jud's friends an' relatives on the jury. Them hill folks are real close, an' it 'pears there's a big parcel o' Moores up that way. So they brung in a 'Not Guilty' verdict an' that was that. Waal, not quite. Local feelin' up there was a mite high an' Jud decided to light out. Sheriff back there got him marked GTT.'

Clay Wallace looked at the big sergeant. 'GTT?'

'Yeah, Gone to Texas! Sorta final note when somebody heads south an' don't come back. Here they come. I'll get the boys together an' send them down to the stable. You hail Pa an' tell him he's got visitors.' He raised his voice. 'Alright fellas, we got work to do. Get down to the stable an' check your gear.' He drew Pete Jensen aside. 'Just take it slow, Pete. I want them mounts rested 'fore we ride.' He closed one eye. 'You follow me?'

Pete Jensen looked at him carefully and nodded. 'Sure do. Reckon we'll have to look at our gear real close 'fore we light out for Trinity.'

Lance slapped the young trooper on the shoulder. 'Now you're talkin'. He turned as the two riders cantered into the yard. 'Oh, howdy Mister Paterson ... Jud. Been a fair spell since we last met. 'Course, patrollin' don't give you much time for socialisin'!'

Dunc Paterson nodded curtly. 'Howdy, Lance. Your pa around?' He swung down and tied his horse to the rail. Jud scowled and followed suit.

'Pa? Yeah, he's just comin'. Reckon' he's talkin' to that Wallace fella. Seems like they've taken quite a shine to each other.'

'I'll bet!' Paterson said angrily as Jim Jordan came through the door.

'Howdy, Dunc ... Jud. Thought you might be droppin' by. Come right in. Ma's got a pot o' coffee and some pie.'

'Ain't got no time for socialisin',' Dunc Paterson said tetchily. 'Me an' Jud got work to do. Come to make you an offer for the Circle J!'

'Waal now.' Jim Jordan paused and looked at the big rancher. 'Seems like this should be kinda private business between the two of us.'

'Any business o' mine, Jud sits in on it.' There was an air of finality in Paterson's tone.

Lance's eyes narrowed. 'Reckon we got to even things up a mite. I ain't in no hurry. I'll sit in with you, Pa.'

Jim Jordan took a long look at his eldest son. 'Reckon you got every right, boy. After all, you're the eldest o' the family.'

'Guess your bounty huntin' brother ain't goin' to be none too pleased when he hears 'bout this,' Jud Moore sneered as they made their way into the comfortable living-room.

'Bull?' Lance grinned. 'You just let me worry 'bout that. What's between him an' me is Jordan business, an' it sure as hell ain't yours!'

Moore looked at him coldly. 'You won't allus have that uniform to save you.'

The big sergeant's blue eyes chilled suddenly. 'Any time, Jud ... any time,' he said softly. 'However, right now I reckon we just sit in an' listen.'

'Waal,' Dunc Paterson looked hard at Jim Jordan. 'I'll give you three dollars an acre for the ranch. That's twelve thousand dollars.'

Jim kept his face carefully noncommittal. 'I was thinkin' more on four m'self. Been thinkin' on what Clay was sayin' 'bout silver ... '

'Damn him,' Paterson exploded. 'What does he know about it? This is cow country.'

'Dunc,' Jim Jordan spread his hands deprecatingly. 'I ain't sayin' you're wrong, but a man's got to look out for himself.' Privately he was happy. Clay had said that if he got three dollars an acre he would have done well. He paused for a moment. 'Alright, it's a deal, provided you take the calf crop. Say three dollars a head?'

'Done!' Paterson's fist struck the table triumphantly. 'We got a deal.' They shook hands. Watching closely Lance saw Jud Moore's face twist in a sneer. Some day Dunc, he thought, you're gonna regret lettin' Jud in on all your plans.

'Reckon you can make it to Fort Worth next week?'

Jim Jordan nodded.

'Right.' Paterson stood up. 'See you there next Wednesday.' He looked round with a proprietary air. 'Allus said I'd get this place some day. Let's go, Jud.' Picking up his hat he strode from the room, followed by his foreman.

'Waal.' Lance stood beside his father watching Dunc and Jud heading along the ridge trail. 'You happy with what you got?'

Jim Jordan shrugged. 'Can't say I'm happy, but I guess it's for the best. Hush up now,' he added warningly. 'Here's your ma an' Clay comin' to see how things went.'

'Waal?' Mary-Lou peered sharply at them, 'everything pan out alright?'

Her husband grinned. 'Yeah, just like Clay said. Dunc offered three dollars an acre, an' three dollars a head for the calves. We're meetin' in Fort Worth next week to draw up the agreement. Then the money'll be transferred into our account an' that's it.'

Lance laughed. 'Seems like everything worked out fine, so I reckon I'll be movin' on. Got a patrol to run.' He kissed his mother and punched Clay on the shoulder. 'Been nice meetin' you, Clay. Mebbe see you again sometime. Oh ... ' he turned back. 'Almost forgot, When you plannin' to pull out?'

His parents looked at each other. 'Reckon three ... four weeks,' Jim Jordan said slowly. 'Time we get the stock gathered, buy a heavy wagon an' team to carry any things we want to take with us, we'll be gettin' near to the end o' July. Don't need a chuck wagon, we can convert that new wagon, no trouble. Yeah, say the end o' July.'

'See you in Arizona then.' He strode towards the waiting troopers. Pete Jensen had the big buckskin saddled and ready.

'He don't change much,' Ma said severely. 'Just as wild as ever.'

'Mary-Lou,' her husband protested, 'that's hardly fair. He's a top sergeant in the cavalry an' that don't come easy. Anyway, I'm glad him an' me got our differences straightened out.'

Together they watched their son settle himself in the saddle and raise his hand. The patrol moved off quietly, Pete Jensen in the lead and Lance bringing up the rear. They splashed across the creek and climbed the bank. Lance twisted in his saddle and waved. For a moment the horsemen were silhouetted against the skyline, then they were gone.

Chapter 26

There was a stillness in the thicket. A brooding oppressive stillness. The sunlight filtered faintly through the leaves of the cottonwoods, and dappled the coat of the giant black bull hidden in the underbrush. He flicked his ears to dislodge the flies that were plaguing him and listened intently. In the distance he could hear the shouts of the Flying W riders, as they hazed stock out of the brush.

Anger flared in the red eyes and the bull rumbled deep in his throat. One of the last of the old cimmarones, the wild black cattle that had originally come from Spain, he was descended from the Andalusian fighting bulls. It showed in the heavy body, the powerful shoulders and the dagger sharp, forward pointing horns.

Now, he pawed the ground and snorted angrily as he listened to the shouts coming closer. The flies settled again on the open wound in his shoulder, and he swung his head at them irritably. Three days ago he had clashed with the only other cimmarone bull left in the brush. That in itself had been unusual. For years they had carefully avoided each other. However, the proximity of a Longhorn cow, unusually late 'in season', had brought them together, and sparked off the battle. At the end the challenger was dead, but not before he had left his mark, a wickedly-deep shoulder slash. Now, the pain of the wound was driving the survivor into a killing rage.

The shouts were getting very close now, as horsemen crashed through the brush. A steer broke out of the scrub on the far side of the clearing, Bull Jordan on the big grey, close behind.

With an angry bawl the cimmarone lunged out of the undergrowth. The steer veered right and lit out across the clearing. Bull took in the situation at a glance. Left-handed he pulled the big horse round, while his right hand flicked the lariat loop onto the saddle horn and drew the big .45 all in one lightning movement. The grey spun sideways like a cat and, as the bull swept past, the big man leaned out of the saddle and pumped two quick shots into its head, just behind the ear. Tiredly the black giant dropped to his knees and rolled over. Bull swept around in a tight turn and waited tensely.

Manuel Ortega crashed out of the brush on his pinto. His eyes widened as he saw the giant bull. 'Madre de Dios!' The Mexican crossed himself reverently. 'Many times the old ones, they tell me about the cimmarones. I thought they were all dead.'

'Let's just make sure that this one is.' Bull drew his Winchester from the saddle boot, and jacked a round into the breech. 'That pony o' yours gun-broke?' he queried as he lined up the rifle.

'Si' Manuel patted his mount's neck. 'Diablo, he is afraid of nothing.'

'Right.' Bull squeezed the trigger. The crash of the shot reverberated across the clearing. Neither horse moved as the bull's head jerked under the impact.

'Waal,' Bull slid the gun back into the boot, "pears like he's dead alright. Hoss,' he stroked the gelding's neck, 'you ain't Red, but you'll do till he gets here. Lost me a steer through this though,' he added. 'Let's ride. Ain't nothin' we can do here now.'

'Si, Boss.' They urged their mounts into the brush. The vaquero frowned as his mount swerved to avoid a thorn bush. 'Mike, he reckoned that there were two old cimmarone bulls left in here.'

'Yeah?' Bull grinned. 'Tell you what Manuel. Next one's yours!'

* * * *

'Cimmarone you say.' Old Tex looked up as he ladled stew onto Bull's plate. 'Pity you hadn't brung the critter in. Way you fellas eat beef we coulda used it!'

The big man smiled tightly. 'I'll bear that in mind, if I run up against the other one that Mike reckons is still around.'

'Not anymore he ain't,' Joe Masterson stripped the saddle from his horse and secured the gelding to the picket line. 'Found him dead 'bout three miles south o' here.' He picked up an empty plate and made his way to the chuck wagon. 'Nigh on an acre o' scrub all tore up. Must've been a helluva fight.'

'Yeah,' Bull looked at Manuel. 'Remember our fella was cut up bad in the shoulder? Reckon they must've fought it out an' he won.'

'Si.' the Mexican nodded. 'It did not do him much good though.'

'Mm.' Bull Jordan chewed for a moment. 'Waal, looks like we've seen the last o' the cimmarones. When m'folks get here we can mebbe risk some o' them Durham bulls down this way.'

'Yeah.' Joe took the loaded plate from Tex and sat down beside Bull. 'We got a lot o' beef out there on the flats. Must be all of a thousand head. Mike an' Sam are ridin' herd on them now.'

Bull rose and poured himself a mug of coffee. 'Who's got the first night trick?'

Joe grinned. 'You an' Manuel. Then Jem an' Jeff.' He waited until the rancher had seated himself again. "Course we still got a lot o' work to do wi' them critters. Calves to cut an' brand. An' there's a lot o' big old steers that should have been beef years ago. Then there's them scrub bulls. Must be thirty at least. Still thinkin' o' sellin' them to the army?'

Bull nodded. 'Yeah. They'll just be a damn nuisance if we don't.' He thought for a moment. "Nother three days you reckon, 'fore we finish here?'

'Guess so. Might be better to say four. Then we can push them up onto the home range. Once we get them up there we can start cuttin' an' brandin'.'

* * * *

Clay Wallace settled into his seat on the stage, and watched the outlying buildings of Fort Worth drop behind. He smiled to himself at the thought of a job well done, and the knowledge that he was heading back to the Flying W. Strange that I should feel like this, he mused. Me, Clay Wallace, who used to become bored so easily. Now I can't wait to get back to the ranch and see what progress Bull has made. At least his parents got a good price for the Circle J. If I never do anything else in my life, I can take some pride in that.

Wouldn't have done to have stayed, though I'd have liked to have been on that trail drive, but no ... He shook his head regretfully.

His mind went off at a tangent. Jud Moore, now there is a dangerous man. He shivered involuntarily. Just as well Lance was there the other week when he showed up.

Lance is quite something. As Jim Jordan says, it's not easy to make top sergeant in the cavalry. Shrewd too, he could see the way Bull would feel if he came back home now. Not like me, I haven't anything like that to worry about.

What would it cost me in pride to go back; to admit I was wrong? Not all that much I suppose. Father has always said in his infrequent letters that, if I came back cured of the gambling habit, all would be forgiven. Well, I'm pretty sure I'm cured, but I don't feel like going back just yet. Not until I've got something to my credit. Maybe I could start up in Tucson, the town looks to have a future, and they could use an accountant.

First though, we've got to get the Flying W up and running. Don't think I could face Miz Jordan and Bull if I let them down. Don't think I'd want to face Bull. Now there is one hard man. Wonder what Father would say if I told him that the man who straightened me out was a bounty hunter! That would go down well with Mother's friends. I can just hear them discussing it. Come to that I couldn't see Mother and Miz Jordan hitting it off. They'd be like oil and water. Don't suppose it's Mother's fault that she's a snob, but she is none the less. 'But Clay dear, they're not our sort of people.' Maybe not, but they're a damned sight better than the snobs she mixes with.

Smiling to himself he recalled Ma's warning about Sara-Jane. His mother would have a fit if she thought there was any danger of him becoming involved with a small-time rancher's daughter. And yet, why not? Sara-Jane was the genuine article, not like the artificial beauties he'd known back east. Look how she'd coped when her mother was in Arizona. Not many girls of her age could have run a house and looked after two little orphans at the same time. But she had done it. She'd make some lucky man a great wife one day.

Not like Ellie-May. Clay frowned as he thought about her. In all his life he had never met a girl so completely unaffected by her appearance as the tall blonde was. She was the only woman he had ever seen wearing levis and he wasn't sure he approved. Sara-Jane had told him of the furious battle there had been between Ma and Ellie-May, before the reluctant intervention of Jim Jordan had forced Ma to concede the point. Still, he admitted grudgingly, Ellie-May pulled her weight on the ranch and she couldn't have done that wearing a dress. Wonder what Father would say about her?

As for her brother John, and Jake Larsen, I wonder if they'll ever fit in. Ten years in a different culture is a long time. Sara-Jane had told him the whole tragic story, and he doubted if John and his mother would ever be very close. In young Jake's case it would depend very much on Jim Jordan whether he would ever be totally accepted into the family.

Jim Jordan was quite a man. The lean, soft-spoken rancher had managed to keep that widely diverse family together, and that couldn't have been easy. His only failure, if you could call it a failure, had been with Lance, and even there he had eventually sorted out their differences. Yes, he mused, watching the interminable miles of sagebrush roll past, there was more to Jim Jordan than met the eye. In fact, the whole family meant a great deal to him, and he just hoped the feeling was mutual. With a smile, Clay Wallace, reformed gambler, tipped his hat forward and closed his eyes.

★ ★ ★ ★

The evening sun, just dipping behind the ridge, drew long shadows from the ranch buildings nestling in the valley below. High on the ridge trail Jim Jordan drew the team to a halt.

Beside him Ma blinked her eyes and blew her nose fiercely.

Her husband put his arm round her. 'Guess I know how you feel. Been thinkin' o' the years we put into that place, an' now we're leavin'. Don't seem right somehow.'

'It's for the best, Jim.' There was sadness in her voice nevertheless. 'This is a chance for the family to make it big. We've had our time, now it's their turn.'

She saw a shadow darken his face and put out a hand impulsively. 'Jim, I didn't mean it like that. If I'd my time again I'd still want to spend it at the Circle J. It was the best thing that ever happened to me.'

Her husband scrubbed at his chin with a calloused hand. 'Never thought I'd hear you say that,' he muttered gruffly. Together they watched two tiny figures at work among the horses in the corral. 'You know Ma, them's two good boys. They're the best horse breakers for miles round. I'd like to see you lighten up on them some.'

Ma sighed. 'I'll try, but it'll take time. Mebbe this move'll help.'

In the distance they could see a lone rider drifting a band of horses down to the creek.

'That's Ellie-May,' Jim Jordan murmured. 'You can tell that palomino o' hers anywhere. I told her to hold the horse herd down by the creek. Want to look them over 'fore we light out on the drive. Anyways,' he shook out the lines, 'time we was rollin', we got a lot to do.' The Clevelands eased into their stride and dust plumed out behind the buckboard.

*   *   *   *

'Sara-Jane, will we be goin' to Arizona with you?'

Sara-Jane shut the oven door and straightened up, pushing a recalcitrant lock of hair out of the way. "Course you will. Ain't no way we can go without you. 'Sides,' she added, unfolding a tablecloth and spreading it on the big kitchen table, 'you got to go an' help Bull run this new ranch.'

'Mm,' Sarah bit into a biscuit and chewed reflectively for a moment. 'Does Mister Bull know we're coming?'

'Yes he does,' her young sister cut in sharply. 'Mister Bull knows everything.'

Sarah looked at Sara-Jane thoughtfully. 'Will Mister Clay be there?'

'I expect so. He went into Fort Worth with Ma an' Pa, an' he was goin' to catch the stage back to Tucson from there.'

'Do you like him?'

'Yes, he's very nice.' Sara-Jane paused with a handful of cutlery. 'Now get yourselves tidied up. Supper'll be ready soon.'

'Maybe Mister Clay will marry Sara-Jane.' Mary Johnson looked up innocently from the book she was trying to read.

'You hush up now,' Sara-Jane blushed scarlet. 'Talkin' such foolishness. Time you were tidied up 'fore Ma an' Pa get back. I'll just go see if there's any sign o' them.'

The two little girls watched her disappear through the kitchen door.

'What did you say that for?' Sarah whispered fiercely. 'Now she's cross with us.'

'Wasn't my fault,' Mary whimpered. 'She said she liked Mister Clay.'

'When you're older,' Sarah said loftily, with the crushing superiority of her eight years, 'you'll find that grown-ups don't like you saying things like that. Hush now, here she comes.'

'Have you finished tidyin' up?' Sara-Jane hurried in.

'Yes,' Sarah said meekly. 'Will we get you another bucket of water from the pump?'

'No, but you're good gals to think of it.' She hugged them both. 'Still, you can help finish layin' the table.'

☆ ☆ ☆ ☆

'Waal,' Jim Jordan looked round the table, 'you know as much as Ma an' me now. The ranch is sold, an' we got a month to pack up an' get on the trail to Arizona. It'll mean hard work for all of us. Anybody got anything to say, now's the time.'

John cleared his throat. His father looked at him enquiringly. 'One of us will need to scout ahead,' John said hesitantly.

The rancher nodded. 'That's true. It's nigh on a thousand miles, an' mighty rough country at that. Whoever scouts it has got to be young an' fit, so I guess it lies between you two fellas. How you gonna decide it? Cut cards?'

Jake Larsen shook his head. 'It would be better if John was scout. I would like it that way.'

There was a long pause, then John Jordan nodded gravely. 'If that is how Jake wants it I am happy.'

'Right.' his father said briskly. That's one thing settled. Now we can get down to plannin' the drive.' He looked at the piece of paper in front of him. 'First of all, we got two hundred an' eighty-nine cows an' six bulls. Plus mebbe thirty steers for beef on the drive, an' in case we have to buy off Injuns. That's just a small herd, but we can't afford to take chances on this trip. So what I aim to do is hire four extra hands. I'll ride into Greenhills next week an' see if I can find any fellas keen to make the trip.'

Ma frowned. 'Ain't gonna be cheap. An' all the top hands'll have gone wi' the northern trail herds.'

Her husband shrugged. 'That's true, but there ain't nothin' we can do about it. This ain't your normal trail herd. It's mainly breedin' stock an' they won't be easy to handle. So, if we get any Injun or rustler trouble on the trail I want to be ready for it. Agreed?' There were nods all round.

'The next thing's the remuda.' He looked directly at his elder daughter. 'This ain't gonna be no easy chore. We got breedin' stock again. There's big Dance, the Cleveland stud, plus twenty mares; eight Clevelands an' twelve Morgans. Then we each got to have a string o' mounts for trail work, so you're talkin' somethin' like sixty, seventy head. Ellie-May, think you can handle it?'

'Sure.' There was a decisiveness in Ellie-May's voice. 'Don't see no problem.'

Jim Jordan frowned. 'It ain't as easy as you think. Dance an' them mares cost a lot o' money. Reckon we need a nighthawk as well. That's why I'm hirin' them extra riders. You can't cover the wrangler's job day an' night.'

Ellie-May nodded reluctantly.

'Then, we got to have a chuck wagon. That new wagon can be converted for that. Old Paint an' Dusty can haul it. They're a steady team.' His eyes twinkled as he looked at Sara-Jane. 'Won't give you no trouble, will they?'

His younger daughter gulped nervously. 'Sure hope not, Pa. Reckon I'll need more practice though.'

Her father laughed. 'You'll get enough practice on the trail. Next, I been thinkin' o' somewhere for Ma an' you gals to sleep, an' I reckon I got just the thing. It's an ex-army ambulance wagon. Belongs to a fella in Crockett, an' I've told him I'll swap the buckboard for it. Seems like he's interested. Anyways, he's bringin' it across. 'Course, we'll have to do some work on it but that ain't never stopped us yet.

'Lastly, we need a heavy wagon, somethin' to haul the things we want to take with us. Don't know where we'll get that yet, but we got to find one somewhere.

'An' that's it.' He looked round their serious faces. 'Right now we all got a lot o' work to do 'fore we head west. Any of you not keen on this move?' There was a concerted shaking of heads.

'Alright, let's get some sleep. Come mornin', me an' Jake'll start out wi' that last bunch o' horses to Fort Concho. John, you get busy alterin' that new wagon. Ellie-May'll help you, an' Ma'll show you what she wants done.'

★   ★   ★   ★

'Six, seven, eight.' Ellie-May halted and turned to survey the lightning-blasted cottonwood she had chosen as a target. Mm, 'bout twenty feet. Should be enough. Off to one side, hitched to a convenient bush, Goldie, her highly-strung palomino pony, snorted suspiciously.

'Easy, boy.' The blonde girl spoke softly, her gaze locked on the scrap of red cloth tacked to the dead tree, six feet from the ground. 'Easy, now.' She drew the slim throwing knife from its sheath. Her arm whipped suddenly back and forward. The gleaming blade flashed in the sunlight and pinned the cloth to the tree.

Ellie-May smiled tightly as she retrieved the knife and untied the snorting Goldie. Swinging into the saddle she turned the pony's head for home. *I'm getting better, John. Some day I'll be as good as you.*

Chapter 27

Captain McMillan rose from behind his desk and extended his hand. 'Nice to see you again, Mister Jordan. The usual number I suppose?'

Jim Jordan nodded as they shook hands. 'Yeah. Twenty head, as agreed. Me an' Jake brought 'em along real easy, so they're in good condition. All gentled an' saddle broke. You won't find a better bunch o' remounts in the country.'

The tall raw-boned captain laughed. 'I've got to hand it to you. You'd make a great salesman.' He glanced at the dark-haired young lieutenant who had come into the room with the rancher. 'You agree with Mister Jordan's assessment?'

'Yes, sir.' Lieutenant Jackson nodded emphatically. 'They're good stock alright, as good as any I've seen. The recruits won't have any trouble with them.'

'Fine,' McMillan stroked his heavy moustache and looked shrewdly at the rancher. 'You must have some good men who can gentle horses like that.'

'Yeah.' There was a flicker of pride in Jim Jordan's eyes 'That's my youngest boy, John an' his sidekick, Jake Larsen. Best in the business.'

'Mm, your son Lance ... Sergeant Jordan, he told me about John being with the Comanches all those years. They say the Comanches are the best when it comes to horse-breaking. That where he learned it?'

The rancher nodded sombrely. 'Yeah, as you say they're the best, an' accordin' to young Jake, Ten Bears reckoned John was better than any o' them.'

McMillan laughed. 'You can't get a higher recommend than that. Does your son talk much about his years with Ten Bears?'

'Hardly ever. Maybe someday, but it'll be in his own good time.'

'I understand.' The captain opened a small safe and took out a wad of notes. 'Fifty dollars a head, subject to satisfactory inspection on delivery. There you are Mister Jordan, a thousand dollars in ten-dollar bills. I'm sorry that it's paper, but the government insists on its use.'

Jordan shrugged as he tucked the money into his vest pocket. 'We'll all be usin' it soon. Sold my ranch last week an' got paid the same way.'

The captain looked at him. 'That's right, Sergeant Jordan mentioned it. Heading out to Arizona I hear.'

'Yeah, m'wife got left a big spread east o' Dorando an' right down on the Border.'

'Pity. We'll miss these mounts of yours. Lot of Apache trouble out that way from all accounts. That bother you at all?'

The rancher shook his head. 'No more than usual. You just got to take them things as they come.'

'Mister Jordan,' the captain came to a sudden decision. 'What I'm about to tell you is confidential, and I must ask for your assurance that it will remain so.'

'Sure.'

'Fine. I've already discussed my idea with Lieutenant Jackson, but putting it into practice will require the agreement of your son Lance and yourself.'

The rancher frowned, 'I don't follow … '

McMillan smiled. 'Bear with me, Mister Jordan.' He walked across to a large wall map of the South-West. 'You're bound for Arizona. That means you'll be travelling the Horsehead route to Emigrant Crossing and from there on up the Pecos to Pope's Camp; here.' A long finger stabbed at the map. 'Most herds cross just above Pope's. Then you'll be heading for El Paso. Right?' The tall captain looked interrogatively at Jim Jordan, who nodded. 'After that you'll swing northwest to Stein's and Apache Pass, then down towards the Santa Cruz and Dorando.' He traced the route as he spoke. 'Nigh on a thousand miles Mister Jordan, over some of the worst terrain in the whole South-West. You'll be facing storms, flooded rivers, drought and stampedes. In addition you're liable to be attacked by Indians, Comancheros and rustlers. Quite an undertaking.' He laughed suddenly. 'Why is it then, that I wish I was going with you?'

Jim Jordan grinned. 'Way you tell it, captain, it don't hardly seem worthwhile startin'. Still, me an' m'family know all this. Can't see what you're leadin up to.'

'Mister Jordan, how would you like to have your eldest son with you on this drive?'

'Waal yeah, I surely would, but it ain't possible. He's a cavalry sergeant, in the last year of a four year hitch … ' he broke off suddenly. 'He ain't in no trouble is he?'

McMillan shook his head. 'Nothing like that I assure you. Lieutenant Jackson and I consider that your son is one of our top sergeants, though I'll thank you to keep that information to yourself.'

'Then what ... ?'

'I want Lance with you as an unofficial observer. Somebody with a military mind who can evaluate conditions all the way from here to Arizona and report back. As you may have gathered, the Army is struggling to get to grips with the Indian problem. Personally I think we're going about it the wrong way and I've never made any secret of my views.' He grinned wryly. 'Maybe that's why I'm stuck here at Fort Concho.

'We've too many corrupt Indian agents, and too many greedy contractors supplying inferior stores. In short, too many vested interests who are perfectly happy to keep the pot boiling and line their pockets at the same time.

'In the field it's no better. Young, raw lieutenants fresh out of West Point. My apologies to Lieutenant Jackson, at least he's listened and learned. Elderly commanding officers who have been posted here to get them out of the way, and I include myself in that category! Finally, the lack of an overall coherent campaign strategy against the finest guerrilla fighters in the world. It's only superior numbers and firepower that enables us to hold our own. Mark my words, one day the Indians are going to surprise us with superior forces, on ground of their choosing. Then the United States Army will have a military disaster on their hands.'

Jim Jordan frowned. 'That's quite a speech. Reckon it'd go hard with you if them generals back east got to hear about it.'

McMillan shrugged. 'Don't suppose it would make much difference. I've never been noted for tact. Bluntly, Mister Jordan, I have no faith in the information that is being passed to me from our sources in New Mexico and Arizona. It appears to totally ignore the fact that Indian activity in this area is actually increasing, that the Comanches are attacking our lines of communication, and that the Apaches themselves are now striking as far south as the Big Bend country.'

Angrily he struck the map with his hand. 'Captain La Salle, in Fort Davis is virtually under siege, his supply columns have to fight their way in. Fort Clark is too far south to help effectively, so it's up to us. That's where Sergeant Jordan comes in. Officially on an extended furlough to assist his parents in their move to Arizona, he will be my unofficial observer. Travelling as a working member of a trail drive, he will be in an ideal position to see for himself and talk to local people along the way. In short, Mister Jordan, an on the spot report, from somebody with a military mind who knows the country. What do you say?'

'Suits me fine, but how about Lance? You talked to him about this?

Mcmillan shook his head. 'Aside from Lieutenant Jackson here, nobody else knows. That reminds me,' he looked at the lieutenant. 'Would you get hold of Sergeant Jordan and bring him across here?'

'Good youngster that,' he commented after Jackson had snapped a salute and gone. 'Sets considerable store by your son. Of course he's biased, Sergeant Jordan saved his life.' He saw the look of surprise on the rancher's face. 'Didn't you know? No, I can see you didn't.'

Jim Jordan shook his head. 'Lance don't say much about his soldierin'.'

Captain McMillan nodded approvingly. 'Glad to hear it. Shows the right attitude. Jackson wanted to recommend him for a medal but he just laughed. Said anybody would have done what he did.'

'That's Lance alright. Surprises me you ever got him to be a sergeant!'

'Yes ... well, it took a deal of persuasion. Ah, here they come now.'

Lance stepped into the office and saluted. His eyes widened when he saw his father there.

'At ease, sergeant.' In a few crisp sentences McMillan outlined his proposition. 'It's up to you Sergeant Jordan,' he concluded. 'I don't intend making this an order, but you'll be doing me a big favour if you agree.'

Lance thought for a moment. 'How does it set with you, Pa?'

'Can't think of nobody I'd rather have sidin' me.'

'And I'm officially on furlough?' The big sergeant looked at McMillan.

'That's right. There are people who know there is a problem, and who want something done. However, they don't want to know how it's done. Then, if anything goes wrong the responsibility isn't theirs.'

Lance grinned. 'That figgers. Alright, sir, I'll do it. When do I start?'

'Well,' the captain looked thoughtful. 'It wouldn't be a good idea if you left here with your father, so I'd wait two, three days if I were you. Let it be known you're worrying about your parents making this drive to Arizona. Then apply for special furlough. That should cover it. One more thing, sergeant. I'll expect a full report at the end of your trip, complete with an assessment of the Indian situation, and how it can be improved.'

'Yes, sir.' Lance came to attention and threw a snappy salute, which McMillan acknowledged.

'Carry on, sergeant.'

He waited until the door closed before turning to Jim Jordan. 'You should see him in about a week. That suit you?'

'Sure. Only thing I need now is a heavy wagon. Big enough to carry anything we want to take with us.'

'A heavy wagon?' McMillan looked at him thoughtfully. 'Maybe I can help you. There's a young man who came into the post about a month ago. Name's Turner; Ben Turner. Hails from Louisiana. Seems he planned to settle out here and build up a freighting business. Sold up everything and invested in a big Studebaker wagon and a team of draft horses. Fine looking animals, Conestogas, I think they are.'

'Sounds good. You don't see many Conestoga teams down here.'

'Mm. Sadly, his wife and baby son took ill and died on the way. Fever I think. He's been here ever since. Does the odd freighting job but his heart isn't in it. Don't think he's got over the loss of his family. Anyway, I suggest you talk to him.'

'Sure will ... an' thanks.'

'Pleasure, Mister Jordan.' The tall captain held out his hand. 'Nice doing business with you. I hope your drive goes well. Goodbye now.'

☆   ☆   ☆   ☆

Ben Turner swept the brush down a shining flank and surveyed his handiwork critically. Yes, that would do. He patted the big draft horse and moved on to the next in line. Reckon I'd be as well selling up and moving back to Louisiana. Nothing for me here. Ain't hardly paying my way. If only Peg and the baby were here. He blinked and rubbed a hand across his eyes. One of the big horses whinneyed softly and he looked up to see two riders approaching. The tall old guy looks 'bout fifty. Gear's well-used but good. Nice piece o' horseflesh, Cleveland I reckon. The young fella, he's more difficult to place. Early twenties I guess. Fair-haired, could be a Swede from his colouring, 'cept for them dark eyes. Medium height. Packin' a knife too. That black cowpony's got a lot o' Morgan in it.

'Howdy, mister. I'm lookin' for Ben Turner.'

'That's me. Can I help you?'

'Yeah. The name's Jordan; Jim Jordan. This young fella here's Jake Larsen. Like to talk to you 'bout some freightin' work.'

Turner nodded. 'Sure. Sorry we got to talk in the open like this, but I ain't got no premises.'

'Yeah,' Jordan looked at the young man critically. 'Seems like you been havin' a hard time from what I hear.'

'That's my business.'

'Sure. Still, it seems to me you could use some steady work. You got a good outfit there, but they ain't earnin' nuthin' standin' idle.'

Turner shrugged. 'Don't seem to have the same interest now. Anyway, there ain't all that much freightin' work round here.'

'Yeah.' Jim Jordan dismounted and stood for a moment deep in thought. 'You ever thought o' movin' somewhere else. Further west maybe.'

'On my own?' Ben Turner shook his head. 'Nah. Buildin' a business don't mean nuthin' to me now.'

'Son, you ain't thinkin' straight. Now, I got a proposition for you. I'm moving my outfit to Arizona an' I need a wagon like yours. Suppose I hire you to freight my stuff out there. Say five hundred dollars, plus thirty a month for yourself. Then, when we get there you can set up in business. Use my ranch as a depot till you get organised. Hold on.' He held up his hand as Turner made as if to speak. 'If that don't set easy with you then I'll buy your outfit as it stands. Say a thousand dollars the lot. How does that strike you?'

Ben Turner frowned as he thought about it. 'That's a fair price you're offerin', but I reckon I'd miss them horses. Ain't nuthin' to hold me here. Mister, I'll haul your freight. You got yourself a deal.'

They shook hands. 'Now,' Jim Jordan gestured towards the wagon. 'How long will it take you to clear up your business here?'

'Nuthin' to clear up. I sleep in the wagon, an' the team is hitched to this picket line here. Everything else I sold off. Didn't seem no point in keepin' it somehow.'

The rancher nodded sympathetically. 'I can guess how you feel. So you can roll any time?'

'Sure. Now if you say so.'

'Right, me an' Jake'll help you hitch up. Then we'll travel with you to the Circle J. That's m'ranch here in Texas.'

Ben Turner nodded, his face suddenly alive. 'Alright, let's get this team hitched up.'

★ ★ ★ ★

'Mister John.'

John Jordan paused, hammer in hand and looked down at the small serious face.

'Is this what Ma calls the chuck wagon?'

'Yeah,' he grinned wryly. 'Well, it will be when I've finished. Let me show you.' He dropped the big tailgate to the full extent of its securing chains. 'This will be Ma's table. Now,' he indicated the shelves and drawers which he had built across the wagon to form a crude cabinet. 'This is where she will keep all the pots, pans and dishes that she'll need. Then back in the wagon she'll have the Dutch oven and all the stores.'

Crouching down he pointed underneath the wagon. 'See this hide I've stretched across the underside of the wagon. That's to hold any wood we find along the way. Firewood can be awful scarce at times.'

'I know,' Sarah Johnson nodded gravely. 'When I was little I had to collect buffalo chips. I hated it.'

'I have collected buffalo chips too, when I lived with the Comanches.'

'Did you really live with the Comanches? Were they very bad?'

John paused, a faraway look in his eyes. 'Yes Sarah, I lived with them for ten years. There were good and bad amongst them, just like other folks.'

'They killed my Ma and Pa,' Sarah said pensively.

The tall young man put his arm round her. 'Yes Sarah, they did, and that was bad.' He searched for a diversion.

'Look,' Sarah pointed. 'There's a wagon coming down the ridge trail, and see, there's Mister Jordan an' Jake.'

'Best run in and tell Ma,' said John thankfully. Times like this, he thought, I don't know what to say.

★   ★   ★   ★

'Ma,' Jim Jordan dismounted stiffly. 'Meet Ben Turner. Ben'll be travellin' with us to Arizona. He's hopin' to start up in business there.'

'Nice to meet you, ma'am,' Ben set the brake and climbed down. The big horses looked about them placidly. 'Sure hope I ain't givin' you too much trouble arrivin' like this.'

'Son, you ain't givin' me no trouble.' Ma smiled, 'just light down. We'll fix you somethin to eat an' a place to sleep. You're welcome.'

★   ★   ★   ★

'So Lance is comin' with us,' Ma Jordan looked shrewdly at her husband. 'Kinda sudden ain't it? And since when did the Army allow a furlough as long as this?'

'Alright,' Jim Jordan leaned against the horse pasture gate and rolled a cigarette. 'I knew I'd have to tell you sooner or later. That's why I brought you out here.' Swiftly he outlined Captain McMillan's plan and the reasoning behind it. 'So you see, Mary-Lou, this is between you, me an' Lance. And,' he added warningly, 'that's how it stays.'

Ma nodded. 'It'll be nice havin' Lance around for a spell,' she said. 'Think the two of you can get along now?'

Her husband scratched a match on the gatepost and lit up. 'Yeah. Him an' me made our peace. There won't be no trouble.'

'You done anything 'bout them extra riders?' Ma queried suddenly.

'Left word in Greenhills with Hannah MaCrae. She said she'd tell any hands lookin' for work that we was needin riders. Anyway, I'll go across an' see. Lance'll be along in a few days, but he'll only replace John. He'll be headin' out in a day or so to scout the Goodnight trail from Fort Concho to the Pecos. Then he'll come back an' meet us at the fort.'

'Jim.'

'Yeah.'

'You right sure John can do this? I mean, it's a big responsibility, scoutin' for a trail herd.'

'An' you think he ain't up to it? Ma, he's our son. For ten years he was a Comanche. He can scout, fight an' live off the country. For all we know he's ridden on a war party. 'Course he never talks about it. He speaks Comanche like it was his mother tongue. He can get by in Apache. Of all the family he's the one best suited for the job.'

There was a long silence then Ma spoke hesitantly. 'Jim, I didn't mean ... '

'I know you didn't, but just remember this. He's had his life messed up, same as yourself, an' so has Jake. Start treatin' them like family an' don't get so uptight when they're around. You can't blame them for what happened to your folks. So act natural wi' them an' maybe they'll do the same wi' you.'

Ma dabbed at her eyes. 'I'll try, but it ain't gonna be easy.'

'Never said it would be, but we got nigh on a thousand miles o' mighty rough country ahead o' us an' we all got to pull together!'

They stood together in silence looking out over the valley. Ma's eyes were misty and she put a tentative hand on her husband's arm.

'Remember when we first came here?' Jim Jordan's voice was gruff. 'The plans we had. We were gonna build a big spread. Only thing was Dunc Paterson got there first! Then, John was taken an' we couldn't think 'bout nothin' else. Finally the war ... Lance away in the Army, an' Bull as well towards the end. Now, when it don't seem to matter, we've got what we want.'

'But it does matter, Jim.' Ma put a hand on his arm. 'It matters for the kids. It's their chance.'

'Yeah, guess you're right at that. Just hope they can take it. Anyway, time we went in or they'll be wonderin' what's happened.' Slowly, they made their way down the slope to the house.

Chapter 28

Jim Jordan looked up at his youngest son. 'You ain't gonna change your mind then?' He said worriedly. 'You can take Bob an' welcome.' Absentmindedly, he patted Red's neck. Ears back, the big horse snapped at him, long yellow teeth just missing the rancher's sleeve as he jerked his arm clear.

'Damn you, you ornery slabsided mule! Can't think what Bull sees in you.'

John grinned down at his father. 'You forget, Pa, Bull saved him from the Comancheros. He's a one-man horse. He just puts up with me and no more. If I leave him he won't let anybody else ride him, and if you put him in the remuda he'll just raise hell generally.'

The rancher frowned. 'Yeah, you're right. He hates folks, 'cept Bull. An' he ain't keen on other horses. He's a loner alright. Whatever the Comancheros did to him must have been powerful bad, 'cause deep down he's a killer an' don't you ever forget it. Only thing I got in his favour is that he'll outrun an' outstay any horse I've ever seen.' He looked closely at his son. 'Just why does he accept you anyway?'

John shrugged. 'It is hard to say. Alright, I am good with horses. I know that, but so is Jake, and he will have nothing to do with Jake. I think he knows that when Bull is not here he must turn to someone. Maybe he senses we are brothers.'

His father nodded. 'Who knows, mebbe you're right. Anyway, you know what I'm hopin' for. Water at Mustang Springs. If they're dry then we got trouble. Look for a waterhole somewhere. One good thing, last o' this year's trail herds headed north 'bout a month ago. Grass'll have caught up again. See you at the fort. Adios now.'

'John!' Ma bustled through the open doorway.

Surprise showing in his face, John reined Red to a halt.

'You take care now, you hear me.'

'Yes, Ma.' Her son smiled broadly, 'I'll be careful. Adios now.'

They stood together watching Red hit an easy lope up onto the ridge trail. 'Thanks, Mary-Lou.' Jim Jordan squeezed his wife's arm. 'That was right nice of you. I could see he was pleased.'

★   ★   ★   ★

Lance Jordan swayed easily to the loping stride of the big buckskin and grinned to himself. This was the life. Freedom from the restricting regulations of the fort and the eternal spit and polish that went with it. Freedom from the worries of command and responsibility. Of wondering whether or not he had made the right decision, and what would happen to the patrol if he was wrong.

His right hand dropped to his gunbelt and rested on the worn handgrip of the holstered .45. For a moment his thoughts were far away. Long time since I wore them guns. El Paso, 'fore the war, if I remember rightly. Good thing I kept all my old gear. At least I look like a cowhand. He shook his head in wry remembrance. Hell, I was a wild young kid in them days. Guess it's as well the folks don't know half the things I did. Waal, maybe I've made up for some o' them in the past three years. Sure hope so.

He came out of his reverie with a start and breathed deeply. The scent of sage filled his nostrils. Beneath him the buckskin sensed his rider's change of mood and bucked slightly to let him know they were in tune. Lance laughed and nudged the big gelding with his heels. The horse got his head down and went into some serious bucking.

'Damn you, Buck!' The big sergeant swore as he fought to keep his seat. 'Just 'cause I'm in a good mood ain't no reason for you to try your luck.' He dug in his heels again and the horse took off at a dead run.

A quarter of a mile down the trail Lance eased his mount back to a canter. 'Alright, you've had your fun. Now, quit foolin' around and start workin' for your hay.' Buck shook himself with spine-jarring efficiency and settled sedately into a mile-eating lope. Wonder what he'll be like herdin' cows, the sergeant ruminated. Still, he's a smart hoss. Don't reckon it'll take him long to pick it up. Change from patrollin' though.

He ran over McMillan's instructions once again. 'I want a complete report, sergeant,' the tall captain had said sternly. 'The Apaches are filtering down into Texas. It's up to you to assess the size of the problem. Are the local tribes, the Lipans, the Kiowas, and the Comanches involved? If they are, then we may have a major Indian uprising on our hands. On the other hand, it may be that the Apaches are under pressure from the Army, or the

Comanches, and are looking for easier pickings down here. If that is the case then how do the local tribes feel about it? Check discreetly with the ranchers and small communities along the trail, and find out if there is any evidence of increased Indian activity. In short, I want to know everything! However, as I said before, if anything does go wrong you're on your own.' The tall fair-haired sergeant scowled. Some things never changed!

The buckskin pricked his ears and whinneyed deep in his throat. Lance narrowed his eyes and squinted ahead. Rider comin' on a big red roan. Could almost be Red, but the rider ain't Bull. Somethin' about him, if it wasn't for the hat an' the cowhand gear I'd swear he was an Injun. Warily he eased the big .45's in their holsters.   The distance between them closed rapidly. Tall fella, blond hair, rangy build, could be ... it is! 'John! Howdy, boy. You're way off your home range.'

The brothers grinned at each other.

'Howdy, Lance. Pa said you were going to help out on the drive?'

'Waal,' the sergeant shrugged. 'Didn't reckon you would ever make it without me!'

They laughed together. Big Red sidled closer and lunged suddenly at the buckskin, teeth flashing.

'Damn you!' Lance pulled his startled mount out of the way. 'Why've you got Red anyway? He's just like Bull, allus lookin' for trouble.'

John shrugged. 'I can't leave him. He will not work for anyone else and he will not settle in the remuda.'

Lance looked curiously at his brother. 'You sure do understand Red. Guess the Comanches gave you their secrets? Everybody says they're the best when it comes to workin' with horses.'

'The Comanches give you nothing,' John said coldly. 'Everything must be earned. When Ten Bears said I was the best with horses, then it was true.'

Lance flushed and bit his lip. 'Me an' my big mouth. John, I'm real sorry, but you never talk 'bout your time with the Comanches.'

John shrugged. 'Lance, I do not find it easy to talk about it. Ten Bears was very good to me. He treated me like a son. I think like a Comanche, I fight like a Comanche, and I can talk like a Comanche.'

Lance looked at him. 'Why did you come back then?'

His brother paused and stared into the distance. 'I am not sure. I had been on a couple of raids as a horse holder. That's how they break you in as a young brave. Then I got to wondering what I was doing, fighting against whites. That was the winter that Sven and Jake moved in with the tribe. All through the winter, whenever I could, I talked to them. They said I should be with my own people.' He shrugged, 'That's how it happened.'

'Mm. How are the folks?'

'Alright. Pa was goin' into Greenhills to see if he could pick up some more hands.'

'How about Ma?'

John frowned. 'It's strange, but since she came back from Arizona she's been different. Quieter and a lot easier to get along with.'

Lance nodded. 'Yeah, I noticed a change in her. Anyways, what brings you over this way?'

'Pa wants me to scout the Goodnight trail from Fort Concho to Horsehead Crossing. He's worried about water.'

'Don't blame him. Still, you might be lucky at Mustang Springs. You comin' all the way back?'

His brother shook his head. 'Pa says to wait at the fort.'

'Don't get into no trouble there. Waal, be seein' you.'

'Adios.' John eased Red into his stride.

☆   ☆   ☆   ☆

'So, you're lookin' for a place with a trail herd?' Jim Jordan scowled thoughtfully at the small youngster standing in front of him. Just a kid, thin an' hungry lookin'. Levis worn an' patched, boots rundown at the heels. Still, he's keen an' that's somethin'. 'You got any experience?' he asked suddenly.

'No, Mister Jordan, though I'm good wi' horses.'

'Where you from, son?'

'Down towards Austin. M'folks got a homestead down there, an' Pa does a little freightin' as well. I'm right good wi' a team.'

'Waal now, I might just take you up on that. What's your name?'

'Allen ... Rafe Allen.'

'What brung you up here?'

'Well, there's six of us at home, an' Pa said there wasn't no way he could keep us all. I'd allus wanted to be a cowhand, so he gave me a horse an' told me to try my luck up north. Only thing is, all the trail herds have gone. I'd just about give up when Miz MaCrae said you was lookin' for hands.'

'Alright, you're hired. Where's your horse?'

'He's picketed back o' Miz MaCrae's place. She said it was alright, an' I ain't got money for the livery stable.'

'Right, saddle up an' meet me here in an hour.'

He watched the small figure hurry away and turned to find Hannah MaCrae regarding him quizzically. 'What you trying to do to me, Hannah? He's only a kid.'

'Jim,' the big woman put a hand on his shoulder. 'We all got to start somewhere, an' he's keen.'

The rancher shrugged. 'Waal, that's somethin' I suppose. Got anybody else?'

'Coupla other fellas saw the notice I put in my window. You'll find them down at Nathan McGraw's livery stable.'

'Any good?'

The widow pursed her lips. 'Gettin' kinda long in the tooth. But then, ain't we all? Clean and polite though.'

'That'll be just fine if the herd starts to mill in the middle o' the Brazos!' He saw Hannah scowl. 'Alright, I'm sorry. It's just that I ain't so young myself. Oh, an' thanks. Don't know what you said to Mary-Lou but thanks anyway. It sure has made a difference.'

'It weren't nothin', Jim. Reckon she was ready to talk to somebody an' I just happened to be handy.'

'Lucky for me you were. Anyways, I'll head down to the livery stable an' check out them fellas. Be seein' you.'

Hannah watched him bow-legging across the street. Jim Jordan, you're gettin' old an' cranky. Still, can't say as it's all that surprisin'. Livin' with Mary-Lou must be hell! Glad things are better now. Sighing, she made her way indoors.

★   ★   ★   ★

'Fellas, Miz MaCrae tells me you're lookin' for an outfit to sign up with?'

'That's right, mister. I'm Mike Glenwood, an' this here's Andy Boone.' The two elderly cowhands looked at him anxiously. Glenwood, lean and stoop shouldered, sported a mustache. Boone was stocky and clean-shaven.

'Jim Jordan, Circle J.' They shook hands. 'What spreads you been ridin' for?'

They looked at each other nervously. Finally Mike spoke. 'Mister, you look like a straight shooter, so I'll give it you straight. 'Fore the war we had a homestead in Louisiana. Nice little place an' it suited us just fine. Then the war came. Our stock was run off an' then the homestead was burned. Somebody torched it one night. So we sold up an' moved down to Texas. Ended up with a little spread just north o' Laredo. Fella who sold it let us have it cheap. 'Course he didn't tell us he'd been havin' trouble with this big outfit, the Turkey Track. Waal, you can guess what happened!'

'They run you off?' Jim guessed.

'Not right away. They gave us a year. Hell, it suited them just fine. We was diggin' beef out o' the brakes, an' they let us build up a nice little herd 'fore they moved in. Said we was rustlers an' that we'd used our JA Connected iron to blot their Turkey Track brand.'

'An' had you?' Jim Jordan queried quietly.

'No sir! Nuthin' like that. Cattle down in the brakes, they been breedin' there all through the war. Most o' them ain't got no brands on 'em.'

'So what happened?'

'Waal, the boss man, name of Arnie McCall, he said we had a choice. Said we could sign over the herd and the spread to him, or we could hang as rustlers. Mister, you ain't long in makin' up your mind when you see a noose danglin' from a branch in front of you! So he wrote out a bill of sale an' we signed. McCall reckoned he was a fair man, he'd give us a hundred dollars, and he did too.'

Mike dug into his vest pocket and brought out a piece of paper which he passed to the rancher.

Jim Jordan read slowly. 'Sale of land and stock comprising the JA Connected Ranch, for $100.' He looked up. 'Them your signatures?'

They nodded shamefacedly.

'Sure makes it legal. So what did you do?'

Andy Boone flushed. 'Mister, we ain't gunnies an' we ain't heroes. We got on our horses an' lit out. Better that than swingin' from a tree, I reckon.'

Jordan sighed. 'Guess you didn't have much choice at that. Some day this country'll be law abidin', but not yet awhile. So, are you ready to ride for me?'

Their faces lit up. 'Mister,' Andy said hesitantly, 'I didn't think you'd want us after what you just heard.'

The rancher grinned. 'Ain't sure but what I wouldn't have done the same. A noose sure does help to make your mind up right quick. Anyways, saddle up, we're ridin'.' He paused for a moment. 'I'm lookin' for another fella. You know anybody?'

The two old cowhands looked at each other. 'Waal,' Mike said slowly, 'there's an' old Mex fella bunkin' here. He's lookin' for an outfit. That's his mule in the second stall there. 'Course, he ain't no cowhand. He was a mule skinner down Sonora way.'

'Was he now? Just might be I got a job for him. You know where he is?'

'Yeah, he's sleepin' back there.' Mike raised his voice, 'Miguel, fella here'd like a word with you.'

There was a long pause, then … 'I hear you, Senor Mike.' A couple of minutes passed and a small stout Mexican appeared from the depths of the stable, rubbing his eyes.

'Miguel, meet Mister Jordan, he'd like to talk to you. Boss, this here's Miguel Jerez.'

'Buenos dias, Senor Jordan. I am sorry to be sleeping when you call, but there is no work.'

Jim looked at the small roly-poly figure, straw still entangled in his hair. Sure am scrapin' the barrel now. Aloud he said, 'Mike here tells me you're a teamster?'

'Si senor. That is true. Mules, oxen, horses, I have handled them all. I, Miguel Jerez, am the best teamster in the whole South-West.'

'Mm.' The rancher gnawed his lower lip dubiously. 'I'm lookin' for a man to drive a wagon to Arizona. Pay's thirty a month an' found. Ain't gonna be easy.'

'Senor.' The small Mexican drew himself up proudly. 'It will not be easy, but I will do it. I, Miguel Jerez, am the best ... '

'Yeah, sure.' Jim Jordan cut in swiftly. 'Now, if you'll just saddle your mule, we'll be on our way.'

'At once, senor.' He slapped the big mule on its hindquarters. 'Come, Pancho. We have work to do.'

Jim Jordan looked at his four new handst and shuddered inwardly. A youngster who ain't hardly dry behind the ears yet, a Mex who don't look as though he'd amount to a row o' beans, an' a coupla old cowhands who look as though they're past it. What the hell, you got some nerve thinkin' like that. You ain't no spring chicken yourself! 'All set?'

They nodded nervously.

'Right, let's go.'

✯   ✯   ✯   ✯

Red blew through his nostrils and champed at the bit, as John studied the trail ahead. Satisfied, the young rider urged his mount forward and swept the surrounding country with a cautious eye. Ain't seen no Injun sign as yet. Should make the Leon soon.

He looked at the sky. Midday, sun overhead, not a cloud anywhere. No chance o' rain an' the rivers are low. Sure hope things change by the time we come through with the stock. Still, grazin's fair. Pa says the crews that made this trail reckoned there weren't no springs from Fort Concho to the Pecos. Just the ponds at Mustang Springs, and in the summer they're dry more often than not. Them breedin' stock won't like it if they can't get water. Well, Pa said this was my job so I'd better do it right. Every sense alert, John Jordan headed west.

Chapter 29

'You think we'll be ready in time, Pa?' Mary-Lou Jordan looked searchingly at her husband. 'Ain't but one more week left.'

'Sure, we'll be ready.' Jim paused in the act of nailing down a box lid. 'Ben Turner's got the makin's of a right good carpenter an' old Miguel ain't no slouch either.'

Ma raised her eyebrows.

'Yeah, I know he ain't much to look at but he's doin' alright. An' he's got them Clevelands eatin' out o' his hand. Ellie-May an' young Rafe have got the remuda gathered, an' Ellie-May's been practisin' leadin' big Dance on a halter. If you remember, when he was a yearlin' he caught that colic. It was Ellie-May that took care o' him, an' she used to walk him on a leadin' rein an' a halter when he was gettin' better. Waal, he ain't forgotten. She reckons if she can get the remuda to follow him it'll make things a lot easier.'

Ma nodded approvingly. 'That's smart thinkin'.'

'Yeah. Her an' young Rafe are hittin' it off right good. 'Course, she bosses him, but he don't seem to mind.

'Lance an' the two old boys, took the calves over to the Triple X this mornin'. Reckon it'll be late 'fore they're back.'

'Mm.' Ma paused in the act of wrapping a plate and frowned worriedly. 'I'll be glad when there's some space between Jud an' Lance. Them two can't abide each other. Anyway,' she concluded acidly, 'I reckoned for sure you'd send Jake. How come you didn't?'

'Damn!' Jim Jordan swore and dropped his hammer. Startled, Ma looked up. It was unheard of for her husband to swear around wimmenfolk.

'Mary-Lou, would you quit needlin' me 'bout Jake.' He sucked at his injured thumb. 'He's gonna be segundo on the drive, an' that means he's got a sight more to worry about than two-three hundred calves. Lance is rusty when it comes to cow work. This is a good chance to break'm in. 'Sides,' he picked up the hammer, 'he's a grown man, and a cavalry sergeant to boot. An' lemme tell you somethin' else. If it ever comes to a showdown 'tween him an' Jud, which God forbid; I'm bettin' he'd be the one to walk away. Right now,' he drove the last nail home with quite unnecessary force, 'I'm more concerned 'bout John findin' water at Mustang Springs.'

Ma finished wrapping her best china and looked at him again. 'What'll happen if there ain't no water there?'

'Waal, it means we drive right through. It'll be rough on the stock an' we might lose a whole lot o' them, but there ain't no other way.'

☆   ☆   ☆   ☆

The calves were skittish, uneasy about the sudden loss of their mothers, and bawling plaintively as the three riders eased them across the flats towards the ranch buildings. Lance Jordan's mount deftly blocked an inquisitive youngster, and, unbidden, lifted into a canter to turn another independently minded individual back into the herd. The big sergeant grinned to himself. Herdin' cows is just like soldierin'. Once you got the hang of it you don't ever forget. Seems like I ain't never been away. 'Course, old Blue knows all the moves. Reckon he could do the job on his own.

The distance was closing fast now and the figures at the corrals were becoming recognizable. No sign o' Dunc. There's Jud though. Damn him, that's one guy I got no time for. He turned the leaders neatly through the open gate, with Andy and Mike pushing hard at the laggards. There was a moment's hesitation, then the mass of bawling calves jostled their way through the opening and they were in.

Lance swung down and stretched himself.

Jud Moore's tall, black clad figure detached itself from the group of Triple X hands and came towards him.

'You findin' cow work a mite hard?' the foreman sneered. 'Good thing you ain't workin' for a real spread. The Circle J's only a two-bit outfit. An' how come you ain't hidin' behind that fancy uniform again?'

'Well now,' Lance grinned tightly. 'Seems like you don't know everything, Jud. I'm on furlough, though I can't see what business it is o' yours. An' the Circle J brand maybe ain't that much, but it sure is a helluva lot better than GTT!'

Moore's face darkened and his eyes narrowed. 'What the hell d'you mean by that?' He eased sideways, away from the corral rails; hands poised claw-like above the ivory grips of his twin Colts.

The big sergeant felt the familiar surge of excitement coursing through his body. It never leaves you, he thought soberly. The same old gunfighter's thrill. He dropped into a slight crouch and set himself.

'You know what I mean, Jud. That's what Sheriff Campbell's got marked against your name back there in Jonesville, ain't it? So Marshall Kilgore said. An' he reckons Sam Easterby's brothers would surely like to know where you're holed up. Guess they feel like evenin' the score some!' Menace hung in the air for a fleeting second.

'Hold it!' Dunc Paterson's stentorian bellow split the silence. The burly rancher came down the ranch house steps on the run. 'That's enough, you damned pair o' roosters. What in hell's got into you both? This here's a business deal and nothin' else.'

'Sorry, Mister Paterson.' Lance relaxed and took a deep breath. Man that was close. Better humour the big fella. 'My fault, I guess. How was I to know Jud wouldn't take kindly to bein' joshed some!'

Paterson rounded on his silent foreman. 'What made you get fired up all of a sudden, Jud? 'Tain't like you at all.'

Moore shrugged, fury still flickering in his cold eyes. 'Guess I don't like bein' hoorawed,' he muttered.

Dunc frowned heavily. 'So it seems. Anyways, this deal means a lot to me, so you two cool it, you hear me?' Lance nodded, and there was a muttered assent from Jud.

'Right.' Paterson switched his attention to the corralled calves. 'They look real good. Allus said your pa knew stock. Two hundred and eighty-nine as agreed?'

'Yeah. We got two late calvers, but two sets o' twins balanced them. Guess we'll have to drop them late calves off along the way.' Out of the corner of his eye he saw Jud make his way across to where Mike and Andy waited anxiously.

The rancher nodded. 'Happens,' he said abruptly. His voice lifted in a shout and he beckoned to his foreman. 'Jud! We'll leave them in the corral for a day, then we'll turn them loose along the valley flats. Right now I want you to go see ... ' he glanced back at Lance and dropped his voice as he and Moore walked towards the ranch house.

The big sergeant frowned. So that's what it's like to be a big-time cattleman. Bull's welcome to it. Me, I like a little fun in m'life. Mounting, he jogged across to where the two old cowhands waited nervously. 'All set?'

They nodded. 'That foreman fella, Jud. Mean cuss ain't he?' Mike said uneasily.

'Yeah.' There was a faraway look in Lance's eyes. 'Jud is bad clean through. Don't ever forget it.'

The two old-timers looked at each other. 'We ain't likely to,' Andy Boone said slowly. 'Didn't seem to bother you none though.'

There was a long silence.

'I didn't mean ... '

'I know you didn't. Alright, I'll level with you. This is between the three of us. 'Fore the war I was a wild young kid. Couldn't settle; allus in trouble. Come to a showdown with Pa in the end. That's when I tore loose an' drifted west. Fetched up in El Paso. Guess I musta been there 'bout a couple o' years. Some o' the things I did ... ' he shook his head, regret mirrored on his strong features. 'Let's just say I ain't proud o' them. Then I found I was a natural when it come to gunplay. Some guys have it; most don't. Mebbe they're the lucky ones. Anyways, there I was with a rep as a flash young gunnie, when the war came along.'

Silence again, then Lance laughed, a short, bitter laugh. 'I was all set to be a general; couldn't wait to get in. 'Course, nobody told me what battles was like. Fellas blown to pieces; good horses wi' their guts hangin' out.' He shook his head, as if to clear away the memories. 'Funny thing was I liked soldierin'. Stayed on after the war. Even made it to sergeant. Back in El Paso they'd forgotten about 'Ace' Jordan, an' I figgered that was for the best.' There was a roughness in his voice and he paused for a moment before continuing. 'Like I said, this is between us three. I wouldn't want my folks to know ... ever.'

Mike and Andy nodded wordlessly. Side by side, each deep in thought, the three riders headed for the Circle J.

✯   ✯   ✯   ✯

Night had fallen by the time they got back. A cool breeze was blowing from the creek, and a crescent moon shone fitfully through the drifting clouds. The ranch was in darkness, though the loom of the buildings showed occasionally in the intermittent moonlight. They stopped to let their mounts drink at the long trough, the ponies sucking greedily at the cool water.

The kitchen door opened a fraction. Moonlight glinted fleetingly on the dull sheen of a rifle barrel.

'That you, Lance?'

Startled, Lance grinned to himself. The old fox! Never reckoned he could be so tricky. Just goes to show.

'Yeah.'

'Ma's left grub an' a pot o' coffee on the stove. See you in the mornin'.'

The others were already in the stable, and Mike had lit the hurricane lamp. It threw flickering shadows on the walls as Lance led the tired Blue into a stall. Working quickly, they stripped the gear from their mounts and rubbed them down.

Lance picked up a bucket. 'We'll grain 'em, then get somethin' to eat ourselves. After that, you fellas go get some shuteye. I'll come back an' turn 'em into the corral.'

★   ★   ★   ★

They ate ravenously until they had taken the edge off their hunger. Over a second cup of coffee Andy Boone looked speculatively at Lance. 'This fella Henderson, across the creek. Him that owns the Rockin' H outfit. He an alright guy?'

The big sergeant took a swig at his steaming cup. 'One o' the best. Him an' Pa go way back.' He paused. 'Why d'you ask?'

Boone frowned. 'Nothin' likely ... 'cept that Jud fella was askin' an awful lot o' questions 'bout him. Like, did we see much of him. Did them two old riders o' his allus go into Crockett at weekends. That kinda thing.'

Lance drained the last of his coffee. 'They do too, every Saturday in life. Cliff now; he likes to sit at home wi' a bottle o' corn licker.' He paused, frowning. 'Queer though. Jud ain't one for socialisin'. Still, mebbe he's tryin' to show Dunc he ain't all bad. Anyways, I'll go see to them broncs. You fellas hit the sack.'

The sky had cleared now, and the moon was riding high. Swinging the big gate open, Lance turned Andy and Mike's mounts into the corral. Got to hand it to the old man, he thought admiringly. Any other spread you'd be wrestlin' wi' slip rails. Damned unhandy things. Not here though. Pa believes in timber and hinges. Gotta go along wi' him. They make life a helluva lot easier.

He made his way back to the stable, mulling over Andy Boone's remarks. Why would Jud be interested in Cliff Henderson? Unless ... unless Dunc is leanin' on Cliff to try an' make'm sell. The night seemed to chill suddenly.

That's it ... that's what Dunc was talkin' about when he said to Jud, 'I want you to go see ... ' He's sicced Jud onto Cliff to push'm hard. Trouble is, Jud don't know when to stop. An' this is Saturday night. Old Cliff's on his own across there, an' he'll be hittin' the booze.

Reckon I'd best check out m'hunch.

The tired cowpony flicked its ears inquiringly at feel of the blanket, then hunched instinctively as the saddle landed on its back. 'Sorry, Blue.' Lance was busy with the cinches. 'I ain't got time to rope another pony. An' I don't want the folks knowin' 'bout this anyway.'

The Rocking H; about three thousand acres all told, was located in a heavily wooded valley, some six miles east of the Circle J. Lance knew his father didn't like the location. 'Don't make sense,' Pa had said to Cliff more than once. 'You're just askin' to be hit by Injuns. All that timber and scrub. They'll be on you 'fore you know it.' But Henderson had disagreed. And surprisingly, down the years his luck had held.

A hundred yards to go. Lance dismounted and tied Blue to a convenient bush. A horse whinneyed softly from the brush. The sound filled Lance with foreboding as he padded across the dusty yard towards the partially open door.

Light showed dimly through the kitchen window, and he could hear voices raised in anger. He had one foot on the porch when gunfire erupted in the room.

Stealthily, Colt at the ready, he eased through the door. The acrid smell of gunsmoke stung his nostrils. His night vision adjusted to the dim light.

Jud Moore, gun in hand, was stooped over the prone form of Cliff Henderson.

A cold killing rage shook Lance. 'Drop that shooter now, an' raise your hands 'fore I drill you.'

There was a tense pause, then the ivory handled .45 thudded to the floor. Slowly, Jud Moore raised his hands.

'Turn around ... easy now. I'd as lief kill you as not.'

The foreman revolved carefully on his heels. 'Hell, if it ain't the soldier boy,' he sneered. 'What you want to come bustin' in here for anyways? Me an' Henderson had words an' he went for his gun. That's the long an' short o' it.'

Lance took a deep breath. Easy now, don't let this lobo get to you. An icy calm gripped him.

'You lyin' son of a bitch!' he said coldly. 'Old Cliff weren't no gunnie. Reckon you needled him till he got mad. Likely he was just lickered up enough to go for his gun, 'cause he wouldn't ha' done it no other way. Now I got to take you in an' I guess I'll be wastin' m'time. Dunc'll square the jury an' you'll walk, more's the pity.'

'Got it all figgered out, ain'tcha,' Moore sneered. 'Like I said t'other day, two-bit outfits don't amount to nothin'. You gotta have muscle. Seems to me, Ace, you'd best let me go!'

Lance froze suddenly. 'What did you call me?' he said carefully.

'Ace.' Jud's confidence was growing. 'Ace Jordan! Ain't that what they useta call you in El Paso when you hung out there?' Emboldened by Lance's silence he went on; 'Was out that way m'self awhile back an' run into a fella that remembers you. Accordin' to him you was right handy wi' them shootin' irons. Then he said Ace Jordan took off to the war, an' that was the last anybody in the Pas heard o' him. 'Course, it was only when he said Ace had kin in this neck o' the woods, that I kinda put two an' two together. Anyways, I guess I hit the jackpot.' He paused and looked challengingly at Lance.

The big sergeant gritted his teeth. 'An' you reckon this changes things?'

'Why, yeah.' Moore affected surprise. 'You surely don't want your folks hearin' that their fine upstandin' soldier boy useta be two-gun Ace Jordan. Don't think the Army would take too kindly to it either. An' that little whore you was shacked up with. Your old ma ain't gonna like that one bit.'

'Shut up!' Blind unreasoning rage gripped the sergeant. Just for a second his finger tightened on the trigger, then slowly, very slowly, he got himself under control. Suddenly the solution was there in his mind. He surveyed it dispassionately. It was the only way.

Moore watched him carefully, alert for the slightest slip, the sneer evident on his dark saturnine features.

'Alright, Jud.' The voice was suddenly, dangerously, quiet. 'Like you say, I was Ace Jordan. An' yeah, I rode wi' the wild bunch. Now, just bend down real slow an' pick up that shooter. Don't make no wrong moves, just finger an' thumb. Now, drop it into your holster, real easy now. There you go. We're all set.'

Uneasiness flared in Moore's eyes. 'What're you aimin' to do?' he queried suddenly.

'Well now.' There was a steely edge to the quiet tones. 'That kinda depends on you. Ever since we first met you been spoilin' for a showdown. Now you got it. I'll count to three an' you can draw in that time. You don't draw I'll kill you anyway. Only one of us walks away. Seems a fair deal t'me.'

Jud frowned. 'Don't see no need for this,' he said slowly. 'You're headin' for Arizona an' I'm stayin' here. We just walk away an' forget it ever happened. Likely we'd never meet again.'

'You're yella, Jud.' Lance said coldly. 'You got a yella streak a mile wide. Reckon you're startin' to wonder if all them stories 'bout Ace Jordan are true. Makin' you sweat, is it? Anyways, it makes no difference. Step back a piece.' He watched tensely as Moore eased himself back to the other side of the room.

'Now,' he holstered the big .45. 'I'll start countin'. When you're ready, make your play.' Hands hovering above the holstered Colts, he set himself and began to count.

'One, two ...' Moore's eyes flickered and they went for their guns together in a flurry of lamp-lit action. Moving with eye-baffling speed, Lance drew and shot in a blur of co-ordinated movement. The big .45 slugs punched Jud against the room wall, his guns still only half-drawn. Slowly, tiredly, he slid to the floor and sprawled there, like a discarded rag doll. There was the faintest sound, as if a candle was guttering in the wind, then silence.

Cautiously, Lance approached Moore's body and prodded it with his foot. Nothing. Face set, he checked carefully. Mhm; twice, dead centre. Looks like I still got the touch. He turned to where Henderson lay. Damn you, Jud. He never even got his gun out. Likely you just up an' killed him outa pure cussedness. Anger flared again within him. An' Dunc, you ain't no better, turnin' this lobo loose.

The implications of his actions jostled in Lance's mind. Hell, what a mess. Damn it, why do I allus go off at half-cock. This could queer Pa's deal wi' Dunc. Then there's the Army. His mouth twisted wryly. They don't take kindly to us shootin' civilians. They'd bust me for sure. Guess I could even finish up doin' time. Anyways, this is Dunc's territory. Ain't no jury round here gonna let me go free. Nah, gotta think o' somethin'.

The germ of an idea grew. Maybe, just maybe, it's possible. Quickly he checked the dead men's guns. Both .45s, thank the Lord. Cliff's gun ain't been fired. Got to fix that. The scenario took shape.

Jud comes through the door; he arranged the body accordingly. Cliff has his gun already out; mebbe he heard somethin'. They shoot together an' kill each other. Waal, it's possible. Now, the only other thing I got to do is fix them shooters. Jud fired two rounds at Cliff, and, his mouth quirked wryly, none at me. Reckon I can leave his iron as it is. Working quickly, he removed the ivory handled Colt and placed the weapon in the foreman's outstretched hand. Its twin he jammed back into the holster.

Reaching for the old rancher's gun, he extracted an unfired round before turning the cylinder to the next load. Stepping outside he listened carefully for a moment. Nothin'. Guess if folks ain't heard the ruckus by now they never will! He was suddenly aware of a dark object hanging from the porch rail. Hey, that's an old saddle blanket! Carefully wrapping it round the gun in his hand, he pointed the weapon at the night sky and squeezed the trigger. Heavily muffled, the sound carried no distance and he nodded, satisfied. Ain't nobody gonna find that slug. Better take the blanket wi' me. Likely there's powder burns on it.

Placing the old Colt in the rancher's calloused palm he swept the scene with a critical eye. 'Tain't perfect, but it might just pass. About to blow out the lamp, he stopped suddenly. Nah, gotta leave it burnin' or they'll know somebody was here for sure. Adios, Cliff. You were an alright guy. Jud, I killed you an' mebbe I should be sorry, but I ain't. You've had it comin' for a long time.

Quietly, carrying the old saddle blanket, he made his way back to Blue. Deep in the brush the unknown horse whinneyed softly again. You'll be alright till mornin', fella. Reckon you're Jud's mount an' he stashed you there. Untying the old cowpony, he eased into the saddle and headed for home.

* * * *

Jake Larsen woke suddenly and lay listening. Something had disturbed him. Silently he slipped out of bed and peered through the window. Somebody was turning a horse into the corral. The tall figure closed the gate and made its way back to the stable. In a few minutes it reappeared and headed for the house. Closer now, the moonlight shone fully on the strong features of Lance Jordan.

Jake relaxed. So old Lance is on the prowl, is he? He grinned suddenly. Mebbe he's got a gal stashed somewhere and don't want the folks to know. Well; he climbed into bed; he's an alright guy an' it ain't none o' my business. I got this drive to think about. Turning over on his side, the young half-breed was soon fast asleep.

* * * *

Lance lit the kitchen lamp and drew his gun. Working carefully, he removed all trace of firing and loaded two fresh rounds. Then, returning the cleaning equipment to its cupboard, he checked the room. Yeah, looks alright, Nothin' for Ma to notice.

Gently blowing out the light, he padded down the passage to his bedroom. Undressing, he slipped into bed, but sleep did not come easily. Wonder what Bull would have made o' this? Likely it wouldn't have bothered him. Hell, he's killed enough fellas on his bounty hunts. Funny, this useta be his room. Now he's in Arizona an' I'm here. Still musing, he eventually drifted off to sleep.

Chapter 30

Sunday was a day of rest at the Circle J. Way back, when they first moved in, Mary-Lou had decreed this and her husband had gone along with it. Only on one point had Jim Jordan dug in his heels. He'd insisted that, once they were old enough, the family had the right to decide for themselves. So, morning chores completed, the family went their various ways.

In the living room, Ma read aloud from the big family bible, while Pa, and anyone else who wanted to, sat around and listened. Strangely enough, of all the family, only John and Jake had joined in on a regular basis. This put Ma in a quandary. It pleased her to see them there, but at the same time it was galling to hear that Injun, as she privately referred to Jake, discussing the Old Testament knowledgeably with her husband.

Of late however, things had been different. Mary-Lou now had a captive audience. Ben Turner, Andy Boone, Mike Glenwood, Miguel Jerez, Rafe Allen, Sara-Jane and the two little Johnson girls, all attended. Ben, Andy and Mike, because they genuinely wanted to. Miguel because he had a tremendous regard for the Senora Jordan. And Rafe because he was too scared of Ma to do anything else!

Sara-Jane, who had rebelled and opted out the previous year, was back because the Johnson girls, Sarah and Mary, had asked her go with them.

Lance, who in his younger days used to sneak off whenever he got the chance, was cleaning a bridle in the stable and listening intently for the first sound of approaching hoof-beats.

Down in the barn, the monotonous thud of metal striking wood indicated that Ellie-May was practising knife throwing; a skill she intended to hone to perfection.

From the corral, old Blue, ears pricked, looked towards the creek and whinneyed a welcome. The faint sound of a running horse increased rapidly. Peering from the stable door, Lance felt his stomach muscles contract. Any time now.

Caleb Stone, one of the two veteran Rocking H riders, swept around the corner of the barn and pulled his lathered mount to a halt beside the porch. Dismounting stiffly, he hammered on the door. It was opened by Pa, with the others crowding behind him.

Time to take a hand. Lance ran towards the ranch house, registering as he did so Ellie-May's startled face in the barn doorway.

' ... both o' them stone dead.' Caleb was saying shakily. 'Never seen nothin' like it.'

'What's happened?' Lance eased his way onto the porch.

Pa turned. 'Cliff an' Jud Moore, both dead. Caleb and Chas found them this mornin', when they went across to the house.'

Ma hustled the wild-eyed old cowhand into the kitchen, the others crowding close behind.

'Pa,' Mary-Lou eased Caleb into a chair, 'get'm a drink. Somethin' strong,' she added darkly.

Nodding, her husband reached into a cupboard, and producing a bottle and glass, poured a stiff shot of Old Crow, which he set in front of Stone.

'Lance.' He motioned to his eldest son, while Caleb downed the fiery liquor. 'Hightail it into Crockett an' get Sheriff Lane. Accordin' to Caleb, it looks as though Cliff and Jud shot each other, but we don't know no more than that.'

'Sure, Pa.'

'Jake.'

'Yeah.'

'Light out for the Triple X an' tell Dunc the same.' Jake nodded silently. He and Lance ran from the room. 'Miguel.'

'Si, Senor Jordan.'

'Hitch up old Dusty and Paint to the buckboard. I'll go see what's happened across there. Mike,' he turned to Glenwood, 'you an' Andy come in late wi' Lance. See anythin' on the trail?'

Mike shook his head. 'Nary a thing.' He reflected for a moment. 'Tell you somethin' though. Moore was askin' an awful lot o' questions 'bout Henderson when we was at the Triple X. Ain't that so, Andy?'

His partner nodded. 'Sure was. 'Member mentionin' it to Lance when we was havin' our grub in here last night. He reckoned maybe Jud was just tryin' to show Mister Paterson that he had a good side!'

Jim Jordan frowned. 'Don't sound like Jud, no way. Still ... .' The buckboard rattled to a stop outside. He raised his voice. 'Folks, we'll play it cool until the sheriff an' Dunc get here. We don't know for sure what happened, an' maybe we never will. Right, Caleb. If you're ready, let's go.'

The old cowhand rose silently and followed him through the door.

✦   ✦   ✦   ✦

'Dunno what Mister Paterson's gonna say 'bout this,' Sheriff Lane said worriedly. They were halfway between Crockett and the Rocking H, and riding hard. 'He set an awful lotta store by Jud.'

Lance nodded. An' if he hadn't made that killer lobo his foreman, I wouldn't be in this mess now, he thought sourly.

'As I recollect,' the thin, sandy-haired sheriff twisted in his saddle and squinted at Lance, his close-set blue eyes narrowed in sudden concentration, 'you an' Moore never did hit it off, did you?'

The big sergeant shrugged. 'That's true. But then, you could say that 'bout most o' the fellas round here.'

Lane grunted non-committally.

✦   ✦   ✦   ✦

His father and the two old riders were waiting at the Rocking H. 'Howdy, Steve. We found Jud's mount in the brush an' brung'm in.' He led the way into the kitchen. 'Nothin's been touched.'

Lane sucked in his breath at the scene. 'Who'd have thought old Henderson could take Jud.'

Jim Jordan frowned. "Pears like you didn't know Cliff all that well. Him an' me go way back.' He looked down at the dead rancher. 'He was a ranger in the old days. Right handy wi' a shootin' iron, Cliff was. Could've had a lot o' notches on that old gun, if he'd been so minded. An' he was cagey too. Anybody that figgered he could sneak up on Cliff was liable to stop lead.'

There was the sound of a hard-ridden horse, and Dunc Paterson pulled his lathered mount to a halt in the yard. Dismounting hurriedly, the burly rancher shouldered his way through the door. His normally florid features changed colour visibly when he saw the bodies.

'Howdy, Dunc. This is a bad business.'

Lance glanced at his father. Jim Jordan's face was grave. What in hell's got into the old man. I know him. He's puttin' on an act. But why?

'Howdy Jim ... Steve.' Paterson was still shaken.

'Was just sayin' to Sheriff Lane; folks round here didn't know it, but old Cliff was a hellion from way back. Reckon you'll be wantin' to look at them guns, sheriff?'

'What ... oh sure, sure.' Hastily Lane examined both revolvers. 'Mm, mhm. Two rounds fired from each gun.'

'That so.' Pa was on his knees beside his friend's body. 'Cliff took two slugs dead centre. How about Jud?'

'The same.' Paterson rose slowly. 'Never knew Henderson was a gunnie.'

Steve Lane coughed nervously. 'Looks like Jud didn't know it either, Mister Paterson.'

The big rancher nodded absently. There was a faraway look in his eyes.

Jim Jordan climbed stiffly to his feet. 'I guess Sheriff Lane's right, Dunc. Seems like another o' them open an' shut cases to me. Still, mebbe Caleb an' Chas can tell us somethin'.'

The two old hands shuffled their feet in embarrassment. 'Ain't much to tell,' Caleb Stone said awkwardly. 'Chas an' me went into Crockett as usual.' He squinted at Paterson. 'You got some real nice fellas in your crew, Mister Paterson. They was buyin' us drinks all night.'

'Were they now?' Jim Jordan nodded slowly. 'That was real nice o' them. An' then what happened?'

'Nothin'. Can't remember gettin' back. Can't remember anythin' much until mornin'. Then I come across an' found 'em.' He shrugged helplessly. 'He was an alright guy, Cliff Henderson.'

Jim Jordan nodded sombrely. 'Yeah, he surely was. Well now, Dunc.' He turned to Paterson. 'You know any reason why Jud should be callin' on Cliff?'

'Uh ... oh no, no,' the big rancher said hastily. "Course, Jud never talked much about any personal business. Likely it was just somethin' that got outa hand. Reckon we'll never know. Like you said, an open an' shut case. Ain't that so, Steve?'

Sheriff Lane nodded vigorously. 'Sure is, Mister Paterson. Open an' shut. Guess we can leave it at that.'

'Lance!' His father voice was suddenly authoritative. 'Take the buckboard and go fetch Ma. She can lay Cliff out decent. Boys here'll give her a hand. Dunc, reckon you'll want to take Jud back with you. Him bein' your foreman an' all.'

Paterson nodded, still looking bemused.

'Right,' Jim Jordan said incisively. He looked at his eldest son. 'Tell Miguel to bring the new wagon over. Then he can go wi' Dunc an' bring it back after. Sheriff, reckon you'll want signed statements from all of us for Judge Smith? Sorta tie things up like.'

'Uh ... oh yeah, sure.'

'Reckon that's it then. Me, I'll go sit on the porch awhile. Cliff was an old friend.'

★ ★ ★ ★

Sunday evening. Shadows were beginning to stretch across the range. Jim Jordan leaned on the big corral gate and rolled a cigarette. The new wagon rattled into the yard, but he did not turn his head. Kids, he thought reflectively as he lit up. You struggle to bring 'em up right, an' when they're full grown you hope you've done a good job. Then, just when you think you've got it made, they up an' do somethin' that scares you all to hell. Shrugging, he broke the spent match between his fingers and flicked it into the air.

Footsteps behind him. His eldest son joined him at the gate. 'Hi, Lance. You all finished, boy?'

'Yeah, Pa. Ma's got Cliff laid out real nice, an' the two old boys are sittin' with'm. Miguel just come in wi' the wagon.'

'He made good time.'

'Yeah ... well, he had Buck an' Star.'

'Uh-huh.' Pa blew a long streamer of smoke. 'Them Clevelands are the best team in this part o' Texas. You know, Lance, life's funny.' He pointed to the old cowpony, watching them from the corral. 'Take old Blue there. I've had'm since he was a colt. I broke him m'self. I trained him. He's the best damn pony I ever had. He can do 'most anything, bar talk. Say,' a thought seemed to strike him, 'mebbe he can talk! Let's see.'

Lance gritted his teeth. Something was wrong here. Ain't never seen Pa like this.

'Here, Blue.' His father unhooked the gate and eased through. 'Easy, boy. Ain't nobody gonna slap a rope on you. Easy now.' The pony minced forward suspiciously and blew through his nostrils.

Patting the glossy neck, the rancher stooped and lifted the animal's near fore hoof. For a long moment his fingers probed the metal shoe, then, lowering the hoof, he straightened his back. Absently he rubbed Blue's ears, before turning and walking back to the gate.

'Alright, Pa,' Lance said slowly. 'What in hell are you leadin' up to?'

His father stood for a moment deep in thought, then ... 'I shoed Blue m'self, three days ago. Run outa nails too!' He laughed suddenly. 'What kinda rancher let's hisself run outa horseshoe nails. Just one was all I needed. Then I remembered them special nails I brought from Missouri. They got stud heads. We used 'em to shoe mules back there. Helped them to get a better grip when they was ploughin'. Didn't think I'd ever use 'em out here, but what the hell. I figgered one wouldn't matter, so that's what I did. 'Course I filed it down some, but you could still tell.

'This mornin', when I was waitin' for you an' Sheriff Lane, I did some scoutin' in the brush. An' what did I find? First off I found Jud's pony, that claybank he allus rode. Then I scouted some more an' I found where another pony had been tethered. There was a hoof-print, plain as could be, an' there was the mark o' a stud nail. Now,' he looked challengingly at his son, 'you mind tellin' me what really happened across there?'

'Ain't much to tell,' Lance said heavily. 'When we was across at the Triple X, Jud started pumpin' the boys about Cliff. Then somethin' I heard Dunc say made me think, an' I went across to warn the old fella.' He went on to describe how he'd found the foreman bending over Henderson's body, with a smoking gun still in his hand. Carefully avoiding any reference to 'Ace' Jordan, he described Jud's sneering confidence that he would walk free if brought to trial. Then the explosion of his own violent temper, culminating in the shoot-out. Finally, his decision to stage the whole thing to look as though Jud and Cliff had killed each other. 'I reckoned Dunc might pull out o' the deal, just to spite you. Then I figgered it could be the end o' my army career. Might even find m'self doin' time. I ain't proud o' what I did, but if I had to do it all over again I reckon I'd still play it the same!'

His father looked at him for a long moment, then sighed. 'Son, I figgered me an' Ma brought you all up to be straight shooters. Seems like we ain't done as good a job as I thought. Alright.' He held up his hand to silence his son's protest. 'Jud was a cold, mean killer. He had it comin'. Just wish it hadn't been you. Still, that's water down the creek. An' Dunc was in it as well. You heard Caleb sayin' how the Triple X boys was buyin' him an' Chas drink all night. That was to keep them away from the Rockin' H. So mebbe there was some kinda justice in what you did. I dunno. Take a better man than me to figger it out. Anyways,' he turned away from the gate; 'let's go see if Ma's made a pot o' coffee.'

'Pa.'

Jim Jordan looked at his son. 'Yeah?'

'I never knew old Cliff was such a gun handy hellion?'

His father laughed shortly. 'Old Cliff couldn't hit a barn broadside on! That was his twin brother, Clifton. Now there was one tough hombre. Texas Ranger, gunman, and raider. Rode wi' Quantrill. Never came back. Likely his bones are bleachin' out there in the brakes somewhere. Damn fool idea, christening twins wi' names like Clifton an' Clifford. Both got shortened to Cliff. So if Lane or Dunc checks on m'story, what're they gonna find? That Cliff Henderson wasn't somebody to fool with!'

'Pa.'

'Yeah?'

'You're one cagey old wolf, ain'tcha!'

'Just doin' m'job, son. Just doin' m'job. Let's go get that coffee.'

★ ★ ★ ★

Sheriff Lane's big sorrel stamped fretfully and swished its tail at the pestering flies.

'Got to hand it to you, Sheriff.' Jim Jordan looked up at its rider in well-feigned admiration. 'You sure got everything buttoned up when it comes to the law. An' Judge Smith said you'd done a good job, did he? Should count for somethin' come election time.'

The thin, sharp-featured sheriff, preened himself. 'Yeah, the judge agreed that it was an open an' shut case, just like I figgered. Anyways, I was on m'way back from the Triple X, an' seein' as how you're leavin' right soon, I thought I'd drop by an' let you know everything's tidied up. Oh, an' thanks for your help.'

'Shucks.' The rancher lifted a deprecating hand. 'Was the least we could do. Us law-abidin' folks got to pull our weight. 'Specially if we got good peace officers.'

Lane smirked self-consciously. 'Right nice of you to say so. Waal, reckon I'll be on m'way. Say.' He frowned. 'The judge did mention one thing.'

Jim Jordan stiffened, every sense alert. 'Yeah?'

'Seems he knew Cliff Henderson too. Knew'm right well from the way he talked. He said old Cliff was a hellion alright. An' that he was real sorry he wasn't here 'fore we buried him. Reckoned he would've liked to have paid his last respects. Anyways, he asked me to pass his thanks on to Miz Jordan, for seein' to the layin' out an' all.'

The rancher expelled a long breath. 'Thanks, Steve. We was just bein' neighbourly, but yeah, I'll tell Ma.'

'Adios then. Hope you have a good drive.' Lane wheeled his mount and cantered away across the yard.

'Whooee!' Jim Jordan mopped his brow. Sure was a good thing the judge never saw old Cliff 'fore we chested him. Smith's a smart old coot, an' he might just have noticed the difference. He headed towards the barn, where his eldest son was helping Ben Turner to load the big wagon. Lance, boy, I reckon the good Lord was watchin' out for us there.

* * * *

Ellie-May unbuckled the halter and reached into her shirt pocket. 'Here, boy.' Dance, the Cleveland stallion, lipped delicately at her open palm, before picking up the piece of molasses candy. Crunching noisily with evident enjoyment, he turned and ambled down the horse pasture towards the watching brood mares.

Rafe Allen watched him go. 'He sure is some stud,' he said admiringly.

'That's right.' Ellie-May looped the halter over her shoulder as the youngster closed the gate. 'An' he's the best breedin' stallion around these parts. Nigh on every service is a foal!' She strode towards their waiting mounts, Rafe at her heels. 'We'll bring the remuda in next.'

Rafe Allen felt his face reddening. She ain't like a gal at all, he thought resentfully, wearin' pants an' guns. An' the way she talks 'bout breedin' an' suchlike. Wonder what Ma would say if she saw her? Or Pa either, come to that!

Surreptitiously, he eyed the tall blonde girl as they swung into their saddles. The sudden effort tightened the checked calico shirt, and her breasts showed boldly against the material. She sure looks nice though. Like Pa said to Ma one time, she goes in an' out in the right places!

Their mounts cantered towards the grazing remuda, and he flicked a glance at the twin .44s belted round the trim waist. They say she gunned down Diamond Jack Anderson, right there in the yard. An' that knife throwin'. She can peg a branch at thirty feet, every time. He shivered.

' ... you ain't listenin', Rafe!' Ellie-May's exasperated voice cut across his thoughts. 'Swing wide an' start driftin' them back to the creek. Don't push 'em too hard.'

'Sure,' he mumbled. Imagine bein' married to her! Sara-Jane now, she's different. Real nice she is. Dresses like a gal, an' talks like a gal. Right pleasant she is too. Still, he eased the grazing ponies deftly into a walk, I ain't got no reason to gripe. The Jordans are good folks, an' Mister Jordan's a fine boss. An' I got the move to Arizona comin' up. That'll be somethin' to tell the family when I write.

Ellie-May Jordan surveyed the ambling spread of horseflesh, and smiled to herself. Just right, she thought. They're gettin' used to us now. Critically, she watched Rafe as he eased the drifting ponies towards the creek. He's doin' alright. 'Course it wouldn't do to tell'm. Men get ideas if you give 'em too much praise. Still, he ain't bad. He'll make a hand yet.

Swaying easily in the saddle, Ellie-May gazed towards the distant ranch. Last night at the Circle J. Tomorrow's the start o' the drive. Sure gonna be a long haul. Wonder what the Flyin' W's like? Ma says it's awful big. Well, it's a new start for all of us.

Picketed in a line behind the barn, the tall girl saw Ben Turner's team grazing contentedly. 'Ben ... ' His name rose unbidden to her lips. He's a real nice fella. You can talk to him 'bout horses an' guns. Shame 'bout his wife an' the boy. Reckon it's a new start for him too.

Halting her mount, she sat pensively, watching the remuda spread along the creek bank. Rafe cantered across to join her.

'They're beginnin' to move real good now,' he said tentatively, uncertain of her mood. You never knew with Ellie-May. Silence. 'I said ... '

'Heard you the first time,' his companion said sharply, reining her mount round. 'Alright, we ain't got all day to sit here gabbin'. You check over Paint an' Dusty's gear. Ma ain't got time, an' Sara-Jane don't know nothin' when it comes to harness. Me, I'll go see the corral ropes have been loaded, an' we can get at them easy. We'll need them twice a day. Let's go!'

Rafe grinned covertly to himself. This was more like the Ellie-May he knew.

Chapter 31

Jim Jordan brought Bob up alongside Jake's mount. He waved a hand at the bawling jostling herd, headed towards the ranch. 'Lookin' good.'

Young Larsen nodded. 'Yeah, they're ready for the drive alright. Good thing we got them yearlin' steers cut out. Andy an' Mike pushed 'em over onto the Triple X, an' a couple o' Dunc Paterson's boys got 'em now. 'Course, we kept back that thirty you wanted to take along.'

'Uh-huh. We got to have beef for the crew, an' we'll likely need to buy off some o' the tribes wi' a few head. Better that way than swappin' lead.' Pa glanced at his companion. 'How'd you feel 'bout this move anyway?'

Jake Larsen shrugged. 'Nothin' for me here. Folks are dead. John and I have talked about it. We feel this move is best for us. In Arizona we can make a fresh start, and forget the past. Sure hope so anyway.'

Jim Jordan nodded approvingly. 'Seems like right good thinkin' t'me. 'Sides, you're gonna get a lot o' experience on this drive. Likely come in handy later, 'cause I reckon Bull will want to drive a herd north right soon.'

Jake hesitated, then ... . 'How do you feel about moving?'

The rancher scratched at his stubbled jaw. 'Waal now, I reckon it's for the best. Gives you young folks a chance to make good. Anyways, it's what Ma wants, an' it is her ranch when you come right down to it.' He grinned suddenly. "Course, Bull is all for it. Got plans, Bull has. Big plans. Trouble is, he sometimes forgets the rest o' us got plans as well!'

'He is a good cattleman though.' There was grudging admiration in Jake's voice.

'Never said he wasn't, son. Just wish he wasn't so damned ornery at times.'

The young half-breed grinned. 'Then he would not be Bull!'

Jim Jordan laughed. 'You got me there, Jake. Anyways, keep 'em headed for that bottom land grazin'. We'll bed them down there tonight. I'll go see how Lance is makin' out.'

The big sergeant watched his father swing round the rear of the herd towards him. The old man an' Jake hit it off real well. Reckon he's mebbe closer to Pa than any of us. Well, his father died for this family, so the least we can do is treat'm as one o' us.

'Howdy, Pa. You come round to see I ain't sleepin' on the job?'

His father grinned. 'Mightn't be such a bad idea at that! Once we hit the trail there won't be a lot o' sleep for anybody. How's that cavalry horse o' yours makin' out herdin' cows?'

'Old Buck?' Lance patted the buckskin's neck. 'He's doin' right well. 'Course, he ain't no top hand's mount, but he's gettin' there.'

They jogged on together, each busy with his thoughts.

'Lance.'

'Yeah, Pa?'

'What you did that night. It bother you much?'

His son reflected for a moment. 'Nah. 'Course I'm sorry 'bout you gettin' mixed up in the mess, but Jud was a lobo an' a mean one at that. I ain't sheddin' no tears 'bout him. Reckon all I can do is draw a line an' start again.'

Pa scowled. 'Oh, he had it comin' alright. Pity it had to be you though. Somethin' like that can nag at you, even if you think it won't. Reckon we'll all be glad to see the back o' Texas.'

⋆ ⋆ ⋆ ⋆

'Sara-Jane.'

Sara-Jane turned from the stove, where she was stirring a pot. 'Yes, Mary.'

Six year old Mary Johnson gazed up at her. 'Are you glad to be leavin' here?'

Sara-Jane nodded. 'Yes I am. We're goin' to somewhere new, an' it's real excitin'.'

'Mister Bull's not new, an' he's there.' Mary said doggedly. She looked suddenly doubtful. 'He is there, isn't he?' she queried anxiously.

"Course he is,' her elder sister Sarah cut in loftily. 'Mister Bull said he'd meet us when we got there. Didn't he, Miz Jordan?'

Ma closed the oven door and straightened up, her face flushed with the heat. 'Can't argue wi' that,' she said briskly. 'That's what he said.'

'There!'

'Ma,' Sara-Jane said cautiously; 'You pleased to be movin'?'

About to start laying the table, Ma paused for a moment. 'Reckon I am at that. It's a chance for us to make it big, only don't go tellin' your pa I said so. If he'd his way we'd be stayin' here. Suppose you're pleased?'

'Mm? Oh sure. Only, there was times when it was nice here too.'

'Huh,' said her mother dismissively. 'You get mebbe one chance like this in a lifetime. We got to take it.'

Sara-Jane nodded. An' Clay Wallace'll be there. She hugged the thought to herself. Maybe we'll be able to spend some time together. Just so long as Ma don't find out! She stirred industriously.

* * * *

Bob, Pa's Cleveland saddle horse, splashed into the creek and lowered his head. 'A'right, you big tank.' Jim Jordan lounged comfortably in the saddle. 'Drink your fill. Might be your last chance. Water could be right scarce on the drive.' The big horse lifted a dripping muzzle and flicked his ears inquiringly at the sound of his rider's voice.

Waal, Jim boy, ain't many more nights on the old Circle J. Seems like only yesterday we come here, all bright eyed an' bushy tailed. Lot o' water under the bridge since then. He sighed. Plenty o' grief an' heartache, but there's been good times as well. In the distance he saw his wife come out onto the porch and look around. An' if it makes Mary-Lou happy then I reckon some good'll have come of it. 'Alright, boy.' He kneed his mount into motion. 'Let's go.' Bob ploughed across the creek and loped towards the distant ranch.

* * * *

John Jordan squatted by the small campfire and gnawed contentedly at the piece of roast meat. Seems to me white folks could learn a lot from the Injuns. I'd just about forgotten how good roast squirrel tasted. Grinning reminiscently he reached up and touched the hilt of the throwing knife, snug in its neck holster. Reckon he thought he was safe in that old dead tree. Nearby, securely picketed, Big Red cropped noisily at the thick grass. Might as well turn in. John settled himself comfortably and pulled the blanket round him. For a while he mulled over the family's move to Arizona. Guess it's a chance to make a new start, just like Jake said. Mebbe it'll change things wi' Ma. A last check; he listened intently. All quiet. Ain't nothin' gonna get near while Red's around. Closing his eyes, the young rancher was soon asleep. The campfire flickered and died.

☆   ☆   ☆   ☆*

'We'll have a couple of extra guests tonight, Lydia.' Miz Jordan, here.' Hannah MaCrae inclined her head in the direction of Mary-Lou, sitting opposite, 'an' her son, Lance. He'll be along later.'

'Yes, Miz MaCrae.' The door closed noiselessly behind the negro maid.

Hannah sipped her coffee. 'You all set then?'

Ma nodded. 'Ready to roll. Just wanted to see you 'fore we go. We've been friends a long time.'

The widow nodded, a faraway look in her eyes. 'Yeah, that's true.' She paused for a moment, deep in thought. 'And Lance?' she queried quietly.

'He's across in the saloon;' Ma shrugged. 'Somethin's needlin' that boy. He's been awful tetchy this past week. Still,' she said thoughtfully, 'he's gettin' along right well wi' his pa, an' that's a blessin'. When Jim told'm to hitch up the team an' bring me across to Greenhills, he just nodded an' went right ahead. Time was when they couldn't look sideways at each other.'

Hannah frowned. 'Mebbe he's missin' the army,' she ventured.

Ma nodded. 'Could be.' Their conversation drifted into other channels.

☆   ☆   ☆   ☆

Lance Jordan took a long pull at his beer and leaned back against the bar. Moodily he surveyed the almost empty saloon. Greenhills don't change much, the sergeant thought sourly. Still the same one horse outfit it was when I was a raw kid. He grinned at the memory. Crockett now, there's a real cowtown.

The batwing doors banged and Lance watched with heightened interest as Dunc Paterson pushed his way into the room. He was followed by a tall clean cut youngster who paused and looked about him uncertainly. Together they made their way to the bar.

'Well, howdy, Lance.' There was a forced joviality in Paterson's booming voice. 'Good to see you.'

Like hell it is, Lance thought wryly. Wonder who the young fella is? 'Howdy, Mister Paterson. What're you an' your friend drinkin'?'

'Whisky straight for me. This here's Asa Hartley.'

Lance flicked an inquiring glance at Hartley.

The young cowhand nodded. 'Beer'll be fine.'

Lance Jordan grinned. 'Beer it is.' He signalled to the bartender.

Paterson swallowed a mouthful of whiskey. 'Well now, didn't expect to see you here.'

Lance shrugged. 'Ma's visitin' wi' Miz MaCrae. Be the last time 'fore we leave.'

The burly rancher gave a perfunctory nod. 'On m'way back from Fort Worth. Hired Asa to run the Circle J, an' the east side o' the Triple X range. Ain't that so, Asa?'

The young cowhand reddened and nodded uncomfortably.

Paterson paused, as though coming to a decision. 'Been wantin' to see you anyway. Now seems as good a time as any. Asa, you hang on here. Got some business to discuss wi' Lance.' He pointed. 'That corner table there.'

Lance scowled. He detested Dunc's hectoring manner. 'A'right.' Reluctantly he picked up his glass and followed the big rancher.

They seated themselves on opposite sides of the rough table. Lance took a swig at his beer. 'So, what's on your mind?'

Paterson frowned. 'Got to find me another foreman right soon,' he said heavily. 'Spread as big as the Triple X can go all to hell if you ain't got a good ramrod.'

Lance Jordan shrugged, 'You got Hartley there.'

'Nah. Good stockman, that's all.' There was a pause, then the big rancher spoke again. 'Been thinkin',' he glanced obliquely at Lance, 'supposin' you was to take the job. Don't reckon the army pays all that much. Fella like you, handy wi' his shootin' irons an' all, I reckon I could run to a hundred a month an' found.'

Lance stiffened, suddenly alert. 'What the hell d'you mean, handy wi' shootin' irons? I ain't no hired gunnie. I'm a cavalry sergeant on furlough. What makes you think I'd want to ramrod for you anyways?'

Rage flickered briefly in the burly rancher's deep-set eyes. "Tain't what you want to do. Might be you ain't got no choice in the matter, Ace!'

'What the hell did you call me?'

'Ace. That was your moniker wasn't it, when you hung out in El Paso?' He tossed back a swallow of whiskey and grinned, a wide-mouthed derisive grin. 'Hell, you don't think Jud kept that piece o' news to hisself. Nah. He told me.' Paterson paused for a moment, brooding. 'We was allus close, me an' Jud. Guess that kinda surprises you.'

He squinted at Lance. "Course, I ain't right sure what happened that night, but I don't reckon Jud an' Cliff killed each other. When I started to think real hard 'bout it I remembered Jud was a two-handed draw man, yet only one o' his guns was fired. 'Nother thing I'd forgot about, old Cliff had downed nigh on a bottle o' corn licker that night. Don't reckon he could'a drawn a gun, never mind pull the trigger. 'Course, I can't prove nuthin', but I reckon once folks know you're Ace Jordan, top gunnie, there'll be an awful lot o' questions asked. Anyways, in the end I'll get what I want.' He grinned again, coldly calculating. 'Reckon that should change your mind some. What d'you say?'

Lance sat for a long moment marshalling his racing thoughts. Finally ... 'It might,' he said quietly, 'an' again, it might not. Seems t'me you might want the whole thing hushed up yourself. You sicced Jud onto Cliff, an' my guess is you just hoped that lobo might kill the old-timer. Yeah, I know.' He held up his hand as the rancher made to speak, 'I can't prove it either, but folks might be right interested just the same.'

Tossing back the last of his drink, Lance twirled the empty glass in his hand. 'An' there's somethin' else, Dave,' he saw the florid features pale suddenly. 'Yeah, Dave Peterson, ex-shotgun guard! Seems like Bull was right after all. Strange ain't it, how you an' that mine payroll disappeared at the same time. Then you come here an' bought the Triple X.' He leaned forward and stared stonily at the silent rancher. 'Guess we both got somethin' to hide, so I reckon this is a stand-off. Anyways,' he rose to his feet, 'here's how she lays. You forget about Ace Jordan an' I'll forget about Dave Peterson. Deal?'

Dunc nodded shakily.

'A'right; just a couple more things.' The hatred in the big sergeant's cold tones was very evident.

Paterson braced himself.

Lance smiled suddenly, a smile which did not reach his cold blue eyes. 'I wouldn't ride for you if the Triple X was the last ranch 'tween here an' hell! An' just in case you're wonderin', Jud never cleared leather!'

✯   ✯   ✯   ✯

Damned bookwork. I sure hate it. Bull Jordan closed the ledger with a bang and rubbed his eyes. The sooner Clay gets back here the better. Wonder how things are goin' wi' the folks?

Yawning, he wandered out onto the porch and leaned on the worn rail. In the distance the sun was just beginning to dip behind Saddle Mountain, and purple shadows were lengthening rapidly from the cottonwoods down by the creek. Hell, I'm tired. Seems like there ain't enough hours in the day.

He watched Joe Masterson turn a pony into the corral and close the gate. Bull waved, and the foreman headed across the wide yard towards him. That's one thing I did right anyways, makin' him foreman. I've met some good ramrods in m'time, but he'll stack up wi' any o' them. Wonder where he's been now.

'Evenin', Boss.'

'Howdy, Joe. Seems like you're allus busy.'

Masterson shrugged. 'First foreman's job I ever had, an' I ain't about to mess it up.'

Bull grinned. 'Work you're puttin' in, that ain't likely. Where you been tonight anyway?'

The red-haired foreman removed his battered hat and mopped the sweat from his brow. 'Went down along the creek. Manuel reckoned he saw an old tom cougar down there t'other mornin'. Thought I might get a shot at'm. Don't want him spookin' that stock we brung up from the brush. Nary a sign though. Reckon he's long gone.'

Together, they watched the shadows lengthen across the horse pasture. The giant rancher glanced curiously at his companion. 'How d'you feel about bein' foreman anyway?'

Joe reflected for a moment. 'When I was a young green kid I fooled around a lot. All I wanted to do was herd cows. 'Member my old man tellin' me I'd never amount to much. Now, thanks to you, I got me a chance an' I aim to take it. I'm foreman for one o' the biggest spreads in the territory. Got a good crew, an' a boss I respect. Hell, what more could a man want.' He stopped abruptly, red-faced with embarrassment.

'Thanks, Joe.' There was a gruffness in Bull's voice that belied the emotion in him. 'Looks like we both feel the same way 'bout things. That bein' so, we'll make the Flyin' W a brand to remember. 'Course it's still Ma's ranch, an' rightly so, but I reckon I'll be runnin' it.' He grinned. 'First time a Flyin' W herd hits the trail we'll give Goodnight, Chisum, an' the rest o' the big outfits a run for their money!'

Together they leaned contentedly on the porch rail and watched the darkness fall.

✯   ✯   ✯   ✯

From the driver's seat of the chuck wagon, Ma Jordan took a last long look at the Circle J. Never thought I'd leave here an' own a place like the Flyin' W. Anyways, too late for Jim an' me now. This one's for the family. There was a lump in her throat, and she swallowed hard before picking up the lines.

On the steps of the ranch house her husband blew his nose noisily and blinked as he looked at Dunc Paterson. 'She's all yours now, Dunc. Been a long time. Never thought I'd leave the Circle J.'

There had been a distinct change in the burly cattleman since Jud Moore's death. His domineering self-assurance had been badly dented. Now he shrugged weightily. 'Just a piece o' land, Jim. Folks buy an' sell it all the time. Reckon you're makin' a good move m'self. Now, I got some o' the boys holdin' our stock back a ways, on the flats. Soon as your herd's onto the ridge trail we'll be movin' in. Young Hartley's got the makin's of a good cattleman an' he'll run this side o' the spread from here.'

He coughed, and looked away. 'Accordin' to Dave Lane, if Cliff Henderson ain't got no relatives, then the Rockin' H will be sold by public auction to the highest bidder. The money'll be used to help pay county expenses.' He turned suddenly. 'Cliff ever mention his family to you?'

Jim Jordan's eyes narrowed and he frowned. 'Far as I know,' he said vaguely; 'his folks died when he was just a kid. Fever, I think. 'Pears he was an only child.' You son of a bitch, Dunc, he thought in sudden fury. Man ain't cold in his grave an' you're plannin' to snap up his place cheap. Ain't nobody gonna bid against you round here, an' you know it. Guess it makes what Lance did set easier with me now.

'You alright?' Startled, he found Paterson looking at him curiously.

'Yeah, just thinkin' about the old place. Adios then, guess we'd best be movin'.' Ignoring the cattleman's attempted handshake he turned away abruptly and waved his hat in the agreed signal.

Jaw set grimly, Ma urged her team forward. Behind her Miguel Jerez, perched high on the sprung seat of the accommodation wagon, spoke softly to the big Clevelands fretting impatiently at their bits. Seated at one of the windows, Sara-Jane wiped her eyes and turned to find the two small girls regarding her anxiously.

'Sara-Jane, why are you crying?'

'I'm not, Mary. There's something in my eye I think.'

Ben Turner smiled to himself as he raised his voice and set his team in motion. Today, for the first time since Peg and little Tim's deaths, he felt as though life was worth living. The big draught horses settled into their collars, and the brightly painted Studebaker wagon started to roll.

Out on the bed ground, beyond the horse pasture, Jake Larsen rose in his stirrups and acknowledged the rancher's signal. Then, waving to Lance on the other side of the herd, he pointed ahead.

Jim Jordan had been explicit about this. He had taken Lance aside and said that Jake would be straw boss on the trail drive. His eldest son had laughed and said that was fine by him, and that he didn't plan to herd cows for the rest of his life anyway. Ma had tightened her mouth disapprovingly when she'd heard, but the look in her husband's eyes had been enough. Where Jake was concerned, Jim Jordan brooked no interference.

Between them, the two riders eased the leaders onto the trail towards the west. Further back, Andy Boone and Mike Glenwood slotted into the swing positions on the flanks of the herd, while Jim Jordan came up at a lope to cover the drag.

At the horse pasture gate, Ellie-May waved as he passed. She waited until the cattle were up onto the ridge trail before swinging the gate wide. Dance, the big easygoing Cleveland stallion, ambled through the opening, looked inquiringly at Ellie-May and then swung west onto the trail, the mares and the rest of the saddle horses streaming behind him. Young Rafe Allen, bringing up the rear, hesitated momentarily. The tall girl waved him on. Closing the gate, she turned her mount and cantered after the remuda.

The accommodation wagon topped the ridge and Sara-Jane took a last look at the Circle J, nestling in the valley below. *I wanted to leave this place more than anything, an' now I'm sad 'cause I am leavin'.* She shook her head determinedly and turned to talk to the girls.

Jake twisted in his saddle and looked back along the herd. Everything was fine. The cattle were moving easily and the riders were all in position. He raised a hand and grinned across at Lance. The big sergeant waved back but his face remained set.

The tiny nagging doubt surfaced again. *Where was Lance the night Cliff an' Jud had their shootout?* Working automatically, his thoughts elsewhere, Jake chivvied a stray bull back into line.

If I hadn't seen him an' his pa at the corral, guess I'd never have thought to look at old Blue's shoes m'self. An' if I hadn't looked, likely I'd never have connected Blue wi' them studded tracks across the creek, headin' for the Rockin' H. An' comin' back.

Still, it ain't none o' my business. Lance ever wants to tell me what happened, reckon he will. Let it ride I guess. He urged his pony forward, grinning as he remembered Ma's last Old Testament reading. *Seems t'me we're kinda like that fella Lot an' his family. Best we don't look back.*

If you have enjoyed 'Jordan Luck,' look out for 'Jordan Land'. The beginning of its first chapter follows.

Jordan Land

Chapter 1

▼

The rattlesnake woke suddenly. Something had disturbed it. Vibrations, and they were getting closer. Raising its head questioningly, the snake searched the surrounding terrain, forked tongue flickering. Sensing that the vibrations were closing fast now, it withdrew carefully beneath a convenient bush and waited there, coiled, silent and deadly.

Angling down the long slope, the red roan gelding blew through his nostrils as he headed towards the few small pools of scummy liquid, all that was left of Mustang Springs ponds. His rider swayed easily to the movement, mind busy with the implications of the scene before him. Mustang Springs was dry!

The horse trampled past the bush and the diamond back rattler sounded a warning. Startled, the giant roan reared and spun away, snorting angrily. At the same moment the snake struck ... and missed.

Controlling his raging mount with one hand, John Jordan drew the slim throwing knife in a blur of fluid continuous movement. The 'Arkansas Toothpick' flashed in the sun and pinned the rattler's wedge-shaped head to the ground.

Holding the snorting gelding on a tight rein, John waited until the snake's thrashing death throes had subsided. Dismounting, he retrieved the gleaming weapon, wiping the blade carefully, before returning it to the riveted leather scabbard lying snugly between his shoulder blades.

A lean, powerfully built, blond six-footer, there was an aura of menace about John Jordan. Taken by Comanches at the age of eight, he had spent the next ten years as their captive, gradually becoming more and more Indian in his ways. Given the name Yellow Panther he had been accepted as the great

Ten Bears' adopted son, blood brother to many warriors, and eventually as a 'dog soldier' (a hunter) known and respected by all the tribe. His escape, and subsequent return to his family, was now part of East Texas frontier lore.

A loner, possessing unparalleled skills as a horse tamer, John Jordan was to all intents and purposes a white Comanche.

Now, he led his mount towards one of the small pools and watched as the gelding sucked greedily at the brown liquid.

Big Red was a moody unpredictable equine giant, who lived only for one person; John's brother, Hardy Jordan. As a two year old he had been beaten and tortured by Comancheros in an attempt to break his spirit. Rescued by Hardy, Red had become a one man horse. The only other person he would tolerate on his back was John, and that was a tenuous partnership at best; one which could be broken at any moment. Only the young rider's superb understanding of horses kept it going. Deep down Red was an outlaw, with a sullen smouldering temperament. As John's father, Jim Jordan had said grudgingly, 'He can outrun and outstay any horse I've ever seen. But,' he had added warningly, 'deep down he's a killer, and don't ever forget it.

Well, John grimaced wryly, looks like we're in big trouble Red. Pa ain't gonna like this one bit. Best thing we can do is push on and take a look at the Pecos. Swinging into the saddle he reined the giant gelding round and headed west. On the ground the first ants moved unerringly towards the dead snake.

Printed in the United Kingdom
by Lightning Source UK Ltd.
134701UK00002BA/1-66/P